DARIUS LOGAN: SUPER JUSTICE FORCE

THE ADVENTURES OF DARIUS LOGAN—BOOK ONE

D. F. Walker

Portland, Oregon

The characters and events in this book are the work of fiction. Any similarity to real persons, living or dead, is purely coincidental and not intended by the author.

Text copyright © 2009, 2011 D. F. Walker
All rights reserved.
Printed in the United States of America

1 2 3 4 5 6 7 8 9 10

FIRST EDITION
March 2011

No part of this book may be reproduced, or stored in a retrieval system, or transmitted in any form or by any means, electronic, mechanical, photocopying, recording, or otherwise, without express written permission of the publisher, except for brief quotations used for review purposes.

Published by Drapetomedia, LLC
2000 NE 42nd; Suite D, #102
Portland, OR 97213
www.superjusticeforce.com

Library of Congress Control Number:
2011923621

ISBN-13: 978-0-9833557-0-0
ISBN-10: 0-9833557-0-3

Portions of this novel were published in a slightly different version on the Internet.

Cover illustration by Robert Love
Cover color by Diego Simone
Interior and cover design by Jim Hill
SJF logo design by Tyson Smith
Character design by D.F. Walker

Dedicated to my favorite superheroes—Darius Weems, Logan Smalley (without whom my hero would have no name), and the rest of the "Darius Goes West" crew (Ben, Andrew, Sam, Daniel, Kevin, Collin, Dylan, Jason, John, John, Barbara, Allison and everyone else). Know about it.

A special dedication to every kid who has ever thought they were alone and that no one really cared or understood. If you have ever felt alienated, dismissed, marginalized, or simply like there was no place in the world where you belonged, then this book is specifically for you.

PART 1: SECOND CHANCE

1

Darius Logan ran for his life. And more than almost anything else, he hated running. His pounding heart drowned out all other sound. Fire filled his lungs. Every muscle felt like it was being torn apart. But the cop chasing after him—barely a block behind and gaining fast—kept him running as if his life depended on it, which it did.

His mind raced almost as fast his legs. He had to get away, even though he didn't know where to get away to. Darius had no real friends. No family. Nowhere to run. He kept running anyway, dashing across a street that cut through the decaying rubble of dead neighborhoods called No Man's Land.

Darius made it to the other side of the street, ran to the end of the block, and turned the corner. A side street stretched out before him, lined on both sides with four and five-story apartment buildings. People used to live in these buildings. That was before The Attack.

No one lived this far into No Man's Land. This far in the buildings were just burned-out shells. Block after block of giant tombstones, marking the graves of entire neighborhoods that had been dead for years. And everywhere it stunk of death and decay, an overwhelming smell—like boiled garbage left out to rot—made worse by the humid night air. Darius breathed deep through his mouth, trying to catch his breath, certain he could actually taste the stench.

One of the areas hit hardest during The Attack, and almost eight years later, nothing had been done to rebuild. And so No Man's Land continued to crumble and stink and fester, and the only sign of life was a desperate black kid who hated running being chased by a cop.

None of the streetlights on the block worked anymore and clouds partially obscured the crescent moon, making it difficult to see. The nighttime shadows cast by the empty buildings stretched out like the bony fingers of a Grim Reaper come to claim all light.

Darius thought for a moment about turning around to see if the cop chasing him was any closer. But he couldn't risk slowing down, not even to look over his shoulder.

Probably can't see anything in the dark anyway, he thought as he kept running.

Halfway down the block, Darius couldn't go anymore. A terrible pain stabbed at his side—like a hot knife jammed deep into his ribs. *Gotta stop and catch my breath—just for a minute.*

Up ahead he saw a narrow alley running between two of the decaying buildings. Alleys like this cut through much of No Man's Land, and Darius spent most of his youth avoiding them. There were too many unknown dangers hiding in the narrow paths. Some of those dangers might still be hiding—a desperate junkie willing to rob anyone to get a fix. Or maybe one of those crazy street people who ate roaches and rats when there was nothing to be found in the garbage. Worse, there might be some of those giant rats that ate people when there was nothing to be found in the garbage.

Darius thought about all of the things that might be waiting in the alley. Nothing he thought of mattered. Nothing changed the fact that a stabbing pain tore at his sides while a cop practically breathed down his neck. He needed to stop. He needed to catch his breath.

Darius stood about fifteen feet back in the alley—far enough away that someone running past wouldn't see him, but not so far back that he couldn't see the dark street he had just turned off of. He worried the cop would hear him panting like a dog. A wave of nausea overtook him as he breathed in the putrid air in the alley—someone or something had recently used it as a toilet. The stench overwhelmed Darius. He fought to keep from vomiting while at the same time trying to figure out how he had messed up so bad.

Ten minutes earlier, Darius had been in an abandoned parking garage, doing something he knew he shouldn't be doing with three other guys. He barely knew Karlito, the one who talked him into what quickly proved to be a mistake. The other two, Mickey and some guy they called Bay-Bay, he knew even less. That didn't stop Darius from tagging along when Karlito asked him if he wanted to make some money.

By nature, Darius didn't talk much. Over the years, as he drifted in and out of foster homes, juvenile detention, and the shelters that housed people like him, he learned that most people really didn't listen to what he had to say, so he didn't say much.

Karlito, by comparison, never stopped talking. "I'm a man of a million ideas," he would say. And even though most of Karlito's ideas were bad, Darius didn't say anything. He should have. But he didn't.

Karlito's latest get-rich-quick scheme involved selling Adrenaccelerate—better known as eXXeLL—in an abandoned parking lot deep in the heart of No Man's Land. On the streets a single dose of eXXeLL fetched more money than five times the same amount of cocaine. Of course, as far as illegal drugs went, possession of Adrenaccelerate with intent to sell was a violation of Homeland Security and a federal offense.

"Cops ain't gonna mess with us in No Man's Land. Besides, it ain't like we're the Masters of D.E.A.T.H. or Doc Kaos," said Karlito—like he knew what he was talking about.

From the beginning, the plan didn't sound that well thought out. The presence of Mickey just made everything worse. Mickey was so stupid Darius wondered if he had been dropped on his head as a child.

"That boy is so ignorant, stupid must be in his bones," is what Darius's mother would have said about Mickey, if she were alive. At the same time, if his mother had been alive, chances were pretty good Darius would never have found himself in the sort of circumstances that brought guys like Karlito, Mickey and Bay-Bay into his life.

When the cops yelled, "Freeze! You're all under arrest!" it took Darius a split second longer than the others to realize that he should run. The others bolted like roaches when the lights are turned on, leaving Darius holding the bag, literally. Karlito thought it would be a good idea. "You the youngest," Karlito said. "Something goes wrong, you a minor."

It can't go much more wrong than this, Darius thought, hiding in the foul-smelling alley, gasping for air.

The doses of eXXeLL Karlito stuffed into Darius's backpack made being a minor irrelevant. The way Darius figured it, he had enough Adrenaccelerate in his backpack to send him away for life. And with two strikes already against him, Darius would be screwed if he got caught. Which is why he ran for his life.

The sound of feet pounding the pavement of the darkened street caught Darius's attention. With nothing else making noise for blocks and blocks, the police officer's running footsteps thundered like rapidly approaching cannon fire. Darius half expected the ground to shake. And just like that, the cop ran past the alley, never breaking his stride.

Darius took off toward the far end of the alley, stopping where it opened up on to the block running parallel to the one he'd just been on. More darkness greeted him. Burned-out streetlights helped hide abandoned and crumbling buildings. He stood in the opening of the alley, looking both ways, trying to figure out what to do, when it suddenly occurred to him. *I still have the eXXeLL on me.* In all of the confusion and running, he forgot to ditch it.

Still fighting to catch his breath, he struggled to get his arms free of the straps, and just as he was about to drop the backpack, Darius heard a voice behind him.

"Freeze!"

The single word seemed to bounce off the walls on either side of the alley.

2

The cop chasing Darius had doubled back and come into the alley. He pointed his gun directly at Darius's face. Darius saw the look in the cop's eyes and knew that he meant business. There would be no warning shot.

This is it. It's all over.

"Drop the backpack and place your hands on your head," said the cop.

Darius stared down the barrel of the gun, weighing his options. He could do what the cop said, and he'd spend more than a few years in prison. Or he could die right there in the alley. Neither option seemed acceptable.

Darius dropped the backpack, slowly putting his hands on his head. *Maybe it wouldn't be so bad*, he thought. *Maybe I won't be charged with carrying felony weight. Maybe this won't be counted as my third strike. Yeah, right*, he thought, grunting with laughter.

The officer moved in closer, grabbed Darius, pushed him up against the side of one of the derelict buildings, and without a word began frisking him. The cop, still winded from the chase, breathed his hot breath on the back of Darius's neck—it smelled almost as bad as the alley itself.

A voice came over the cop's walkie-talkie. "You got a twenty on the suspect?"

The cop grumbled to himself, fidgeted with something, and a second or two later spoke into his radio. "Copy that."

Using his left hand, the cop pushed Darius hard against the wall. But if the officer was pushing against Darius using his left hand, then it meant that he was using his right hand to hold the radio.

Where's his gun? Darius wondered, before realizing the cop must have holstered his weapon. *Now's my chance. If I'm gonna get out of this, it's gotta be now.*

Running wasn't Darius's thing—he wasn't good at it. But he did know how to fight. His father saw to that, teaching Darius to defend himself after he had come home with a bloody nose given to him by a schoolyard bully. He was six at the time, and small for his age. Even now he wasn't that big, but back then, he was tiny. And the other kids picked on him. So his father taught him how to defend himself.

Darius took a deep breath, reminding himself that his life was on the line. *Three strikes and you're out.* And then he remembered what his father had taught him: "In a fight, your greatest strength will always be the weakness of your opponent."

The weakness of the cop, who weighed at least seventy-five pounds more than Darius, and stood at least five inches taller, was that he wasn't paying attention. The cop only had two things over Darius—his gun and his undivided attention. Neither one was trained on Darius. The cop underestimated the sixteen-year-old kid he had pushed up against the wall of a crumbling building. Darius didn't need any more advantage than that.

Darius elbowed the cop in the ribs as hard as he could—hard enough to knock the wind out of the police officer. The radio fell to the ground. Gasping for air, the cop reached for his gun. Darius knocked it out of the officer's hand with a kick, sending it flying into the darkness.

Shocked, sucking in air, the cop fought to regain himself. He had been in worse scenarios, faced down more dangerous felons than the scrawny black kid that caught him off guard with an elbow to the ribs. He was ready for a fight.

Darius was ready for a fight as well. If he knew anything at all, he knew how to fight—it came as naturally as breathing. He'd spent over half of his life fighting. He fought back against the bullies at school. When his parents were killed and he found himself living on the streets, he fought to stay alive.

The officer took a swing at him, and Darius ducked the punch. With nothing for the cop's fist to connect to, he spun around, losing his balance. Darius took advantage of the moment, body slamming the cop into the side of the building.

The cop let out a loud grunt, the wind knocked out of him for a second time. Off balance and gasping for air, the cop was running on empty. Whatever fight he had in him disappeared. Darius slammed the officer again into the wall of the building. A small cloud of concrete erupted as part of the wall crumbled to dust against the force of impact. Grabbing the cop by the front of his uniform with a classic jujitsu hold, Darius used the man's own weight against him, driving him to the ground. He almost felt bad for the cop, but not so bad that he was willing to go to jail.

Darius took off running, stopping when a stray beam of moonlight glinting off the cop's gun caught his eye. *Last thing I need is to get shot*, Darius thought.

Darius grabbed the gun and looked over at the cop. The officer, picking himself up from the ground, saw Darius holding the gun. Even in the darkness, Darius could see the look of fear on the cop's face. *Did I look that scared when the gun was pointed at me?* Darius thought to himself.

He wondered if the cop had a family. Maybe the cop thought of them as he stared down the barrel of his own gun, wondering if he'd ever get to see his kids again.

Maybe he was just another bully that only felt safe when the odds were in his favor. None of it made a difference to Darius. He wasn't about to shoot the cop. Someone like Karlito might use the gun. Darius wasn't Karlito. He wasn't about to make a bad situation worse.

With all his strength, Darius threw the gun into the building across the street. He took off running before the gun had a chance to land somewhere amidst the rubble. It would only be a matter of moments before more police arrived for backup. Darius's freedom depended on his next moves. It had been one thing when he had the backpack full of eXXeLL. He had just beaten the hell out of a cop, which made getting away all the more important.

The success of Darius's escape depended on one simple fact: he knew where he was. People once lived in No Man's Land, his family included. He had grown up not far from the burned-out block he ran down, and though many years had passed, he still knew the streets. Five, maybe six blocks away was a subway station.

If I can get to the subway, I can get to the Caves, he thought.

The "Caves" were what people called the abandoned subway tunnels and derelict stations that had been left to rot after The Attack caused parts of the city to collapse on itself. Some stations and tunnels were repaired, but those that weren't—those that cut through the heart of No Man's Land—had been transformed. Instead of the hustle and bustle of commuters moving through the city, the stations became caves that had been taken over by those with nowhere else to go. There was no telling who you might find living in the Caves, anyone from junkies desperate for a fix to rogue metahumans that refused to register.

Darius hated the thought of seeking refuge in the Caves—it was too dangerous and just plain scary. He lived down there for nearly six months and seen things he never wanted to see again. It was a whole different world, requiring a special strength just to survive. The fact that Darius made it out with so few scars always amazed him.

Most people thought the worst thing about the Caves were the metahumans living down there. The law required anyone with "enhanced abilities and unusual attributes" to be registered with the Federal Bureau of Metahuman Affairs, and there were a lot of people who thought of metahumans as monsters.

The metahumans didn't bother Darius—he actually got along with mutants better than he did most "normal" people. It was the giant killer rats he couldn't deal with. But if it came down to hiding in the abandoned subways and dealing with giant rats, or going to jail, there was no question. The cops would never find him—they never went into the Caves unless they absolutely had to.

The Caves it is, he said to himself.

Before he could take another step, two police cars came tearing onto the street, one on either end of the block, lights flashing, sirens blaring, boxing Darius in. He looked to his right, then to his left, and knew he couldn't go in either direction.

Instead, he went straight ahead, right into the derelict building in front of him.

It smelled worse in the building than in the alley—a combination of piss and crap and the rotting stench of dead dreams and forgotten lives that once called No Man's Land home.

This is stupid, Darius thought, angry there was nowhere else to run. He quickly moved further into the building, his eyes adjusting to the dark. Something scurried past him on the floor. *Please don't be a rat,* he said to himself. *Anything but a rat.* The last thing he needed was a hungry rat the size of a dog trying to chew his leg off.

Outside, Darius could hear cops moving toward the building. He could either make his way to the basement, where he could try to hide from the cops, or he could try something nearly as stupid and definitely more dangerous. Darius opted for the second, found the stairs, and ran as quickly as the darkness and rotting steps would allow him up to the second floor, then the third, fourth, fifth and finally to the roof of the building.

Out of breath again, his heart pounding, Darius felt the stabbing pain in his side return to taunt him like one of the bullies who used to pick on him at school.

Darius quickly surveyed his surroundings. All of the buildings on the block were tightly stacked with only a few feet between them. He could jump from rooftop to rooftop until he reached the end of the block. He had no idea what to do after that. *I'll deal with it when I get there.*

Darius ran from one rooftop to the next. The cops must have been looking for him inside the building he'd run into, because by the time he had jumped across five rooftops, they had yet to show up. He raced to the roof of the last building on the block and looked over the edge. He didn't see any cops in the darkness below. He did see a fire escape, and he knew how to get back down to the street.

Darius climbed on to the fire escape. Old and rusty, the fire escape made a terrible creaking sound and. as he began his climb, Darius wondered how sturdy it was. He didn't have to wonder for long.

As he lowered himself down four rungs from the top, the concrete in which the ladder was anchored simply crumbled to dust. The rusted metal of the ladder seemed to scream as it bent and broke, the whole thing falling away from the building.

It was a six-story drop to the ground. *I'm dead*, was the only thought in his mind. But then something grabbed Darius by the back of his sweatshirt, hoisted him high into the night air and flew off.

Darius knew exactly what had saved his life—or rather, *who* had saved his life. It only made him wish he'd fallen to his death.

3

Sitting in the interrogation room at the police station, Darius Logan knew he was in serious trouble. *This isn't going to be like the other times*, he said to himself.

Technically he was still a minor, but that wouldn't matter. He already had two strikes. Had already done time. And this was much more serious—backpack full of eXXeLL, running away from the scene of the crime. And of course, he had beaten up a cop.

I wonder if I'll be charged with resisting arrest or assaulting a cop—or both. I'm screwed either way.

He didn't know how long he'd been in the interrogation room. From where he sat, Darius couldn't see the clock on the wall. All he could do was listen to the tick, tick, tick, sound of the second hand as it moved. He figured it must have ticked at least 7,200 times. That's how many times it would tick in two hours, and he knew that he had been in the interrogation room at least two hours. At least it felt like two hours.

I hope time doesn't move this slowly in prison.

A sign on the wall read "No Smoking," yet the interrogation room smelled of stale cigarettes. Maybe smoking wasn't allowed in the room, but it had been at one point, and the stink still lingered like a ghost. It mixed with another smell—more powerful and foul than the cigarettes that had been smoked years ago.

Darius couldn't figure out what it was. And then he realized it was him. He stunk of body odor mixed with the residual funk of No Man's Land. Somehow, the way he smelled made a bad situation worse.

Four other people were in the dingy interrogation room that stunk of cigarettes and sweat. The room seemed big to Darius—at least big enough to fit the small table where he sat, and the four others who were in the room.

Two of the people were the detectives who had taken Darius into custody. One of the detectives called the other one Bob; but Detective Bob never used his partner's name. To Darius he was Detective No Name.

Detective Bob talked more than Detective No Name, who reminded Darius of a cop Clint Eastwood played in these movies he watched with his father. Darius's father loved Eastwood movies—"Dirty Harry," "Magnum Force," "Sudden Impact"—and so did Darius. That didn't mean he liked being in the same room with a detective doing his best Clint Eastwood impersonation.

An older woman sat between Detective Bob and Detective No Name. Darius had never seen Edith O'Malley looking so old or disappointed. He could see her fighting back the tears, which only made Darius feel worse. He wanted to tell her that everything was going to be fine, but they both knew better than that.

Edith had been Darius's caseworker ever since his parents were killed in The Attack when he was nine years old. Almost eight years later, she remained the most consistent person in his life—the only consistent person in his life.

The Attack had been brutal. Thousands of people of all ages and walks of life were killed, leaving behind thousands more to grieve. Only a few dozen kids like Darius were orphaned in The Attack, especially surprising considering the number of casualties. The newspaper even did a story on them, called "Orphans of the Attack," but Darius wasn't included in that article. It had been the sons and daughters of people who mattered—doctors and lawyers and people like that. Over the years he wondered if that was why nobody other than Edith cared about him.

At first Darius stayed with his only living relative, his father's older brother, Kenny. Darius's father and Uncle Kenny were never that close, but there was no other family. In the weeks and months following The Attack, Uncle Kenny paid close attention to all the news relating to death benefits awarded to families who had lost someone. "We gonna get paid offa this," Uncle Kenny would say with a big grin. And every time Darius would grow to hate him more and more. It got to the point where a fire of rage and resentment burned in Darius's gut every time he looked at his uncle, which only got worse every time Kenny talked about "gettin' paid."

It took almost a year for Darius to start getting the settlement that came in the form of twelve monthly checks. Before the checks started coming, while the government worked with insurance companies to develop a compensation package for the families of victims, Uncle Kenny would say, "If that money don't come soon, you know you gotta go." And when the checks finally came, Kenny would wave the envelope in Darius's face and say, "This is all your worthless ass is good for."

For a year, Uncle Kenny cashed the checks, spending most of it on booze, dope and gambling, while complaining that Darius's parents weren't worth much. He'd get drunk, swear at Darius, and once in a while put out his cigarettes on his nephew.

One night, Kenny didn't come home. Two days later, Edith O'Malley showed up at Kenny's apartment with a police officer. "Your Uncle Kenny has been arrested," she told Darius. "You're going to be placed in a foster home."

The first two or three foster homes weren't much better than staying with his uncle. Darius hated Kenny, but at least his uncle acknowledged his existence—even if it was only to smack him around or put out his cigarette butts on Darius's arm. His foster families were strangers who went back and forth between ignoring him and treating him like dirt. None of them cared that Darius lost his parents in The Attack.

By the time he moved to his fifth foster home—just before his fifteenth birthday—Darius knew that it was him against the world. Edith O'Malley was the only one who showed any caring or understanding. "I know this has been a difficult time, but you need to try and fit in at this home," she said every time he went to live with a new family.

Darius didn't see Edith O'Malley that often, but she always came by on his birthday with a card and a present, no matter where he lived. Edith O'Malley was the only person to remember or acknowledge Darius's birthday since the death of his parents, making her the closest thing to family he had. He'd never thought about her that way before, until he sat across from her in the interrogation room at the police station, with her fighting back the tears of disappointment. He knew his mother would not be able to do the same.

If Janae Logan were alive, sitting between Detective Bob and Detective No Name, she would be crying her eyes out to see her son in that interrogation room.

Thinking about his mother just made Darius feel worse—as if that were possible. He tried to push his mother out of his mind, but he couldn't do it. His parents were hardwired in his brain, even after being dead all these years.

"Darius, do you know how much trouble you've gotten yourself into?" asked Edith O'Malley.

"Yes, ma'am," replied Darius in a quiet whisper. Years of hard living and abuse had not taken away the lessons his parents had given him in how to be respectful. Sure, he'd been busted with a backpack full of Adrenaccelerate and been in a fight with a cop, but that wasn't going to stop him from showing some respect where respect was due. In a weird way, it brought Darius some sense of comfort, fleeting though it may have been. He knew he had screwed up. He knew he was going to prison. But part of the decent person his parents raised him to be still remained.

"I don't think you do know," said Detective No Name. He hadn't said a word since putting the handcuffs on Darius and placing him in the back of an unmarked police car. "This isn't shoplifting or boosting car stereos."

Detective No Name didn't take his eyes off Darius. An open folder sat on the table in front of him, and Detective No Name quietly tapped his finger on papers inside. The detective's tapping finger and his wannabe Clint Eastwood stare spoke to Darius without saying a word.

Edith glanced down at the file containing Darius's criminal record. When she looked back up, the tears she'd been fighting back flowed freely. "How would your parents feel if they could see you sitting here like this?" asked Edith.

My parents are dead.

And then, even though he didn't want to, Darius wondered how his parents would feel if they could see him sitting in the interrogation room. *They wouldn't be pleased.*

Until he was nine, Darius had been the only child of Dwayne and Janae Logan. The most beautiful woman Darius had ever seen, his mother gave birth to his baby brother two days before The Attack.

Darius's father dropped him off at school, and then went to pick up Janae and Dwayne Jr. from the hospital. And then came The Attack, and the world ended. In all of the chaos and confusion that followed, he wondered if his parents were all right.

The first parents started showing up to pick up their children within a few minutes of The Attack, while the city was still being torn apart. They rushed off, fleeing the city in hopes of avoiding the slaughter. In some cases it was other relatives who showed up at the Langston Hughes Elementary School, but it seemed like someone came to pick up every boy and girl who went to that school—except for Darius.

Up to that day, Darius never thought things like "What if my parents died?" But by the time it was dark, and everyone else had been picked up by a parent or a grandparent or a neighbor, Darius knew that his mother and father and baby brother were dead. He just knew it.

He tried not to spend too much time thinking about the family he'd lost, because it filled him with emotions he couldn't control—an explosive mix of sadness and anger that got him into too much trouble over the years. Gradually the sadness became less and less, until it was just a dull ache that Darius lived with and barely noticed most of the time. The anger, on the other hand, never left. He felt it whenever it flared up. And it flared up often.

But sitting in the interrogation room, with the clock ticking loudly behind him, the sadness that Darius lived with, to the point he hardly noticed it anymore, suddenly crashed over him like a massive wave. He'd squandered everything his parents had done for him and dishonored their memory. "They'd be upset," said Darius, his voice filled with shame over what he had become and profound sadness over the all he had lost.

"What is he being charged with?" asked Edith O'Malley.

"He was carrying Adrenaccelerate," said Detective Bob. "That's a violation of Homeland Security and considered an act of terrorism. And that's for starters. There's resisting arrest. Assaulting an officer."

Edith looked away from Darius, her eyes fixed on the silently tapping finger of Detective No Name. She let out a sigh that reminded Darius of the sad sigh his mother would make whenever he did something wrong. Only he had never done anything this wrong when his mother was alive. But his mother was dead. So were his father and baby brother. He had been alone for a long time, and as the files under Detective No Name's tapping finger clearly showed, Darius Logan did what he needed to survive.

Darius knew it didn't matter that he barely knew the guys he was with, that he'd never sold drugs before, never done drugs, or that he was still a minor. None of it mattered.

All that matters is the fact you got caught, he said to himself. *This is all on you, and you're gonna have to carry it yourself.*

"Young man, haven't we met before?" asked the booming voice of the only person in the room yet to speak.

This was the person who intimidated Darius the most—the person that left him feeling small and worthless, causing him to stare down at his hands nearly the entire time he sat in the interrogation room. This was the person that caught him when the fire escape tore away from the side of building, rescuing him from the inevitable death that would have followed a six-story fall.

He never said a word to Darius. But Darius knew who it was. As if getting caught by the cops wasn't bad enough, he'd been caught by Him.

The lights in the interrogation room weren't that good—long fluorescent bulbs, one of which was burned out, and one that would flicker from time to time—making it difficult to see Him. He stood in the far corner of the room, hidden by shadows—as if he had been trying to hide, to not call attention to his presence. But try as he might, Darius could not ignore Him.

"I'm good with faces," said the man, moving out of the shadows.

Darius tried not to look at him, but couldn't help himself. It looked like the man floated across the room instead of walking. "And you look very familiar. Do I know you?"

"Yes, sir," said Darius.

The man stood nearly seven feet tall, his head almost scraping against the ceiling of the room. His wide, muscular build made him equal to two men, and though Darius was intimidated, he could not help but look up from his hands and stare at Captain Freedom, the greatest superhero in the world.

4

Captain Freedom was the leader of Super Justice Force, a team of superheroes and crime fighters committed to protecting the world. His bright blue costume, made out of material that could not be burned or torn, fit him like a glove. The bald eagle emblem on his chest stared out at Darius, and even though there was no breeze in the room, his cape seemed to flap in the breeze nonetheless.

Capes looked stupid on most superheroes and had been out of style for years, but somehow Captain Freedom still managed to look cool. And while other heroes and crime fighters hid behind masks, Captain Freedom made no attempts to hide his face, making him that much more of a badass.

As far back as Darius could remember he worshipped Captain Freedom. He learned how to read with Captain Freedom comic books. He slept in Captain Freedom pajamas that he wore over Captain Freedom underwear. He saw the movie based on the Captain's life at least ten times, and even owned the whole line of Captain Freedom action figures, which his mother and father would argue about him playing with.

"I don't want him playing with a toy that doesn't look like him," his mother said. "Why can't he be into someone like Human Tornado or the Uptown Avenger?"

"Baby, you've got to be kidding me. I can't believe you'd even mention those names," his father responded.

"You know what I mean."

"Look, there are worse role models for him to have than a white guy in a silly suit who fights crime," said his father.

At the time, he didn't understand what his parents were talking about. All Darius knew was that his mother wanted him to play with action figures of guys like Human Tornado and Uptown Avenger, who had stopped fighting crime and didn't even have their own line of toys or comic books. His father, on the other hand, would say, "I don't care what color dolls you play with, as long as you understand what these men stand for in real life."

Darius didn't know what his father meant by that—especially since he didn't play with dolls, he played with action figures. And even though his parents didn't agree over what he should play with, neither of them had a problem with him reading Captain Freedom comic books. Once a week his father came home from work with one or two new books, and he would always say the same thing: "Don't just look at the pictures."

After he read the comic books—some of which were the adventures of superheroes other than Captain Freedom—Darius recounted for his parents what happened in each issue. And this led to Darius becoming obsessed with Captain Freedom and the rest of Super Justice Force. The thing he liked best about Captain Freedom and the others—as opposed to superheroes like Spider-Man and Superman—was that the heroes in Super Justice Force were real. The comic book adventures of SJF were based on real things, and that was so much cooler than the make-believe superheroes in other comic books.

When he was eight years old, Darius wrote an essay about Captain Freedom and Super Justice Force—"How Captain Freedom and Super Justice Force Keep the World Safe." His teacher submitted the essay to a citywide competition, and it actually won.

Darius met Captain Freedom for the first time at an award ceremony for students being honored for academic excellence. Darius earned his place at the ceremony for the essay he'd written and for being a straight-A student. His teachers all said he was "unusually bright." He skipped second grade altogether, and halfway through third Darius was bumped up to fourth—all of which factored into his being named Student of the Year, much to the surprise of him and his parents.

The school superintendent gave a speech about Darius and his essay, and then announced him as Student of the Year. The room erupted in applause, his mother burst into tears, and his father never looked more proud. It was definitely the best moment of Darius's life, one he thought could not get any better. But when Captain Freedom himself came out to give Darius his award placard, he knew that his life would never get better than that moment.

Nine years later, sitting in the interrogation room at the police station, Darius was reunited with Captain Freedom. If his first meeting with the Captain was the best moment of his life, the second meeting was one of the worst.

"You wrote an essay about me," said Captain Freedom.

"Yes, sir," said Darius. *How can he possibly remember that?*

"And you were Student of the Year, isn't that right?"

Darius should have felt proud. After all of the years, after all of the things Captain Freedom had done and all the people he met, the superhero still remembered him. Instead, he felt ashamed.

"What happened to you? Where did you go wrong?" asked Captain Freedom.

Darius didn't have the answers. He didn't know where he went wrong. He didn't know what happened to him. All he knew was that one day he was happy, living with his mother and father and waiting for the birth of his baby brother who he was going to share all of his toys and comic books with. And then came The Attack. In one instant his family was killed, his life destroyed.

Is that what you want me to say? Darius wondered. *Do you want all the details of my crappy life these last eight years?*

Darius didn't know what to say, so he said nothing. And he and everyone else in the room remained silent, while the second hand on the clock ticked. Darius counted thirty-five ticks before someone said something.

"It was The Attack. His parents were killed in The Attack," said Edith O'Malley. She paused, while the second hand ticked by ten more times. "He's had a very difficult time since then."

The sadness in Edith's voice reminded Darius of how many people sounded after The Attack, when they talked about people who'd been killed. To Darius, it almost sounded like Edith was talking about someone else—someone dead. And as he sat there in the interrogation room in the police station, Darius wished that he was dead. He wished that he died with the rest of his family, which would have been better than living without them.

"A lot of good people were killed in The Attack. That's not a reason," said Captain Freedom. "It's an excuse."

His lower lip began to tremble, and Darius could feel the tears welling up in his eyes—the first tears he had cried in many, many years. He couldn't tell if they were tears of sadness or anger. He dealt with many bad things since the death of his parents, but few were worse than this. And as he fought to keep from crying, for a very brief moment, Darius began to realize that *this* was the worst time of his life—even worse than the death of his family. He couldn't explain it. He just knew it.

For so many years he wished he died alongside his mother and father and baby brother, but now, sitting in the interrogation room, he realized that his life really was ending. He would be going to prison for possession of the most controlled substance on the planet. For resisting arrest and assaulting an officer. For being unlucky enough to not die with his parents and baby brother who was only two days old when Darius's whole world crashed down around him.

"What would your parents say if they could see you now?" asked Captain Freedom.

Darius sat for a moment and searched deep within himself for an answer. His parents worked hard to raise him proper. His mother pushed him to get the best grades possible. His father taught him how to defend himself. They taught him not to lie, and how to be respectful, and all the other things good parents teach their children. But sitting in the interrogation room, one thing his father always said to him stood out more than anything else, echoing in his head.

"Don't be a stereotype or a statistic," said Darius. His voice trembled with too many years of nothing but sorrow and rage. Darius recognized the words, but he didn't even recognize the voice as his own, nor did he notice the first tear as it began to roll down his cheek.

"What's that? I can't hear you," demanded Captain Freedom.

"Don't be a stereotype. Never become a statistic," said Darius. His voice louder, repeating what his father said to him since as far back as he could remember.

Dwayne Logan told his son that there would be times in life that people would ask and expect many things from him, and the only thing Darius had to remember was to "not be a stereotype and never become a statistic."

"Looking at you, sitting there, it seems to me that's exactly what you are," said Captain Freedom. For a brief second, his voice almost sounded like Dwayne Logan. "What happened to the kid who was Student of the Year? Was he killed in The Attack as well?"

Darius sat, waiting for someone else to answer the question.

"Was he killed in The Attack as well?" Captain Freedom asked again—his voice louder and more demanding. The walls in the interrogation room actually shook. And it wasn't just Darius that noticed; the others felt it as well. Even Detective No Name, who tried to look tough and act like Clint Eastwood, looked a little shocked and scared.

But no one in the room was more scared than Darius. Every day since his parents had been killed was a fight to simply stay alive—bouncing around from one foster home to another, spending time locked up in juvenile detention, living on the streets. There were nights when he went to sleep with his stomach empty and days when he woke up to rats or roaches scurrying around whatever floor he slept on. It had been nearly eight years of living hell, with no one to care whether his next meal was cooked in a kitchen or came out of a garbage can. No one to care if he lived or died. And no matter how scared he felt at any given moment, he never gave into the fear, because that would have meant he had lost.

Sitting there in the interrogation room, Darius couldn't hold back the volatile mix of emotions—fear, sorrow, rage—any more than he could hold back the tears. And as he cried, he thought about what Captain Freedom had asked him: "What happened to the kid who was Student of the Year? Was he killed in The Attack as well?"

As much as he wished he'd been killed with his family, Darius didn't die on that terrible day. He was very much alive, and about to face the consequences of his actions.

"No, sir. He wasn't killed in the attack," said Darius, crying for the first time since the day his parents died.

5

The detectives and Captain Freedom left Darius alone in the interrogation room with Edith O'Malley. She sat silently watching him as he ate the fast food that had been brought to him. *Not much of last meal for a condemned man*, Darius thought as he chewed the cold, greasy hamburger.

"There's nothing I can do for you this time," said Edith, her voice sounding tired and sad.

Darius wanted to apologize to Edith. He knew that she cared about him, maybe even more than most social workers care about their clients. And for whatever reason, he felt like he'd let her down. He couldn't think of anything to say—at least not anything that would have mattered—so he just offered her some of his food.

"No thanks," she said with a faint smile.

Of all the clients Edith O'Malley had—more than she could adequately take care of—Darius was one of her favorites. Despite his troubles, she knew that he was a good person. And considering all that he'd experienced over the years, Edith was often amazed at how well he had managed to keep himself together. She had nearly two-dozen other clients, all of them strung out on drugs, drowning in booze, and in and out of jail. She was pretty sure Darius had never done drugs, and even when he went to juvenile detention on assault charges, part of her knew that he was justified in what he'd done.

"It's cool if you don't visit me in prison," Darius said.

"What are you talking about?" Edith asked.

"Could you just send me letters or something? Not all the time—one or two a year would be fine. Just something to remind me that I was once somebody who had someone that cared."

Edith reached out and took Darius's hand. They both sat in silence, angry and sad at the cruel world that brought them together. In a better world, Darius and Edith would have never met. And though neither said it to the other, they both wished their lives had been different. Darius wished his life had never fallen apart. Edith wished she didn't have to spend her life holding together the broken pieces of kids like Darius.

The door to the interrogation room opened, and a uniformed officer led Darius out of the room and down the hall. Edith began to cry, wondering if she would ever see him again.

The police officer escorted Darius to a different room—a larger conference room, with better lighting, more comfortable chairs, and no stale scent of cigarette smoke. Captain Freedom sat waiting with two other people Darius didn't know. *They're not cops,* he thought. *Probably lawyers.*

"Sit," said Captain Freedom, pointing to a chair.

I'm not a dog, Darius thought as he sat in the chair next to the one Captain Freedom pointed to.

"This is Oliver Porter with the Public Defender's office and this Adalyne Oldham with the District Attorney's office," said Captain Freedom.

A pudgy black man with a shaved head, Oliver Porter looked like a darker version of Elmer Fudd from those old Bugs Bunny cartoons. He wore a suit that looked less than new, and a tie with little green cartoon frogs that looked like a Father's Day gift. His briefcase sat in front of him, a disorganized pile of papers overflowing onto the table.

"You can call me Ollie. I'll be representing you," he said, extending his hand.

Ollie Porter looked like a soft man. But his handshake was surprisingly strong, and his voice was probably an octave lower than his looks would have indicated.

Sitting across from Ollie, with a pile of papers slightly more organized, sat Adalyne Oldham, an older white woman with dark circles under her eyes and glasses about to slide off her nose. "You can call me Ms. Oldham," she said in far less friendly tone.

Aside from the brief introductions, neither lawyer wasted any time getting to the heart of the matter. Ollie shuffled through his stacks of papers, looking for something that didn't seem to be there. "You're a ward of the state," he said in more of a statement than a question.

Darius assumed that Ollie was talking to him and nodded his head. "Yes."

"And you turn seventeen later this month?" asked Ollie, shuffling through the papers.

Darius nodded again. "On Wednesday," he said.

Ms. Oldham cleared her throat as if she had something to say. Everyone turned to look at her, except for Captain Freedom, who never took his eyes off Darius.

"Mr. Logan, given your past record, and the nature of the crimes you've been charged with, it is the belief of the District Attorney's office that despite your age, you be charged as an adult," said Oldham, pushing her glasses back further up to the bridge of her nose. Her voice rasped from too much smoking, and her lips barely moved when she talked.

The world around Darius began to crumble, while he felt like he was collapsing in on himself.

"Do you know what that means?" asked Ollie.

"Serious time," answered Darius.

"I'm afraid so," said Ollie. "If you'd been in possession of cocaine, it might have been different. But possession of Adrenaccelerate is a federal offense, and the amount you were carrying bumps the charges up to possession with intent to sell. And then you throw in resisting arrest and assaulting an officer. That's very serious time."

"We'll need to confer with the federal prosecutor's office, but the D.A.'s office will be looking for the maximum sentence," said Oldham. Her voice sounded tired, like the last thing she wanted to talk about was how much of Darius's life would be spent in prison. "Fifteen years, minimum, is what we're going to ask for."

Fifteen years? Darius felt like he had just been hit in the face with a brick.

"Would you excuse us for a few minutes?" asked Captain Freedom.

Both Ollie and Ms. Oldham mumbled something, and then left Darius and Captain Freedom sitting across from each other at the large conference table. Except for the sound of the clock ticking, the room was uncomfortably silent.

"Congratulations, Darius," said Captain Freedom, breaking the awkward silence. "You have officially become both a stereotype and a statistic. You're a three-time loser headed to a life in prison. Not much of a way to honor the memory of your parents, is it?"

Alone with the superhero he worshipped in his childhood, Darius no longer felt scared or ashamed or confused. He simply felt angry. Darius burned with anger over Captain Freedom's words and what they said about him and his life.

Even though he stood only five-feet, seven inches tall, and weighed only 135 pounds, Darius wanted to fight. Captain Freedom pissed him off, and it didn't matter that the superhero had single-handedly defeated supercriminals like Doc Kaos and the Masters of D.E.A.T.H., or that he led Super Justice Force in defending Earth against the forces of the Ad-Ahlen Empire. It didn't matter that Captain Freedom could bend steel with his bare hands, or that he could fly, or that a copy of the first issue of his comic book had sold on eBay for over $10,000. All that mattered was that Darius wanted to tear his head off.

Darius quickly glanced around the room looking for some sort of weapon. *I wonder how much damage it would do if I hit him over the head with one of these chairs,* Darius thought. *Probably not much. Bullets bounce off him.*

"I can tell you're pissed off," said Captain Freeman, a slight smile on his face. "And you know what?"

Darius stared directly into the eyes of Captain Freedom. He might not be able to go toe to toe with him, but Darius wasn't going to back down. "What?"

"I don't care. I really don't," said Captain Freedom staring right back at Darius. "All I want to know is what are you going to do?"

And with that, Captain Freedom got up from the table, leaving Darius alone in the conference room.

Darius stared at the clock on the wall as the seconds ticked away, turning into minutes, and he thought about the minutes turning into years. *Fifteen years is a long time. I won't get out of prison until I'm almost thirty-two. Maybe I can get time off for good behavior,* he thought, trying to be optimistic.

After what felt like hours alone, with only the ticking of the clock to distract him from thinking about his inevitable fate, the door opened. Ollie Porter and Ms. Oldham came back in, followed by two other men Darius didn't recognize. One of the men looked to be in his mid-forties, the other, maybe twenty years older than that. Both men carried briefcases, and neither introduced himself.

Darius's head started to pound in pain—feeling like his brain would explode at any moment. He just wanted to get it all over with.

Captain Freedom entered the room. He sat directly across from Darius. "I'm going to make this very simple," he said. "You can either become a better person, or you can go to jail."

Simple? Nothing is simple. What the hell is he talking about?

"What Captain Freedom is trying to say is that you are being given a choice—a choice you need to make before any of us leaves this room—that will very likely determine the rest of your life," said Ollie Porter.

Reaching into his briefcase, the older of the two men pulled out a large folder and slid it across the table. Darius picked up the folder and examined the contents, but he had no clue what he was reading.

"Darius, my name is Dr. Samson Omatete, but you can call me Dr. Sam," said the older man. "My colleague is Chuck Maslon."

Darius glanced at both men, not saying a word. Dr. Sam looked gruff, more like an ex-Marine drill sergeant or a retired boxer than a doctor. When he talked it sounded like an angry growl of an old grizzly bear. He reminded Darius of Jim Brown, a football player his father used to talk about.

Maslon, the younger of the two, was the opposite of Dr. Sam. His suit fit better than Dr. Sam's, and he carried himself with more of a sense of importance. But something about the way he looked at Darius—almost glaring at him—didn't sit well.

Watch out for this one, Darius thought.

"I work for Super Justice Force," said Dr. Sam, "heading up a special rehabilitation program for select offenders called Second Chance. After discussing your case with your lawyer, Ms. Oldham and Captain Freedom, we've decided that you are an excellent candidate for the program."

Darius studied the papers in the folder. Pages and pages and more pages—so many pages there was no way he could read them all right there. Nothing made sense. He had a terrible headache, making it especially difficult to concentrate. It almost sounded like he might be able to keep from going to prison. "I'm not sure I understand," Darius said.

"There's a lot of information in the packet, and I know it can get confusing, so I'll try to explain it as simply as possible," said Dr. Sam, trying to sound compassionate. It didn't work. He simply wasn't the type who made you feel comfortable with his presence, no matter how hard he tried. "Super Justice Force believes that locking criminals up is not enough. We believe that the best way to prevent future crimes is to provide rehabilitation opportunities to key offenders. That's what Second Chance is. We provide jobs and career training for convicted felons, hoping that these opportunities will lead them away from a life of crime and to a more productive role in society."

"And you want me to be part of Second Chance?" asked Darius.

"I want you in Second Chance," said Captain Freedom.

"Okay, I'll do it," said Darius without a second thought. He really had no clue what Second Chance was about, and frankly he didn't care. If it meant staying out of prison, he was all for it.

"Well, here's where it gets a bit complicated," started Dr. Sam. "Until now, every person who has gone into Second Chance came out of prison, already having done time."

"But you haven't done any time," said Maslon. The tone in his voice made Darius uncomfortable. "That makes you an exceptionally difficult case."

"Exceptional, yes," said Dr. Sam, "but not necessarily difficult."

Maslon shook his head as he looked at Darius. "We're not set up to be a viable alternative to incarceration. Sam, I get where you want to take the program, but this punk kid is too young, and he's not the way to take the program to a new level."

Darius clenched his fists under the table.

"Let's start helping people before they become hardened criminals," said Dr. Sam.

While Dr. Sam and Maslon continued to argue, so too did Ollie and Ms. Oldham. The lawyers could not agree on what a reasonable amount of time served in Second Chance would be, as opposed to time served in prison. Ms. Oldham felt that because the D.A.'s office wanted fifteen years, fifteen years in Second Chance would be a reasonable amount of time served. Ollie wanted three years and probation.

The arguing went on and on and on. Finally, everyone came to an agreement. Or at least it was something close to an agreement. Dr. Sam and Ollie were happy; while Ms. Oldham was relieved the conversation had ended. Maslon was the only one not pleased. If he had it his way, Darius would not be going into Second Chance at all, period. But that's not how it was going to be.

It didn't matter how Chuck Maslon felt about the issue. Darius Logan was going to work for Super Justice Force, the world's most powerful team of superheroes.

6

Technically, Darius Logan had been placed under arrest, although the paperwork he filled out referred to it as a "term of service." Instead of being tried and convicted, he was remanded to the custody of Super Justice Force to participate in Second Chance, a rehabilitation program operated by SJF.

Second Chance had been started by SJF over twelve years earlier as a way to help ex-convicts start a normal life after prison. Dr. Samson Omatete ran the program, which worked with everyone from petty crooks to super powered villains—it didn't matter as long as they were committed to going straight.

Once Darius agreed to enter into Second Chance, and before the final details could be worked out, Captain Freedom left the conference room at the police station, saying, "Don't screw this up."

Filling out the stacks of paperwork took almost an hour. Everything had to be signed by six people—Maslon, who was the Head of Security for Super Justice Force, Dr. Sam, both of the lawyers, Darius, and eventually Edith O'Malley, who, as his caseworker, had permission to act as a custodial guardian. When the last of the forms had been signed, Dr. Sam arranged all of the papers and placed them back in his briefcase.

"So, you'll make sure his case worker signs off, process the paperwork today, and send copies over to both offices?" Ollie asked Dr. Sam.

Dr. Sam nodded at him and waved his hand as if to say, "It's all taken care of."

"I'll need my copies first thing Monday morning," said Ms. Oldham, closing her briefcase with a thud. She looked over at Darius, pushed her glasses back up, and spoke in her raspy voice. "Well, Mr. Logan, you've dodged a bullet. I sincerely hope you make the most of this tremendous opportunity. This is not a 'get out of jail free' card. Any violation of the terms spelled out in the forms will constitute a breach of your term of service, in which case you will go directly to jail. You will not pass go. You will not collect $200. Am I understood?"

"Yes," said Darius.

"Good," said Ms. Oldham with the closest thing to a smile Darius had seen on her face. "Good luck to you."

Ms. Oldham left the room. In a way, Darius felt sad to see her leave. She had been far from friendly, but compared to Maslon, she was downright motherly.

Next, it was Ollie Porter's turn to leave. He rose from his seat and extended his hand to Darius. "Good luck with everything, Darius," said Ollie. He handed Darius a business card. "If you have any problems at all, just call me."

As Ollie Porter left the conference room, Maslon removed something from his briefcase. It was an object that looked like a black plastic bracelet. "This is your cage," said Maslon, handing Darius the black object.

Darius had no idea what he held in his hands. It was made of some sort of smooth black material. It felt heavier than it looked, and as near as Darius could tell, it was one solid piece. A small display of lights came on—something electronic inside the black band had been activated.

Darius looked up at Maslon, talking into his cell phone. "I need you to go live with Logan, Darius R., number 005-1381."

Red electronic characters appeared on the band's display screen that read, "Logan, Darius R., 005-1381."

"Now I need you to open the door," said Maslon.

A moment later, an invisible hinge on the band opened. Maslon walked over to Darius, took the band from him, and squatted down like a shoe salesman helping a customer try on a new pair of sneakers. He placed the band around Darius's ankle, and closed it. Standing back up, he spoke into the phone one more time. "Now lock the door."

A small beeping sound came from the band around his ankle, and before Maslon could explain, Darius knew exactly what was happening. The black band was some sort of LoJack, or tracking device, or something along those lines.

Nothing like a high-tech ball and chain to keep you in line, Darius thought.

"It's called a Security Transmitter and Tracking Unit, STATU for short," explained Dr. Sam.

"Does everyone in Second Chance where one of these?" asked Darius.

"Not everyone. But some," answered Dr. Sam. He offered a smile that Darius figured was supposed to be reassuring.

7

Darius felt exhausted. He'd been awake for over twenty-four hours, and even though he usually had trouble sleeping, he felt like he would fall asleep in the backseat of the car being driven by Chuck Maslon. Dr. Sam sat in the front passenger seat.

"Where are we going?" Darius asked.

"Your new home," answered Maslon, a hint of contempt in his voice.

Darius couldn't tell whether Dr. Sam noticed Maslon's tone. The doctor seemed to ignore much of what Maslon said.

"We're going to Super Justice Force Headquarters," said Dr. Sam. "There is, among other things, housing facilities at HQ. You'll be staying there."

"What about my stuff?" asked Darius.

"What stuff?" asked Maslon.

Darius didn't own much. A few tattered books and some beat-up clothes that made him look homeless were about all he had as far as worldly possessions went. But there were also the pictures—a handful of old photographs he had managed to hold on to over the years that provided the only proof he once had a family. The pictures meant more to him than anything else. "I have some stuff, clothes and pictures and things."

He tried to downplay how important the photographs were. Darius could go the rest of his life wearing just the clothes on his back, but he had to have the pictures that he'd found in the bottom of a box in his Uncle Kenny's closet.

He had asked Kenny many times if there were any pictures of his mother and father, and his uncle told him there weren't. The thing was that Darius remembered his mother sending at least one picture. It had been taken a few weeks before his parents died, and Darius remembered his father arguing with her about it. "Do you really think my brother cares?" Dwayne asked.

But Janae sent it anyway, and even though Uncle Kenny claimed he had no pictures of his brother, sister-in-law and nephew, Darius was convinced otherwise. It took him a long time of secretly rummaging through Kenny's stuff, before he found the photos in a box filled with junk. He wasn't going to lose them now. He didn't care if the STATU around his ankle made his whole leg explode, or if going after the pictures meant going to prison, he couldn't live without the photos.

"We'll make arrangements to get your things in the next few days—after you get processed," said Dr. Sam as the car pulled up to the world headquarters of Super Justice Force.

Darius had spent a lot of time doing research for the essay that won the citywide competition when he was eight. Part of his prize included a guided tour of Super Justice Force World Headquarters. And even though he hadn't read many comic books in the last seven or eight years—or many books, for that matter—he still felt he knew a lot about Super Justice Force and their HQ.

The largest man-made structure in North America, Super Justice Force World Headquarters had been named one of the modern wonders of the world. The original headquarters had been built nearly forty years earlier, when the first Captain Freedom, a man named Jake Kirby, Sr., originally formed Super Justice Force.

Jake Kirby was the son of Dr. Jacob Kurtzberg, the foremost scientist in the study of metahumans and super powered humans. It was Kurtzberg who identified the "twenty-fourth chromosome," the genetic disorder resulting in Kurtzberg-24 Syndrome, which gave human beings super powers. Considered by historians to be the first real costumed superhero, Kirby used his powers to help fight crime and protect humanity as Captain Freedom. His comic book adventures thrilled a generation, and his real-life adventures gave them hope for a better tomorrow.

There were other superheroes at the time, dressed in colorful costumes, fighting crime and defending justice, but none were as recognizable or popular as Captain Freedom. The Protector fought crime using a high-tech suit, and became the first crime fighter to get a major corporate endorsement deal, turning superheroics into a viable business venture. Validus was rumored to be an alien from another planet. The original Super Justice Force consisted of Captain Freedom, the Protector and Validus, who joined forces with five other lesser-known heroes to thwart the first of two alien attacks.

Over the years, Super Justice Force grew into the largest team of superheroes and crime fighters in the world. With over one hundred fully active members and another fifty affiliate members—not including Teen Justice Force—SJF maintained operating headquarters in six cities, and had at least one hero on active duty in all fifty states. Recognized by the federal government as a privately owned law enforcement agency, SJF worked in conjunction with local, state and federal agencies, and every member of Super Justice Force was fully licensed and deputized. Both the team itself and individual members earned money from endorsement deals and royalties from film, television and comic book revenue, not to mention action figure sales and whatever they earned from personal appearances.

The massive structure looming before Darius had been built twenty years after the construction of the original HQ, and took up the equivalent of six full city blocks. HQ consisted of four buildings clustered together, with a fifth building on the other side of Super Justice Force Memorial Park. The original headquarters, called "the Mansion," looked almost like the White House with its grand columns and sense of importance, and served as the main entrance to HQ. Directly behind the Mansion, "the Tower" stood thirty stories tall. "The Dome" stood to the east of the Tower, and it looked like a high-tech sports arena. Wedged between the Tower and the Dome, only five stories tall, stood "the Bunker." And on the other side of the park stood the fifth building that comprised SJF Headquarters, "the School."

The five buildings comprising HQ were a sight to see. At a glance, the buildings looked separate—especially the School. But the four main buildings connected on the ground level, the second floor, first basement, and through an intricate series of tunnels and corridors, while the School was connected to the other buildings by series of underground passages. All of this made the five buildings one massive structure.

Within the walls of the HQ were living quarters for active members of Super Justice Force, housing for participants of Second Chance, SJF corporate offices, a fully functioning medical clinic with a trauma center, and the most elaborate communications network in the galaxy. The maintenance shop serviced the various vehicles used by SJF members, including the SJF interplanetary ship, which could take off and land from the Dome when the retractable roof opened. The Kurtzberg Metahuman Research and Training Center, located in the School, was the leading research facility for both metahumans and those with Kurtzberg-24 Syndrome, offering full training for mutants and those with powers, as well as a private school for students in grades five through twelve.

The most recognizable part of HQ, the Mansion served as the main public entrance. Everyone entering HQ passed a giant statue of the original lineup of Super Justice Force members. Both impressive and beautiful, the inscription at the base of the statue read, "Justice For All."

A security station inside the main foyer greeted all visitors checking in, while uniformed men and women directed people to their destinations. Visitors taking the guided tour of HQ moved to the right, toward the SJF Museum, gift shop and restaurant. Other visitors moved to the left, going toward the SJF research library and the primary entrance to the corporate offices.

Dr. Sam and Chuck Maslon led Darius into the building just as a busload of tourists arrived. The tourists stood in a single-file line, taking pictures as they waited to pass through the security station, which looked like the x-ray machines at airports—only more high-tech. Only four of the five x-ray machines were being used. Dr. Sam led Darius past the tourists to the fifth machine, flashed some sort of identification badge, and he and Darius were waved through.

Darius looked behind him and saw Chuck Maslon still at the security station. Maslon made a show of removing a gun from his shoulder holster and handing it to one of the security guards before passing through the x-ray machine.

Who needs a gun in a building full of superheroes? Darius thought. It just made Maslon that much more of a joke.

"I'm sure you've noticed by now, Chuck doesn't have the most endearing personality," said Dr. Sam. "He takes his job as Head of Security very seriously. And he doesn't trust anyone."

"Sounds like he's fun to be around," said Darius, trying not to sound too sarcastic.

"Not everyone can be the life of the party," said Dr. Sam with a smile. Dr. Sam smiling looked like an old bulldog baring its teeth before attacking.

Maslon caught up with Darius and Dr. Sam at an elevator that faced the gift shop.

"We taking him to processing?" asked Maslon. He adjusted his gun in the shoulder holster in a way that seemed to be a show for Darius's sake.

"He can be processed tomorrow," said Dr. Sam. "He needs some rest."

"I think it's a mistake to not process him now," said Maslon. He talked to Dr. Sam, but looked directly at Darius.

"Processing will take at least four hours, and Darius hasn't had any sleep," said Dr. Sam. "I'm taking him to Detention. Tomorrow he can be processed."

Dr. Sam led Darius on to the elevator, but Maslon did not follow. "He's wearing his STATU. There's nothing to worry about," said Dr. Sam as the elevator door closed.

Darius knew it wasn't the last he'd be seeing of Maslon, but for the moment, he felt relieved to have him out of sight. He had no idea what the days—and even years—to come had in store. He did know for certain that at some point in time he would have trouble with Maslon.

"He's going to be waiting for you to mess up, Darius. And if you do, he'll know about it," Dr. Sam said, as if reading Darius's mind. The elevator moved, but Darius couldn't tell which way it was going. At first it felt like the elevator moved horizontally instead of vertically.

When the elevator doors opened, they arrived somewhere that looked like a futuristic version of a small-town jail. Two men sat at a security station. Both looked a lot like cops. Dressed in dark uniforms with an official-looking badge pinned over the left breast of their shirts, name tags and photo identification over the right, they wore the same uniform as the security guards at the entrance to HQ. Neither man had a gun, but one had an UltraStun 500 in a holster on his belt. And with an UltraStun 500, he didn't really need a gun.

On the other side of the station were what looked like jail cells—only without bars. Darius looked around the room to get a better sense of his surroundings. The lack of windows made him wonder if they were underground. There was little by way of decoration, although a large clock on the wall told him it was almost four o'clock.

Even without the bars, this place looked a bit too much like a jail, which made Darius uncomfortable. "Is this where I'm going to be living?" he asked.

"No, this is Detention. It's primarily used for holding suspects until they can be transported to jail," explained Dr. Sam. "And sometimes, we hold people here right after they get out of prison, before they get processed into Second Chance."

Dr. Sam greeted the guards, Sullivan and Martin, and then introduced Darius. "I'll be taking Darius to Processing in the morning," said Dr. Sam. "In the meantime, make sure he gets some dinner, and tell whoever comes on for the next shift that I'll be back at eight in the morning."

"We'll make sure they have him ready," said Sullivan.

"If you need anything, just ask Sullivan or Martin," said Dr. Sam, getting back on the elevator. "I'll see you tomorrow morning."

As the elevator doors closed and Dr. Sam disappeared, Martin led Darius to one of the holding cells. They waited a moment while Sullivan deactivated a force field.

The room looked just like a jail cell, complete with a small bed, a sink and a toilet. Darius dreaded the thought of using the toilet with no privacy at all. The look on his face must have said it all.

"There's a bathroom right down the hall, if you want some privacy," said Martin. "We'll be right outside if you need anything."

Darius sat on the bed and waited for the force field to be reactivated, but it wasn't. He heard Sullivan and Martin outside talking about the baseball game from the night before. And then he fell asleep.

8

Chuck Maslon liked to think he ran the whole show at Super Justice Force World Headquarters. As the head of security, he was in fact one of the six most powerful SJF employees. Only the "supes"—superheroes like Captain Freedom, Nightwatcher and Kid Spectacular—had any real authority over him. But there were a handful of others that could call the shots just like Maslon, and every once in a while something reminded him that the show he fancied was his to run wasn't really his, and that he was nothing more than a player. A big player, with a lot of power, but a player nonetheless.

Sitting in Detention, at a few minutes past seven in the morning, Maslon was reminded that there were others at SJF with power to rival his own. The two security guards stationed in Detention were, as far as he was concerned, not real security guards. Yes, both the guards had Level Three clearance, but both had gone through Second Chance, which made them criminals. Neither of the guards was a member of Maslon's elite Security One team—made up mostly of ex-cops, all of whom answered to him and him alone. He knew that Dr. Sam must have pulled some strings to get "Big" Mike Epting and Theo "Butchie" Pirro stationed in Detention.

Maslon came to work for Super Justice Force as head of security six months after The Attack. Before that he'd been the lead detective in the police department's "Super Squad." That's what everyone called the unit of detectives that worked on cases related to metahumans, anyone with super powers, or simply the nut jobs that put on costumes and ran around the city.

Maslon's actions in the Super Squad during The Attack thrust him into the public spotlight, and during the fifteen minutes of fame that followed, plenty of job offers came his way. He could have taken a job on any police department in the world, and the private sector offered him more money than most people could realistically imagine. But it was the job at Super Justice Force that lined up most with his personal goals.

The aftermath of The Attack wasn't his first time in the public eye. Long before he had been a cop, Chuck Maslon had been in the Marines, a member of the First Earth Infantry—the first unit of the United States Military deployed on another planet. This was years before the formation of the United Terran Defense Initiative, and just before the legendary Battle of Enceladus.

Earth's first and only off-world colony had been built on the Saturn moon of Enceladus, where nearly two thousand humans lived and worked alongside an equal number of extraterrestrials from four other planets. Maslon was the youngest member of First Earth Infantry stationed on Enceladus when the Ad-Ahlen Empire attacked; resulting in the human race's first and most deadly conflict with an extraterrestrial race.

As one of the few survivors of the Battle of Enceladus, and as a veteran of the toughest city in the world—with more superhero and metahuman activity per capita than anywhere else—Chuck Maslon had long since learned how to identify trouble. And as far as he was concerned, Darius Logan was trouble.

Sitting quietly at the guard station, not saying a word to either of the guards, Maslon studied the folder full of files that chronicled the life and times of Darius Logan. When he arrived at Detention, one of the guards, "Butchie" Pirro, had been studying the files, which told the head of security that Dr. Sam, and not some scheduling error, was responsible for the guards on duty.

Dr. Sam had a sneaky habit of making sure his new recruits in Second Chance were looked after by veterans of the same rehabilitation program, who all shared some immoral code of honor. Maslon knew this was part of the reason Second Chance enjoyed such a high success rate—Dr. Sam manipulated the program and bent the rules to ensure that jokers who belonged behind bars stayed in the program, instead of going to prison. This was not, however, going to be the case with Darius Logan.

When Maslon took over as head of security for SJF, Second Chance was already in place. In theory, he didn't have that much trouble with the program, and if all Second Chance served was petty criminals and small-time losers who were relegated to mopping floors and doing laundry, then he'd have no problem at all. But Second Chance worked with the worst of the worst—hard-core offenders like Magnetic Mauler, the Oblivi8or, El Toro Loco and Otto Rekker—all of whom had a bit too much power and authority at SJF. It was only a matter of time before the program took in someone beyond redemption, and that person would ultimately threaten the security of all that he had worked for. And though he couldn't explain it, Maslon worried Darius Logan could very well be that person.

Darius showered in the bathroom across from the holding cells in Detention. He'd woken up after the soundest sleep he'd had in years, and it took him a few seconds to figure out where he was. The guards stationed in Detention told him it was okay to use the shower, handing him a towel, a neatly folded pile of clean clothes that must have come from the SJF souvenir shop, and a bag for his dirty clothes.

"You can wear these until we get a chance to wash your clothes," said the older of the two guards.

Catching a glimpse of himself, Darius stared at his unwashed reflection in the squeaky-clean mirror of the sterile bathroom, and realized that he looked like what his mother used to call "leftover mess gone cold."

He stood in the shower, letting the hot water rain down his body. It felt like forever since he'd taken a shower, and it had been forever since he'd been in a room that clean.

No roaches. No rats. This is high living. If I could just spend the next few years right here in the shower, everything would be cool.

As the water washed away the dirt and funk, Darius's head began to ache. A dull pain at first, just behind his eyes, that he figured was from hunger. He always got a headache when he was hungry. But as Darius dried off, the pain quickly escalated. In a matter of moments he had one of the worst headaches he had ever known.

Something is wrong, he thought, slipping into the clothes he had been given. *My head feels like it's going to explode.*

The gray t-shirt read "Property of Super Justice Force," and the dark blue sweatpants had "SJF" printed on one of the legs. The clothes were too big, but not to the point that they made Darius look ridiculous. Truth be told, Darius didn't care how the clothes made him look, or even that they were clean. All he could think about was the pain—it was too intense, making him dizzy and nauseous. It was more than just being hungry. *Maybe I'm having a brain aneurism or something like that.*

Darius walked back out into the main area of Detention. He struggled to keep his balance as much as he struggled to keep from crying out in pain. "I think something is wrong," he said.

"And what would that be?" asked a familiar voice.

Darius looked up to see Chuck Maslon sitting at the security station.

"There's no soap in the shower," Darius lied.

"Is that all?" Maslon asked. The tone of fake concern in his voice sickened Darius.

Darius nodded his head. He wasn't about to tell Maslon about the excruciating pain. Something told Darius that his pain and suffering would be Maslon's pleasure, so he kept it to himself and focused on the moment.

"I thought I'd pay you a visit before you start your new life here," Maslon said. "I'm concerned we got off on the wrong foot yesterday."

"If you say so."

Despite Maslon's cordial tone and smile, Darius wasn't buying whatever he was selling. There was something about the way Maslon looked Darius directly in the eye. It was the way a bully stared at someone they were trying to intimidate.

"My views on Second Chance are no secret around here," said Maslon. He shot a quick glance at the guards, looking at them with the same disdain he showed Darius. "I've seen the program work for some people, while others fail miserably. Personally,

I don't like Second Chance. I don't like the people in it. And if I had my way, the program would be shut down. Am I making myself clear?"

"Yes, sir," said Darius.

The fake smile on Maslon's face faded. Darius knew it wasn't a good idea to piss him off. Clearly he didn't like Darius. And clearly he had come to bully Darius—to intimidate him. That wasn't going to happen.

Maslon slammed the file he'd been reading shut, and tossed it to one of the security guards without looking. "I'm going to be watching you. Everything you do, I'm going to know about it. And when you screw up, and you will, I'm going to bounce your ass out of here and off to prison so fast it will make your head spin."

My head is already spinning. And pounding. And burning, Darius thought. The pain felt like a hot knife digging into his brain. But the pain was a good thing. It kept him distracted enough that he didn't say exactly what was on his mind to Maslon, which would have only led to trouble. "Is that it?" asked Darius.

Maslon stood up and walked to the elevator, pressed the button, and the doors opened. He stepped inside. Holding the door open, he turned back to face Darius. "Don't get too comfortable here," he said. "You won't last. Bits like you never do."

The elevator doors closed and Maslon disappeared. Darius returned to his holding cell and sat on the bed. The headache started to fade almost as quickly as it had come.

This place sure is going to be fun, he thought, *with this tracking device around my ankle and that idiot breathing down my neck.*

"Maslon is a ball-bustin' sonovabitch."

Darius looked up to see the older of the two security guards standing in the entrance of the cell. The guard's name tag read "Pirro."

"I hadn't noticed," Darius said.

"The name's Butchie," said the guard, extending his calloused hand to Darius.

"Darius."

"First rule at Second Chance: don't let Maslon bust ya balls," Butchie said. "And believe you's me, he'll try. He tries to break everyone."

"What's his problem?" Darius asked.

Butchie shrugged. "Beats me. I'm thinkin' he's got cape envy."

"Cape envy?"

"Sure, cape envy. Ya ain't never heard of cape envy?" said Butchie. "That's what happens to some guys when they spend too much time around the supes—people in capes that can bend steel in their bare hands and leap over tall buildings and all that crap. They start to feelin' inadequate, so they do things like yell at their wife or kick their dog."

"Does Maslon have a wife or a dog?"

"Probably not. Which is why he picks on guys like you's."

A giant mustache covered Butchie's upper lip and part of his mouth, making it impossible for Darius to tell if the guard was smiling or not.

"Hey, my coffee's getting' cold," said Butchie. "You's wanna come out and join us?"

Darius followed Butchie out of the cell, and the two joined the other guard at the security station. "That's Big Mike," said Butchie, pointing to the other guard.

Big Mike offered a half-hearted wave and went back to reading his magazine.

"How old are ya, kid?" asked Butchie.

"I'll be seventeen in a few days."

"I didn't know they took 'em that young in Second Chance. They send ya here straight outta juvie?"

Darius didn't quite know how to explain his unique position in Second Chance. But sitting at the security station, it dawned on him that he might be explaining it a lot, whether he wanted to or not. He couldn't hide his situation from others—not without being a liar. And not without being a fool for thinking others would believe his lies.

"I got sent here instead of going to jail," said Darius, keeping it simple.

"Ya came here *insteada* going to jail?" asked Butchie.

Darius nodded, figuring it better to say too little than too much.

"No wonder Maslon was up in your face like that," said Big Mike, putting down his magazine. Suddenly the conversation interested him. "He must really hate you. Normally he doesn't pay personal visits like this."

Not knowing what to say, Darius shrugged, hoping his silent would say whatever it was Big Mike wanted to hear.

"Something you's'll learn 'round here is that there's two types of people," said Butchie. "There's them that hate Chuck Maslon, and them's that don't like him much."

"Maslon is a scumbag," said Big Mike. "He hates all Chancers—don't matter who they are or what they did."

"What's a Chancer?" asked Darius.

"Anyone who's been in Second Chance," said Big Mike. "Maslon treats all 'em like they're guilty until proven guilty. Once a criminal always a criminal, in his book. And the worse the crime you did, the more he'll hate."

"Yeah, well, I got caught with eXXeLL," said Darius.

"eXXeLL? Wow. That's big time," said Big Mike. "I could see him developing a special hate for you."

"And I beat up a cop."

"You beat up a cop? Were you high on eXXeLL or something?"

"No. I just know how to fight."

Big Mike looked Darius up and down, trying to imagine him beating up a cop. "Look kid, I don't know you," he said. "And I may never see you again after today—HQ is a big place—but let me tell you this: watch out for Maslon."

"Don't let this clown freak ya out, kid," Butchie said. "Just keep ya nose clean, and do ya best to stay outta Maslon's way."

"How hard will that be?" asked Darius.

"Impossible."

9

Darius sat with Butchie and Big Mike for over thirty minutes, while the two security guards gave him a crash course in how things worked at Super Justice Force HQ. Big Mike did most of the talking. Once in a while Butchie would look up from the file he was studying to say something. "The stuff we're tellin' ya ain't gonna be in the Employee Handbook or covered in orientation," Butchie would interject.

"There's a lot of Chancers working 'round here," said Big Mike. "Make sure you know who's who. A Chancer always gonna have your back. Especially if you get into a beef with a Long Arm."

"What's a Long Arm?" Darius asked.

"Lotta ex-cops work here at HQ. Most of 'em work on the Security One team, with Maslon," said Butchie.

"Okay, but what's a Long Arm?" asked Darius.

"You know—long arm of the law," said Big Mike.

"That's a stupid name," said Darius.

Butchie shrugged, like he'd never given it much thought. "Most times Chancers and Long Arms get along—ain't too much beef," he said. "But you get two guys workin' together, one's an ex-con and the other useta be the cop that busted him, and sometimes it gets dicey."

That would suck, Darius thought. *I'd hate having to work with the cop from the other night.*

"Does that happen often—Chancers and Long Arms working together?" Darius asked.

"Depends on where ya get placed," said Butchie. "You's gonna take some tests, depending on how ya score, depends on where ya work."

"Pray you don't score low on the tests," said Big Mike. "Otherwise you'll be a Scrubber—and it doesn't get any worse than that. If it's cleaned, polished, mopped or scrubbed in any way, shape or form, it's done by Scrubber."

"There's nuthin' wrong with bein' a Scrubber—it's honest work," said Butchie. "It just ain't career work. Some guys, they get into Second Chance, they test low and get stuck scrubbin' toilets, and that's what they do. They scrub toilets the entire time they're on probation, and when probation is up, they either keep scrubbin' toilets here, or they move to scrub 'em some other place. And that's what's really wrong about bein' a Scrubber—when that's all you's ever try to be."

It seemed clear to Darius that Butchie had been a Scrubber. It also seemed that despite the gruff way he talked, the older of the two guards had a bit more wisdom to share. Darius had questions for Butchie, but before he could ask, the elevator doors opened and Dr. Sam entered the Detention area.

Dr. Sam greeted everyone, mentioned something about getting breakfast, and then told Darius to leave his dirty clothes in the cell. While Darius placed the bag with his dirty clothes back in the small holding cell, Dr. Sam had a brief conversation with Big Mike and Butchie.

Stepping out of the cell, Darius saw Butchie handing Dr. Sam the file he had been looking through all morning. Darius noticed that his name was printed on the tab.

"I'll need you to do a favor for me later today," Dr. Sam said to Butchie.

"No problem," said Butchie as the elevator doors closed on Dr. Sam and Darius.

This time Darius was certain—the elevator moved horizontally instead of vertically. Then it moved vertically. He looked at the panel where in a normal elevator there would be numbers for each floor. This panel was more complex. There were thirty-six buttons on the panel. One for each letter in the alphabet and the numbers zero through nine. Above the panel a digital display flashed an ever-changing combination of two letters followed by four numbers.

The elevator stopped, and the doors opened leading to a hallway of polished marble. Dr. Sam led the way, motioning for Darius to follow. "I feel like pancakes today," said the doctor.

Darius followed Dr. Sam down a hallway to the employee cafeteria. Dr. Sam ordered pancakes with sausage, and coffee with enough room for extra cream. "Get whatever you want," said Dr. Sam.

As they ate their breakfast, Darius wondered what was in the file that had his name on it. He tried not to stare at it, but it taunted him.

"At nine, I'll take you to processing," said Dr. Sam. "It starts with a complete physical. I've taken the liberty to order a dental exam for you as well. Your fingerprints will be taken, a retina scan, voiceprint and full DNA bio-scan. The fingerprints, retina and voice scan are for identification. The DNA bio-scan is for security."

"What kind of security requires a DNA bio-scan?" Darius asked.

"It's the only way to keep out unwanted bio-morphs. Shape shifters. A powerful bio-morph could shape shift to look just like you, right down to your fingerprints—provided they had access to the information. But they can't fake your DNA."

Never seen a bio-morph before, Darius thought. *At least I don't think I've seen one. It's not like I would know—they can look like anyone.*

Aside from what he'd read in comic books, Darius didn't know much about bio-morphs. He was pretty sure that there were no human bio-morphs at all, and that shape shifting was something that could only be done by a select few extraterrestrial races.

After they finished eating, Dr. Sam and Darius made their way back to the elevator, which took them to what looked like the waiting area of an emergency room. "This is the Medical Trauma and Surgery Unit—MTSU," explained Dr. Sam. "There is a health clinic that provides a variety of medical services, as well as a fully operational trauma center."

Dr. Sam led Darius to an exam room, where they were greeted by another man.

"Dr. Amir is the head of MTSU," said Dr. Sam. "I'll leave you with him, and be back to get you when you're done."

Over the next four hours Dr. Amir and other medical staff poked, prodded and scanned Darius's body, took blood samples, monitored his heart, tested his vision, hearing and muscle strength, and had him pee into a cup. "You look to be in good shape. A little malnourished, but nothing serious," Dr. Amir said. "Make sure you eat enough. I want to see you again in three months, and you had better have packed on a few pounds."

Dr. Sam returned after Darius had completed the medical portion of processing, and escorted him back to the employee cafeteria. They sat quietly, Darius eating a double cheeseburger and fries, Dr. Sam having the soup of the day—chicken noodle—half of a turkey club sandwich and a cup of coffee with plenty of room for extra cream.

"There was a mistake in your paperwork. You were supposed to be assigned living quarters, but the order didn't go through," said Dr. Sam. "I'm afraid you'll have to spend another night in Detention."

"That's fine," said Darius. He had spent the night in worse places. Detention was a luxury hotel compared to the abandoned subway stations across the river.

Dr. Sam slurped his soup, broth dribbling down his chin. Darius wondered if Dr. Sam personally escorted around every person entering Second Chance. The thought had kicked around Darius's mind most of the day, and he started to wonder what Dr. Sam's real motives were. The harsh truth of the world Darius came from was that no one did something for nothing, and he doubted this world would be any different. Everyone had a motive.

"You do this with everyone?" asked Darius.

Dr. Sam looked up from his soup. "Do what?"

"This," said Darius. He pointed at the lunch, looked around the cafeteria and motioned his hands to indicate everything surrounding them. "All of this—the lunch, being led around personally."

Dr. Sam stopped eating. He stared at Darius for a moment, just long enough for the silence to be awkward.

"I've been waiting a long time for you, Darius," said Dr. Sam.

"Waiting for me?"

"Okay, not you, but someone just like you. Second Chance started twenty years ago with a simple: offer jobs and training to ex-cons that they could use when they got out of prison. It took five years just to get the program up and running. The first three years we only offered training and counseling in the prisons. Then we expanded the program to include pretty much every aspect of operations at Super Justice Force. This guaranteed that the guys who went through the program would have jobs waiting for them on the outside."

"Where do I come in?" asked Darius.

"I knew seven years ago that Second Chance was working. I proved it could work with a ninety-five percent success rate," said Dr. Sam. "I knew that if we could rehabilitate the people we had been working with—and we've worked with some people that seemed impossible—we could help anyone. We could stop career criminals before they became career criminals."

"And I'm the guy to prove Second Chance can do that?"

"You better be," said Dr. Sam. "There were others that we could have taken into the program before you came along, but Second Chance didn't need them."

"I don't understand. Why does Second Chance need me?"

Dr. Sam leaned across the table, a fire in his eyes. "Because the mayor's nephew, who keeps getting busted for buying crack, or some corporate bigwig's son doing dirt will be catching breaks their whole lives. The entire system is designed to help privileged punks who get into trouble. The moment I took some silver-spoon-in-his-mouth white boy into Second Chance, that's all the program would be good for.

"If you went to prison, Darius, the chances of you doing anything good with your life would be slim to none. A Bit like you—you'd have been chewed up and spit out. They'd turn you out and pass you around, trading you for a pack of cigarettes. And when you finally got out of prison, you wouldn't be a man. You'd be a thief, or a hustler, or just some jive-ass animal that preys on those weaker than him."

"You don't know me," said Darius. "You don't know that's what would happen to me."

"It happens to all of them, in one way or another. Prison turns all men—no matter what color they are—into animals," said Dr. Sam. "Second Chance is barely even putting a dent in the problem. But I'll be damned if I let this program try something new and it isn't for those who need it most."

Dr. Sam went back to slurping his soup.

Darius sat quietly thinking about everything Dr. Sam said. Dr. Sam's words had weight to them—a weight that Darius could already feel pushing down on him. More than his personal freedom seemed to rest on success or failure in Second Chance.

Nothing like a little pressure, he thought.

10

After lunch, Dr. Sam and Darius took the elevator back to MTSU for Darius's dental appointment. "When you finish up with your dental exam, someone other than me will come get you—I'm not sure yet who it will be," said Dr. Sam. "Whoever it is, they will take you to get your stuff. I'll see you tomorrow."

Considering he couldn't remember the last time he'd been to a dentist, Darius's teeth were in pretty decent shape. X-rays revealed three cavities, all on the left side, which the dentist filled on the spot. The dentist asked Darius about the missing molar on the right side. Darius lied, saying the tooth had broken while eating something. It was easier than telling the truth—the tooth had been knocked out in a fight.

It took just over an hour for the dentist to clean Darius's teeth and fill the cavities. Thanks to the novocaine, Darius couldn't feel the left side of his mouth.

Butchie the security guard waited for Darius in the lobby area of MTSU. His uniform had been replaced by a pair of faded jeans and a t-shirt that read "Fuhgetaboutit," which made Butchie look like a dad on his way to coach a little league game. "Dr. Sam asked me to take ya to pick up yer stuff," said Butchie.

From the time they left MTSU to the time they got in the car, neither Darius nor Butchie said a word to each other. The car looked just like the one that had been used to drive Darius from the police station to HQ, only this one smelled slightly different. The front passenger seat was also more comfortable than the backseat.

"How'd it go today?" asked Butchie as he pulled the car out of the vehicle pool and into traffic.

"I peed in a cup."

"Get used to it. You'll be peein' in a cup at least once a week."

"What for?"

"Testin' for drugs and alcohol."

"What happens if you fail the test?" Darius asked. Not that it really mattered to him. He didn't drink or do drugs.

"Depends. If yer a straight employee, ya get fired. Zero tolerance and all. If yer a Chancer, on probation or parole, it's a violation. You's goin' back to da joint."

The two of them sat in silence for a few more minutes. Not being much of a conversationalist made idle chit chat difficult for Darius. But having entered a new world, he had too many questions to keep quiet.

"What's a Bit?" Darius asked.

"Where'd ya hear that?" asked Butchie.

"Earlier today, Dr. Sam called me a Bit. So did Maslon."

"Bit is a two-bit –like a two-bit criminal," said Butchie. "Lotta guys in Second Chance is Bits. I was a Bit."

"Is that how you ended up Second Chance?"

"I got into Second Chance way back in the beginnin'—before there was even guys workin' at HQ. Dr. Sam was startin' up this rehab program for guys in the joint. Didn't know at the time what it was about, but I needed something different. Dr. Sam's a good guy. A stand-up guy. I owe him a lot. I'd been in an outta the joint since I was a kid—younger'n you, even. Worked as hired muscle for big-time guys like the Jester and that crazy broad that useta dress like a spotted cat."

"You mean Sheetah?" asked Darius.

"Yeah, that's her. All the big-timers, they'd make ya dress up in some silly outfit. Sheeta made us wear these freakin' stupid cat masks. The Jester had us wearin' clown makeup. And then you'd get busted by Nightwatcher or the Incapacitator, and you'd be dressed like a freakin' idiot cat or a clown, and you'd feel like a tool. Once, I got my ass handed to me by this broad called herself the Ballerina."

"Yeah, the Ballerina. She was a member of Teen Justice Force."

"Yeah, cute little thing, wore a pink outfit. But try gettin' your ass kicked by some chick in pink who's got legs stronger'n a horse," said Butchie. "That's when I knew I needed to change my life. Every freakin' guy in the joint is lookin' at me and sayin', 'You's the guy that got clocked by the Ballerina.' If that ain't a clear signal that yer life's gotta change, I don't know what is."

The rest of the drive was made in silence, except for Butchie pounding on the horn and screaming profanities in Italian at other drivers. It took them over thirty minutes in traffic to travel the mile or so that separated SJF Headquarters from the place Darius had been calling home, but they may as well have gone to another planet.

11

Until his arrest, Darius lived at Sloane House, a run-down building on the west side of the city. Originally built as a hotel in the 1920s, it had since fallen on hard times, eventually coming to be used for "transitional housing." For Darius that meant living in a fifteen-story building with only one working elevator, populated by a variety of odd characters ranging from psychiatric outpatients to ex-cons on parole to people who weren't exactly homeless but still had no place to really call home.

After he was released from juvenile detention, his caseworker couldn't place Darius in another foster home. He was too old and had a history of violence. Somehow, Edith got him a room at Sloane House. On the one hand he appreciated all she did for him—it was, after all, a roof over his head. But on the other hand it was a terrible place to live. He occupied a single room on the ninth floor so small he could stand in the middle of the room, stretch his arms out, and touch the walls on either side. The two bathrooms down the hall—one for men and one for women—both had roaches and rats scurrying around.

Darius lived at Sloane House for two months before meeting Karlito, who lived on the third floor. Darius would see him from time to time, either in the lobby, or passing each other in the stairway. One day Karlito asked Darius for money to buy cigarettes. When Darius told him he didn't have any money, Karlito told him that he knew a way to make some cash. Things fell apart from there.

Butchie followed Darius into the lobby of Sloane House. Decades earlier, when it was the lobby of a hotel, it might have been a nice place. But any trace of that was long gone, obscured by the stink of urine and so many layers of filth that only a wrecking ball could effectively clean the place. A sign on the only working elevator indicated that it, like the other two, was "out of order."

"You feel like walking up nine flights of stairs?" Darius asked Butchie.

"I'll wait for ya down here."

Darius hoofed it up the stairs as quickly as he could. He hated Sloane House, and wanted to get out of there as soon as possible. He also didn't want to run into Karlito, who no doubt had been looking for him ever since the night Darius took off running with all the eXXeLL in his backpack. Karlito claimed to know Tiny Biggs, and had even implied that he was peddling the eXXeLL for the notorious crime lord.

By the time he got to the ninth floor, Darius was winded. Climbing nine flights of stairs was too much like running, which he hated. He made his way down the hall, past the bathroom filled with roaches and rats, and came to a stop in front of his tiny room in the far northeastern corner of the building. The door was open. Pried open. Probably with a crowbar.

Someone had gone in his room and stolen everything he had—not that he had much. And Darius knew exactly who had stolen his few belongings—Karlito. *No one else would break into my room and steal worthless junk like mine.*

Darius raced out of the room, down the hall, and ran down the stairs much faster than he ran up them. A million thoughts ran through his head as he tried to come up with a plan to find the photos of his family—the only things that mattered to him.

I need to explain this to Butchie. What if he doesn't understand about the pictures? I could try to sneak past him. How long will it take for Butchie to call someone if I take off? How long before they track me down and send my ass to prison?

Darius made it to the landing of the first floor, pushing open the door leading into the back corner of the lobby. Karlito stood in front of the door, waiting for him. Darius screeched to a halt, his breathing labored, his blood boiling.

"Lookin' for this?" asked Karlito.

Karlito held a pillowcase—the pillowcase from Darius's room—no doubt stuffed with everything he had stolen. Bay-Bay stood a few feet behind Karlito, trying to look menacing.

Where's the stupid one, Mickey? Darius thought. *Did he get busted, or is he hiding, waiting to jump me?*

Darius knew the deal. Karlito wanted the Adrenaccelerate. Darius didn't have it.

"Made a few calls down to the po'leese station, 'cause that's the kinda dude I am, always lookin' out for a brotha," said Karlito. His fake sincerity made Darius angrier. "They got papers filed on Mickey, but they ain't got no record of you bein' booked. Figure you musta got away, jus' like me an' Bay-Bay."

Darius didn't say a word. He kept his eyes directly on Karlito, but he could still see Butchie on the other side of the lobby. Any chance of the situation ending well—without someone getting their ass kicked—depended on Butchie.

"You got my stuff, nigga?" demanded Karlito. He dropped the pillowcase to the dirty floor of the lobby, a sure sign he was going to make a move.

Darius knew he could take Karlito in a fight. He wasn't so sure about Bay-Bay—Karlito's back-up plan in case he had trouble with Darius. Bay-Bay was a monster. And Darius had to get through Karlito first.

How far will things go before Butchie makes a move to break it up? Darius thought to himself.

The answer came when Karlito slammed his right fist into the left side of Darius's jaw, knocking him to the floor. Darius saw the punch coming from a mile away and simply rolled with it. In fact, he didn't even feel the right hook, his jaw and mouth were still completely numb from the novocaine.

Karlito mistakenly thought his punch had really done some damage. "That's what I'm talkin' 'bout, beeyotch," he said.

Basking in the glow of his perceived triumph, Karlito never saw Darius land on the floor. Rather than dropping to the floor in an unconscious lump, Darius hit the floor, spun himself around, and caught Karlito with a sweeping kick, knocking his legs out from under him.

Karlito crashed to the floor, flat on his back. Darius scurried around and pounced on top of Karlito. Darius delivered three powerful jabs to Karlito's face with such speed and force Karlito didn't know what hit him. Bam! Bam! Bam!

With a fourth punch came a cracking sound of either bone or cartilage, followed by an explosion of blood. Karlito's face looked like raw hamburger, blood flowing from his nose and mouth.

Before Darius could get in one more punch—just for good measure—Bay-Bay tackled him.

Bay-Bay knocked Darius off Karlito, and tried to get him in some sort of hold he must have learned from watching professional wrestling. But for a guy his size, Bay-Bay wasn't all that strong. Darius had learned from being bullied by guys twice his size that being big didn't always go hand in hand with being strong.

Bay-Bay struggled to keep Darius in a chokehold that may have looked impressive on live pay-per-view wrestling matches, but was completely useless in the real world. Darius grabbed hold of one of Bay-Bay's wrists with his right hand, and brought his left hand down like a hammer, smashing Bay-Bay below the belt.

"If you're fighting for your life, there's no such thing as fighting dirty," Darius's father used to say.

Bay-Bay let out a high-pitched scream and loosened his chokehold. Still holding on to Bay-Bay's wrist, Darius spun around and got back up on his feet. Pure, blind anger kept Darius from letting go of Bay-Bay's wrist. He knew that Karlito would have likely killed him for the drugs, and Bay-Bay would have helped. At least that's what he told himself as he twisted Bay-Bay's arm until the shoulder dislocated. Bay-Bay screamed even louder.

Bay-Bay lay on the floor of the lobby of Sloane House screaming in agony. Next to him, Karlito cried like a baby, blood flowing from his face. Darius picked up the pillowcase and checked to make sure his pictures and the other things that constituted the worldly possessions were inside.

Butchie stood at the far end of the lobby near the main entrance. He had not moved once during the fight.

Darius walked over to the Butchie. "That all your stuff?" Butchie asked.

Darius nodded.

The two of them left Sloane House without saying a word, and got into the car. They sat in silence for a few minutes while Darius's mind raced. *If Butchie reports what happened, I'll be in so much trouble. It'll be over for me—no Second Chance.*

Darius looked at his hand, already starting to swell. He clenched and unclenched his fist, wondering if anyone would notice.

"We should get you some ice. It'll keep the swellin' down," said Butchie.

12

Darius sat in the main reception area of Personnel. He had eaten breakfast with Dr. Sam, and considered himself lucky that his face and hands weren't swollen. Butchie had given him some ice packs to keep the swelling down, and taken his clothes to make sure Karlito's blood was washed off.

He didn't know why, but Darius felt nervous. For too many years his life had been lived one uncertain moment to the next. This moment, sitting in the Personnel office at Super Justice Force Headquarters, shouldn't have been any different. And yet it was.

He had gone largely ignored and unnoticed more than half of his life. No one expected anything from him, because no one cared. All of that changed overnight. There were people watching him—waiting to see if he succeeded or failed. He wasn't invisible anymore.

When he walked through the two large glass doors that led into Personnel, the receptionist talking on the phone held up a finger to him, indicating that it would be a moment before she could help him. She pointed to the plate of cookies sitting in front of her, motioning to Darius, letting him know to take one.

It's too early for a cookie, Darius thought. He picked one up anyway, just to be polite, and took a seat.

The receptionist finished her phone call and turned her attention to Darius. "How can I help you, sweetie?"

Darius waved the piece of paper Dr. Sam had given him, his mouth still full of cookie. "I'm here for orientation," he said as soon as he swallowed.

The receptionist didn't even look at the paper. "You're scheduled to see Trang Nguyen. Her office is down that hall, second door on the left."

"Thanks," said Darius.

"Take another cookie."

"Really?"

"If you don't eat it someone else will. Besides, you're too skinny."

Darius ate the second cookie in three bites as he walked down the hall. It had been a long time since he'd had a homemade cookie. Uncle Kenny certainly didn't make cookies, and there weren't any in juvenile detention. In fact, he was pretty sure none of the foster families had cookies either, especially not homemade ones. He tried to remember the last time he'd had a homemade cookie, but he couldn't.

Darius knocked on the second door on the left, and a woman's voice told him to come in. An Asian woman dressed in a bright red sweater that matched her red lipstick and red earrings, sitting behind a desk cluttered with paperwork, greeted Darius. .

"You must be Darius," said Trang, motioning for Darius to sit on the other side of her desk. "I'm Trang Nguyen, your contact in Personnel here at HQ. My official title is Status Supervisor. Think of me as a cross between a guidance counselor and parole officer."

"Guidance counselor and parole officer," Darius repeated. He quickly looked around the room, taking in the certificates and photos on the wall with a single glance.

"That means I will be your best friend and possibly your worst enemy as long as you participate in Second Chance," said Trang, her matter-of-fact tone balancing out her smile. "Every participant in Second Chance comes here from prison, either after time served, or while they are still on probation, and as such they are all bound by certain rules of conduct. All Second Chance employees report to a Status Supervisor."

Trang shuffled through the pile of papers on her desk until she found just the right one. She studied it for a moment, and then placed it on top of the cluttered mess.

"I don't know how much was fully explained to you, so I will give you a quick rundown," she said. "You've opted to enter into Second Chance, a rehabilitation program operated by Super Justice Force. This program is designed for convicted criminals who have already spent a significant amount of time incarcerated. In the history of this program, we have never had a participant who has come to us without first serving time."

"I'm also the youngest," said Darius.

"Also the youngest," repeated Trang. The smile faded from her face as she stared intently at him.

An odd feeling came over Darius that he hadn't felt in a long time, not since he'd lived down in the Caves with the metahumans.

"Are you a telepath?" Darius asked.

"No," said Trang. "I'm an empath. I can read true emotions, and to a certain extent I can feel what others feel."

"To a certain extent."

"My empathic powers aren't strong, thankfully."

"Yeah, that would suck," said Darius. He had briefly known a telepathic metahuman who had been driven insane by the thoughts of other people. Darius couldn't imagine reading other people's emotions would be good for someone's sanity either.

"Darius, how much has been explained to you?"

Darius stared into Trang's eyes. "I will be your best friend and possibly your worst enemy," is what she had said to him. With her empathic abilities that was more than some dramatic statement. Darius wondered how much of his emotions she could feel.

"I'm the great experiment," he said.

Trang nodded her head. "I might have phrased it differently, but that sounds about right. You will report to me three times a week for the next sixth months. After that, we will drop down to once per week for six months. You will also have one group counseling session a week, and one private counseling session—most likely with Dr. Sam. Expect random drug tests frequently. Whatever department you are assigned to, the supervisor will be filing weekly reports. If there are any problems, if for some reason things don't work out, you will go to jail."

Darius nodded his head. "I'll be fine."

"Have you had a chance to study your Employee Handbook?" asked Trang.

"No, ma'am. I never got one."

Rolling her eyes, Trang let out a sigh. At first Darius thought he'd done something wrong, but then she muttered to herself, "We work for an organization that has battled the Masters of D.E.A.T.H. and hostile aliens, but they can't get the new guy an Employee Handbook."

She turned around in her swivel chair to face the bookshelf behind her, and grabbed something off of it. She turned back around to face Darius, typed something into her computer, and then handed him the "Super Justice Force Employee Handbook."

"Read this," said Trang. "It covers everything you are going to need to know as an employee of SJF. That is yours to keep as long as you work here, but we ask for all copies back from employees who leave the company."

Darius flipped through the book. The size surprised him—over three hundred pages.

"Since you didn't get an Employee Handbook, can I assume no one has explained your housing situation or food to you?" asked Trang.

"Not really, ma'am. Dr. Sam said I'd be staying here. Somewhere."

Once again, Trang rolled her eyes and let out a sigh. This time Darius knew it had nothing to do with him.

"Please, call me Trang. Ma'am makes me feel old."

"Okay. Sorry about that."

"While you're participating in Second Chance, you will be staying in the Transitional Employee Housing Program. Some of the people who come here do so directly from getting out of prison, and they have nowhere to live. TEHP provides them with temporary housing until they can get a place of their own. Normally, a person can only stay in TEHP for up to six months. You, Darius, will be our first permanent resident."

"Beats a prison cell."

"That it does. You will also be provided a Meal Voucher Card that will cover your food. Usually those are only good for a month. I guess I'll have to look into how that will work for you."

Trang shuffled through some more papers, said something about making sure Darius had his identification badge before he left Personnel, opening an account for him at the credit union, and then found what it was she was looking for. She handed two packets of stapled pages across the desk to Darius.

Darius glanced at the packets: "Level One Security Protocol and Regulations" and "Second Chance Code of Conduct."

"These are the rules that would apply to you if you had come to Second Chance as a parolee. Honestly, we're going to be making up the rule book for you as we go along," said Trang. "But assume that everything spelled out in those packets applies to you, because it does. Just know that there will be more additions as the needs arise."

They don't even have rules for me yet, he thought.

There was a knock on the door, and the receptionist came in to the office carrying a large manila folder that she handed to Trang. She smiled at Darius as she left the office—the kind of smile a grandmother would give.

Trang opened the folder and pulled out a stack of papers. "Well, it looks like you passed your physical exams," she said examining the papers. "That means you're cleared for orientation."

"That's good," Darius said.

He never doubted he would pass the medical exams.

Trang reached into the folder and pulled out a plastic card with a metal clip on the back. "Keep this with you at all times," she said, handing the card to Darius.

Darius studied his identification badge. The front of the badge had a holographic image of Darius that turned from one side to another—like he was slowly nodding his head—giving a full view of his face and both sides of his profile. His name appeared directly under his picture, and under his name green letters spelled out "L1 Trainee." The back of the badge had a metal clip on the end of a thin, retractable wire.

"Congratulations," said Trang. "You are officially an employee of Super Justice Force. Now we just need to get you through orientation, and get you an assignment."

13

Shortly after Darius got his identification badge, he was taken to a small classroom with two-dozen desks. The top of each desk was actually a computer screen that tilted upward. Sitting at eight of the desks were five men and three women—all waiting for the new employee orientation. Darius wondered if any of them were in Second Chance.

A woman dressed in a gray skirt and white blouse stood in front of the blank cyber-chalkboard at the head of the classroom. She looked almost human, but clearly she wasn't. Her skin was an odd shade of dark red, like a brick that had been faded by the sun. Her unusually large eyes were completely black, she had no visible ears, and as she shuffled through a pile papers, Darius could see she only had three fingers and a thumb, all of which were noticeably longer than those of a human.

Darius had seen other aliens before, but he had never been this close to one. He tried to remember how many extraterrestrial races lived on Earth. He'd read three chapters on aliens in his sixth-grade social studies class. There had been a test and everything, but he simply drew a blank. *Is it five or six?*

"My name is Xangtha," said the woman, her voice revealing no hint of being anything other than human. She used a piece of cyber-chalk to spell her name on the board. The tiny electronic device never touched the board, but the letters X-A-N-G-T-H-A each appeared, as if by magic. "I will be your orientation supervisor. The first order of business is a test that will take approximately two hours to complete. Don't be concerned about passing or failing, this is not that type of test. This is more to determine personality, interests and aptitude, which will then be used to determine your assignment."

The test broke up into several sections, with the first part covering math, spelling and language skills. *They want to make sure I'm not an idiot*, Darius thought as he answered questions like "fish is to water, as bird is to (fill in the blank)."

The remainder of the test was some sort of personality evaluation. There were hundreds of questions, mainly multiple choice, some true or false, all answered by touching the appropriate box. Some of the questions were the same, only phrased slightly differently. And some of the questions were kind of weird, like the one that asked if he ever felt like being alone, or if he ever felt like people did not understand him. He had to choose between answers like "all the time," "sometimes," "occasionally," and "never." He wasn't even sure of the difference between "sometimes" and "occasionally," so he just decided to alternate between the two whenever he needed to.

There were a handful of essay questions at the end of the test. The last question on the test perplexed him the most. "When is it acceptable to break the law?"

This has got to be a trick question, Darius thought. *Answer this one wrong, and they'll haul my ass back to jail.*

He stared at the computer screen for what seemed like a long time. He thought and thought and couldn't come up with an answer, and then something popped in his head from when he was much younger.

In the back of his mind, Darius recalled an old memory of his father trying to fix something. Darius couldn't even remember what it was, just that there were parts and pieces all over the kitchen floor, and his mother was yelling at his father. "You made it worse," Janae Logan said.

"Sometimes you gotta break it in order to fix it, baby," said Dwayne.

Darius wondered if that kind of thinking applied to the law. And then another memory popped into his mind. His mother, ever the lover of history, sat him down to watch a documentary film about the Civil Rights movement. The image of black kids his age, in the streets of Birmingham facing down police dogs and water hoses came clearly into focus in his mind's eye, and he had the answer to the question.

"It is acceptable to break the law when the law needs to be fixed," he typed.

14

It took Darius and the others two hours to complete their tests. Once they were done, Xangtha gave the group a brief lesson in how the elevators worked—which was surprisingly complicated and confusing—and then she escorted the small group to the employee cafeteria.

The employee cafeteria, she explained, was different from the restaurant located on the first floor next to the gift shop. The cafeteria remained open twenty-four hours a day, but the kitchen was only open from six in the morning until ten at night.

They all ordered their lunch, and sat together at a table big enough for eight. Eating in silence, Darius listened to the conversations going back and forth between the others. One of the guys asked Xangtha about payday, and if the credit union at SJF was any good. Another one of the guys seemed more concerned about whether he should have ordered something different for lunch.

For a moment, Darius thought about joining in the conversation, but he had nothing to say. *I have no idea if the Yankees have a chance of making it to the World Series*, he thought. *And I don't care.*

"You don't talk much, do you?"

Xangtha's voice pulled Darius out of his private world, bringing him back into the moment.

"Not really," he said.

"This whole place can be pretty intimidating at first. If you have questions, don't be afraid to ask."

"Thanks."

Both Xangtha and Darius went back to eating their lunch. Darius thought about asking a question, anything to make him appear to be more social, but then one of the other guys asked about parking, and there was no longer the pressure to make conversation.

The cafeteria was crowded, mostly with people wearing some type of uniform, although some were dressed in business suits. At one table sat a man dressed in a bright green suit with yellow trim that matched the yellow mask he wore. Darius didn't recognize the costume or the hero wearing it, but he recognized the woman sitting with the guy in green as Smoking Ace. Her costume had changed, but the cloud of smoke that hovered around her was a dead giveaway.

On the other side of the cafeteria five people sat together at a table—three women and two men. They looked to be around the same age as Darius, and seemed to be friends. Darius couldn't hear what they were saying, but their laughter traveled across the room.

The uniforms they wore all looked the same—black pants, a magenta, button-down shirt and a black tie. Darius had seen others wearing the same type of uniform giving tours when he first arrived at HQ.

He tried not to stare at the five people laughing loudly, looking like they hadn't a care in the world, but he couldn't help himself. The most beautiful woman he'd ever seen sat at the table, and he couldn't take his eyes off her. She wore her long, curly black hair pulled back in a ponytail, and when she laughed, Darius could see her perfect smile.

At some point one of the other girls at the table noticed Darius staring, and must have said something to the others, because they all looked over at him. Mortified that he had been caught, he quickly looked down at his food. When he looked up, they were no longer looking at him. He had only mattered in their world for a brief moment. But then the beautiful girl looked back over in his direction, and even though she smiled at him, he felt totally embarrassed.

The beautiful girl and her friends all got up to leave at the same time. Darius tried not to be too obvious as he watched them walk past. The beautiful girl looked over at him, smiled, and offered a tiny wave. Darius didn't know what to do. He wanted to wave back, but fear left him paralyzed, and before he knew it, she was gone.

All Darius could think about as he finished his lunch was the beautiful girl. And when he returned to the classroom, he still thought about her. His life, up to that moment, had been all about surviving. And when you're rummaging through a garbage can looking for edible discards, or trying to avoid getting punked in the shower at juvenile detention, there isn't much time to think about girls.

Back in the classroom, Darius and the others sat in front of their computers. Over the next few hours, they watched a series of training videos. Captain Freedom hosted a video about safety on the job that covered everything from emergency evacuation procedure to lifting with your knees instead of your back. Each training video ended with a recap of everything that had been presented.

"Don't forget to lift with your knees, and if it's too heavy, get someone to help you," said Captain Freedom. "And don't forget, the first step to safety on the job begins with you."

By the time they were done with the training videos, Darius was ready to call it a day. Xangtha excused the others, telling them to be back at nine the next morning.

She told Darius to report back to Trang Nguyen's office, and told him what code he would need to enter for the elevator.

Darius arrived at Trang's office to find her and Dr. Sam in the middle of a conversation.

"No one ever said this was going to be easy, but we will make it work," Dr. Sam said, his back to Darius.

Trang caught sight of Darius standing in the doorway, acknowledged him with a slight smile, and returned her attention to Dr. Sam. "I'm sure we will."

"The lady from orientation said you wanted to see me," Darius said.

Dr. Sam turned to face Darius. The doctor looked exhausted. "Good to see you, Darius," he said, sounding as tired as he looked.

"How was orientation?" asked Trang.

"Seems to be going good. I learned about lifting with my knees."

Dr. Sam seemed to brighten up a bit. "Good. Very good."

Trang shuffled through some of the papers on her desk. "Tomorrow after lunch, you need to come back here for a special meeting."

"What kind of meeting?" Darius asked.

"Well, we are going to finalize some of the guidelines of how to deal with you," said Trang.

"What Trang is trying to say is that in addition to giving you your work assignment, we'll be coming up with a schedule for you to follow," said Dr. Sam.

"We will also be finalizing protocol for how your day-to-day life will be while you're living here."

"Speaking of living here, your apartment is ready. You have a new place to call home."

15

Darius and Dr. Sam didn't say much to each other as the elevator moved vertically, then horizontally, and then, it seemed, diagonally. The doors opened on to the eleventh floor of the Tower. Dr. Sam led the way down a long hallway that looked like a hallway in any other apartment building. Except this wasn't any other apartment building.

"There are one hundred and fifty residential spaces here in the Tower, and I'm guessing half of Super Justice Force lives here. This floor is all transitional housing for Second Chance," said Dr. Sam, stopping in front of apartment 11-J.

"Use your identification badge to unlock the door," said Dr. Sam, pointing to the key-card lock on the door.

Darius inserted his identification badge, the door to apartment 11-J opened, and he stepped inside. Dr. Sam remained in the hall.

"I'm going to leave you to get settled in your new home," said Dr. Sam.

Darius's new apartment was small, but more than big enough for him. The furnished studio space had a bed, desk, chair, a clock and a small dresser. The kitchen area had a mini refrigerator, a two-burner stove, and a sink with a cabinet over it. The best part had to be the bathroom—his own bathroom. Most of the foster homes only had one bathroom, and it was always a fight just to get a few minutes to yourself.

It took him less than a minute to "unpack" the pillowcase filled with his belongings. He threw his second-hand clothes into one drawer in the dresser, and placed his pictures on top of the desk. The pictures on the desk made Darius's apartment feel like home.

Darius kicked off his shoes and lay down on the bed. Opening up the Employee Handbook, he started to read, first the introduction, then "A Brief History of Super Justice Force," which wasn't all that brief. Halfway through the section "How Things Work at Super Justice Force Headquarters," someone knocked at his apartment door.

The clock on the desk told him it was a few minutes passed 8:00.

Someone knocked on the door again.

"Be right there," said Darius.

When he opened the door, Darius almost didn't recognize the man holding a brown paper bag. Dressed in regular clothes, and not his bright costume, Captain Freedom looked almost like a regular person. Almost.

"Am I disturbing you?" asked Captain Freedom.

"Just reading the employee handbook."

"Can I come in?"

"Sure."

"I figured you might not have any food, so I brought you some—sort of a 'welcome to your new home' meal," said Captain Freedom, entering the studio apartment and handing Darius a brown bag.

Darius looked inside the bag. There were two boxes of Captain Freedom Breakfast Cereal—both the fruit-flavored and the chocolate kind—and a half-gallon of milk.

"Didn't know which you preferred, so I brought both," said Captain Freedom.

"I like both. Thanks," said Darius. He hadn't had Captain Freedom Breakfast Cereal in years—not since his parents died.

"I get cases of that garbage for free," said Captain Freedom. "You ever want more, there's a storage closet full of it. Just go help yourself. Personally, I don't eat it. Tastes like shit to me."

It took Captain Freedom three steps to walk through the entire apartment. Small as it was, he made it seem smaller. He pulled up the only chair and sat down, letting out a loud sigh that reminded Darius of his own father.

Darius sat on the end of his bed. Less than a week earlier he had been listening to Karlito's big plans for getting rich. Now he sat across from the man he worshipped as a child. The whole scenario struck Darius as surreal—Captain Freedom, showing up at his new apartment with boxes of cereal and milk. *A lot can change in a week.*

"You ready to get assigned tomorrow?" Captain Freedom asked.

Darius opened one of the boxes of cereal. He had no bowls in his apartment, so he used his hand. "I just hope I don't have to be a Scrubber," he said, stuffing a handful of dry cereal into his mouth. It tasted terrible.

"That's the last thing you should worry about," said Captain Freedom.

The momentary surreal feeling passed, replaced by an awkward quiet where the only sound was Darius crunching bad tasting chocolate cereal. He held the box out to Captain Freedom. "You sure you don't want any?" he asked.

Captain Freedom reached into the box and pulled out a handful of crispy bits of chocolaty nastiness. "I really do hate this crap," he said, and then shoved the cereal in his mouth. He winced as choked down the dry cereal. "I guess I shouldn't complain though. The endorsement deal on this garbage alone paid for my kids' college tuition and my summer home."

Something about Captain Freedom struck Darius as odd. And it had nothing to do with him being out of costume, or complaining about the foul-tasting cereal that bore his name and likeness. If Darius didn't know better, he would swear that he smelled a hint of booze coming from Captain Freedom.

"Do you have any idea what it's like, hawking crap like this cereal, knowing that it tastes terrible and contributes to child obesity?" asked Captain Freedom. "Jesus, I've probably killed more innocent people with this garbage than the Jester has with his laughing death ray. I mean, do you know how many people die of diabetes every year?"

Captain Freedom snatched the cereal from Darius, dug his hand into the box, and pulled out another fistful that he crammed into his mouth. "I tell kids to stay in school and keep off drugs," he said, his mouth full of cereal. "And then I tell them to eat this stuff. You know what that makes me?"

"What?" asked Darius.

"A hypocrite. A goddamn hypocrite."

They didn't say a word to each other for what felt like a long time. Captain Freedom continued to eat the chocolate cereal, mumbling to himself about how he'd "sold his soul for breakfast cereal."

In the meantime, Darius opened the fruit-flavored box of cereal—which tasted much better than the chocolate—and washed it down with milk he drank straight from the carton. He felt increasingly uncomfortable the longer they went without conversation, and the longer the silence lasted, the more Darius wondered if Captain Freedom had been drinking.

"Captain Freedom?" said Darius.

"Call me Jake—at least in private," said Captain Freedom. "When people call me Captain Freedom, it sounds like bad writing in a comic book."

"I just wanted to tha …," Darius started to say, but Captain Freedom cut him off.

"Don't thank me just yet."

"Why not?" Darius asked.

"Because it doesn't mean anything right now. It's just words. And words without action are empty and meaningless."

"I just wanted to thank you for helping me," Darius said. "For getting me into Second Chance."

"You want to thank me? Don't screw this up," Captain Freedom said. "Don't make me regret going to bat for you like this."

Captain Freedom reached out and took the box of fruit-flavored cereal. He stuffed a handful into his mouth. "The fruity stuff tastes better," he said. "At least it doesn't taste like it fell out of a dog's ass."

"Why did you go to bat for me?" Darius asked.

Captain Freedom grabbed the milk carton and took a swig.

"What do you want me to say, Darius? That you're special? Is this where I give you some sort of pep talk about how much I believe in you?"

"Not if you don't mean it."

"When I saw someone falling from that building in No Man's Land, I didn't know it was you. I just thought it was another loser. Honestly, I was tempted to let you fall. I've seen enough losers to know that one less won't make the world a worse place," Captain Freedom said.

Darius snatched the box of fruity cereal from Captain Freedom. "I'm not a loser," said Darius.

"So you say," Captain Freedom said, taking another sip of milk. "All I know is that when I recognized you and realized who you were, my heart broke just a little bit. And for a second—maybe less than a second—I wished that I'd let you fall."

The box of cereal fell from Darius's hands. He could feel his anger rising. Anyone other than Captain Freedom would be swallowing their own teeth by now.

"Is this your idea of a welcoming party?" Darius asked. "I know you think I'm being an asshole," Captain Freedom said. "And I'm sure this is the last thing you want to be hearing."

"Not at all," said Darius, hoping his sarcasm had come through loud and clear. He grabbed the carton of milk away from Captain Freedom, and raised it in a mock toast. "It's not every day Captain Freedom calls you a loser, says you broke his heart, and wishes he'd let you fall to your death."

"You might not believe this, but I've thought about you a lot over the years."

"You're right. I don't believe you."

"I was seriously thinking about giving it all up—the fight for truth, justice and all that other junk. It all seemed pointless," said Captain Freedom. "And then I met this kid who was so inspired by me that it reminded me why I would put on that stupid costume and fly around and help people, even when it seemed pointless."

It never occurred to Darius that the essay he'd written might have made some type of impact on Captain Freedom. After all, here was a guy who had his own breakfast cereal—nasty tasting though it may be—a comic book series, line of action figures, animated television show and a hit film.

"Can you imagine what it was like for me, seeing that kid after all these years?" Captain Freedom asked.

"Can you imagine what it was like being that kid all these years?"

Captain Freedom and Darius sat silently staring at each other—no crunching of dry cereal to interrupt the quiet. They both sized each other up—looking for something they could believe in.

Captain Freedom looked at Darius, hoping to see some sign of the child who had inspired him when he had been filled with personal doubts.

Darius looked at Captain Freedom and saw him as something far less than the hero he had worshipped his whole life.

Both wrestled with their own disappointments.

Captain Freedom looked at his watch. "It's getting late," he said. "I'll leave you to study the Employee Handbook."

He stood up and walked to the door. "Sorry I ate all the cereal," he said.

Darius couldn't tell if Captain Freedom was apologizing or talking to himself.

Captain Freedom opened the door and stepped out into the hallway. "Do your time here and make the program work for you. If you can do that, then your thanks will mean something," he said, and closed the door behind him.

16

The second day of orientation went very much like the first. Darius and the rest of the new employees watched more training videos, after which they got sized for their work uniforms, and then ate lunch together.

Once again, they sat as a group, talking amongst themselves, with Darius saying very little. Xangtha explained that they'd be getting their assignments after lunch. Darius paid attention to everything she said, all the while keeping his eyes peeled for the beautiful girl from the day before.

By the time he and the others got up to leave the cafeteria, Darius had given up on seeing her. When the doors to the elevator down the hall from the cafeteria opened, the beautiful girl was there with the same people she had been with before. At least Darius thought it was the same people as before. If he had to be perfectly honest, he hadn't paid attention to the others.

The beautiful girl caught sight of Darius, as did her friends, who giggled when they saw him. He could feel his face flush, and was thankful that his skin was dark enough that she couldn't see it turning red.

As the beautiful girl and her friends stepped off the elevator, and Darius and his party stepped on, the two locked eyes for a brief moment. Darius felt almost as terrified as when the fire escape broke away from the side of building and he thought his death was imminent. In fact, that moment might not have been as bad as the awkward glance he shared outside the elevator.

The doors closed, and Darius could breathe again. His heart rate slowed down. He hoped that Xangtha and the others hadn't noticed his ridiculous reaction. When they got back to the orientation classroom, Trang Nguyen, Chuck Maslon and Dr. Sam sat waiting. For the second time in a matter of minutes, Darius's heart skipped a beat and he had trouble catching his breath. Only this time it had nothing to do with a pretty girl. This time it was panic-induced fear.

Darius knew he had a meeting after lunch with Trang and Dr. Sam—he was supposed to go to her office. But there she was, waiting with Dr. Sam and Chuck Maslon in the classroom.

Did I misunderstand something? Darius wondered. *Did I screw up somehow? Are they here to personally escort me to prison?*

"We need to talk to Darius," Dr. Sam said to Xangtha. "Are you done with him?"

"He's done with orientation," said Xangtha. "He just needs his assignment and his uniform, but I was under the impression you were handling that anyway."

"Great. Thank you," said Trang.

Dr. Sam led Trang and Maslon out of the classroom. Darius followed as Xangtha wished him luck.

I'm going to need it.

Darius followed Dr. Sam and the others to a small conference room down the hall. They all sat around the table, a feeling of dread clinging to Darius like a cold wet shirt. Or maybe it was just the nervous sweat that he felt.

Trang started the conversation off. "The test results are back from the exam you took yesterday."

"The lady, Xangtha, she said it wasn't a pass or fail kind of test," Darius said. He tried to sound cool, despite feeling nervous and his head starting to hurt.

"And it isn't a pass or fail test," said Trang. "But that said…"

"That said, you scored exceptionally high," Dr. Sam cut in. "The academic portion is only part of the exam, but still, you managed to score in the upper two percentile."

So I scored well, thought Darius. *So what? Any spazz could've answered most of those questions.* But he kept that to himself. Instead, he simply said, "I thought you wanted to meet at Trang's office."

"We're here because Chuck insisted on being part of this meeting, and there's more room here than in my office," said Trang.

Suddenly, as if reading Darius's mind, Dr. Sam realized how it all must have looked to Darius. He smiled his reassuring smile that looked like an old bulldog getting ready to attack. "There's nothing to worry about. You're not in trouble."

"We're here to discuss the terms and conditions of your service here at SJF," said Maslon, doing his best to keep Darius feeling afraid.

"I've already explained standard operating procedure to Darius," said Trang. She sounded annoyed.

"These are special circumstances," countered Maslon.

"Is there anyone here not aware of the special circumstances?" Trang shot back. Clearly she liked Maslon as much as Darius did.

"Darius, have you finished high school?" asked Dr. Sam. He had no need to further discuss anything that had already been discussed at length.

Darius wasn't sure what his graduating high school had to do with anything, though as a matter of fact, he hadn't graduated. He felt no pride in it—especially given how important education had been to his parents—and it wasn't like he hadn't tried. He'd stayed in school as long as he could, but bouncing around to different foster homes, and in turn transferring to a different school every time, didn't help his grades. And at some point, none of it seemed to matter anymore.

"No, sir. I didn't finish high school."

"That's what I thought." Dr. Sam jotted down a quick note on a piece of paper. "Super Justice Force operates a continuing education program in conjunction with City University. There is a program that will allow you to get your GED. This is one of the terms of your time spent in Second Chance. You must get your GED. You'll only be working eight hours a day, which means we need to find other productive things for you to do. Understood?"

Maslon fidgeted in his chair. Darius could tell he didn't like where the conversation was going. Maslon didn't even want Darius in Second Chance, let alone finishing up high school.

"I'll get all the information together for you, and by the time we meet next week, you can get started," said Trang. "We'll come up with a schedule that doesn't conflict with work, your meetings with me, or your counseling sessions."

"Does he know about his movement restrictions?" Maslon asked.

"Chuck, how is he supposed to know about something we just decided this morning?" Trang asked.

She let out an audible sigh, and made no attempts to hide the roll of her eyes. Her contempt for Maslon almost brought a smile to Darius's face.

"I know you've heard this a million times, but I will repeat it to make others happy," said Trang, shooting an icy glance at Maslon. "You are unique to Second Chance, and the rules and regulations that apply to others are different for you…"

"Because technically you are under arrest and in the custody of Super Justice Force," finished Maslon.

"I'm also the youngest person to go through Second Chance. And the first to skip prison altogether. The future direction of the program depends on me," said Darius. "Is there anything I'm forgetting?"

Darius wanted to throw in a swear or two, but thought it might be best if he didn't. His head pounded, and Maslon only made matters worse.

Still, Maslon's negative attitude inspired Darius in a weird way. Any doubts Darius might have had about himself were slipping away, if for no other reason than to prove Maslon wrong.

"As long as you are in the custody of SJF, you will adhere to movement restrictions that have been determined for you," said Maslon. He sounded like he had been rehearsing his little speech.

"Movement restrictions?"

"You are allowed to move throughout the buildings of this facility as your security status permits. You may only leave the buildings of this facility if you are accompanied by a SJF employee with Level Four security clearance or higher."

"Is that all?"

The challenging tone in Darius's voice upped the tension in the room. He wanted the conversation to be over. He wanted to be as far away from Chuck Maslon as possible.

"Your STATU has been programmed to allow you to go no more than two blocks in any direction outside of SJF property. Anything more than two blocks will be considered an escape attempt on your part."

"Which side of the second block do I have to stay on to keep from attempting an escape?"

Trang did her best to stifle a laugh. She enjoyed the show between Darius and Maslon, and especially appreciated the fact that Darius wasn't backing down. If Darius had any hope of getting through Second Chance, he couldn't let Maslon bully him.

"We tried to come up with something that was fair, while taking into consideration your status," said Dr. Sam. "You can be granted special consideration for movement outside of these facilities, with prior approval of two employees with Level Four clearance or higher."

All things considered, Darius didn't have it too bad, especially considering the alternative. Having to stay within two blocks of Super Justice Force Headquarters sounded better than any prison he could imagine. Not being able to venture more than a couple of blocks past a building where he had his own private apartment was a small price to pay, and much easier to deal with than getting shanked.

"Is there anything we've discussed that doesn't make sense to you?" Trang asked.

They had already talked to him about how well he had scored on his test. *I'm not as stupid as some people think.* They also talked about him getting his GED. *That would make Mom and Dad happy.* Finally, they had discussed where he could and could not go. *I've had less freedom.*

Only one thing had not come up yet. He almost didn't want to ask, afraid of the answer. He asked anyway. "Where have I been assigned?"

"Well, that's something we need to talk about," said Trang. "We have a potential problem."

That doesn't sound good. What kind of problem? he wondered. *With my luck, I'll be sent off to be a Scrubber.*

"Captain Freedom called me first thing this morning, wanting to know the results of your tests," Trang said. "When I told him, the only thing he said was, 'Put him with Manny.'"

"How's that a problem?" Darius asked.

"Three weeks ago, Manny was promoted and transferred to night shift," said

Trang. "He works from eleven at night to eight in the morning. That can be a brutal shift."

"We're concerned about your ability to work those hours," said Dr. Sam.

"Who is Manny and why does Captain Freedom want you to put me with him?" Darius asked.

He thought he saw a glimpse of irritation on Maslon's face. It was hard to tell, because Maslon always looked irritated.

"Manny is the new night shift supervisor of Operations Crew. He came up through Second Chance—one of the program's biggest successes," said Dr. Sam. "He's one of the best employees here at SJF."

"Manny Ortiz is a crook and a thug," said Maslon. "I fail to understand why no one else sees this. Putting a Bit like this with a Bit like Ortiz is a joke. The only good that will come out of it is we'll be rid of this punk sooner, because there's no way he won't screw up working with Ortiz."

Trang and Dr. Sam tried to ignore Maslon's little rant as best they could. Dr. Sam seemed to tune Maslon out completely. It wasn't as easy for Trang, who shot him a quick look of anger, then quickly turned her attention back to Darius. She gave him a forced smile of reassurance, as if telling him to not worry about anything Maslon had said.

Nothing Maslon said phased Darius. If anything, it gave him confidence. Captain Freedom wanted Darius to work with Manny, but that meant nothing compared to Maslon's hostility. Maslon's disdain for Manny Ortiz—whoever he was—told Darius something important.

Any enemy of Chuck Maslon is a friend of mine, Darius thought.

Darius looked Maslon directly in the eye. He had his doubts about being able to handle the hours, not to mention whatever job he might have to do. But he had no doubts about pissing off Maslon. *I might as well give him a real reason to hate me.*

"No problem," said Darius. "I can handle the night shift."

17

Darius arrived for his first night of work ten minutes early. Knowing he'd be working from eleven to eight, he tried to take a nap, but it didn't happen. He had trouble sleeping as it was, and taking a nap in the early evening simply wasn't meant to be. Instead, he spent the hours leading up to his first shift studying the Operations Crew section of the Employee Handbook. If he couldn't be well rested, at least he could have a clue about what his new job was all about.

```
Super Justice Force is a privately owned, government sanctioned
organization committed to the enforcement of the law, protection
of the innocent, and fighting to ensure justice for all. This
is not easy work, and the super-powered heroes, costumed crime
fighters and metahumans that make up Super Justice Force cannot
do it alone. This is where you, the SJF employee, come in. You
are part of a valuable team that we at SJF call Operations
Crew, for without you, the most powerful team of heroes in the
world would not be able to protect the world.

Operations Crew is responsible for the day-to-day operations at
Super Justice Force Headquarters, as well as all Super Justice
Force Secondary Bases of Operation, or SBOOs for short (more on
SBOOs in the next section). The duties and responsibilities of
Operations Crew are varied, ranging from building and vehicle
maintenance, mid- and low-level security, laundry services,
cleaning up spills, shoveling snow, and anything else you
could possibly imagine. Even the factories that manufacture the
Super Justice Force action figures are overseen by Operations
Crew. The food prepared at the employee cafeteria is cooked
by Operations Crew, who wash all the dishes. And that is just
the beginning. Let's take a look at how Operations Crew really
works.
```

Some people get confused by the term "Operations Crew," mistakenly thinking it is a single department within Super Justice Force. In reality, Operations Crew is a collective made up of three different "service teams." Each of these service teams breaks down into different departments and sub-departments, known as "service branches." As a member of Operations Crew, you will receive basic training within all three service teams. Eventually, you will be given a permanent assignment on a team, with specific duties related to a particular branch of the team.

Security and Observation (SAO) is the biggest of the three service teams at Super Justice Force, and plays a crucial role in the fight against crime and the struggle to enforce justice. SAO maintains security at all facilities and performs all of the duties associated with protecting SJF, its properties and its employees. Utilizing a massive network of surveillance systems, SAO also monitors for criminal activity and possible threats to innocent lives. Oftentimes, it is SAO team members who discover wrong-doing in progress before their super-powered co-workers. It is for this very reason that SAO is such a crucial component in the fight for justice.

Maintenance and Services (MAS) workers are the unsung heroes at Super Justice Force, keeping all the facilities clean and in working order. But MAS is not just about mopping floors and doing laundry. No, there is more to MAS than that. The MAS team maintains every vehicle used by Super Justice Force, from the company cars to the interplanetary SJF Starcruiser. MAS prepares all of the food that is cooked in the employee cafeteria and at the highly rated Justice Café. The employees working the assembly lines that manufacture SJF action figures are all MAS. Even the tour guides and clerks at the Gift Shop of Justice at SJF Headquarters are valuable members of MAS.

Communication and Dispatch (CAD) is the service team that keeps things running smoothly throughout Super Justice Force. CAD maintains the lines of communication between all the service teams and service branches within SJF. The CAD team also operates the elaborate communications network SJF shares with the military and every law enforcement agency in the country. CAD handles every piece of mail that comes to or goes out of any SJF facility, the shipment of action figures from the factories, and even comic books from the printer. All of these responsibilities and more make CAD another crucial component in the successful operation of Super Justice Force.

Darius read the entire Operations Crew section of the Employee Handbook, as well as the individual sections for each service team, which went into greater detail. By the time he finished reading everything, it was time for him to go to work, and he still had no idea what he would be doing.

He got dressed, putting on his official work uniform and making sure that his identification badge was properly affixed to his shirt—the Employee Handbook had a diagram showing proper badge placement. Darius didn't know how long it would take to walk from his apartment in the Tower to Operations Command Central in the Bunker, so he decided to give himself plenty of time.

Nothing Darius had seen in real life could compare to Operations Crew Command Central—O3C. He thought of pictures he'd seen of mission control at NASA, but that didn't look nearly as impressive. And "impressive" didn't really begin to describe it. "Overwhelming" was more like it.

This place looks like something right out of a comic book, Darius thought, stepping into O3C for the first time.

Located in the first basement level of the Bunker, O3C was massive. The hexagon-shaped room took up more space than a full city block, standing two stories from ceiling to floor with a mezzanine dividing half of the space into two levels. A massive display of video monitors lined the three walls separated by the mezzanine. The video monitors on two of the walls provided surveillance feeds and news broadcasts from all over the world—a thousand views all broadcasting live. The third wall of monitors showed nothing but feeds from security monitors stationed throughout SJF Headquarters and the Secondary Bases of Operation.

Standing in the middle of O3C, it was possible to see all the monitors at once. Video feeds from security cameras all over the planet flashed across screens. Darius watched the world from his vantage point. It all made him feel tiny and insignificant.

Super Justice Force employees moved around Darius as if he wasn't there. He had never seen a more eclectic collection of people in his life. His co-workers came in every size, shape, and color imaginable, both women and men, and at least three races of extraterrestrials.

"Can I help you?"

The voice coming from behind him brought Darius back into the moment. Transfixed by everything around, he'd almost forgotten why he was there. He turned to face a man, or something close to a man. Darius was terrible at identifying extraterrestrial races, so he had no clue what he was talking to.

"I'm looking for Manny," Darius said.

"Have you tried the supervisor's office?"

The alien pointed to a glass-encased room directly behind Darius.

"Thanks," said Darius.

Compared to the rest of O3C, the supervisor's office seemed unimpressive. It sat along one of the six walls, strategically placed across from the middle wall of surveillance monitors. Glass walls on three sides made the office look like a fish tank pushed up against a wall. Inside looked like a typical office, complete with cubicles and work stations.

Darius knocked on the glass door before entering. A woman sitting at one of the cubicles held her finger up to Darius, letting him know she'd be with him in a moment. "Look, just run a full diagnostic for now, and we'll have someone from MAS get down there right now," she said to no one in particular.

The woman touched a finger to her ear, then pulled something out of it. Darius couldn't see exactly what it was, it looked almost like a hearing aid.

"If it's not one thing it's another," said the woman. "Now, how can I help you?"

"I'm supposed to report to Manny," Darius said.

"He's running late. Should be here in a few minutes," said the woman. "Have a seat."

The woman pointed to a chair at one of the cubicles.

"I'm Amina, one of the other night supervisors," said the woman.

"I'm Darius."

Darius extended is hand. Amina shook his hand, all the while sizing him up. A beeping alarm sounded from the small electronic device sitting on the desk in front of her. "Excuse me," she said, placing the tiny object back in her ear.

Amina began talking to someone, engaging in what sounded like a one-sided conversation about a clogged toilet as she continued to look Darius over. She had a hard stare and a no-nonsense attitude. She didn't make Darius feel uncomfortable the way Chuck Maslon did, but at the same time he hoped Manny Ortiz was friendlier.

Darius sat at one of the cubicles, trying to ignore Amina staring at him by looking out at O3C. A row of clocks on one of the walls displayed every time zone on the planet. It was 12:05 in the afternoon of the next day in Hong Kong.

The door to the supervisor's office opened. A large man rushed in, out of breath. "Sorry I'm late," he said.

"No worries. Everything's under control," said Amina. She returned to her one-sided conversation without missing a beat.

The man looked at Darius. "You must be Darius," he said. "I'm Manuel Ortiz. Call me Manny."

Manny held out his hand for Darius to shake. He didn't look anything like what Darius expected—even though Darius wasn't sure what he expected. Certainly not someone with a face as weathered by age and battle.

Manny looked like he had seen his share of fights, his crooked nose showed signs of having been broken several times, and a half-circle scar cut a line that curved from above his left eyebrow around his upper cheek. At four inches over six feet, and close to three hundred pounds, Manny looked like an ex-football player who hadn't bothered staying in shape. His frame was still muscular—far from being a flabby mess—but his stomach was bigger than it should have been, and it pushed ever so slightly against the shirt of his uniform, threatening to bust out. Some time in the near future he would either need to get a new shirt, or lose some weight, but he could still probably hold his own in a fight.

"Good to meet you," said Darius, surprised at the strength of Manny's grip. Manny's massive hand swallowed Darius's hand, clamping down on it like a killer whale biting down on a goldfish.

"Give me a minute to get settled, and then we'll get started," said Manny.

Manny set the paper bag he brought with him on top of a desk, typed something into one of the computers and walked over to Amina's cubicle. He waited for her to finish her conversation, but she continued to talk, either ignoring him, or feeling he wasn't important enough to acknowledge. Manny turned his back to Amina and faced Darius, rolling his eyes and shrugging his shoulders.

Darius fought to keep from laughing.

Manny continued with his act. He held his hand up to the side of his head, pantomiming like he was talking on the phone.

Darius looked away. It was all he could do to keep from bursting out in laughter.

Amina finished her conversation. "Sorry about that," she said.

Manny turned around to face Amina, acting perfectly normal, as if seconds earlier he hadn't been making fun of her.

"That toilet down in VMB1 is clogged again, and we're short-staffed in MAS tonight," Amina said.

"Any other crises to deal with tonight?" Manny asked.

"There was an energy surge about an hour ago on the main power grid down near the Cage," said Amina.

"Probably a standard techno-plasm discharge. We're about due for one anyway," said Manny.

"Probably. Still, I've dispatched a MAS crew to run a full diagnostic, and sent down two extra bodies from SAO to babysit," Amina said. "I planned on running down there later, just to check things out for myself."

"I'll go," said Manny. "I've got to show Darius around anyway."

Amina glanced at Darius. The cold, hard stare she'd given him when he first came into the office faded, replaced with something else. Darius couldn't tell, but she almost looked worried.

"You're taking him to the Cage? On his first night?" she asked.

Manny nodded and said something about it being better to get "these things out of the way sooner instead of later."

"C'mon, amigo, follow me," Manny said to Darius.

Manny walked to the back of the supervisor's office. The entire back wall of the office was a massive vault. He pressed his right palm to the security pad next to the door, and then punched a series of numbers into the keypad next to the scanner. The heavy steel door opened. Manny stepped inside, motioning Darius to follow him.

"This is where we keep the expensive toys," said Manny.

Darius quickly scanned the room. To the left was a case filled with weapons—machine guns, UltraStun 500s, and portable techno-plasm cannons.

"They don't trust me enough to let me play with those," Manny said, pointing to the guns. "Don't matter to me though, 'cause only a puta uses a gun."

Manny moved to the other side of the vault. He opened a storage cabinet, pulled out a leather belt, a large black flashlight, and a box. He handed the belt and flashlight to Darius. "I'm sure you know how these work," he said.

"I think I can figure it out."

Darius followed Manny out of the vault. The door closed automatically behind them.

"It's got a safety feature. The door can't close if anyone is inside," said Manny. "It didn't used to be like that. But two years ago someone got locked inside and suffocated to death."

"Really?" asked Darius.

"Of course not. I'm making that up," Manny said with a laugh.

Manny returned to the cubicle where he'd set his paper bag. He pulled up a second chair, motioned for Darius to sit next to him, and then logged on to the computer. He handed the box he brought with him from the vault to Darius. "Open that up, while I set you up on the computer," said Manny.

Darius opened the box and pulled out an electronic device that looked like an old-school smart phone. The device was a bit too big to fit in the palm of his hand, and couldn't have been more than a quarter of an inch thick.

"Looks like some kind of cell phone or something," said Manny. "But it ain't."

"What is it?"

"That, amigo, is your Personal Communication Unit—PCU for short. It needs to be activated before it'll work," said Manny. "But believe me, that's the most valuable tool you got. Keep it with you at all times. Once it is activated, it's plugged into the entire SJF communication grid. You can access any video surveillance unit here at HQ, or at any Secondary Operational Bases. Its got a built-in video feature, so you can capture and transmit information live, directly into the system. There is also an emergency transmitter and GPS."

"Darius, make sure he shows you how to disable the live video feed," said Amina. "The last thing you want to do is transmit a signal of yourself sitting on the toilet."

"Thanks for spoiling the fun," Manny said.

Manny had Darius read off the serial number on the back of the PCU. He entered the numbers into the computer, and a moment later Darius's PCU activated.

"Now, you just need to enter a personal access code," said Manny.

He scooted his chair out of the way, turning his back so he couldn't see the password Darius entered into the computer. Darius typed D-W-A-Y-N-E into the computer. His PCU beeped. The Super Justice Force logo appeared on the screen with a message that read, "Welcome to the Super Justice Force Communication Network."

"You're now plugged in and live, homes" said Manny. "That's an amazing piece of technology, but very simple to operate. Read the manual, and if you have any questions, ask anyone. But here's the best part."

Manny took his PCU from the holster on his belt, dropped it on the floor, and then smashed his foot down on it. He picked it up and handed it to Darius.

"These things are pretty indestructible." Manny said.

Darius examined Manny's PCU. It looked as new as the one he had removed from the box. Darius handed the unit back to Manny.

"Okay, make sure you get this out of the box," Manny said. He held up a small, cylindrical device and placed it in his ear. "If you see people walking around, talking to themselves, either they're using one of these, having a conversation with Invisiguardian, or they're crazy."

Darius removed the device from his box. It was just over a half inch long, tapered so that it could fit easily in the ear canal, with a button set into the larger end.

"It's a two-way remote transmitter—sends and receives signals," said Manny. "Allows you to keep your hands free. I'll show you how to use the whole thing once we get started. You ready to do this, amigo?"

Darius nodded his head.

"That's all you got for me? That little baby nod?" asked Manny. He nodded his head, mocking Darius more than imitating him. "You're rollin' with Manny now. You can't act like no puta."

Manny laughed and slapped Darius on the back. It was a gentle slap—meant in good fun—but it almost knocked Darius off his feet.

I'd hate to have him hit me for real, Darius thought. *He'd turn my bones to dust.*

"Now, one more time. You ready to do this, amigo?" Manny asked.

"Yeah," said Darius.

"I don't know," said Manny, shaking his head. "Sounds kinda weak. We'll have to see."

18

They started their tour at O3C, with Manny giving Darius a basic overview of everything, spending more time on the break room and the bathroom than anywhere else. "When you got business to handle, you gotta handle your business," Manny said.

Manny walked Darius through O3C, introducing him to everyone on duty. There were too many people for Darius to remember, not to mention more people than he felt comfortable being around. Manny, on the other hand, liked everyone and everyone seemed to like him. Making the rounds through O3C, introducing Darius, constantly cracking jokes—Manny was in his element.

"I'm not going to be able to remember all of these people," Darius said after being introduced to his thirty-third co-worker.

"You think I know everyone's name?" asked Manny. "That's why God invented the name tag."

"I didn't know God invented the name tag"

"Now you know. Make a note of it. There'll be a test later," Manny said with a laugh. He laughed at most of his jokes. "Seriously, though, don't worry about remembering names. Everyone has an identification badge—you can't go anywhere without one. There's more important things to remember—like where the nearest bathroom is."

"The nearest bathroom?" Darius asked.

"I already told you—when you gotta handle business, you gotta handle business."

Darius didn't know what to make of Manny, or if he was the right person to train him. As much as he hated to admit it, Darius worried that Maslon might have been right. In the half hour Manny spent showing Darius around O3C, Manny had done very little other than crack jokes. The jokes were funny, but Darius didn't have a clue as to what he was supposed to be doing.

Manny led Darius to the middle of Operation Crew Command Central. Activity swirled around them. Events of the world played out on the video monitors in front of them. Darius felt like he was standing in the center of the universe.

"Kinda overwhelming, ain't it?" Manny asked.

"Just a little," said Darius.

"Everyone gets overwhelmed at first. This is how it all looks to you right now," Manny said, stretching out his arms as wide as he could. "You need to learn to see it like this." He held up his hand, his thumb and forefinger two inches apart. "Comprende?"

"Not really."

Manny stretched out his arms again. "This is what's going on here right now—at Super Justice Force, in O3C. All of this," he said. "But all of this, is made up of all of these." He held up his hand again, thumb and forefinger two inches apart.

"A lot of small parts, making up the big part," said Darius.

"Exactly. Think of Operations Crew as all the small parts, instead of the one big part," said Manny. "Don't think of it as this big giant thing. You start thinking about the big part, and that's how you get overwhelmed."

"You mean like the service teams—SAO and all of that?"

"What do you know about service teams?" Manny asked.

"Just what I read in the Employee Handbook," Darius said.

"Really? You read that thing?" asked Manny. "I don't know anyone who's actually read that thing. I bet you were the kid that always turned in his homework on time."

"I want to do a good job," said Darius.

"You're with Manny, amigo. You watch, four weeks from now you'll see."

"What happens in four weeks?" Darius asked.

"That's how long your training lasts. You train with me for a week. After that, you spend three days a week floating in other departments and two days with me. At the end of the month you'll be evaluated. Right now you're a L1T—a Level 1 Trainee. You read about that in the Employee Handbook?"

"Yeah. It means I have limited security clearance"

"Limited don't really begin to cover it," said Manny. "Sixty-five percent of HQ is off limits to L1Ts unless they're with a L1 or higher."

"The Employee Handbook said that after training I'd be moved up to a Level 1."

"If you pass your evaluation—prove you've learned something in training—then yeah, sure, you move up to a standard L1."

"What happens if I don't get past L1T?" Darius asked.

"You'll be sent to wash dishes in the cafeteria. But that ain't gonna happen, amigo," said Manny. "You're being trained by Manny. El francaso no es una opción."

"What's that mean?"

"It means that failure ain't an option," said Manny. "You're gonna do good here, 'cause if you don't, it makes me look bad. And I never look bad."

Manny laughed and slapped Darius on the back, once again almost knocking him off his feet.

Manny and Darius walked around SJF Headquarters for almost two hours, wandering along corridors, up and down stairways, riding the elevators, and generally exploring all the buildings. In addition to the regular hallways and corridors that ran through each building, HQ also had a series of "Emergency Access Paths" that allowed quicker, more direct passage to various locations throughout the entire facility.

"There's a lot of corridors that look the same—it's easy to get lost or confused. Especially in an emergency," said Manny. "You know where we are right now?"

Darius looked up and down the long corridor he stood in with Manny. It looked like the other dozen or so long hallways they had taken from location to location.

"I don't even know what building we're in," said Darius.

"Neither do I," said Manny. "I guess one of us better figure out where we are and how to get outta here."

Darius fumbled with his PCU, trying to make sense of the map on the screen. Manny had already showed him how to use the device to determine location, as a guidance system and how to tap into the main surveillance system. More than anything, Darius struggled to work the touch-pad screen. Every time Darius tapped the screen of the PCU he would zoom in on the map so tight he couldn't tell where he was, or he would accidentally activate some other function. It felt like playing a video game that he kept losing. Finally, he managed to pull up the information he needed.

"We're in Sector 3, at coordinates 1-A53," said Darius. "I think."

"I don't know," said Manny, shrugging his shoulders. He pointed to the juncture at the end of the corridor. "What happens if we go right or go left?"

Darius touched the screen again. "We go left, and it takes us to the stairwell at co-ordinates 1-A55. To the right is an access point to VMB1. What is VMB1?"

Manny shrugged his shoulders again. "I don't know, esai. You're the one who read the Employee Handbook," he said. "Maybe you should access a security feed, and we can figure out what VMB1 is."

Once again, Darius fumbled with the PCU, this time trying to access the proper security feed. He struggled, activating incorrect functions, accessing the wrong feeds, and swearing under his breath.

"You know, you can always smash that thing on the ground. It won't break," Manny said.

"I've almost got it," Darius said.

"Oh, I can see that," said Manny. He made a show of looking at his watch. "You know, our shift is over in about six hours."

"Is this how you train everyone?" Darius asked.

"Most people usually ask for help by now."

"Well, I'm not most people. I don't need help," Darius said, holding out his PCU for Manny to see the screen. "Vehicle Maintenance Bay One."

"Very good," said Manny, clapping his hands. "And you thought you couldn't do it."

You're right, Darius said to himself, *I didn't think I could do it.*

Manny started walking toward VMB1. He didn't say a word to Darius, just motioned for him to follow. Manny stopped in front of a set of double doors that looked like countless other doors they had passed while wandering the halls. "The video surveillance feeds don't do this place justice," said Manny. "This place will blow your mind."

Manny opened the door leading from the corridor to rear of Vehicle Maintenance Bay One. He hadn't been exaggerating.

Darius stared in wide-eyed wonder at VMB1, a massive space the size of a football field. Along the far wall were a series of garage doors big enough to drive either a tank or a semi-truck through—both of which were parked inside the space. Ten individual hydraulic lifts took up half the floor, and could be locked together, forming one huge lift that rose all the way to the ceiling—five stories up—where it doubled as a landing pad once the retractable dome roof opened.

In addition to the semi-truck and the tank, a small fleet of vans and cars sat parked in service bays. None of those vehicles impressed Darius. It was impossible to be impressed by ordinary cars, vans, trucks and tanks, when parked in the same space were things Darius never thought he would see in real life.

Nightwatcher's Nightmobile was probably the most famous car in the world. Darius had a die-cast metal replica of the legendary crime fighter's tricked-out car when he was a kid.

A small team of men dressed in red jumpsuits, stained with dirt and grease, worked on the Nightmobile. Darius could see that the car was banged up pretty bad. He walked over to get a closer look, but something much bigger caught his attention.

Standing not ten yards from the Nightmobile was the Super Justice Force Starcruiser. The heavily armed tactical ship looked like a smaller version of the space shuttle crossed with a jet fighter. Capable of space travel at incredible speeds, two earlier versions of the Starcruiser had been destroyed during the Battle of Enceladus, years before Darius was born. He still remembered reading about it in "Tales of the Super Justice Force." And he'd begged his parents for the toy version of the Starcruiser, but it was too expensive.

"Maybe for Christmas," his mother told him.

Christmas never came that year.

Lost in the moment, Darius felt like a little kid. He couldn't remember the last time he'd been as excited by anything. He thought about his parents, and his brother Dwayne, and how excited they would be if he could tell them about everything he saw—at least his father and brother would be excited. His mother would just smile and say, "That sounds wonderful," although she would really be wondering what all the fuss was about. His brother, on the other hand, would be asking a million questions, first and foremost being if he could get a ride on the Starcruiser.

"Earth to Darius. Come in Darius."

Manny's voice snapped Darius out of his fantasy.

"You okay?" Manny asked.

"Just thinking."

"Don't strain yourself," Manny said, chuckling. "C'mere. I got someone I want you to meet."

Manny stood beside the Nightmobile, next to someone working on the engine. Darius couldn't see the mechanic who had crawled under the hood of the car, but he could hear him swearing up a storm.

"This is Otto Rekker," Manny said, pointing to the man cursing under the hood of the car. "Otto, get out here."

Otto grumbled a string of profanities that sounded like every single swear word ever spoken, mashed into one long super curse. He pulled his head out from the tight space under the hood, his face smeared with slightly less grease than his hands, He wiped his right hand—his real hand—on red, grease-stained coveralls with the sleeves torn off.

"Otto, this is Darius," said Manny. "Darius, this is Otto."

Otto Rekker needed no introduction. Standing nearly seven feet tall, his head shaved completely bald, the ever-familiar handlebar mustache creeping down both sides of his mouth, Darius recognized Otto from the comic books he'd read as a kid. An elaborate tattoo of a dragon wrapped all the way around Otto's right triceps, bicep and forearm. The head of the dragon rested on the back of his hand, its mouth open, spitting fire that came out onto Otto's fingers. Otto's left arm had no tattoo, because he had no left arm—at least not a real one. His left arm was completely mechanical—a high-tech fusion of lightweight metal alloys and experimental plastics crafted into an incredibly powerful machine attached to his body.

The leader of the notorious gang of criminals called the Rekking Crew, Otto Rekker was one of the worst supercriminals of all time. Darius remembered when he was kid, Otto Rekker had broken the back of Nightwatcher in a fight, leaving the crime fighter out of commission for two years.

"Big D, good to meet you," said Otto.

Darius mumbled a response, reluctantly shaking Otto's hand. Something about Otto made Darius uncomfortable. It had nothing to do with the fierce-looking tattoo or the bionic arm. It had to do with the bad man he knew from comic books—the supercriminal whose face had flashed across the television screen for weeks after a near-deadly encounter with Nightwatcher.

Darius never much cared for Nightwatcher. As far as he was concerned, Nightwatcher wasn't even a real superhero—he had no real powers. He was just some guy who dressed up in a weird costume with a bunch of high-tech gadgets.

Still, what Otto Rekker did to Nightwatcher was wrong.

"Now that is a bad man," Darius's father, Dwayne, had said while watching a news report about Otto Rekker.

Like Darius, Dwayne Logan had never cared much for Nightwatcher. "Can't trust a man who hides behind a mask like that," he would say. But his feelings for Nightwatcher changed after Otto Rekker had broken his back. It was the same way for much of the country. Nightwatcher had been a dangerous crime fighter who played by his own rules, and it made people uncomfortable. But the savage beating he took from Otto Rekker made him a public favorite, eventually leading to his first endorsement deal and membership in Super Justice Force.

"I wasn't expecting to find you here this late," Manny said to Otto. "I was just showing the kid around."

"I was supposed to be home hours ago. Anna is pissed. But this old girl is tore up pretty bad," Otto said, pointing to the Nightmobile. "And you-know-who needs it for some charity event this weekend, so I'm stuck burning the midnight oil."

The left side of the Nightmobile didn't look that bad. The right side was another story altogether. The entire right side had crashed into something—something big. Parts of the car were actually missing—like the door, the front quarter panel and the front tire. The rear tire was simply a shredded mess of rubber.

"Didn't you just fix this thing?" Manny asked.

"Last month. Completely rebuilt the whole damn thing," said Otto.

"Was he drunk?"

"We're talking about Nightwatcher here, not Captain Freedom," Otto said. "I swear, every time he takes the old girl out he crashes her into the side of a building or drives her off a freakin' bridge. Then I fix her, and that sonovabitch just wrecks her again. No respect at all. I'm telling you, someone needs to revoke his license."

"You say the same thing every time," laughed Manny.

"And I mean it every time. You know he's practically blind in one eye? I'm serious. Everyone thinks he squints all the time to look tough, but it's because he can't see out of that one eye. The guy can barely see! My dead grandmother has better eyesight! But he's still toolin' around like he doesn't have a care in the world."

Manny laughed uncontrollably. Darius didn't understand what was so funny. Otto's jokes made him feel kind of uncomfortable.

"Do you think I want to be here, when I could be home in bed with my wife? I keep telling him replace that bad eye of his with a bionic one, but he doesn't listen to me," Otto complained. "Our health plan doesn't cover biomechatronics, and he's too cheap—that's the problem. He says it's because he doesn't want to be laid up recovering that long. Hell, it wouldn't be like the time I broke his back. But I'll tell you this much, if he wrecks this thing again, I'm gonna rip out that bad eye of his, and then he'll have no choice but to get a new one."

Manny gasped for air, tears rolling down his cheeks. "Please...please...stop," he begged. "I can't take any more."

"I'm glad my misery brings you so much joy," Otto said.

"Go home, amigo. Get some sleep." Manny said, slapping Otto on the back. The same slap that almost knocked Darius off his feet didn't budge Otto. Manny took a deep breath, wiping tears of laughter from his cheeks. "We need to get back to work."

"Hey, don't forget: a week from this Saturday, barbecue at my place. I just got a new grill," Otto said. "And don't forget to remind Elladia. I know Anna sent her an email, but you remind her."

"Thanks. I'll be there. Not too sure if Elladia can make it—she's been swamped with school. But I'll be sure to pass along the invite," said Manny.

"Big D, you're welcome to come by too," said Otto. "We'll have plenty of food. You like barbecue?"

Darius nodded his head. He felt like he had nothing to say to Otto. He certainly didn't plan on going to his house for a barbecue.

Manny led Darius out of VMB1, into a different corridor from where they had come. He showed Darius where all the janitorial supplies for Sector 3 were stored, and then showed him an emergency access corridor that led to the Medical Trauma and Surgery Unit.

Darius heard everything Manny told him, including how MTSU offered free courses to all employees in first aid and CPR—something Darius would need to know to move up in rank. But something ate away at Darius, stealing his focus, making him more and more uncomfortable. His mind kept wandering back to the stories he'd read in comic books like "Supercriminal Showcase" and "Tales of Villainy"—all starring Otto Rekker.

How can a guy like that be allowed to work here? Darius wondered. *Maybe no one knows it's him. Maybe he used some sort of mind control device to keep people from realizing who he is.*

"Manny, do you know who that guy back there was?" Darius asked.

"Which guy?"

"The guy back there, with the tattoo and the bionic arm"

"Sure, that was Otto, head of vehicle maintenance."

Darius stared in disbelief at Manny. *It must be some sort of mind control device—like the one Professor Necromance used on Humdinger.*

"No, man, that's Otto Rekker—of the Rekking Crew," said Darius. "The guy is like one of the worst super criminals of all time. When I was a kid, he nearly killed Nightwatcher. Don't you know that?"

"Everyone knows who Otto Rekker is," said Manny. "And everyone knows what he did."

"If everyone knows who he is, and everyone knows what he did, then what's he doing here? How can they just let someone like him in here?"

"Someone like him? What about someone like him?"

"He's one of the bad guys," said Darius. "What do they call 'em around here? A Bit? He's a Bit."

Manny fixed a hard stare on Darius, who was clearly upset. He reminded himself that Darius was new on the job, not to mention young—very young. Which is why he kept his cool. The old Manny would have torn into a kid like Darius for being so disrespectful—maybe even hit him. But the old Manny had been laid to rest for a long time. Still, Darius needed to know the score.

"Listen to me very carefully, 'cause I ain't ever sayin' any of this to you again," Manny said, his sense of humor replaced with a hard seriousness. "Otto Rekker has been many things, but he ain't ever been a Bit. You don't know him, which means you don't judge him. You don't judge anyone. Ever. Unless you're ready to be judged. Comprende?"

"What're you talking about?" Darius asked.

Manny pointed to the STATU around Darius's ankle. "You wearin' that as some sort of fashion statement?"

Darius looked down. For a moment, he had forgotten.

"I don't let anybody on my crew if I ain't read their files," said Manny. "You got pinched last week when you didn't run as fast as your loser friends. You were carryin' enough eXXeLL to keep the wannabes in No Man's Land juiced up for six months. I know all about you, esai. At least Otto Rekker was able to go toe-to-toe against Nightwatcher. You couldn't even out-run some flat-foot cops. If anyone is a Bit, it's you, kid."

"Those were mistakes. I'm getting my life together."

"I'm sure you will. That's what Second Chance is all about. The reason you're here right now is because at some point the supes realized that catchin' bad guys and lockin' 'em up wasn't doin' the trick," said Manny. "Otto, he's First Ten—one of the very first Chancers. Him and Butchie Pirro, EZ Manigo and Quincy Boone and the guy that dressed like a beaver, and all them other guys, Second Chance wouldn't exist if it weren't for them. There would be no second chances. Not for you. Not for me. Not for anyone."

Darius had thought about Second Chance a lot ever since he entered the program. But he hadn't thought of it the way Manny was talking about it. For Darius, Second Chance would be an opportunity to turn his life around. The lives of others hadn't much occurred to him. He wondered about guys like Butchie and Big Mike, but those thoughts were only in passing.

"I'm sorry," said Darius. "I never really thought about it like that."

"You never thought of yourself as malo hombre?" Manny asked with a smile.

"Malo hombre?"

"One of the bad guys"

It sounded weird to Darius, Manny calling him "one of the bad guys."

"No, I never thought of myself as malo hombre."

"Most people never do. Someone breaks the law, you can bet they got their reasons—reasons they can justify. Reasons that make sense—at least to them," said Manny. "Hell, Doc Kaos can probably make a compellin' case for tryin' to destroy the human race."

Manny's words got Darius to thinking. Every time he broke the law—every time he did something wrong—he felt justified. He stole because he needed to survive. Stealing meant money. Money meant food. Food meant staying alive. It was better to steal than it was to starve—even if stealing was against the law. He never thought of himself as a bad guy for doing it. He did what needed to be done to get by.

"I'm sorry if I came down hard on you," said Manny. "You need to keep some things in mind. First, there are a lot of people who work here that used to be one of the bad guys. Don't ever judge them for what they did, unless you're prepared to judge yourself the same way."

"But how did he end up in Second Chance after everything that happened with him and Nightwatcher?" asked Darius.

"Ask him at his barbecue next weekend. In fact, Nightwatcher will probably be there, so you can ask him too. It's always better hearing the story from the two of them at the same time," said Manny.

"I don't think I can go to the barbecue. I'm not really supposed to leave HQ."

"You ain't supposed to leave HQ without the approval of two Level 4 employees or higher," corrected Manny. "I think we can find some L4s to give their approval."

Manny slapped Darius on the back. This time Darius braced himself. He still felt like he was going to be knocked to the ground.

19

"It don't matter what section you're assigned, there's reports to be filed," said Manny. "Make sure you keep on top of your paperwork."

After their tour of HQ, Darius and Manny returned to O3C, where Manny explained the proper way to file reports for different service teams and service branches. Everything was done electronically, and everything had to be reported. Mopping a bathroom floor or changing a light bulb required reports that needed to be filed.

I can't believe there's this much paperwork, Darius thought.

Everything at Headquarters operated on a set schedule, from security sweeps to sweeping the floor in the main lobbies. Using both a computer and a PCU, Manny showed Darius how to access different schedules.

Darius tried to keep his mind from wandering to other topics. Lack of sleep made it difficult to focus at three in the morning. He needed something other than filing reports and checking schedules to keep him from nodding off.

"How did you get in Second Chance?" Darius asked.

He regretted asking the question the moment the words were out his mouth. It violated the sacred rule—never ask a convict what they did. Locked up in juvenile detention, no one asked anyone what they'd done. Some guys bragged about their crimes—they were idiots. Others proclaimed their innocence—many were liars. But no one ever asked anyone what they did. Everyone knew that.

"I'm sorry," said Darius. "I shouldn't have asked."

"Ain't nothin' to be sorry about, amigo," said Manny. "You've gotta own the things you do. Even the bad things. And back in the day, when I was El Toro Loco, I did some loco mierda."

"That was you?" Darius asked in disbelief. He remembered reading an issue of "Supercriminal Showcase" that featured El Toro Loco—the Crazy Bull. "You had that mask with the thing! You were like…like…"

Manny cut him off. "I was a malo hombre—a very bad man. Selfish. Reckless. I hurt a lot of people, amigo. My older brother would beg me to quit—but I loved the life too much. Then him and his wife were killed in The Attack, and their little girl was left an orphan. I was the only family she had, and I had to do right by her. Turned myself in, right here in this very building."

"And just like that they gave you a job?"

"It's more complicated than that. Let's say I was given 'special consideration,' and my first job that didn't involve stealing," said Manny. "Some day I'll tell you the whole story."

Darius wondered what his life would have been like if someone stepped up to take care of him the way Manny did for his niece. Instead, he got Uncle Kenny, an endless parade of foster families, and the dirty floor of an abandoned subway station.

"Your niece is lucky she had someone like you to look out for her," Darius said.

"No, I'm the lucky one. If it wasn't for her, I probably never would have turned my life around. She's grown into a beautiful woman, works here part time, getting ready to start school at State University. And that's my story."

"She's beautiful?" asked Darius. He thought briefly about the girl he'd seen the in the cafeteria, wondering what department she worked in.

"Gorgeous," said Manny. "Anyone goes near her, I'll kill 'em."

After touring much of HQ, lessons in using the computer systems, PCUs, filing reports and accessing schedules, exhaustion had set in. Only halfway through his first shift, Darius didn't know if he could make it. He fought to keep from yawning as he followed Manny to the employee cafeteria.

Darius had never seen the employee cafeteria so empty. Usually it was crowded, staff hustling in the kitchen, Operations Crew members grabbing a meal during a break, conversations between co-workers. But with the exception of two people leaving as Darius and Manny entered, only one person sat in the cafeteria, eating Chinese food out of to-go containers.

Darius didn't recognize the lone diner, but there was no mistaking his costume. He wore a tight-fitting suit that looked like it was made out of space—outer space.

Pictures of the elite Galaxus Alliance Corps were one thing; Darius had seen plenty of those. Seeing an actual member of GAC in person was something different. If he wasn't so tired, Darius might have been excited.

With members from all over the universe—and according to the comic books, other dimensions as well—the Galaxus Alliance Corps enforced the law throughout the known galaxies. The GAC were police officers and soldiers, patrolling the cold vacuum of space, fighting for justice on distant planets in alien star systems. The incredible powers of each Galaxus came to them from the Mhadra Turas, an ancient race of symbiotic life forms that bonded to host bodies.

Everything Darius knew about the GAC he had read in comic books. "Adventures of the Galaxus Alliance Corps" was one of his favorite comics—after the Captain

Freedom comics. Every issue of "Adventures of the Galaxus Alliance Corps" featured the daring exploits of a team of Galaxus, led by a human named Max "Galaxus" McKool. The guy sitting at the table, eating Chinese food, looked nothing like Max McKool. With his shaggy blonde hair and barely noticeable stubble of a beard just starting to grow in, this particular Galaxus looked more like a rock musician or professional surfer than he did a cosmic defender of justice.

The Galaxus looked up from his food, saw Manny, and broke into a huge smile. He stood up from the table, grabbed Manny, and wrapped his arms around him in a huge bear hug. "Manuel, amigo! Como esta?" asked the Galaxus.

Manny, who wasn't exactly small, looked like he might break from the embrace of the Galaxus. "Muy bien," he gasped.

The Galaxus released Manny from his bone-crushing embrace. Turning his attention to Darius, he extended his hand. "Hey, my name's Zander. Zander Boeman. Everyone calls me Z-Boe."

"I'm Darius," he said, gripping Zander's hand. A sudden energy surge, the likes of which Darius had never felt before, pulsed through his body. It felt intense—like fireworks going off inside his body—and happened so quickly Darius wasn't even sure if it had happened. He wondered if everyone who shook hands with a Galaxus felt the same energy surge, and for a moment, Darius worried about contracting some sort of cosmic cancer.

Z-Boe didn't even seem to notice. And as quickly as the sudden rush of energy had moved through Darius's body, it vanished. Darius convinced himself it had something to do with the symbiotic life forms that gave Z-Boe his power. Or maybe he was just really tired.

"Mind if we join you?" asked Manny.

"Hey man, mi casa es su casa, or something like that," said Z-Boe.

"Mi mesa es la mesa," corrected Manny.

Darius and Manny joined Z-Boe at his table. Zander offered the others some of his Chinese food—there was more than enough for everyone. Manny already had his meal, packed in a brown paper bag, and Darius felt self-conscious.

"I don't see you carrying your lunch like Manny here," said Z-Boe, noticing Darius hadn't packed a lunch. "Dude, you on some kind of diet?"

"I've got a meal voucher card. I was going to use it to get something out of the vending machines, but I forgot it," Darius said.

"Blah, blah, blah," said Z-Boe. "If you don't eat some of this stuff, there's gonna be trouble, bro."

"You better eat something, amigo," Manny said. "You don't want to piss off Zander Boeman on your first night."

"No doubt, man," said Z-Boe laughing. "No doubt."

Since there were no plates, Darius ate out the boxes. He tried to stuff some pork fried rice into his mouth using chopsticks without looking foolish. It was a futile attempt, even though Z-Boe kept showing him what to do. "Hold it like a pencil, bro," Z-Boe said.

Despite his help, it still didn't work. Darius spilled food all over himself, while Z-Boe handled the chopsticks like a pro, or at least like a guy with super cosmic powers that made him one of the most powerful men on the planet.

Manny rummaged through his paper bag, pulling out his meal—a sandwich, bag of chips, hardboiled egg, an apple and a slice of cake. "Oh, I almost forgot," he said, sliding the plastic-wrapped piece of cake over to Darius.

"What's this?" asked Darius.

"My niece baked a cake the other day," Manny said.

"What're you giving it to me for?"

Manny smiled at Darius. "Think about it."

Darius thought for a moment, but had no clue. He looked over at Z-Boe, but he didn't know either and just shrugged.

"I give up," said Darius.

"Happy birthday," said Manny.

Darius had forgotten. It was his birthday—seventeen years old—and he had completely forgotten.

"Dude, no kidding? It's your birthday?" asked Z-Boe.

Darius nodded. He couldn't believe he had forgotten his own birthday.

"Well, happy birthday, bro," said Z-Boe, high-fiving Darius.

The moment the palms of their hands slapped together, another surge of energy passed through Darius's body. And again, the Galaxus didn't seem to feel a thing.

"Sucks that you gotta work on your birthday," Z-Boe said.

"Beats being in prison. Ain't that right, vato?" said Manny.

"Word up," said Z-Boe, this time hi-fiving Manny.

In his entire life, Darius had never met anyone like Zander Boeman. Loud and gregarious, with a smile that never seemed to fade and a booming laugh that needed very little to get going, Z-Boe was the complete opposite of Darius. The sort of person that was everybody's new best friend, Z-Boe made whoever was around him feel like there was nothing to worry about.

A reserve member of Super Justice Force, and the official liaison between the GAC and SJF, Zander lived in an apartment at Headquarters, but seldom fought crime the way other members did. He spent more than six months out of the year away from Earth, which made his life difficult. "I miss my girlfriend," he told Manny and Darius. "And do you know how hard it is to get decent Chinese food when you're not on Earth?"

Darius always imagined the life of a Galaxus as being one of non-stop adventure, but Z-Boe made it sound lonely, boring and uneventful. Instead of tall tales of battles with the Ad-Ahlen Empire, Zander talked about being stuck doing mostly administrative work at the Enceladus Colony on the moon of Saturn.

"Enough about my paper-pushing in the far reaches of the solar system," said Z-Boe. "What's going on here?"

"Same old stuff. The big news is that Barb Smalley got promoted. She transferred out to San Francisco, runnin' the whole facility out there," said Manny.

"Get outta here," said Z-Boe. "Who did they replace her with?"

Manny's face split with an ear-to-ear grin. He pointed at his identification badge. "Me," he said.

"No way! You made L4 Supervisor?"

"Me and Otto—the only two Chancers to make L4 Supervisor," Manny said, not bothering to mask his pride.

"What did Chuck Maslon have to say about you getting promoted?" Z-Boe asked.

"He crapped a brick sideways," said Manny. "He fought it every step of the way—wanted one of his Long Arms to get the position."

"Look at you," said Z-Boe, his smile bigger than Manny's. "Congrats, bro. That is awesome!"

Z-Boe high-fived Manny, and then high-fived Darius—as a matter of principle. "This guy is the Man," Z-Boe said to Darius, pointing at Manny. "They don't get more righteous than this guy here."

"Gracias," said Manny. "But I gotta tell you, these new hours are killing me."

"I heard that," Darius said, stifling a yawn.

"There'll be plenty of time to rest when we're dead," said Z-Boe. "Any other news?"

"Tunneller and Firepower are back," said Manny.

"I thought they quit and joined that operation down in Florida."

"Yeah, the Florida League of Power went bankrupt and fired everyone," said Manny. "Most of these small-time hero teams can't stay in business. They can't get decent endorsement deals, especially when their best guys are Firepower and the Tunneller. Captain Freedom felt bad, so he brought 'em back."

Z-Boe laughed. "Well, I guess the city can breathe more safely knowing those clowns are around. Remember the time Tunneller accidentally cut through that gas line uptown, and then Firepower ignited the whole thing?"

Manny buried his face in his hands and shook his head. "It was blind luck no one got hurt in the explosion," he said.

"Individually, Tunneller and Firepower are just your average do-gooders with great intentions but limited intelligence," Z-Boe explained to Darius. "But you get these two together, and I swear its like Stupid and Stupider."

Darius didn't know much about Tunneller or Firepower. They were newer heroes who'd come onto the scene when Darius had other things to pay attention to, like staying alive.

"What about Lady Themis? She still around?" asked Z-Boe.

"Where is Lady T gonna go?" Manny asked.

"Dude, the last time I talked to her, she was talking about giving it all up. She was dating some football player or something."

"That didn't last," said Manny.

"Watch out for Lady T, bro," Z-Boe said to Darius. "She's cool. And dude, she looks even better in real life. But don't let her start talking to you, or she'll bend your ear all night about her man problems. How a chick that hot can have such bad taste in men is beyond me. They teach 'em how to fight in Amazon Land—or wherever she's from—but they don't teach 'em about picking decent guys."

According to all the magazines, Lady Themis—the Warrior Woman of Justice—was the most beautiful woman in the world. It struck Darius as unbelievable that she would ever have problems with men.

"He's not kidding," said Manny. "She'll go on forever. It doesn't matter who you are. Sometimes, she'll call my niece at two in the morning, crying over some guy."

"She calls Elladia for advice?" asked Z-Boe.

"Yeah, at two in the morning, Lady Themis is calling my seventeen-year-old niece for dating advice. I don't even let Elladia date, but Lady T still calls her," said Manny.

"Okay, you guys have convinced me, I'll stay away from Lady Themis," said Darius.

20

The doors to the elevator closed, and Darius had no idea where they were going. He'd finished his lunch break with Manny and Z-Boe—if you could call it a lunch break at four in the morning—when Manny said it was time for the most important part of the tour. Manny asked Z-Boe to come along as they went to someplace called the Cage.

For the first time since Darius had met him, Z-Boe stopped smiling. "Why would anyone want to go there?" asked Z-Boe.

Darius remembered Amina mentioning something about the Cage earlier. With Z-Boe's reaction, he wondered if he wanted to go there—even though he didn't know what it was.

The elevator passed the first sub-basement, followed by the second and third. Darius watched as the readout on the control panel signaled the passing of the fourth sub-basement. He looked over at Z-Boe for a moment, and if he didn't know better, Darius would have sworn the Galaxus looked scared.

The elevator doors opened to reveal a security outpost, and a long corridor that stretched almost one hundred yards beyond it. Darius immediately noticed that the six men standing at the security outpost were heavily armed and dressed in body armor. He had yet to see anyone armed at HQ—let alone wearing body armor—and the sight of six men standing guard in the fifth sub-basement made Darius unnerved.

Whatever these guys are guarding, I don't want to see it, Darius thought, visions of giant mutant rats or the blood-serpents of Doc Kaos running through his brain.

Manny greeted the six men by name—no jokes, no friendly exchanges. He didn't even bother to introduce Darius to the guards—which was fine with Darius. None of the guards could be defined as friendly, their deadly seriousness making them standoffish and intimidating.

"Heard you were having trouble," said Manny.

"Standard techno-plasm discharge," said one of the guards. The name on his identity badge read Manigo. Of the six guards, he was the only one who didn't look like he wanted to shoot Manny. "A crew from MAS came by, ran a diagnostic, and everything checks out."

"I'll go over the report later," said Manny. "In the meantime, I wanna show this trainee here what's in the Cage."

"Really? Why?" asked Manigo.

"That's what I said," added Z-Boe.

Darius didn't like the tone in either man's voice. They sounded nervous, which made him nervous.

"We can always come back some other time," said Darius.

"No," said Manny. "You need to see this tonight."

Manny led the way down the long corridor, followed closely by Darius, Z-Boe, Manigo and a second guard, Seavers. Half way down the corridor, Manny stopped beside a security control panel on the wall. He motioned for Darius to come stand by his side.

Manny pointed down the corridor. "What do you see?" he asked.

There was a huge double-door at the far end of the corridor that looked big enough to drive a truck through.

"A big door at the end of the hall," said Darius.

"Look carefully," said Manny.

Darius didn't know what he was supposed to be looking at or looking for, but he felt certain that there was nothing else to see in the corridor. Then he noticed, less than two feet in front of him, the slightest of reflections. He almost couldn't see it, but once he finally noticed, it became quite clear—a reflection of himself, Manny, Z-Boe and the guards. He took two steps forward, reached out to touch what felt like a piece of glass, vibrating with an energy source.

"It's a force field," said Manny.

Manny swiped his identity badge along the security panel, and followed it up by punching in a series of numbers into the keypad. In an instant, the force field disappeared, and in that same instant, a series of overhead red lights came on and lit up the corridor.

Darius grew increasingly nervous. Having no idea of what was going on, where he was, or what he was about to be shown, made him very uncomfortable. The red lights only made it worse, like they were all in a hallway to Hell.

He walked beside Manny, not saying a word, with Z-Boe and the security guards following behind. They reached the massive door at the end of the corridor.

"I hate this place," said Z-Boe.

Darius heard something that sounded like fear in Z-Boe's voice.

Manny turned to face Darius and placed his hand on the young man's shoulder. "That force field back there is the exact same strength as the ones used at SJF Moon Outpost and at the Enceladus Colony. A blast from a bazooka at point-blank range wouldn't put a dent in that thing," said Manny. "The room I'm about to show you—I want you to know the entire room is surrounded by a force field five times stronger than the one back there. State-of-the-art Tess-Tech design, reinforced with a techno-plasm infusion."

Darius felt sick in the pit of his stomach. *Whatever he's about to show me, I don't wanna see it,* Darius thought. *Let's just keep it locked up here, underground, behind a techno-plasm infused force field, and pretend that I saw whatever it is.*

A second security panel rested on the wall, just by the massive double-door. Manny motioned for Manigo to come by his side. The guard swiped his identity badge along the security panel, and then punched in a code. Manny did the same thing, explaining to Darius, "It takes two people to open the Cage at all times."

At first Darius didn't even know what he was looking at. It appeared almost like a huge warehouse full of scrap metal. But after a moment, the metal looked like some*thing*. Mannequins. The scrap metal looked like mannequins—for a few seconds anyway. Then the mannequins looked more like skeletons wrapped in metal. *Or maybe those killer robots from that one movie,* Darius thought. And then he knew what he was looking.

When the full realization of what Darius saw dawned on him, he threw up his lunch.

The smell of his vomit quickly filled the corridor as Darius Logan stared into a room full of Automated Combat Units, model 64. And ACU-64s were what murdered his family.

21

"This can't be real," said Darius, more to himself than anyone else. He stared at an underground warehouse full of lifeless ACU-64s, the most deadly weapon since the atomic bomb. Some people called them Killbots, a pretty accurate name.

If he could throw up again, he would. But his stomach was empty. Darius felt a wave of emotions that he could not even begin to categorize. Fear and anger and hate and sadness and just about every bad feeling he had experienced over the last eight years, all rushed through him at the same time. His body shook. His fists clenched and unclenched, over and over again.

None of this makes sense, he thought.

He tried to look away, or at least close his eyes, but he couldn't stop staring. "What is this?" he asked. His voice sounded distant to him—like it came from someone else very far away.

"They can't hurt anyone. They're deactivated. Dead," said Manny.

He stood next to Darius.

"Dead? My parents are dead!" Darius exploded. "My brother is dead! That's what killed them! Those things killed my family!"

"Those things killed a lot of people," said Z-Boe, trying to reassure Darius. "And a lot of us lost people we loved."

"And that's supposed to make me feel better?" asked Darius.

Life hadn't been easy since his family had been killed in The Attack. In fact, Darius's life had been terrible. He fought for many years to get to a place where he felt in control of his emotions—a place where the anger and fear didn't run out of control—because he knew whenever he didn't keep his cool, he always got in trouble. But standing there, in front of the massive underground warehouse filled with deactivated Killbots—the same machines that had butchered his family—he felt himself losing all control.

A fire burned in his eyes when he looked away from the machines, staring directly at Manny. Darius felt all control slipping away, the rage coiling around his brain like a boa constrictor, squeezing out all rational thought. Anger and pain screamed inside of Darius, demanding to be expressed in the language he spoke most fluently—the language of violence.

Darius wanted to hit something. He wanted to hit Manny. He needed to hit Manny, the person who brought him to see the things that had killed his parents. Manny had brought him face to face with the monsters that haunted his dreams, chasing him night after night to the point he hardly ever slept.

You hit him, and it's all over, Darius said to himself, trying to calm down. *You'll go to prison. Maslon will have won.*

"You can hit me if you want to," Manny said.

Manny stood beside Darius, staring at him the way Darius's father used to do. He made no jokes, and didn't smile. He just stood there, a calm picture of strength, seeing all the things inside Darius that threatened to rage to the surface—the anger and the hatred and the fear and the sadness. Manny saw the ticking time bomb that called itself Darius Logan, and prepared to take the brunt of the explosion.

"Hit me if you want," Manny said a second time, speaking more clearly, making sure he was understood. "I'm cool with it."

Darius slowly shook his head, searching for the right thing to say. The smell of his vomit helped push aside all other thought. "I need to clean up my puke," he mumbled.

"Don't worry about it," said Manigo, already cleaning up the mess. "It happens more than you'd believe."

Darius watched the guard mop up the pool of vomit. He looked over at Manny, trying to find just the right thing to say. "Why?" Darius asked.

"Why is Manigo cleaning up your vómito?" Manny asked.

"No," said Darius. He turned back to look at the lifeless ACU-64s. "Why?"

"Because you needed to know, and you needed to know now, not six months from now," said Manny.

"Some people can't be in the building knowing they're here," said Z-Boe.

Darius had forgotten that Z-Boe was standing there.

"And if you are one of those people, we might as well find out now," said Manny. "No point in wasting your time."

Darius wanted to tell Manny that there had to be a better way of telling him about the ACU-64s. But he knew there wasn't. Even if Manny had given him some sort of warning, Darius knew his reaction would've been the same. What would Manny have said? "Hey, Darius, down in the fifth sub-basement we have a warehouse full of deadly robots that killed your family. Wanna see?"

Manigo finished cleaning the vomit off the floor. Darius self-consciously mumbled his thanks to the guard. He felt like a kid for having puked—like some little sissy who pissed his pants after having seen the bogeyman hiding in the closet.

"How you feelin', amigo?" asked Manny.

"How do you think I feel?" Darius replied.

"Like cagada?"

"Yeah. Whatever that is," said Darius.

"It's kind of what you smell like right now," said Manny.

"Those things should've been destroyed," said Darius.

"I agree one hundred percent," said Manny.

"Then why are they here?"

"Even if we tell you why, it won't make sense," said Z-Boe.

"Try me."

"You sure you don't wanna hit me instead, amigo?" asked Manny with a slight smile. "That would be easier than tryin' to make sense of this."

"I still may hit you, but first I want answers."

"That sounds fair to me," said Manny.

"They're here because of money," said Z-Boe. "These things represent billions of dollars the government spent developing a new weapon. Believe me, there were a lot of us that wanted to see them properly destroyed."

"Doc Kaos hacked into the control mainframe of those things. They went crazy and killed what…8,000 people? And you're telling me that they're down here because someone is worried about how much they cost?" said Darius.

"That's exactly what he's tellin' you," replied Manny.

"Those machines killed 8,000 people! They killed my parents! My kid brother—he was only a day old!"

"I told you it wouldn't make sense," said Manny.

Z-Boe placed his hand on Darius's shoulder, and gave it gentle squeeze. Again, a strange surge of energy raced through his body—both overwhelming and soothing at the same time.

"I've been through a lot. I was on Enceladus—lost my whole family there," said Z-Boe. "Honestly, The Attack was the most brutal battle I've ever experienced. And I'm telling you—man to man—that no one was more vocal than me about seeing these things destroyed. But the government wasn't going to let that happen. It took months to come an agreement."

"What kind of agreement?"

"The ACU-64s that weren't completely destroyed were deactivated. Super Justice Force would store the ACU-64s here, under heavy guard, until someone figures out how to make 'em operate correctly," said Z-Boe. "That was the best compromise that could be arrived at."

"So they want to try and use them again?" asked Darius.

"Not if I have anything to do with it," said Z-Boe.

"Not if any of us have anything to do with it," said Manny. "These things are the deadliest weapons ever created, but as long as they exist, if they're here—in this building—I feel safe. Much safer than if the government held on to them."

Darius turned back to face the open room. The cause of every bad thing that happened to him over that last eight years lay motionless in the giant containment facility. He had countless nightmares of ACU-64s chasing after him, coming to finish off what they had started when they killed his family. These machines were the things he feared the most. The things he hated the most.

He walked into the warehouse. Neither Manny nor Z-Boe nor the guards made an attempt to stop him. Darius reached out and touched one of the machines. It felt smooth and cool and lifeless. Darius knew exactly what he touched; but the lifeless machine knew nothing of Darius. It had no clue how much Darius hated it and all the others just like it. And though Darius knew this, and though he knew the ACU-64s could not hear him, it didn't stop him from calling the machines the most vile curse words he could think of.

22

Darius found getting used to his new schedule incredibly difficult. His first week on the job he only worked three shifts in a row—Wednesday, Thursday and Friday—with Saturday and Sunday off. Saturdays and Sundays were Manny's days off, and since Manny was training him, Darius kept the same schedule.

After the weekend off, Darius found himself struggling to adjust to his schedule when Monday rolled around. He stayed up late Sunday night into Monday morning, but he still woke up early. He ate breakfast at the same time most people were eating lunch, and at 4:00 he reported to Trang Nguyen's office for what would become part of his regular routine.

Darius fought to stay awake during his meeting with Trang. She could tell that he was exhausted.

"Are you going to be able to handle the night shift?" Trang asked. "We can find a spot for you somewhere else."

Darius thought about switching to a different shift over the weekend, but decided against it. He liked Manny, and that went a long way for him. And the fact that Captain Freedom had personally recommended him for training under Manny meant Darius would do what he needed to do. "I'll adjust," he said.

"Next week you'll start an online class to get your GED. I'll take you down to the library and introduce you the Miss Evelyn, who will help set you up on the computers," Trang said. "It's a self-paced program, which given your schedule seemed like the best plan."

On Tuesday, Darius had his first private counseling session with Dr. Sam. His weekly schedule included two required counseling sessions—one with Dr. Sam, the other a group session with other Chancers. Darius had yet to attend a group session, but given his feeling about crowds of people and anything that appeared social, he wasn't looking forward to it.

He wasn't looking forward to his first session with Dr. Sam either. Darius didn't like talking, especially about his feelings, and Dr. Sam would no doubt want to talk about feelings.

I know that I'm messed up. But this works for me. I don't need to put my pieces back together again.

Dr. Sam's immaculate office looked like it wasn't used often. On one of the walls there were framed pictures of Dr. Samson Omatete in his Marine uniform, confirming what Darius had suspected all along. Other pictures of Dr. Sam hung on the wall, photos with celebrities, superheroes and presidents of the United States dating back forty years —encounters with power and fame creating a biography of images frozen in time.

The first counseling session with Dr. Sam went well, more casual than Darius had expected. Dr. Sam asked Darius how his first few shifts had been, if he felt like he was adjusting to his new life. No conversation about Darius's innermost feelings. Not a word about the anger he sometimes had trouble controlling. Nothing of how he often wished he had died with his family during The Attack. Instead, Dr. Sam encouraged Darius to attend the barbecue that Otto Rekker had invited him to.

The rest of the week Darius spent getting a basic overview of how nearly everything at HQ worked. He ate lunch with Manny everyday, who alternated between cracking jokes and quizzing Darius with job-related questions.

For the first time in eight years, he felt like maybe he'd found a place where he belonged. He made friends—including Z-Boe, who had come by just to see how he was doing—and met new people everyday. One afternoon, while heading down to the cafeteria for breakfast, he rode in the elevator with Amazing Grrrl, who looked much shorter in person, and Kid Spectacular, who looked at least twenty-five. Both Amazing Grrrl and Kid Spectacular introduced themselves, asked Darius how he was doing, and wished him well.

"It's all pretty crazy," Darius said. "I haven't even been on the job two full weeks, but I feel like I've been there my whole life. In a way, I guess I have been there my whole life—this new life anyway."

He wasn't really talking to anyone in particular, just to the tombstone that marked the gravesite of Dwayne and Janae Logan and their newborn son, Dwayne Jr.

The cemetery wasn't located in the city, making it difficult for Darius to get there. It took one subway and two buses, and over an hour to make the trip on a Saturday, when the buses ran with less frequency. But the last bus he had to take to get to Otto Rekker's house passed by the cemetery, so Darius had to stop.

Manny had insisted that Darius go to Otto's barbecue. Dr. Sam also thought it would be a good idea. "It will give you chance to get to know your co-workers and help you assimilate to life at SJF," said Dr. Sam.

He and Manny filled out the proper paperwork, so Darius could travel beyond the two-block radius that confined him to HQ. The STATU around Darius's ankle was calibrated to allow him to travel nearly twenty-five miles from HQ, and gave him until midnight to return.

The cemetery had a special section just for victims of The Attack, their names carved into the huge stone monument. It didn't matter what time of day it was, or what day of the week, someone was always at the monument, or at one of the thousands of grave markers, laying flowers down for someone they had lost.

Darius never had flowers to bring. The first few times he went to the cemetery, when Edith O'Malley brought him, he felt guilty about it. In those days the cemetery was crowded all the time, littered with flowers and plants and ribbons and crying people. But Edith told him that it didn't matter to his family if he brought flowers or not. She told him that his parents could see him, and all that mattered to them was his being there.

He never fully believed that his parents could see him standing at the grave—especially because they weren't really buried there. Like so many other victims of The Attack, there was nothing left of them to bury. But he needed to do something, and visiting the grave of his mother, father and baby brother a few times a year seemed like the best thing to do.

When he was younger, he would talk to his parents and his brother, but he hadn't said a word at their graves in years. Those earlier conversations came from the hope and desire that his family could actually hear him, and maybe, somehow, his words could bring them back to life. But as he grew older, and life grew more difficult, he accepted the grim reality that he was just talking to himself. Nothing Darius said could bring the dead back to life.

He had no intention of talking to his family, but for some reason, he just began to open up. He told them everything.

"I'm sorry for the things I've done these last few years. I know you raised me better than that. It's just...it's just...," Darius struggled to find the words. "I guess it doesn't really matter, does it? Things are going to change. You'll see."

Dwayne and Janae Logan, and their newborn baby son—dead for eight years and counting—couldn't hear a word Darius said. That didn't matter. For the first time, he didn't wish he had died with them. For the first time, Darius almost felt good about being alive.

23

The suburban home of Otto Rekker was not what Darius expected. It was just a plain house—nothing fancy or sinister—with a minivan parked in the driveway. A bumper sticker on the minivan read, "Proud Parent of an Eisner Elementary School Honor Student." Certainly not the sort of thing you would expect from a notorious supercriminal.

Darius felt nervous about going to the barbecue. He wasn't the most social person in the world, and he didn't feel comfortable in large crowds, especially with food being served. To him, large crowds and food meant the cafeteria at juvenile detention, where someone might try to stab you with the business end of a plastic spoon or the handle of a toothbrush that had been sharpened into a knife. He had a scar on his left forearm from blocking such a knife.

Despite his apprehension about socializing and his concern about being stabbed, Darius had been cooped up inside HQ ever since he arrived—confined to the two-block radius dictated by the security tracker around his ankle. Cabin fever had set in. He needed to get out, and had promised Manny and Dr. Sam that he would go to the barbecue.

Besides, if I'm really going to start a new life, I need to get used to being around other people, he told himself.

He heard the sounds of a party coming from the backyard—people laughing, children running around playing—and worried that he wouldn't fit in. Darius stood there, on the sidewalk in front of Otto Rekker's house, terrified of going around to the backyard.

"Sounds like a party to me," said a familiar voice.

Darius turned to see Z-Boe landing in front of the Rekker house. Dressed in a pair of baggy shorts and loud Hawaiian shirt instead of his Galaxus uniform, he looked more like someone who had just gotten back from a day at the beach than a cosmic-powered champion of justice.

"You flew here?" Darius asked.

"Course I did," said Z-Boe. "Why wouldn't I?"

Darius didn't have an answer. It just seemed weird to him to see superheroes and crime fighters walking around dressed up like everyday people, but still doing superhero things.

"What're you waiting for, bro?" asked Z-Boe. "Food's 'round back."

Darius followed Z-Boe to the backyard. He felt a little bit more comfortable showing up with someone else, especially someone who could divert attention.

There must have been close to fifty people in the backyard. Darius recognized a lot of them from HQ, but there were just as many that he didn't recognize. He figured some of the people must be the families of his co-workers, or neighbors of Otto Rekker. Everyone looked like they were having a good time—like they belonged. It all made Darius feel that much more out of place.

Z-Boe wasted no time jumping right into the mix. He disappeared into the crowd, leaving Darius standing by himself, wondering what he should do.

Otto stood in front of a grill, cooking up hamburgers and hot dogs, using a bizarre-looking metal spatula attached directly to his bionic arm. He wore a large apron with a floral design that said, "Kiss the cook." The apron looked ridiculous on him, what with one of his arms being mechanical, the other covered with a dragon tattoo, and Otto looking like he could rip someone's spine from their body and not give it a second thought.

A black woman stood next to Otto, barely coming up to his shoulder. She held a large plate and looked to be arguing with Otto about something. He waved his real hand dismissively, while removing sizzling hamburger patties from the grill and dropping them on the plate. Otto leaned down to kiss the woman, and caught sight of Darius standing near the entrance to the backyard.

"Big D!" yelled Otto, motioning to Darius to join him at the grill. Otto had started calling Darius "Big D" at their first meeting, and he seemed intent on making sure the nickname stuck.

Darius walked over to Otto and the woman. "Big D, I'm glad you made it," said Otto, grabbing Darius and giving him a hug. Darius worried Otto's bionic arm with the odd cooking utensil attached to the hand would crush him.

"Darius, this is my wife, Anna," said Otto, introducing Darius to the woman holding the plate of food. "Anna, this is Big D."

"Nice to meet you, Big D," said Anna. "You want a hamburger?"

"I'm not too hungry right now. Maybe later."

"Well, we've got plenty of food. And you look like you could use some meat on your skeleton," Anna said.

Anna left Darius and Otto at the grill, taking the plate of hamburgers to the picnic table in the middle of the backyard.

"You want something to drink? Lemonade? Soda?" asked Otto. "I would offer you a beer, but you're too young. Besides that, I don't keep beer around the house—4,682 days clean and sober."

Darius tried to do the math in his head. "Thirteen years?" he asked.

"Almost thirteen years—still have a few months to go."

Darius watched as Otto flipped the hamburgers using the attachment on his bionic hand. Up close, Darius saw that Otto's bionic hand had been replaced altogether with the odd cooking tool.

"You like the hand?" asked Otto. "Check this out."

Otto pulled his mechanical hand off, separating if from the bionic arm. "It's detachable," said Otto. "I've got a whole bunch of these things—a fishing pole, flashlight, leaf blower. I've even got one with a buffer, if I want to wax the car."

Darius studied the detachable hand more closely. The spatula extended out from a housing unit that attached to Otto's arm at the end of his wrist. He pressed one of the buttons on top of the unit, and the spatula retracted into the unit itself. Darius pressed another button, and barbecue tongs extended out. "This is pretty cool," said Darius.

"I build junk like this with my kids," said Otto, reattaching the hand to his arm. "It beats playing video games or watching television. My daughter thought this one up."

"How old are your kids?" Darius asked.

"They're both eight. Twins. They're running around here somewhere—you'll meet them soon enough. They look like their mom, thank God."

A man Darius didn't recognize walked up to him and Otto. Dressed all in black, wearing a baseball cap and dark sunglasses, he looked strangely out of place among the other partygoers. "Otto," said the man, his voice a deep whisper. He looked at Darius, and nodded his head ever so slightly. "Darius."

Who is this guy? Darius wondered. He had no idea who the man was.

The mystery man handed Otto a paper bag. "Veggie burgers. Make sure they don't touch any meat," he said.

"Are you sure you even want me cooking them on the grill? There's meat on the grill," said Otto, sounding annoyed.

"Just make sure they don't touch any meat," said the man. He walked off to join the others at the party.

"I swear, he's such a pain in the ass," said Otto.

"Kaebel giving you a hard time again?" asked Manny. He had arrived at the party unnoticed by either Otto or Darius.

"That was Kaebel Kaine? Nightwatcher?" asked Darius, trying to spot the serious-looking man in the sunglasses. Darius saw him talking to Anna Rekker, and even though she was smiling and laughing at whatever they were talking about, his expression never changed.

"That's him," said Otto. "He gets on my nerves so bad. I swear, there are times when I just want to…"

"Break his back?" said Manny, finishing Otto's sentence.

"No, I already did that once," said Otto. "I just want to serve him some red meat, and see the look on his face when he realizes he's chewing a piece of cow."

Manny and Otto both laughed, but Darius didn't quite get the joke. Most of the time he didn't get the joke. "If you hate him so much, why would you even invite him over?" Darius asked.

"It's more of a love-hate relationship between Otto and Nightwatcher," explained Manny.

"Yeah, we love to hate each other," said Otto with a laugh. "But I'll tell you what, when I decided to clean up my act—to lay off the drinking and go straight—there's not a person on this planet who did more for me than that man. I owe him my life."

With that thought, Otto put one of the veggie burgers on the grill, and took extra care to make sure it touched one of the hamburgers.

Darius still didn't understand the dynamic between Otto and Nightwatcher, but gradually it started to make sense to him. He'd read enough comic books to know that every superhero needed an arch nemesis—someone to balance them out. He just never thought about what it would be like if two sworn enemies ever decided to stop fighting and make peace. Darius supposed that the relationship might be like that of Otto Rekker and Nightwatcher.

"Big D, can you go get a plate for the food?" Otto asked.

"Sure," Darius replied, leaving Otto and Manny to talk about a baseball game that had been on television earlier.

Not knowing where to find plates, Darius instead looked for Anna. She stood by the picnic table, talking to a small group of people, including a woman standing with her back to Darius.

The woman talking to Anna had curly dark hair that flowed to the middle of her back. She turned as Darius approached, and his heart skipped a beat. He'd thought about her a lot since first seeing her in the employee cafeteria. And there she stood, in the backyard of Otto and Anna Rekker.

"Um...," stammered Darius, too nervous to speak in front of the beautiful girl. "Um...Otto...um...Otto needs a plate for the...um...food."

The pretty girl smiled at Darius, just like she did when she caught him staring at her. He felt like a fool.

"Oh, can you get a plate for Big D out of the kitchen?" Anna asked the beautiful girl.

"Sure," said the beautiful girl. She tugged on Darius's sleeve and said, "Follow me."

Darius followed behind her, more nervous than he'd ever been in his life. He wanted to say something, but couldn't think of anything cool or clever. When they made it into the house through the back door, and into the kitchen, he finally asked, "Do you live here?"

"No, I live across the street with my uncle," said the beautiful girl. "I babysit sometimes."

"Uh huh," was all Darius could think to say.

"Haven't I seen you at HQ?" asked the girl.

Darius wanted to say that she caught him staring at her in the employee break room, and that he wasn't doing it to be rude, it was just that she was the most beautiful girl he'd ever seen. That's what he wanted to say, but all he could muster was, "Uh huh" for a second time.

"I'm Elladia," she said.

"I'm Darius," he said, fighting to get the words out.

"Oh, you're Darius," said Elladia, as if the name meant something to her. "My Uncle Manny told me all about you."

"You're Manny's niece? The one he talks about all the time?"

Elladia reached inside one of the kitchen cabinets and pulled out a large plate that she handed to Darius. "That would be me. You better get that plate out to Otto before the food starts to burn."

Darius turned to leave the kitchen, and was almost out the door before he thought to say something. "Um…it was good…um…meeting you."

"It was good meeting you too. I work in the gift shop after school. You should come by sometime."

Darius didn't know how to respond. He could only think of Manny mentioning his niece and threatening to kill anyone who even tried to talk to her.

"And don't worry about my Uncle Manny," said Elladia, as if she knew what he was thinking. "I'll protect you from him."

Darius left the kitchen with a smile so big his face hurt. He had just met the most beautiful woman in the world. He felt like he was on fire and walking on clouds at the same time. He didn't know what it felt like to be in love, but it had to be close to what he was feeling. And if he could just get the courage up to have a real conversation with Elladia, life would be perfect.

24

The following Monday, Darius woke up earlier than he had hoped. He'd had the nightmare again—the same nightmare that had been plaguing him for years. Rather than try to get back to sleep, he decided to get an early start on his day, hoping he might get a quick nap in before going to work.

Darius started his day at the Super Justice Force Research Library. Located on the first floor of the main building—across from the gift shop—the library looked, at first glance, like a standard collection of books, periodicals and movies. But the massive digital collection at the library is what made it one of the most impressive places Darius had ever been. Thousands of publications—maybe even millions—were stored in the digital files. It was supposedly the biggest digital library in the world. Darius could access any book he could think of on the library computers, the pages appearing on the monitor in front of him. He could read digital copies of classic comic books dating back to the adventures of the first Captain Freedom.

After his first trip, the library became Darius's favorite place at HQ. The head librarian, Evelyn Bartee, was an older woman, with long dreadlocks peppered with grey. The ugly scar running down the left side of her face made Manny's scar look like a scratch.

Evelyn Bartee called Darius "Mr. Logan," and he called her "Ms. Evelyn." She helped him set up an account on the library computers, in preparation for his online GED class. "Study hard, Mr. Logan," said Ms. Evelyn. "There's no such thing as too much knowledge."

Ms. Evelyn reminded Darius a bit of his mother. It wasn't that the two women looked alike—because they didn't. It was just that Darius's mother never stopped emphasizing the importance of education. "Ignorance is not an option for you, young man," his mother would say. From the moment he started school, his mom expected nothing less than straight A's.

As his life spun out of control over the years, his grades slipped. It was hard to get decent marks when you went to three different high schools in one year, and equally hard to worry about getting decent grades when living to see the next day was in question. Still, despite all that happened, Darius understood the importance of learning.

The Monday after the barbecue marked Darius's first day in the on-line GED program. He spent two hours setting up his student account and doing course work, and an hour reading "My Life as a Do-Gooder: The Autobiography of Jacob Kirby," by the original Captain Freedom. With an hour until his mandatory meeting with Trang Nguyen, and feeling hungry, he headed to the employee cafeteria.

Because he couldn't eat anywhere else—unless he cooked in his apartment, which he didn't do—Darius ate all of his meals in the employee cafeteria, making him the most regular customer. After his first week he knew almost the entire staff of cooks and dishwashers at HQ. Ezekiel "EZ" Manigo ran the cafeteria. An old-school Chancer—one of the First Ten—EZ Manigo had moved his way up on the job, and oversaw one of the biggest crews at SJF. There were more than a dozen members of the Manigo family who worked for Super Justice Force, including EZ's nephew Julio, whom Darius had met his first night on the job.

Darius sat by himself as he did much of the time, having just started eating his lunch, when a small group came up to the table. "Mind if we join you?"

Darius's heart pounded at the sight of Elladia standing by his table with three of her friends. His mouth dried up so much he had trouble swallowing his food. Breaking out in a cold sweat, part of him wanted to tell Elladia and her friends to go away. With her this close, he couldn't concentrate on the simple things—like breathing. Instead, he choked down his food, said "sure," and tried to look as cool as possible, even though he knew that was impossible.

Elladia introduced Darius to her friends—Rayven, Lillette and Chico. They all smiled politely, and said how great it was to meet Darius, and he pretended it was great to meet them as well.

Darius wasn't sure if Elladia's friends were ignoring him, or if he had suddenly turned invisible. Either way, he wasn't part of the conversation, which was fine with him. It all had to do with television and fashion and music, none of which mattered to Darius. He couldn't remember the last time he'd watched television, he only owned two pairs of pants—not counting his work uniform—and his taste in music had not progressed beyond what he listened to with his parents.

There was no denying the fact that Darius did not fit in with Elladia and her friends—not that he wanted to. He felt a certain disappointment, however, that Elladia would keep company with people like this, who could prattle on and on about nothing at all. But as the conversation dragged on, Darius noticed that Elladia barely said a word. She smiled, and nodded her head in agreement, and kept up the appearance of being part of the conversation, but she hardly said a word. From a distance, Elladia looked like she belonged with these other people. Up close it was a different story.

I wonder if she thinks her friends are as boring and annoying as I do, Darius thought, smiling for the first time during the entire conversation.

Elladia noticed his smile, and the two of them made eye contact while her friends engaged in a heated exchange about who was being voted off of this show and that show. She smiled at him. It was a different smile than the one she had with her friends, and the only way anyone would ever notice the difference would be if they really paid attention to Elladia's face.

It could have easily been a magical moment—the start of a great romance—except it was interrupted by a voice coming directly behind Darius. "Darius Logan, you're under arrest."

Darius turned around to see Chuck Maslon, flanked on either side by two SJF security guards and four police officers.

"What's going on?" Elladia asked.

"You shut your mouth, little lady," said Maslon. "This doesn't concern you."

Darius thought about jabbing his fork into Maslon's eye. *What's the worst they can do, arrest me?*

"You can't just come in here and arrest him. What's the charge?" demanded Elladia.

"The charge against you, señorita, will be obstructing justice if you don't shut up," said Maslon.

One of the cops grabbed Darius by the shirt and hoisted him out his chair. He shoved Darius up against the nearest wall, frisked him, and then slapped the handcuffs on.

He couldn't cry, because even though Darius knew he would never see any of these people again, and that he was headed off to prison, he didn't want them to think of him like some kind of sissy. The humiliation of the moment was bad enough—dragged off in handcuffs in front of everyone. In front of Elladia.

The cops pushed Darius forward, shoving him toward his new life in prison. Maslon got directly in Darius's face. "This didn't last long," said Maslon, sounding satisfied.

From where he stood, Darius could have head-butted Maslon. *I'd probably break his nose*, Darius thought. *At the very least, I could hack up a nasty loogie and spit it in his face.*

Darius chose, instead, to not become the punk Maslon wanted him to be. It didn't feel as good as kicking Maslon's ass would've felt, but given the circumstances it had to do.

25

By the time Darius arrived at the Twelfth Precinct with Maslon and the arresting officers, the others were already waiting. Maslon looked surprised to see Manny there, along with Dr. Sam, and both the lawyers—Ollie Porter and Ms. Oldham.

Manny flew into a rage, cutting loose with a string of profanity in both English and Spanish directed specifically at Maslon. "Chingada su madre, I was asleep, and my niece calls me hysterical!"

"Who's your niece?" Maslon demanded.

"She's the one you told to shut up at the cafeteria," said Manny. "You ever disrespect her like that again you cabeza de mierda, and I'll rip your head off! You hear me?"

Dr. Sam tried to calm Manny down, but it did no good. Manny was furious. And it wasn't just that Maslon had disrespected Elladia. Manny was angry that Darius had been taken away by the police. And the sight of Darius—his face bruised and bloody—only made Manny more livid.

After the cops escorted Darius out of HQ—through the front entrance for everyone to see—they put him in the back of a police cruiser. Before bringing him to the precinct, they stopped in an alley and worked him over with Maslon watching in silence. Darius didn't recognize any of the cops, but he knew what the beating was all about—it was payback for what had happened in No Man's Land.

It had been one of the most terrifying moments of Darius's life. Fists and feet slamming into him, knowing that nothing could stop the cops from beating on him. He was pretty sure they'd broken one of his ribs, and two of his teeth were loose. He knew they could kill him if they wanted to—just shoot him and then say he resisted arrest. It wasn't like he hadn't resisted arrest before.

Nobody at the precinct said a word about the bruises. There were more pressing matters to discuss.

"What the hell is going on here?" asked Dr. Sam.

"He tried to escape," said Maslon.

"When?" demanded Manny.

"On Saturday."

"That's a load of crap," said Manny. "Darius was at Otto Rekker's house with me and at least fifty other witnesses."

"Is this true?" asked Ms. Oldham. She still had the same tired look she'd had less than three weeks earlier.

"I personally put through the authorization to allow him to leave HQ," said Manny.

"And I signed off on it," said Dr. Sam. "I thought it would be good for Darius to socialize with fellow employees outside of work."

"Then what's the problem?" Ms. Oldham asked. She directed her question at Maslon, not bothering to hide the growing annoyance in her voice.

Maslon handed a piece of paper to Oldham, who had no idea what she was looking at.

"He was cleared to go from HQ to the residence of Otto Rekker, and that's it," said Maslon. He pointed at Darius like he was something less than human. "Security reports that he went somewhere else first, and stopped some place he wasn't authorized to stop."

"Meaning what?" asked Ollie.

"Meaning he tried to escape," said Maslon.

Manny fumed. He looked ready to kill Maslon. "Let's see if I got this straight," said Manny, his voice trembling with anger. "Darius left HQ, stopped somewhere on his way to Otto's, and then returned to HQ—and you call that tryin' to escape? He came back, pendejo!"

"If he wasn't trying to escape, then what was he doing?" demanded Maslon.

"Well, if he was tryin' to escape, he'd be a complete moron for comin' back," said Manny. "This is ridiculous. Two L4s signed off on Darius leavin' HQ. He didn't try to escape."

"Darius, where did you go on your way to Otto's house?" asked Dr. Sam.

On the long list of things Darius never talked about, going to the cemetery topped the list. The most personal and private thing he did was not the business of anyone else—especially Maslon. Maslon had no right to know that Darius had been to the cemetery, because, as far as Darius was concerned, that let Maslon know too much about him and his emotions. Still, Darius knew his freedom was on the line.

"I stopped at the cemetery," said Darius.

"What cemetery?" asked Maslon, the tone in his voice condescending and accusatory.

"*The* cemetery. The one where my family is buried. It's on the way to the Rekkers' house."

An awkward silence filled the room, and it wasn't broken until Ms. Oldham scooted her chair back and stood up. "Don't ever waste my time like this again," she growled at Maslon. Then she turned to Darius and handed him one of her business cards. "If you want to file charges against the officers that did this to you, call me. I will personally see to it that at the very least they lose their jobs."

Darius had yet to see this side of Ms. Oldham, and he liked it. As she left, Maslon stopped her. "I want him arrested. End of story."

"Get a life," said Ms. Oldham.

"You don't understand. I don't want this punk at Super Justice Force!" Maslon shouted. He had passed the point of losing his cool, which brought Darius nothing but pleasure.

"You don't understand, Chuck," said a voice new to the room. "It's not your place to get rid of Darius."

Zander Boeman stood in the doorway to the interrogation room, looking like he had just strolled in on his way back from a day of surfing. He wore baggy shorts with an ugly floral pattern, flip-flops, and a t-shirt that said, "Party Naked."

"What're you doing here?" growled Maslon.

"Your boss, Captain Freedom, sent me," said Z-Boe. "He's stuck in a meeting, but he says if Darius isn't back within the hour, you're fired."

Maybe it was because Z-Boe wore flip-flops that were being held together by duct tape, or maybe it was because he hated Darius for some inexplicable reason, but either way, Maslon refused to admit defeat. He wanted Darius gone from SJF and sent to jail. That was it. End of story.

"You have no right to take him back," said Maslon.

"You can talk to the big guy about that," said Z-Boe. He stood aside while the others cleared the room, giving Darius a high-five when he passed. Z-Boe leaned in close to Maslon, so no one else could hear. "Forget Manny, or Jake Kirby, or anyone else. You mess with that kid again, and I'll kill you. And I do mean kill—as in dead."

"Don't threaten me," said Maslon.

"It's not a threat, assface," said Z-Boe. "And tell your friends who worked him over, I'll be paying each of them a visit."

By the time Darius got back to HQ it was almost nine at night. Maslon and the cops had taken him away just before four. When the cops escorted him out the building, very few people at SJF knew Darius Logan. By the time he had returned, his face bruised and swollen, the rumors had started to swirl.

There was some new guy; a Chancer—a really young black kid—and the police and Chuck Maslon had hauled him away in cuffs. Five hours later, he came back, looking like he'd been in a fight. A few hours after that he reported to work like nothing had happened.

For two days, there wasn't much else people could talk about. Darius noticed people noticing him, pointing him out to others. For other Chancers who had been bullied by Maslon and his Long Arm loyalists, Darius became a symbol. For those who supported Maslon, Darius was an enigmatic force that had knocked their leader down a few pegs.

Maslon's plan to get rid of Darius had backfired. And in the process, the Legend of Darius Logan had been born.

PART II:
A YEAR &
SOME CHANGE

26

In the beginning, Darius worried about handling the job. He had a lot to learn, the hours were brutal, and Chuck Maslon lurked around every corner, waiting for him to mess up, which of course would mean a one-way trip to prison.

During those first four weeks, Darius struggled with an incredible doubt chewing away at his insides. Night after night, he went through training and performed his duties, always in doubt of everything. He would return to his apartment in the Tower early in the morning—much of the world just getting up and going to work—and he would lie in bed questioning himself, convinced it was only a matter of time before he messed up, lost the job, and went to prison.

Some of the time Darius worked directly with Manny, especially during the first two weeks, but he spent much of his third and fourth week on the job with different assistant supervisors and team leaders. He reported to Manny at the beginning of his shift, but then went off to work in other sections. "It helps to have a sense of how other people do things," Manny told him.

Despite spending little time working together during his third and fourth weeks of training, Manny and Darius ate lunch together every day. Manny would tutor him, making sure Darius knew as much as possible about working in both SAO and CAD. Manny reminded Darius that his future in Operations Crew was dependent on his ability to move up in rank from a L1 to a L2.

After the initial training period, it took most employees three or four months of consistently working on the same service team to move up to L2. If for whatever reason an employee could not demonstrate the skills and knowledge needed to perform the duties of a L2, they would be permanently transferred to a low-security L1 position with MAS. The last thing Darius wanted was to be transferred to the cafeteria, where he would be stuck washing dishes until his time was served, or in the mailroom, sorting ingoing mail from outgoing.

Moving up in security ranking had nothing to do with tests or exams. Instead, an employee had to, according to the Employee Handbook, "demonstrate basic proficiency within all service teams of Operations Crew, including all required protocols and procedures affiliated with the prescribed duties of both individuals and departments." This worried Darius, because he had no idea what "demonstrate proficiency in all sections of Operations Crew, including all required protocols and procedures affiliated with the prescribed duties of both individuals and departments" meant.

After four full weeks of training as a floater, Darius moved to Security and Observation for his "probationary placement." If he could move up from a L1 Trainee to a regular L1, and then L2, he would be permanently placed on the SAO service team. This suited Darius just fine, because he preferred SAO duty to everything else.

Ever since the night he had to wash Rocky Feldman's stinking clothes, Darius knew that Maintenance and Service was not for him. It was his third night on the job, MAS was short-staffed, and so Manny took Darius on an emergency call to Facility Services. A horrible smell greeted them from down the hall as they approached. It stunk of raw sewage, reminding Darius of No Man's Land.

"What is that smell?" Darius asked.

"That, amigo, is the lovely aroma of crime fighting," replied Manny.

They entered Facility Services, a brightly lit room lined with industrial washing machines and driers, only to find Rocky Feldman standing in the middle of the room, naked except for the over-sized towel wrapped around his waist.

One of the most popular heroes of all time, Rocky also happened to be one of the most recognizable, in part because he looked more like a rock than an actual man. A giant rock for a torso, with a smaller rock on top of it for a head, Rocky's face looked like an unfinished sculpture someone started to carve out of a piece of granite before becoming distracted.

Manny introduced Rocky to Darius—not that Rocky needed any introduction. Aside from being a hero for nearly thirty years, Rocky Feldman was an outspoken advocate for metahuman rights. He authored three best-selling memoirs, starred in the hit sitcom "Mutant in the Family," and had been the Secretary of Metahuman Affairs under two different presidents.

"You smell terrible," said Manny.

"Got into it with some clown from Mutationation, calls himself the Instinkerator," said Rocky. His voice sounded like rocks grinding together, and Darius wondered if Rocky's vocal chords were also made of stone. "Sorry about the stink. I don't even have a nose, and I can smell it. I need to go get myself cleaned up. You guys can deal with the clothes?"

"That's what Operations Crew is here for," said Manny.

Between washing Rocky's uniform three times that night, and mopping up the bathroom near Vehicle Maintenance Bay One with the toilet that seemed to get clogged three of four times a week, Darius quickly got his fill of working MAS. As far as he was concerned, he would rather stare at security monitors, as boring as that may have been, than clean up after a clogged toilet.

Darius had been on probationary placement in SAO for three weeks when things got crazy following an escape from Kirby Island Maximum Security Super Penitentiary. The most high-tech prison on the planet, Kirby Island hosted some of the most dangerous criminals and villains of all time. Located on a man-made island accessible only by either a single bridge or a helicopter, the prison had been called "escape-proof."

All in all, twenty-seven convicts escaped Kirby Island Maximum Security Super Penitentiary, including Squid Vicious, Madame Melancholy, Bo Constrictor, Flying Guillotine, Billygoat Gruff, at least three members of the Masters of D.E.A.T.H. and four of the five members of the Corrosion Crew.

With that many criminals loose, things became very hectic. Stixx and Stone, a husband-and-wife crime-fighting team from the Chicago branch of Super Justice Force, came to town to help out. Teen Justice Force got called into action, as did auxiliary SJF members Slapious Maximus, Invisiguardian and Joe Smith—the most unoriginally named hero of all time. Meanwhile, Operations Crew became swamped.

It took an incredible amount of work to capture the escaped convicts, and while Captain Freedom and the other heroes worked hard at rounding up the bad guys, Operations Crew worked just as hard to make sure SFJ ran smoothly. With shifts working overtime, and resources being shuffled from one section to another, not everything got done by the book.

Several weeks after the escape from Kirby Island, Darius was stationed at a remote security checkpoint with one other person, even though checkpoints were to be manned by at least three people. Two people would have been a problem even if one of them wasn't as new as Darius, but his relative inexperience on the job created a serious security risk. This was especially true when Boom-Boom Kaboom tried to blow up SJF Headquarters.

Boom-Boom Kaboom, by the definition clearly stated in the Super Justice Force Employee Handbook, was a "supercriminal." There were others, like Limbo Maniac, who were criminal masterminds, or Hatchet Head Forbes, who were criminal geniuses. Boom-Boom Kaboom, however, was a run-of-the-mill supercriminal, which by definition didn't pose as big a threat as a mastermind or a genius. Because of this, no one would have expected him to try and blow up SFJ Headquarters.

But it wasn't the mere fact that Boom-Boom Kaboom planned to blow up HQ that surprised people—it was how he planned to do it. Boom-Boom Kaboom, whose real name was Marvin Hemmelsucker, hoped to destroy the SFJ Headquarters using bio-engineered rats. Each rat had been created in a lab, grown with small explosive charges grafted into its tissue, turning it into a walking bomb that could be remotely controlled by microprocessors implanted in the brain.

Boom-Boom Kaboom unleashed the rats in the sewer system nearly two miles away from Super Justice Force Headquarters, programming them to move to various locations directly beneath the facilities. He planned to detonate the rats simultaneously, which would ensure the destruction of Headquarters.

The plan was ingenious in that the rats were a mix of organic material and bio-mechanics that could not be detected by conventional scanners as anything other than normal rodents. It was a perfect plan that could have worked, with the rats destroying HQ and likely killing everyone inside, if it weren't for two simple things: there were too many rats, and rats were the one thing that truly terrified Darius Logan.

Security and Observation at HQ maintained an elaborate and thorough surveillance grid that included not only the buildings but all of the immediate surrounding area. The surveillance grid tracked the movement of all living creatures that entered within the security grid, accounting for every bird that flew past Headquarters and every rat that scurried through the sewers under the buildings.

Darius performed a Routine Checkpoint Security Sweep—RCSS—when he noticed an unusual amount of rodent activity at one of the remote checkpoints, with a concentration of movement that indicated a "non-random migratory pattern." At least that's how it was stated later in his report. At the time he just knew that more rats than he'd ever seen before were heading his way. And rats scared the hell out of him.

Rats hadn't scared him until he lived underground in the abandoned subway tunnels. Darius had heard the stories about giant rats that attacked people, but he thought it was all just urban legend—like the alligators in the sewers. And though he couldn't speak to the alligators, as he had never seen one, Darius did see giant rats during his time in the Caves. One had attacked him, taking a chunk out of his leg, and leaving behind a scar as a reminder of the deadly vermin.

Darius thought of being attacked by rodents the size of dogs the moment the RCSS detected an army of rats heading for HQ. Rather than checking with the immediate SAO watch commander—who was using the bathroom—Darius pretty much freaked out. Panicking at the thought of facing hundreds of giant rats, Darius opted to initiate a Code Yellow security sweep of the sewer.

Code Yellow security sweeps were only initiated during suspected breaches of security. When the security system went to Code Yellow, more elaborate security systems were deployed, including powerful microsensors powerful enough to detect bio-mechanical parts hidden within the organic exterior of the rats.

From the time Darius noticed the unusual number of rats, to the time he initiated a Code Yellow, to the time the microsensors detected the bio-mechanical parts of the rats, to the time the security system automatically initiated a Code Red, all of thirty seconds had passed. It would have taken the explosive rodents thirty-five seconds to reach a juncture in the main sewer line where they would then be dispatched in two different directions. From there, it would take the rats another ninety seconds to split off three more times, until they all had reached their pre-programmed destination, at which time Boom Boom Kaboom would set them off, bringing the entire Super Justice Force HQ crumbling to the ground.

Because of his actions, Darius prevented a major catastrophe. Back at O3C he became a hero, with slaps on the back, handshakes and high-fives. Darius didn't tell anyone he had acted out of blind terror—no bravery had been involved. If anything, it was the opposite. He panicked, and in the process saved Headquarters and the lives of everyone inside.

Let them think I'm a hero, he thought to himself.

Two weeks after he saved the day, Darius moved up from a Level One to a Level Two. The way he handled the situation with the explosive rats convinced Manny to move Darius up in rank, making him one of two employees to ever move up in security ranking in less than three months.

27

Meetings with his Status Supervisor and his counseling sessions took up a good part of Darius's week. The meetings with Trang Nguyen never lasted long, but his two weekly counseling sessions seemed to take forever. The one-on-one counseling sessions were meant to help him cope with whatever he needed to cope with. Darius knew that the sessions were to ensure he adjusted to life in Second Chance and at SJF, and to help him work out whatever issues had led him to a life of crime.

The thing Dr. Sam and the other counselors didn't seem to understand was that Darius had never been a career criminal. He'd been a criminal by necessity. The moment he had a decent roof over his head, a nice place to sleep and food to eat, his necessities were taken care of. He didn't need to be rehabilitated the way guys like Otto and Manny and most of the other Chancers needed to be rehabilitated. Still, he went along with the one-on-one therapy sessions, talking about whatever came to mind. He even talked about the loss of his family, although it took months for him to get around to it.

All things considered, the one-on-one sessions weren't that bad. The same thing couldn't be said about the once-per-week group counseling sessions. At these meetings Darius sat around with a group of other guys—all of them Chancers—and they talked about anything and everything. At least the others talked. Darius had little to say. He chimed in every now and then, to keep up the appearance of participating.

Darius always went to the meetings on Saturday afternoons, which were led by Butchie. He had gotten to know Theo "Butchie" Pirro as well as anyone else he'd met at SJF. A failed boxer who turned to a life of crime, Butchie wasn't much better at crime than at boxing, and soon found himself serving a series of stints in prison. A seasoned veteran among Chancers, he started out as a Scrubber back before the term even existed, and managed to get himself transferred to SAO. Butchie stuck around Super Justice Force long after completing Second Chance, becoming a valuable person when it came to helping others get through the program. Other Chancers loved him, but Chuck Maslon hated him. Maslon felt Butchie had a habit of "looking the other way" when it came to Chancers violating the rules of conduct.

It only took Darius one meeting to know that he hated group sessions. The problem was the group itself. Darius didn't fully understand the point of the sessions, although he suspected it provided some people the opportunity to whine and call it "therapy." Every week he listened to the same thing—this guy talking about his wife nagging him, or that guy talking about how bad he wanted a drink. Everyone would pat each other on the back, and say that everything would be okay, and Darius would want to scream at all of them.

The most annoying member of the group sessions had to be a guy named Francis Feeney. His "professional" name, as he liked to say, was the Safecracker.

The Safecracker? That's the worst supercriminal name of all time, Darius thought every time he heard the name. *That's like calling yourself the Bankrobber or the Carjacker.*

Darius knew nothing about Francis Feeney's ability to crack safes, but his ability to avoid being arrested was evident. Francis served seven years before being paroled and accepted into Second Chance. His biggest problem, aside from a bad choice in a professional name, was his status as a Scrubber. Every counseling session he whined about the same things. "I'm the Safecracker," he would say. "Do you know many safes I've cracked? And now I'm stuck mopping floors for a living. That shows you there's no justice in this world."

Darius didn't much care what the other guys in the group had to say, but at least they switched things up a bit. Sol Solenberg, a white-collar criminal who had done time for embezzling, always complained about his health, but at least he had a different ailment from week to week. Vin "Anvil Head" Matushki, a second-rate supercriminal with a head that looked like an anvil—at least from certain angles—had terrible luck with women, and every week he had some sad story to tell. But Francis Feeney just said the same thing over and over again. "I was the Safecracker. Do you know how many safes I cracked? And now I'm stuck mopping floors for a living. That shows you there's no justice in this world."

After four months of hearing the same thing, Darius couldn't take it anymore.

"What's your problem?" he asked.

"What do you mean?" asked the Safecracker.

"Everyone in this group is here because we got caught and we're moving on with our lives," said Darius. "When are you gonna man-up and move on with your life? So you were the Safecracker. So what? You're the Scrubber now. Shut up and deal with it."

It was the most Darius had said in any of the group counseling sessions. And it didn't sit well with the Safecracker. "Who do you think you are?" demanded the Safecracker.

"I'm the guy who's sick of you whining every week about how you were the Safecracker, and now you're stuck mopping floors," said Darius. "And I bet if you asked everyone else in this group, they'd say the same thing."

A murmur of agreement made its way through the group, which only made the Safecracker angrier.

"No one is forcing you to mop floors," said Darius. "You could always quit. Go crack a safe or two and make enough to retire on. Oh wait…I forgot. You can crack a safe, but you can't keep from getting caught."

That was it. Darius pushed the right button, everyone else in the group laughed, and Francis Feeney flew out of his chair in a rage.

Let him hit you first, Darius told himself. *That way it'll be self-defense.*

The Safecracker grabbed Darius by his shirt and yanked him out of his chair. As soon as Darius was on his feet, the Safecracker pushed him back and threw the most pathetic punch Darius had ever seen. Darius blocked the punch with ease, and then delivered a punch of his own to Francis's face. The Safecracker dropped to the floor, knocked cold.

The rest of the guys in the group applauded Darius. Apparently, none of them much cared for the Safecracker's whining either.

Butchie reported the incident, but his statement made it very clear that Francis Feeney had attacked Darius Logan, and that Darius acted in self-defense. Everyone in the group backed up Butchie's story, which should have been enough to quash any inquiry. It wasn't enough, however, to stop Chuck Maslon from calling for a full investigation. Maslon hoped the incident would be enough to get Darius kicked out of Second Chance, but he was wrong.

The day after Darius knocked Francis "the Safecracker" Feeney cold, Butchie found Darius in the library doing course work for his GED. Butchie had seen Darius in action before—seen the way he handled two guys in a fight. He'd also read Darius's file, and knew about some of the other fights—like the one that landed him in juvenile detention. He hadn't said anything, because there had been no need. All of that changed when Darius clocked Francis.

"We both know that Mr. Safecracker was a pain in the ass. And ya only did what we's all wanted to do," said Butchie. "But you's and me both know that ya made it happen."

"I don't know what you're talking about," said Darius.

"Don't talk to me like I'm some kinda freakin' moron. You were lookin' for a fight and you's got one" "That's crazy. Why would I want to start a fight?"

"Maybe 'cause it's what ya do best. It's the one way ya know to get yer point across. And in the world ya came from—the world out there—it might've worked. But here, in this world, guys like you's and me, who talk with these," Butchie held up his fists for Darius to see, "we gotta find a better way to say what's on our minds."

Butchie's words made sense. No one ever listened to Darius when he talked, but he definitely had ways of getting his point across. And truth be told, Darius had reached a point in his life where he found it much easier to express himself with a few-well placed blows to the face, instead of words that could be easily ignored.

"Promise me, you ain't gonna go startin' no more fights," said Butchie.

"I promise."

True to his word, Darius didn't get into any more fights in the group counseling sessions. At the same time, he still hardly said a word during the meetings. But fortunately, neither did the Safecracker.

28

With his freedom of movement still limited, Darius spent a significant amount of time in the library, working on his GED or simply reading. He read a ton of comic books, and became obsessed with the difference between the superheroes he read about and how the same heroes were in real life. In the comics, Lady Themis was the most confident woman of all time; but in real life she lacked self-esteem, and her inability to date a decent man made for many conversations. There wasn't anyone who remotely resembled Z-Boe in a single issue of "Adventures of Galaxus Alliance Corps." And the Captain Freedom in the comics was a tireless champion of justice, whereas the real Captain Freedom seemed to spend more time in meetings and dealing with the business of running SJF than with fighting crime, while people whispered behind his back about his drinking problem.

When he was a kid Darius hadn't read many issues of "Supercriminal Showcase" or "Tales of Villainy," but those became his favorite books. Both comics featured stories of supercriminals threatening the world or pulling off some major crime, and they all ended the same—with the bad guy getting caught and a "crime doesn't pay" message at the end. There were no less than fifty issues of "Supercriminal Showcase" dedicated to the crimes of Otto Rekker, who had become one of Darius's closest friends. The same was true of Manny, whose exploits as El Toro Loco filled the pages of "Tales of Villainy." Darius even found an issue of "Tales of Villainy" with a back-up story called "Muscle for Hire," and though he couldn't be sure, he suspected the character had been based on Butchie.

If all that the library offered to Darius was enough material to read for the rest of his life and access to enough information that he could fake his way out of seeming stupid, he would have been happy. Darius loved to learn and he forgot that somewhere along the way—or maybe he'd just been distracted from it.

Darius spent as much time as he could at the library, but the books, comics, computers and Internet were only part of the reason he enjoyed being there. If he sat in the right spot in the library, Darius could see across the main lobby and into the gift shop, where he could catch a glimpse of Elladia, Manny's niece, walking past on the days she worked.

He felt stupid, almost like a crazed stalker, desperately looking up from his books in the hopes of seeing her for a brief moment. He longed for the courage to say something, anything to her. Instead, he just got mad at himself for being such a chicken, justifying his fear because of Manny's threats to kill anyone who even looked at Elladia. And the lingering sting of humiliation of Maslon and the cops dragging him out of the employee cafeteria didn't help. Both were reason enough for Darius to keep his distance from Elladia and remain silent.

Besides, there's no way she would ever go for a guy like me, he would tell himself.

Adjusting to his new life at Super Justice Force HQ was more than getting used to a new sleep schedule, reporting to mandatory meetings, peeing into a cup once a week for his drug tests, and spending time at the library, hoping to catch a glimpse of Elladia. With each passing day, Darius found himself more and more drawn into the lives of those around him and feeling more and more like he was part of something.

Darius's new sense of belonging became most apparent when Thanksgiving rolled around. He had been at Super Justice Force for almost six months, saved HQ from being destroyed by Boom-Boom Kaboom, and moved from L1 to L2 in record time. He had gotten to know many of the superheroes he'd read about in comic books, and even had people he honestly considered friends. But it wasn't until he stared at the giant turkey on the dinner table at the home of Otto and Anna Rekker that Darius began to fully comprehend how much his life had changed.

It had been nine years since he last had a Thanksgiving dinner. His parents were still alive then, his mother pregnant with his baby brother. A few months after that came The Attack, followed by years of not being thankful for anything.

Otto Rekker had invited Darius to Thanksgiving dinner, although it was more of a demand. Sitting between Reinier and Aziza Rekker, Otto and Anna's children, Darius couldn't help but recall his first thoughts about their father. He felt ashamed for being so quick to judge.

Gathered around the table were the Rekkers, Manny and Elladia Ortiz, and Kaebel Kaine, better known to the world as Nightwatcher. Anna had prepared a tofu turkey for Nightwatcher, because he was a strict vegetarian, and Otto took great pleasure in teasing him about it. "Real men eat meat," he said.

Before they started eating, Otto stood at the head of the table, tapping his fork against his metal hand. It made an odd clanging sound that almost sounded like a bell. "We want to give thanks for all that we have in our lives—family, food and friends in abundance. We've all been through bad times, but they've been outweighed by the good. We're thankful for the second chances that have been given to all of us, and have brought us together as a family. Amen."

Darius couldn't have said it better himself. He was thankful for second chances and Second Chance.

After dinner, Darius helped clear the table, and without realizing it, he found himself alone in the kitchen with Elladia. His heart raced and he became flushed. *Keep cool*, he told himself. But keeping cool this close to Elladia was impossible.

"Hey," said Darius.

"Hey," replied Elladia. "You enjoy dinner?"

"Yeah. It's been a long time since I've had a Thanksgiving dinner. Not since the…"

Darius cut himself off. He never talked about The Attack. Pretty much never mentioned it out loud. That's just how he was.

"I lost my parents, too," said Elladia. "Luckily, I had Uncle Manny to take care of me."

Darius didn't have anyone to take care of him, but bringing it up would be a conversation killer, so he kept his mouth shut and nodded, as if to say, "Yeah, you were lucky."

"How's it going with your GED?" asked Elladia.

"Just took my last test."

"So does that mean you won't be hanging out at the library anymore?"

"I'm going to take some more classes…you know…some online college classes."

"You know, the library is right across from the gift shop. In fact, you can see right into the gift shop if you sit at the right spot," said Elladia.

Darius's face flushed in embarrassment. *Oh crap, she knows I've been spying on her from the library. She must think I'm some kind of psycho. Please, don't let her tell Manny—he'll kill me.*

"It's not that far of a walk from the library to the gift shop. You should make the trip one of these days," said Elladia.

She went back to washing the dishes, as Darius rushed out of the kitchen. He had just had his longest conversation ever with Elladia, and it had taken its toll on him.

29

By the time Christmas arrived, Darius had been in Second Chance for over six months. His meetings with Trang Nguyen were cut to once a week, he'd received nothing but positive job performance reviews from Manny, and been named both New Employee of the Month and Operations Crew Employee of the Month. Dr. Sam confided in Darius that because of his successes, Second Chance would be moving into a more proactive phase.

Things had gone well for Darius Logan, but as the holidays quickly approached, he became more and more aware that when all was said and done, he was still a prisoner. His prison could be very deceptive, because it afforded him more freedom than a real correctional facility ever would. As a Level 2 employee, he had access to seventy-five percent of SJF Headquarters. His meals were taken care of, and he actually got paid for the work he did. He didn't even need to go to a bank to cash his checks, because there was a credit union located at HQ. If he needed to buy something, he could always shop online using the computers in the library.

Twice a week, Anna Rekker dropped the kids off at the Kurtzberg Metahuman Research and Training Center for an afterschool program. The program itself always ended at least an hour before Otto got off work, and Reinier and Aziza Rekker always ended up at the library, waiting for their father while doing their homework. This is how Darius came to spend time almost every week with Aziza and Reinier, and how they came to know him as Uncle Big D. Reinier regularly invited Darius over to read comic books, and Aziza, who had a crush on Darius, asked him to the zoo, the movies, bowling and ice skating. But Darius remained restricted in his movements outside of HQ.

Darius did get special permission to leave HQ to attend the holiday school play at Eisner Elementary School, where Reinier played a donkey and Aziza was in the choir. After the play, despite the bitter cold of early December, everyone went out for ice cream. But because the ice cream parlor wasn't on the pre-approved agenda submitted for Darius's leave, Chuck Maslon made a second feeble attempt to have him removed from Second Chance and sent to prison.

Rather than have Darius hauled away by the police, which had backfired on him last time, Maslon charged Darius with an escape attempt and called for a review panel. It was a pathetic move on Maslon's part, but Darius saw it as a reminder that he better watch himself. Not much came from the review panel, other than the decision that Darius would no longer be granted any sort of personal leave time from HQ, even with the STATU monitoring his every move and the approval of L4 supervisors.

Maslon had his small victory, which only served to win more people to Darius's side. There were even Long Arms who had trouble siding with Maslon. Darius had done nothing other than go out for ice cream with Otto Rekker and his family after a holiday play, and Maslon's attempt at busting him just seemed petty and personal.

After the review panel, his freedom became more limited, and HQ felt even more like a prison. Still, Darius knew he could be much worse off, and resigned himself to make the most of what he had. He would enjoy life—as much as he could. And that included the holidays.

The holiday party at Super Justice Force was insane. It wasn't so much a Christmas party, as there were people at SJF who didn't celebrate Christmas, but it was festive event of epic proportions. Vehicle Maintenance Bay 2—the third-largest space in all of HQ—had been transformed. Decorations hung on the walls and from the ceilings. A massive buffet served more food than Darius had ever seen in one place. And at the far end of room, a live band performed, while SJF employees and their children danced.

Massive Man, standing nearly ten feet tall, was dressed as Santa Claus, handing out presents. Not to be outdone, a Sesstarian Darius recognized from the credit union also handed out presents, dressed as whatever the equivalent to Santa Claus was on Sesstar IV.

Otto Rekker, with his family in tow, caused the biggest commotion of the party when he gave Nightwatcher his present. Otto had taken up a collection, raising enough money to pay for a bionic eye to replace the half-blind eye that caused Kaebel Kaine to constantly crash SJF vehicles.

Darius mingled at the party for about an hour, making sure he greeted the coworkers that he got along with, and avoiding those who really bothered him. He struggled with trying to be more social and outgoing, but it was difficult. People still got on his nerves. Little things still threatened to set him off. And by the time he'd made the rounds at the party, the walls were closing in. As much as he hated being alone, he had also gotten used to it, and he needed to leave.

He made his way through VMB2, saying goodbye to people as he left, when he bumped into Manny.

"Where you goin'?" Manny asked.

"I gotta get out of here," said Darius.

If it were anyone else, Manny might have argued, trying to convince them stay. He didn't argue with Darius though. Manny knew that Darius was still adjusting to living his new life. Manny hadn't gone through the exact same thing, but he'd gone through something similar enough to understand.

"You gotta do what you gotta do, amigo," said Manny. "Did Elladia find you? She said she had something for you."

Knowing that Elladia was looking for him made leaving the party that much more necessary. Darius became a compete fool around her, stammering and stuttering like an idiot. And that was when things went well. Sometimes he couldn't even remember how to form words when she was around.

Darius almost made it to the exit when he heard Elladia calling his name. For a brief second he contemplated ignoring her—pretending like he didn't hear her and just getting out of there. And he most likely would have done it, except she was too close, and she managed to grab him by the shoulder and spin him around.

"I've been looking all over for you," said Elladia. Her smile looked more beautiful than ever.

"Um...really?"

"I have something for you," she said.

Elladia closed her eyes and took a deep breath. She slowly exhaled, opened her eyes, and mumbled more to herself than anyone else, "Okay, here goes."

From seemingly out of nowhere she produced something tiny and green that she held over Darius's head with her left hand as she grabbed him and pulled him close with her right. It happened so quick, that Darius didn't even register that the tiny green thing was a piece of mistletoe. All he knew was that Elladia's lips pressed hard against his. Darius's mind spun out of control as she kissed him. Elladia pulled away, looking him in the eye. "Merry Christmas," she said.

30

The six months between the Christmas holidays and Darius's 18th birthday were more eventful than he could've ever imagined. After nearly a decade, plans were announced to begin rebuilding No Man's Land, which meant actual efforts were being made to fight crime in the lawless wasteland, including regular patrols by Super Justice Force. Captain Freedom thwarted an attempt to blow up the Statue of Liberty by the Masters of D.E.A.T.H., who may or may not have been working under the orders of Doc Kaos. There were rumors that the Galaxus Alliance Corps had intercepted an Ad-Ahlen spy ship in the outer regions of the solar system, reigniting fears of a potential invasion. And a massive shipment of Adrenaccelerate hit the streets, setting off an epic crime wave fueled by the illegal drug that temporarily gave "normal" people super powers.

Complicating matters was the fact that Kaebel Kaine was still recovering after replacing his bad eye with a bionic eye, leaving him out of commission for several months. Without Nightwatcher patrolling the worst parts of the city, crime increased by alarming proportions. Rival gangs, high on Adrenaccelerate, waged a brutal war for control of the streets.

On one side of the battle lines was notorious kingpin Tiny Biggs, whose crew of eXXeLL-addicted thugs controlled most of the crime in the city. On the other side was gang leader Vi$e Gripper, whose crew consisted of eXXeLL users and metahumans. And just to make things interesting, Mutationation, a gang of unregistered metahumans that controlled most of the crime in No Man's Land, jumped into the fray in an attempt to expand their enterprises to other parts of the city.

Darius couldn't believe how quickly parts of the city fell apart without Nightwatcher out on patrol. Nightwatcher was just one man—who didn't even have superpowers—but he kept several large parts of the city in check. Without him on the streets, things quickly got ugly, as Darius observed night after night.

He also witnessed for the first time the effects of eXXeLL. Darius had seen users of Adrenaccelerate before, and he had a grasp of how the drug altered the body chemistry and gave its users superhuman powers, but it wasn't until the deadly gang war began tearing the city apart that he really understood how dangerous the drug truly was.

Terrorist plots, a possible alien invasion, and a gang war of epic proportions kept the members of Super Justice Force working day and night to protect the city. And it wasn't just the costumed crime fighters and super-powered heroes of SJF working around the clock. Surveillance and Observation became pushed to the limit, with SAO crews working overtime and pulling double shifts.

Just when things seemed like they couldn't get any worse, a major crisis erupted, resulting in the formation of a Fast Response Unit. The FRU consisted of crewmembers from both SAO and Communication and Dispatch. Normally, SAO would use its elaborate surveillance resources to look for and track illegal activity, which it would report to CAD.

This system had been in place for many years, and in general it worked. Unless, of course, there was an extreme emergency, like the escape from Kirby Island Maximum Security Super Penitentiary—when nearly every member of Super Justice Force was called into action and Operations Crew was operating beyond its capacity.

The formation of the Fast Response Unit came as a direct result of Kid Spectacular being abducted by his arch nemesis, Creepy Crawler.

Kid Spectacular had been, for a time, one of the most popular heroes in the world. His powers manifested when he was only thirteen, and after a few high-profile adventures, he was thrust in the national spotlight. He got a major sponsorship deal, a television series and his own line of comics and action figures. By the time he was sixteen Kid Spectacular had become one of the most successful superheroes in the business.

For a time, Kid Spectacular could do no wrong. He only dated supermodels and famous actresses, and every bit of merchandise with his name and likeness became a best seller—even Kid Spectacular acne cream and Kid Spectacular toothpaste. But after a few years things started falling apart. Rumors that he had slapped around his girlfriend, a teen idol in her own right, were compounded by talk of drug and alcohol problems.

Things spiraled hopelessly out of control for Kid Spectacular just after he turned nineteen. Jazzmin Fyne, Kid Spectacular's girlfriend, publicly came out and accused him of physically assaulting her. She left him for another hero named Chisel, one half of a crime-fighting team known as Hammer and Chisel. Neither Hammer nor Chisel were ever taken seriously in the world of heroes—they were a team put together by a marketing company, and never really became a hit with the public. Most people saw Chisel's relationship with Jazzmin Fyne as a publicity stunt to breathe life into his and Hammer's failing career.

The big problem came during a live broadcast of some silly teen-focused awards program honoring both Kid Spectacular and Jazzmin Fyne, who was there with Chisel. Fueled by tequila and cocaine, Kid Spectacular flew into a rage and attacked Chisel. But because Chisel was nothing more than a failed male model name Dirk Barangus, who had no real powers, just a fancy suit and some high-tech gear provided by the marketing team that created him, the beating he took from Kid Spectacular was in and of itself quite spectacular. And of course, it happened on live television with millions of impressionable teenagers watching.

Kid Spectacular's popularity tanked after that. Kicked out of Super Justice Force, dropped by his sponsors, his show cancelled, he was charged with assault and sued by Chisel. Nineteen years old, and he lost everything.

For almost three years, there had been no word on Kid Spectacular, other than the occasional tabloid news story. It didn't matter that Jazzmin Fyne came out and admitted she had lied—she'd made up the story to get sympathy after her latest movie had died at the box office. No one was interested in Kid Spectacular anymore.

Then, on his twenty-second birthday, Kid Spectacular went into rehab. Suddenly, he was all over the news again. A reality television series, "Getting Straight with Kid Spectacular," became one of the highest rated shows on television, and the Kid was reborn. On the second-to-last episode of the show, while at a twelve-step meeting for recovering addicts, someone calling himself Creepy Crawler attacked Kid Spectacular. The final episode of the show featured a fight between Kid Spectacular and Creepy Crawler, watched by more people than the Super Bowl.

Some people believed that the fight between Kid Spectacular and Creepy Crawler was real, while others believed it to be a publicity stunt to relaunch his career. Whatever the truth, Kid Spectacular managed to make a comeback. At first he tried to re-brand himself as Mr. Spectacular, but the media and the public refused to call him anything other than Kid. He was never as popular as he had been in his glory days, but he never tried to be. Gone was the endless line of merchandising deals. He spent his time simply fighting crime, falling in love, and settling down to raise a family.

Five years after his comeback, Creepy Crawler captured Kid Spectacular during early-morning rush hour, minutes before Darius's shift ended. In fact, Darius witnessed the whole thing, caught on video by a television news helicopter. A fight between Mutationation and members of Vi$e Gripper's crew took an unusually destructive turn when one of Gripper's men threw a car at Optiblaster, a metahuman with the power to shoot energy blasts from his eyes. Optiblaster hit the car with his energy blast, causing the car to explode, setting off a chain reaction of exploding cars and buses on a bridge in the Upper East Side. CAD had intercepted the initial 911 calls, and SAO patched into surrounding security camera feeds and television news broadcasts. The two departments worked together, with CAD issuing a general distress call to any Super Justice Force members who could respond.

Within minutes, Kid Spectacular, Blue Shield, Lady Themis, Invisigaurdian, Stixx and Stone were all on the scene, helping police and rescue workers evacuate the area.

Darius manned a SAO post scanning live video feeds from the scene of the accident, which was a lot like watching a dozen versions of the same movie, shot from different points of view, and looking for the difference in details. SAO scanning required a certain knack for noticing the smallest, seemingly most insignificant details, and Darius had that knack. He could look at five or six video feeds simultaneously, and see something crucial that only appeared for a split second on a single feed.

Darius watched as police, rescue workers and SJF members scrambled to contain the chaos at the scene of the accident. Their efforts were hampered by a second series of explosions. By this time, citizens were involved in the rescue, helping to carry the injured. Of the five television news cameras on the scene, one focused briefly on Kid Spectacular as he carried an older woman to what appeared to be a firefighter. The camera panned away less than a second after the firefighter did something to Kid Spectacular. It happened so fast, Darius couldn't see what happened—not definitively anyway—but his first instinct told him it was something bad.

Darius immediately checked in with his SAO team members and CAD. "Did anyone just see something happen to Kid Spectacular?" he asked. "I need an immediate fix on Kid Spectacular."

CAD didn't respond. They were swamped with incoming and conflicting reports. Seconds passed with Darius frantically scanning every video feed coming from the scene of the accident. Lady Themis lifted a bus with one hand, pulling free the car pinned underneath. Blue Shield carried two children, crying for their mother. Stixx helped firefighters with the raging inferno caused by the explosions, while her partner, Stone, tore the side off a burning school bus to rescue the children trapped inside. And in all of this destruction, Kid Spectacular was nowhere to be seen.

Darius checked his PCU, making sure it was set to the proper channel—everyone needed to hear him, not just CAD. "We have a situation. Kid Spectacular is down," said Darius. "We need to send someone in now."

"There is no one else," said a voice over his PCU.

"Find someone. I think Kid Spectacular has been shot. He's not showing up on any feeds."

"We need confirmation," said a disembodied voice.

"Screw confirmation! I saw something. I saw Kid Spectacular go down."

No one responded. Darius felt helpless. He thought about leaving his station and personally going to the scene of the accident to look for Kid Spectacular.

Maslon would love that. He'd bust me for an escape attempt. He'd probably say I staged the accident as a cover.

Darius faced a difficult decision. His gut instinct told him something had happened to Kid Spectacular. No one would listen to him. He couldn't sit by, scanning video feeds for danger, when he knew something dangerous had already slipped past. He made the decision to violate protocols, and give up scanning live feeds.

Darius pulled up the video feed he witnessed minutes earlier. It took him a minute to find the proper feed from the right news camera. He watched the footage of Kid Spectacular carrying the old woman. Kid Spectacular reaches a firefighter. *Something happens. The camera pans away.*

Darius watched the footage five times, still unclear about what he'd seen. The second time he thought he saw the firefighter point something at Kid Spectacular. The third time he realized the firefighter was wearing a protective mask. None of the other firefighters on the scene wore their masks. The fourth time he watched the video, Darius saw Kid Spectacular start to drop the old woman before the camera panned away. The fifth time Darius watched the footage, he felt like a fool for not thinking to watch it in slow motion.

Replaying the video for the sixth time, Darius finally saw what happened. Kid Spectacular moved in slow motion, carrying an old woman in his arms. For the first time, Darius could see their faces. The woman, either unconscious or dead, bled from a gash across her face. Kid Spectacular was saying something to the old woman. Maybe telling her that everything would be fine. Maybe praying for her soul.

Kid Spectacular approached a firefighter—the only firefighter at the scene with his face covered. The firefighter pointed something at Kid Spectacular. Even in slow motion, Darius had trouble seeing what it was, but he had a good guess. Police officers often used the UltraStun 500 to subdue superpowered criminals. The UltraStun 500 could take down anyone with a power rating of four or less. Kid Spectacular had a power rating of three.

The firefighter pointed something at Kid Spectacular—quite possibly an UltraStun 500 stun gun—and then it happened. The firefighter shot at Kid Spectacular. In slow motion you could see the look on Kid Spectacular's face as he was hit. He dropped the old woman to the ground, and collapsed himself a fraction of a second later, just as the camera panned away.

31

Darius had never seen Captain Freedom so furious before. He'd seen Captain Freedom irritated, amused, bored, and possibly even drunk, but Darius had never seen him outright furious. Captain Freedom let loose with a stream of profanity the likes of which Darius had never heard—which said a lot, because Manny, Otto and Butchie were seasoned professionals when it came to swearing.

The moment Darius was sure of what he had seen—an attack on Kid Spectacular—he followed every single guideline required of him. CAD ignored him, claiming there was too much going on to confirm something no one else had reported. An hour later, after the fires were put out and the worst of the injured had been dealt with, CAD decided to look into Darius's emergency call.

It only took a few minutes of reviewing the footage to realize that in fact there was an emergency. An investigation and emergency rescue operation kicked into high gear moments after that. But Captain Freedom wanted to know why Darius's first report had been ignored.

"A valuable member of Super Justice Force is missing," said Captain Freedom. "Only one person in SAO noticed, and no one in CAD—not a single person—did a damn thing when he called it in! If anything happens to Kid Spectacular, heads will roll!"

Within an hour, every news channel ran a story about the attack on Kid Spectacular. Captain Freedom appeared at a press conference, asking the public to come forward with any information.

Four hours after Kid Spectacular was attacked, the first video appeared on the Internet. Kid Spectacular, chained to a chair, being tortured by Creepy Crawler, popped up on KillingKidSpectacular.com. Creepy Crawler promised that by the time he finished, Kid Spectacular would be dead. "But not before I have some fun carving him to pieces," Creepy Crawler said into the camera.

Reserve members of Super Justice Force were called in to help with the search and rescue operation. Several freelance heroes and crime fighters volunteered their services, and an emergency hotline was set up. The best team members from SAO and CAD were pulled together to form a Fast Response Unit consisting of twenty two-person teams, one from SAO and the other from CAD, working directly with a rescue team. Nightwatcher, still out of action because of his eye surgery, led the FRU operation. Even without his costume, Kaebel Kaine was still the best detective in all of Super Justice Force.

Based on the time between when Creepy Crawler captured Kid Spectacular and when the first video appeared on the Internet, search parameters were established. The parameters covered a dauntingly large area that represented an endless possibility of hiding places where Creepy Crawler could be torturing Kid Spectacular. Each of the FRU teams was given a quadrant that they were responsible for monitoring.

It came as no surprise that Maslon didn't want Darius on FRU. He cited Darius's age, a lack of time on the job, and the fact that Darius had violated procedure during the initial crisis, when he stopped scanning live feeds to rewatch the news footage. "Logan's participation will jeopardize the entire operation," said Maslon.

Manny Ortiz responded by swearing at Maslon in Spanish, telling him what to do with his mother.

Captain Freedom had no time to waste with arguing. "If CAD had listened to the kid in the first place, we might not be in this mess," he said.

Darius's FRU partner, Oegheneo-chuko, was a Tessarian that worked CAD. Darius had seen Tessarians around Headquarters, gotten to know a few in passing, and though he'd never worked closely with any, he knew a bit about Oegheneo-chuko.

Oegheneo-chuko came to Earth on one of the Tessarian refugee ships that arrived a decade before Darius was born, got a job at Super Justice Force through the Extraterrestrial Employment Initiative, earning a reputation of being difficult to work with. Because Tessarians were not quite male or female, many of them had trouble assimilating to life on Earth, where so much emphasis was placed on gender. Most humans never quite knew how to refer to Tessarians, since the usual gender-specific pronouns didn't fit. Known for working hard, Tessarians tried to avoid conflict as much as possible, including making a fuss when referred to in any sort of way that implied male or female gender. Oegheneo-chuko was the exception to the rule, primarily because he/she stood up for him/herself.

As a team, Darius and Oegheneo-chuko, who went by Oeghe for short, worked well together. Maybe it was because neither had much to say to the other. Neither of them cared about sports or television or anything else that would have made for idle chitchat on the job. Both had one mission and one mission only: to find Kid Spectacular before Creepy Crawler killed him. This was especially important to Darius, because he felt a sense of responsibility for the Kid's safety. For reasons he couldn't explain, Darius shouldered guilt over what had happened.

"Get that crap outta your mind," Manny told him. "What happened to Steve ain't your fault."

Steve was Kid Spectacular's real name. Steven Hampton.

The chaos of O3C that surrounded Darius and Oeghe didn't bother them as they focused on the far end of the search perimeter—an area that seemed unlikely to contain Creepy Crawler's hiding place given its distance from the scene of the crime. They worked twelve-hour shifts and reported directly to Black Fist and his new partner, White Dynamo, neither of whom were that well regarded in Super Justice Force.

I've been put on the team most likely to fail.

Forty hours after Kid Spectacular's abduction, hope faded fast. Two-dozen torture videos appeared on the Internet, and in each one the Kid looked closer and closer to death. Darius and the rest of the SAO team were forced to watch the torture videos, looking for clues. The videos made Darius sick and angry. *What point is there in me watching this?* Darius asked himself. *If the police, FBI and the rest of Super Justice Force can't find anything, there's nothing I can do.*

Black Fist and White Dynamo were following up a lead that led nowhere. After investigating screams reported by an old woman who lived with sixteen mangy cats, Black Fist and White Dynamo stopped to get something to eat at a place called Hot Diggity Dogs, a tiny fast food joint that specialized in hot dogs.

Darius and Oeghe were in direct communication, both audio and visual, with Black Fist and White Dynamo, while they were eating at Hot Diggity Dogs.

"Where are you?" asked Darius.

"Hot Diggity Dogs," said White Dynamo. "You want us to get you one to go?"

"No, thanks," said Darius. "What is that right behind Black Fist?"

Darius referred to the sign for Hot Diggity Dogs in the background. Two hot dogs with faces, feet and hands, danced around in the middle of a fire. It looked stupid, but somehow oddly familiar to Darius.

Black Fist explained the sign for Hot Diggity Dogs, sending a live video feed, when the blast of an approaching train whistle drowned out most of the sound. But Darius didn't need to hear what Black Fist was saying, because in that instant, all the pieces fell into place.

Darius quickly accessed the torture videos. He looked and listened for something very specific. First he found the video with the noise. Brief and hard to make it out because of the horrific screams from Kid Spectacular, it sounded like a train whistle in the distance.

"What is it that you are looking for?" asked Oeghe.

"Not sure. Give me a minute," said Darius.

Darius sat through three more of the torture videos that made him want to vomit before he found what he was looking for. It was one of the first videos that Creepy Crawler had posted, when Kid Spectacular still had some fight in him. Kid Spectacular and Creepy Crawler struggled. Kid Spectacular managed to push Creepy Crawler away, who in turn knocked over the tripod with the camera videotaping everything. The camera remained on the floor for about thirty seconds, while Creepy Crawler took out his rage on Kid Spectacular. The out-of-focus image made it difficult to determine what the camera was pointed at, but to Darius it looked like a blurry sign for Hot Diggity Dogs.

The torture video continued as someone, most likely Creepy Crawler, set the camera back upright. In the swift motion captured by the camera, it looked like there was a paper bag on the floor. A paper bag with the Hot Diggity Dogs logo on it.

Darius pointed it out to Oegheneo-chuko, who couldn't be sure.

"I'm sure," said Darius. Maybe the sound on the video hadn't been a train whistle. And maybe the out-of-focus image on the camera wasn't a bag from Hot Diggity Dogs. But for Darius, it was enough.

"I've got him," Darius reported back to Black Fist and White Dynamo. "I don't know exactly where, but I think he's close. He's somewhere close enough that you can hear the train whistle. And Creepy Crawler, he's been getting food from Hot Diggity Dogs."

32

It had been like something right out of a movie, or maybe even a comic book—an evil villain about to bring to fruition his dastardly plan, resulting in the death of a beloved hero. But just in the nick of time, the villain's plans are foiled by a pair of superheroes busting through the wall and saving the day. It didn't always happen like that. But it did happen that way with Kid Spectacular.

Creepy Crawler pressed record on his camera. Kid Spectacular, already beaten to a bloody pulp, had one foot in the grave. Creepy Crawler stared into the lens of the camera, his demonic mask splattered with blood and looking rather ominous, and said, "Here's the moment you've all been waiting for, folks." Then he fired up a chainsaw.

And as he moved in with the chainsaw to enact his last bit of torture on Steven Hampton, Black Fist and White Dynamo burst through the wall of the abandoned building serving as the torture chamber. Creepy Crawler moved toward White Dynamo with the chainsaw, swinging it high in the hopes of a decapitation. But White Dynamo avoided the attack, catching Creepy Crawler by the wrists. The two men struggled for control of the chainsaw. Creepy Crawler kicked White Dynamo in the groin, dropping the superhero to his knees. Creepy Crawler raised the chainsaw and started to bring it down on White Dynamo.

Before the chainsaw could connect with White Dynamo, Black Fist tackled Creepy Crawler, knocking the chainsaw from the villain's hands. The two men wrestled on the floor for a few moments, broke apart, and got to their feet. Black Fist delivered a punch to Creepy Crawler that would have leveled a normal man. Creepy Crawler took the punch, and threw one back.

The two men continued to fight, slamming into each other, flinging each other across the room. While all of this went on, White Dynamo picked himself up off the floor and got his hands on the chainsaw. And then he did what much of the world wanted to do ever since the torture videos started appearing.

The video camera captured all of it, the rescue, the fight, and White Dynamo bringing the chainsaw down on Creepy Crawler. And even though the final part was eventually edited out—because it wouldn't do for a superhero dressed all in white and splattered with blood and guts to be seen playing judge, jury and executioner—the video made it to the Internet. Within twelve hours the rescue video had been viewed over ten million times.

When it was all said and done, Black Fist and White Dynamo signed the biggest endorsement deal ever offered to a dynamic duo. They quickly became the most popular heroes of the day, even more so than Captain Freedom, who just weeks earlier had saved the Statue of Liberty from being blown up.

But the real hero behind the rescue of Kid Spectacular was Darius Logan, not that anyone would have known this. The marketing and publicity department of Super Justice Force made sure that White Dynamo and Black Fist got all the credit for what happened. This would move both of them up to the big league of superheroes.

Darius got a special commendation, but his wasn't a story worth telling to the public. He didn't have any endorsement deals or his own line of comics, which meant there was no money to be made by having him be the hero. No one would be rushing out to buy a Darius Logan action figure. And to be perfectly honest, it didn't bother him. He just did his job with no interest in being a hero.

Five days after his rescue, Kid Spectacular woke from his coma in terrible condition. The doctors feared that even though he had regained consciousness, he might not make it.

Kid Spectacular asked to meet Darius. The two had exchanged pleasantries before, passing each other in the hall or on the elevator. They didn't really know each other, but someone told Kid Spectacular who really saved his life.

Mary Hampton, Kid Spectacular's wife, greeted Darius outside the hospital room. Visibly pregnant, Mary thanked Darius for saving her husband, which only made him uncomfortable.

Darius had no idea what to expect when he went into the hospital room. There wasn't much of the man known as Kid Spectacular left. Creepy Crawler had smashed the Kid's left hand so bad that it was a useless mass, likely to be amputated. All of Kid Spectacular's toes had been cut off, one by one, as had two of the fingers on his right hand. He had lost one of his eyes, and Creepy Crawler had cut and slashed Kid Spectacular's body so much that he was wrapped in bandages from head to toe.

He looks like a mummy, thought Darius.

Darius looked down at the gruesome sight that was Kid Spectacular. "You wanted to see me?" he said.

Kid Spectacular looked up at Darius, tears flowing from his one good eye, and he extended what was left of his right hand. Darius gently gripped Kid Spectacular's hand. The Kid squeezed Darius's hand as best he could, and through the clenched teeth of a jaw that had been wired shut, he faintly mumbled, "Thank you."

Darius wanted to run from the room. Seeing someone this broken and battered made him think of victims of The Attack. It made him think of his parents and his baby brother, whose bodies were destroyed so completely there wasn't enough left to bury. But Kid Spectacular wouldn't let go of his hand, and even if he did, Darius would not have left his side.

No other words were spoken as Darius stood next to the man he had helped rescue. Mary Hampton came into the room. She took her husband's good hand in her right hand, and gripped Darius's hand with her left, quietly sobbing.

Darius wasn't sure how long he was in the room, holding Mary Hampton's hand while she cried over her husband. It seemed like a lifetime. Eventually, Kid Spectacular fell asleep and his weak grip on his wife's hand loosened.

Kid Spectacular never woke up again. He died two hours later. The last words he ever spoke were to Darius Logan.

33

For days, the media talked about nothing but Kid Spectacular. His life—the good and the bad and everything in between—became the subject of talk shows, news specials and countless articles appearing on television, in print and all over the Internet. Tributes poured in from all over the world, and everyone attended his funeral, including Darius.

If it weren't for the fact that Mary Hampton, Kid Spectacular's widow, asked Darius to be a pallbearer, he would have skipped the funeral all together. Darius hated funerals. But Mary asked, and Darius couldn't refuse.

With no proper clothes to wear to a funeral, Darius needed to go shopping for a suit. Of course, getting the required clearance to leave HQ became an ordeal, with Chuck Maslon dead set against Darius going anywhere but prison. The usual arguing between Dr. Sam and Maslon, and Manny and Maslon, and Captain Freedom and Maslon went on, until finally, Darius got the clearance he needed.

Anna Rekker took him shopping for a suit, and the kids tagged along. Darius felt odd shopping for clothes with the Rekker family as if he was some distant cousin come to town for a visit. It took three stores before he found a suit that looked acceptable to Anna, which she insisted on paying for. "Arguing with me is pointless," Anna said when Darius tried to pay for the suit himself. "If Otto can't win a fight with me, what makes you think you can?"

Darius couldn't tell the difference between the suit Anna picked out and the other five he had tried on—all of them were black, and he looked the same in all of them. Still, he felt good about having something nice to wear at the funeral, even though he didn't want to be there. He felt out of place, especially as a pallbearer, walking along with Black Fist, White Dynamo, Captain Freedom and Kid Spectacular's father, as they carried the fallen hero to his final resting place.

News crews and reporters from all over the world had flocked to the funeral, and much of the world watched the event live on television as tears rolled down their cheeks. Reporters speculated over the identity of the young man helping carry the coffin. Everyone knew who the costumed heroes were, and most people even recognized Thomas Hampton, Kid Spectacular's father, who had been a regular on the reality series "Getting Straight with Kid Spectacular."

After the funeral, friends, family and fellow crime fighters gathered at Super Justice Force HQ for a somber reception. Darius didn't participate. Ten months into his job at SJF, and just two months away from turning eighteen, the death of Kid Spectacular hit him hard. He was almost the same age Kid Spectacular had been when his life flamed out of control. Most of the world had given up on Kid Spectacular, but he managed to turn things around for himself. He'd been given a second chance—for all the good it did him.

Maybe it meant nothing. Or if there was significance to it all, Darius certainly couldn't find it. All he knew was that Kid Spectacular had fallen to great depths, and managed to pull his life back together again, only to be slowly murdered with the entire world watching on the Internet. Superheroes weren't supposed to have lives like that.

Darius sank into a deep depression in the days following the death of Kid Spectacular. With everything going on, no one noticed that Darius had become more quiet and withdrawn than usual. Only Elladia noticed the change in his behavior.

Things had changed since she kissed him at the holiday party. Darius still got nervous around her, but not like before, when he would just stare from his spot in the library.

On the days she worked at the gift shop, he would stop in and say hello. They often ate lunch together, even though he hardly ever said a word. It was an odd relationship to be sure, but for reasons she couldn't really understand, Elladia cared deeply for Darius. And if sitting around with him not saying a word was all she could get, it would have to do.

When Darius didn't come by the gift shop in the days and weeks after Kid Spectacular's death, Elladia became concerned. He hadn't gone to the library either, and he *always* went there. She wanted to ask Manny about Darius, but her uncle didn't know about the kiss at the party, or that Elladia had feelings for Darius. Maybe Uncle Manny would get mad. Maybe he wouldn't. It didn't matter either way. Elladia couldn't make sense of the feelings she had herself, which meant she couldn't explain them to her uncle.

Not sure what to do, Elladia went to Darius's apartment in the Tower. It was a bold move for her. Sure, she had kissed him at the holiday party, and sure, they were spending time together, but he was far from her boyfriend. There had been no other kisses, no holding hands or any of the romantic things she thought she would have with her first boyfriend. Of course, Darius wasn't even her boyfriend.

Darius wasn't surprised to see Elladia when he opened his apartment door. And he wasn't nervous, which is what she expected, or happy, which is what she wished for. He simply left the door open for her and went back to lie on his bed.

Elladia entered the tiny studio apartment and sat at the desk. The awkward silence wasn't all that awkward because they hardly spoke to each other anyway. They could eat lunch together and sometimes not say a word. So silence was nothing new.

Elladia had never been in Darius's apartment. She looked around, hoping to get a better sense of who he was. The studio was almost as sparse as when he'd moved in nearly a year earlier. No new furniture, just piles of books. Fiction. Non-fiction. Comic books and text books. Darius had his own private library, an eclectic collection of bound pages with written words that told the story of a young man far more complex than he appeared. The books said everything and nothing about Darius all at the same time.

She looked at the pictures on his desk, thoughtfully studying the framed photo of Darius and his parents when he was much younger. He looked so happy. Elladia had never seen him look that happy. If there was any of the happy young boy left inside the brooding young man laying just a few feet away from her, she desperately wanted to see it.

Elladia studied the picture in the frame more closely. Darius's mother was beautiful, and his father was handsome. She thought of her own parents. There were feelings inside of her that she worked very hard to bury, but for some reason they were coming to the surface.

Elladia admired the way Darius kept cool. Sure, he was a nervous wreck around her, but when he wasn't around her, and Elladia watched him from a distance, he seemed so in control. She, on the other hand, fought to keep it together on a daily basis. She always smiled and laughed, but it was little more than a mask. Deep down inside, she was broken, just as Darius was broken, only she didn't know that about him. Just like she didn't know that Darius had often wished that he had died with his parents, the same way Elladia wished that she had died with hers.

"How do you cope?" Elladia asked.

"With what?"

"With all of it. With not having parents."

"You think I'm coping?" Darius asked.

"I guess. You look like it," said Elladia.

"I only sleep three or four hours a night. And most nights, I have nightmares."

"Still? After all these years?"

"Yeah," said Darius. "After all these years."

"I don't have nightmares anymore," said Elladia.

"Then maybe I should be asking you how you cope."

"Mostly I fake it. I smile a lot, and laugh a lot, and I pretend everything is fine, but I really want to break down and cry," said Elladia.

"I fake it too. I don't talk much, and I avoid people, and I pretend everything is as fine as it can be, but I really want to…"

"Want to what?" asked Elladia.

Darius clenched his fists, trying to think of the best way explain himself. "I don't really know."

"You haven't been coming around the gift shop. I was worried."

"I'm fine."

"I've missed you."

"It's this whole thing with Kid Spectacular. It's got me messed up," said Darius.

"You could talk to someone," Elladia said.

"I don't talk to people."

"Not even me? You can't talk to me?"

"No. Not now. Maybe. Someday. I hope."

Darius and Elladia sat silently in the room for quite some time. Eventually, Elladia started to cry. She cried for her parents and Darius's parents. She cried for herself and Darius, because they both seemed so broken. And while she cried Darius lay on his bed, wishing he could do whatever it took to make her happy.

After a time, Elladia stopped crying. She got up to leave, but stopped half way to the door. "Darius, do you like me?" Elladia asked.

Darius sat up on the edge of his bed. "Yeah. I do."

"I like you too. A lot," said Elladia.

And with that, Elladia left Darius's apartment. Neither of them felt good, but they both felt better than before.

34

Thursday, June 19, was pretty much a day like any other, except for two things. First, it marked the one-year anniversary of Darius Logan's first day on the job at Super Justice Force. Second, it was his birthday. That Darius's birthday and the day his whole new life began in earnest were the same seemed somehow appropriate to him. *If your life is going to start twice, it might as well start on the same day*, Darius thought. *Makes things easier to remember.*

Although Darius remembered his own birthday, he didn't expect anyone else to. In the years since the death of his parents, not many people remembered. Edith O'Malley, his caseworker, was the only person who never missed it. True to form, she remembered, her card arriving a few days early. Because Edith's schedule wouldn't permit coming by on his birthday, she came by to have lunch with Darius the day before.

Darius had only seen Edith twice since entering into Second Chance. He talked to her a few more times than that on the phone, and he emailed her about once a month from the computers in the library.

They sat across from each other in the restaurant next to the gift shop at SJF Headquarters. Darius would have preferred to eat somewhere else, but his options were limited to the restaurant and the cafeteria.

"You look absolutely wonderful," said Edith.

"Thanks," said Darius. "You look good, too."

Edith blushed and waved her hand dismissively, as if to say, "Oh stop."

"Are they treating you well?" Edith asked.

He could complain about the two-block perimeter surrounding HQ that served as his prison walls, or that Chuck Maslon was a total pain in the ass. But Darius had no real reason to complain, especially considering what his options were. "No complaints," he said.

"I appreciate the emails you send, Darius. I really do," said Edith. "You mentioned something about taking more online classes."

"Yeah, I just started a history class and a literature class. I'm not really sure what I'm doing right now."

"It looks to me like you're improving your life, even if you don't know what you're doing," said Edith.

"I've been thinking about what I want to do—you know, when I'm done with this place," said Darius. "This is a good job and all, but I don't want to be here forever. I'm thinking about becoming a teacher. I don't know. What do you think?"

"You would make a wonderful teacher. I think you'll do well no matter what you decide."

They sat and talked for almost an hour, which for Darius was a long time to talk to anyone. When they were done with lunch, Darius escorted Edith out the building, walking her to the park in front of HQ. They stopped in front of the statue of the original Super Justice Force, the sun shining down brightly.

"Edith, I just want to thank you for all you've done," said Darius. "I wouldn't have survived all those years if you didn't have my back."

Proud of the man Darius had become, of the incredible changes he had undergone, Edith cried tears of joy.

"Your parents would be so proud of you, Darius. They really would," she said.

Darius took Edith in his arms, giving her a strong hug. "You've been the one person who's cared about me when no one else did. As long as I live, I won't forget that," Darius said. "I love you, Edith." It was the first time he had said those words to anyone since the death of his family.

Darius started June 19 like any other day, going about his normal routine. He received a call on his Personal Communication Unit a little before two in the afternoon. The assistant supervisor of day shift wanted to know if he could come to work early.

"Sure," said Darius. "You need me in SAO?"

"Actually, no. They need someone to cover for a few hours in MAS."

Darius hadn't worked in Maintenance and Services since his trainee days. He hated working in MAS, which always included mopping up a restroom, or doing someone's laundry. But he agreed to do it, and it would mean extra hours on his paycheck.

"Where do you want me to report?" asked Darius.

"Report to the Banquet Hall 2. They'll be setting up for a conference tomorrow. Can you be there at seven?"

Darius agreed to be at Banquet Hall 2 at 7 pm. He wasn't thrilled about working a half shift with MAS, but setting up for a conference wouldn't be that bad. At least it wasn't mopping floors or scrubbing toilets. Still, it was no way to spend his eighteenth birthday.

35

Darius had spent his sixteenth birthday locked up in juvenile detention. He'd been sent there for assaulting Richard, the foster father at the group home where Darius lived. Richard was a worthless excuse for a human being, an alcoholic who abused the kids. Darius had ignored the verbal abuse, but when Richard started hitting one of the other kids—whose name Darius couldn't remember—something snapped.

It had been a brutal fight, due in no small part to the fact that Richard was so drunk he couldn't feel a thing. Darius learned a valuable lesson about fighting with drunks that night: don't do it. Darius and Richard had traded a few pretty good punches, but the drunk refused to go down. Somehow, Richard managed to get a butcher knife from the kitchen. Darius thought for sure Richard would stab him with the knife, which is why Darius smashed him over the head with a folding metal chair.

With Richard lying unconscious on the floor, Darius quickly packed his stuff and took off. That was how he came to live in the abandoned subway stations. He lived down there for months; when through a random set of bizarre circumstances he got caught shoplifting a bottle of peroxide, some bandages and anti-bacterial ointment. With an outstanding warrant from his assault on Richard, Darius ended up in juvenile detention.

It bothered Darius that he could not remember the name of the kid getting beaten at the foster home. He'd gotten in a fight protecting the kid, but couldn't remember his name. *Was it Marcus? Marquis?*

Every now and then Darius wondered whatever happened to the kid. He was probably still living in some group home, getting beaten for no reason by some drunken jackass. That was no way to live life.

Maybe, when I'm done working at SJF, I can open some sort of group home of my own. It would be some place safe for kids like whatshisface, where they wouldn't be afraid all the time.

Darius was thinking about what it would take to open a group home when he got off the elevator and walked down the corridor to Banquet Hall 2. The more he thought about it, the better the idea seemed. He had spent enough time in group homes and foster homes to know what sucked the most. *My place will be nothing like those others. Good food. More than one bathroom. No rats or roaches. And if anyone lays a hand on one of the kids, or yells at 'em, I'll personally beat the living hell out of 'em.*

He opened the door to Banquet Hall 2, practically jumping out of his skin when the room full of people yelled, "Surprise!"

Two banners hung from the ceiling. One read "Happy Birthday." The other read "Happy Anniversary." Both were more than Darius expected, or could have ever wished for.

But it wasn't the banners that meant so much to Darius—it was the people packed into the room. As near as he could tell, nearly all of the night shift had crammed into the banquet hall. There were also members of the other shifts—people he had gotten to know over the last year like EZ Manigo, most of his cafeteria crew, and all of his family. Otto and Anna Rekker and the twins were there, as well as Manny and Elladia Ortiz. Butchie, Dr. Sam, Trang Nguyen, Evelyn Bartee and everyone from his group counseling sessions—except for the Safecracker—had come to wish him a happy birthday. And then there was Super Justice Force. Most of the heroes he had gotten to know were there—Captain Freedom, Nightwatcher, Marvelous Man, Black Fist, White Dynamo, Rocky Feldman, Lady Themis and at least a dozen others, including Stixx and Stone from Chicago, and most of Teen Justice Force.

Nine years had passed since he last had a birthday party, and Darius had given up on ever celebrating again. Not only that, he had also given up on having anyone to celebrate with.

Darius had grown close to several people since starting at SFJ HQ, building strong friendships he never imagined possible. Manny had become a mentor and close friend. Otto Rekker and his family had practically adopted Big D.

In the beginning, Darius couldn't understand why guys like Manny and Otto and Butchie and all the other Chancers were nice to him—why they all wanted to see him succeed. He was just a nobody—a Bit. He didn't understand that the others saw in him their own Second Chance—a chance to get it right. He was young and the odds had been against him, but Darius had been given an opportunity to make the wrong things right, before the wrong things became so bad that the guilt choked the life out of him. All the other Chancers saw in Darius a good guy who could go bad, as opposed to a bad guy trying to make up for all the terrible things he'd done.

The most surprising and unusual friendship Darius had made was with the one person not at the party, Zander Boeman.

Darius and Zander hit it off almost from the start. They shared a common bond in that they were both orphans. Darius lost his parents in The Attack when he was nine. Z-Boe's parents were scientists stationed on the Enceladus Colony located on the moon of Saturn, where he practically grew up. He lost his parents during the legendary Battle of Enceladus, only surviving the battle because the Mhadra Turas had chosen him to become a Galaxus. Sixteen-years-old, orphaned during a war between Earth and an alien empire, Zander Boeman became the youngest member of the Galaxus Alliance Corps.

Z-Boe knew all too well about having no family, about being alone and struggling to survive. If anyone bothered to question his friendship with Darius, or why Z-Boe had taken Darius under his protective wing, all they would have to do is take a close look and see that both were made of similar stock.

Three months before the death of Kid Spectacular, Z-Boe and his longtime girlfriend officially broke up—she simply could not handle the pressure of dating a superhero who spent six months out of the year in space patrolling the galaxy. When they broke up, Z-Boe needed someone to water his plants and take care of the fish in his aquarium.

Technically, Z-Boe could have asked anyone. In fact, he could have put a request in through MAS, and his plants and fish would have been taken care of. Instead he asked Darius to do the job. Zander gave Darius a key to the apartment, which Darius used to let himself in to water the plants and feed the fish, which really weren't fish at all.

Zander had a massive aquarium in his apartment with Vissoam aqua-singers, strange-looking creatures that needed to be fed every four days.

Vissoam aqua-singers looked more like miniature dragons than anything else. The largest of the aqua-singers measured ten inches long from the tip of its beak to the end of the longest of its two tails. Only two of the five aqua-singers had more than one tail, and all had colorful wings, each with its own elaborate patterns. Z-Boe named them Jackie, Jermaine, Marlon, Tito and Michael, but Darius didn't know which ones were which.

Aqua-singers were known for the melodic noises they made, which almost sounded like humming, but not really. They were smarter than fish, and could be taught songs that they harmonized as a group. Darius couldn't really describe what the harmony sounded like, because the aqua-singers didn't sound like anything he had ever heard before. He could, however, name every song the strange creatures sang, because they only sang songs by the Jackson Five. It was the oddest yet most beautiful thing Darius had ever heard, and he looked forward to the days he went over to Zander's apartment to feed Jackie, Jermaine, Marlon, Tito and Michael. And when Darius sank into his depression after the death of Kid Spectacular, feeding the aqua-singers kept him going.

Even though Z-Boe couldn't be at the party, he made sure Darius got his present—his own Vissoam aqua-singer. The creature was red—at least mostly red—with spots of yellow and orange that ran along its spine. Compared to other aqua-singers, it wasn't that big, although its wings were unusually large for its size.

There weren't many other presents for Darius, but considering the fact he wasn't expecting any, all of them were pleasant surprises. The biggest surprise—aside from the aqua-singer—was the present Captain Freedom handed to him personally. "A bunch of us chipped in and bought this," said Captain Freedom.

Darius tore the plain brown paper off the rectangular box. His eyes went wide at the sight of a brand-new laptop computer. And not just any new laptop. Darius had been given an advance version of the Super Justice Force Signature Series Intellipad with chromatanium casing. It was so state-of-the-art it wasn't even on the market yet.

The party began to wind down a little after ten, which was fine with Darius. Most of night shift had to report for duty in less than an hour, and Darius felt a little overwhelmed from all of the socializing. Being a loner didn't take nearly as much energy as putting on a smile and talking.

"You should take the night off," said Manny. "Something tells me your boss would be cool with you callin' in sick."

"No thanks," Darius said. "Besides, it's not like I would be getting any sleep. I'm going to get all my stuff and take it up to my apartment. I may be a few minutes late."

"No worries, amigo," said Manny. "I'll see you soon."

Darius left Manny, and started gathering up his presents, most of which were books. Anna Rekker had bought him clothes, and the twins, Reinier and Aziza Rekker, gave him a collection of Super Justice Force action figures. He struggled to balance everything in his arms, worrying he would drop the tank with the aqua-singer in it.

"Do you need help with that?"

Elladia watched as Darius tried to hold on to everything. The tank with the aqua-singer started to slip from on top of the pile of books, and she grabbed it before it could fall.

"Thanks," said Darius.

"Let me just go tell Otto and Anna real quick—they're giving me a ride home," said Elladia.

Darius watched her as she jogged over to the Rekkers to tell them she was helping Darius take everything back to his place. He wasn't sure, but it looked like Anna had broken into a huge grin, and like Otto had winked at Elladia.

They rode the elevator in silence, making it no different than most of the time they spent together. Elladia carried the tank with the aqua-singer. Darius carried everything else.

He opened the door to his apartment, and dropped everything on the bed. Elladia placed the tank gently on the desk, staring at the odd creature inside.

"Thanks," said Darius. "The cake was delicious."

"You liked it?" Elladia asked.

"Yeah."

"I baked it," said Elladia, looking up from the tank with aqua-singer inside.

"I know."

"How come it isn't singing?" asked Elladia, pointing to the tank.

"It's lonely," said Darius.

"Lonely?"

"They tend to only sing in groups. No one knows why. Some people think it's because they need to be around others in order to really be what they need to be. This one may never sing."

"That's sad," Elladia said.

"That's how it is," said Darius. "I know how it feels."

"You're not a Vissoam aqua-singer, swimming alone in a tank, Darius. You don't have to feel lonely ever again. You know that, right?"

"Elladia," said Darius. "I...I..."

Elladia held her finger to her lips, telling Darius he didn't need to speak. "I know," she said.

Elladia pulled Darius close, or maybe it was the other way around. They looked each other in the eyes, and said nothing, just like they always did. Their bodies pressed together and they could each feel the heartbeat of the other. And then they kissed—a kiss deeper and more passionate than either had expected—which seemed to say all that needed to be said.

36

Manny Ortiz left Darius's birthday party and headed over to O3C. As he left the party, he saw Elladia and Darius getting on an elevator together. He knew it was only a matter of time before they got together romantically, if they hadn't already. Elladia tried to hide her interest in Darius, but her uncle could see through it.

Manny kept thinking he should be more upset. He had, after all, thought of a thousand different ways he would kill Elladia's suitors. Nothing mattered more than protecting Elladia—she was the only family he had. Still, he remembered what it felt like to be young, and have your heart racing over that special someone.

Despite his talk about killing anyone who went near Elladia, Manny wasn't going to deny her that incredible feeling that came from being in love. Still, he needed to sit down with the two of them and lay down some ground rules. And then there was the conversation about birth control—not exactly something he looked forward to. He thought about the time he had to take Elladia to buy her first training bra. That almost killed him. Her first period was even worse. He needed the help of both Anna Rekker and Lady Themis to get through that experience.

Training bras, menstrual cycles and feminine hygiene products had been difficult enough. Each experience had been enough to make Manny wish his niece had been a nephew. Deep down he knew that he'd avoided the issue of sex for longer than any man raising a teenage girl could ever hope.

Part of the reason he had managed to dodge the subject for so long was Elladia's fear of how Manny would react to her having a boyfriend. At least that's what he told himself. For all he knew, she may have already had a boyfriend. But even if there were past boyfriends, there was something different about Darius, and it showed in the changes in Elladia. She wasn't crying as much as she used to, and Manny knew the reason why.

In the beginning, when Elladia first came to live with Manny, she cried all the time. They barely knew each other, living in a tiny apartment in the Tower at SJF

Headquarters, and although he loved his niece and wanted to be there for her, he wasn't sure if he'd done the right thing.

Manny was still living a life of crime as El Toro Loco when The Attack happened. Like the rest of the world, he watched in horror as an army of ACU-64 Killbots, designed to protect the human race, went berserk. But unlike ninety-nine percent of the population, Manny Ortiz was born with Kurtzberg-24 Syndrome, a genetic disorder that made him different than most people. He couldn't fly like some people, or breathe under water, but he had a natural-born strength others didn't possess. It had never occurred to Manny to use his enhanced strength for anything other than what he called "survival," and that was whatever it took to put money in his pocket.

But as an army of ACU-64s rampaged throughout the greater metropolitan area, and the combined forces of the Super Justice Force, European Alliance, unlicensed crime fighters and a contingent from the Galaxus Alliance Corps struggled to stop the deadly machines, Manny had to get involved in the fight. It didn't do much good. He saw firsthand how powerful the Killbots really were.

El Toro Loco fought side by side with Great Defender, a hero second only to Captain Freedom. It didn't matter that Great Defender had personally arrested El Toro Loco twice. All that mattered was stopping the deadly machines—machines that killed Great Defender as El Toro Loco watched, unable to do a thing.

When The Attack finally ended, and the Killbots had been either destroyed or deactivated, El Toro Loco prepared to go back to business as usual. This meant a life of robbing banks, ripping off armored cars, and doing whatever it took to make sure he got paid. But then word got to him that his brother and sister-in-law had been killed, and that his niece had been orphaned. And in that moment, all of Manny's priorities changed.

El Toro Loco turned himself in on the front steps of Super Justice Force Headquarters. The special consideration given for his actions during The Attack, in conjunction with the testimony of Otto Rekker, who had been a former partner in crime, meant an incredible opportunity for Manny Ortiz. Rather than going back to prison for a third time, he was placed on probation and entered Second Chance. From that moment on, Manny's sole priority in life became the care and protection of Elladia.

Manny wasn't certain if Elladia was in love with Darius, but he would support her one hundred percent. Her life had been rough, and all he wanted for her was the best. He just didn't want his eighteen year-old niece getting pregnant or having her heart broken, or both. If either of those things happened, he might just kill someone.

The stack of paperwork piled high on Manny's desk threatened to take up hours of his shift. He couldn't concentrate on the task at hand, his mind wandering back to Elladia and Darius. He finally made a decision about how to deal with their budding romance, when the worst sound in the world brought him back to reality. Something had triggered a Red Alert.

Manny got up from behind his desk and raced outside the supervisor's office to the main room of O3C. Bodies hustled back and forth while voices shouted over communication units in a chaotic scramble of activity that only came during times of extreme emergency.

"Somebody talk to me," said Manny.

"There's a Red Alert down in Detention!"

"Did you just say there's a Red Alert in Detention?" Manny asked.

On the list of things Manny never expected to hear, a Red Alert in Detention placed somewhere at the very top. Red Alert meant an immediate and deadly threat. A plane had crashed into a football stadium. A dam had burst and flooded a city. Squid Vicious and his crew had hijacked a cruise ship full of diplomats from the United Nations and were executing passengers. These were the things that warranted a Red Alert. But Manny couldn't think of a thing that could possibly happen in Detention that would result in such a thing. Chances are it was all some sort of mistake. Still, Manny had to act as if there were a real emergency.

"What do we have on the monitors?" he asked.

"Monitors are offline."

"For how long?"

"It looks like they went offline thirteen minutes ago."

A lot could happen in thirteen minutes, and without any video surveillance, they were blind. Anything could be happening in Detention.

"Lock this whole place down. No one goes in or out until we know what's going on," Manny said. "Dispatch two security crews. Scramble the Fast Response Unit and have four of them meet me in Detention."

Manny raced to the elevator. In all the years he had worked for Super Justice Force, he could count on one hand the number of times there had been Red Alert related to something at HQ. And that included the time a few months back when Boom-Boom Kaboom tried to blow the place up.

By the time the elevator arrived at Detention, Manny had convinced himself that the Red Alert was a false alarm. Either it was a computer glitch caused by a reaction to the surveillance feeds going offline, or maybe someone overreacted to a rowdy punk being held in one of the cells spitting on the floor.

And because Manny had convinced himself no real threat existed, he was that much more stunned when the elevator doors opened. Whatever happened, it had been brutal. It looked like the handiwork of Otto Rekker and his crew, before Otto had reformed. Everything in the room had been broken and smashed, from the desk and chairs to the surveillance cameras to the two guards who had been on duty.

Manny rushed to the aid of Ron Yackley, who struggled to lift himself from a pool of his own blood.

"Don't move," said Manny. "Help is on the way."

"Len," gasped Yackley. "They killed Len."

Manny looked over at the body lying motionless on the floor. The pulverized face of Len Vittmier looked nothing like the blood-splattered image on his identification badge.

37

Darius checked the time on his Personal Communication Unit. He walked Elladia to the employee parking lot where the Rekkers waited to give her a ride home, and now he was late for his shift. Being late didn't have him concerned. Explaining his relationship with Elladia to her uncle is what had him troubled.

Elladia gave Darius a final goodnight kiss as they parted ways. It would have been a great moment, except that Otto and Anna Rekker were right there, and they saw the kiss. Anna gushed, and Darius was sure he saw tears of joy in her eyes—she couldn't be happier for them. Otto's feelings weren't as clear.

Otto had the face of a sinister super villain—even though he'd given up his life of crime. With the grim stare of a man who committed more than his share of mayhem, never backing down from a fight with the costumed do-gooders he'd slugged it out against, Otto watched Darius and Elladia kissing. His face showed nothing but a menacing intensity that intimidated the crap out of Darius.

Otto gave Darius a slight but knowing nod. Someone not paying close attention would have missed the nod completely, but Darius saw it. Otto's nod told him that the time had come to let Manny know about this developing romance. Otto wouldn't say a word to Manny, Darius knew this. But that didn't give Darius an excuse to put off what needed to be done.

At the end our shift, I'll tell Manny about me and Elladia. No need to ruin his whole shift, or mine.

All the different ways he could start the conversation with Manny ran through Darius's mind. He could come right out and lay it on the line—*Manny, Elladia and I, we've got something going.* Or maybe he could take a more indirect approach—*That birthday cake Elladia made sure was delicious. Hey, speaking of Elladia, I'm kind of her boyfriend. I hope you're cool with that.*

Darius entered HQ at the rear security entrance closest to the employee parking lot. He recognized one of the guards at the entrance, Coleman, an ex-cop and one of Maslon's Long Arm stooges. Darius flashed his identification badge and passed through the security scanner.

"Late for work?" Coleman asked.

It sounded like a sneer to Darius, and more important, like potential trouble. After a full year, Maslon still wanted him out of Second Chance, and would use whatever excuse he could to make life difficult. Darius could already see his showing up late making it into some report. Maslon would want to know why Darius was late, why he was coming in to HQ from the employee parking lot, and no matter what, it would be considered an escape attempt.

If HQ was on fire, and I left the building to avoid getting burned, Maslon would accuse me of trying to escape.

"Manny knows I'm running late," Darius said.

"I'm sure he does," said Coleman. "This is still going in my report."

Coleman didn't have to report Darius being late. It wasn't like being late breached security. But with nothing else to harass Darius with, Maslon and his cronies used whatever excuse they could get.

"Make sure you send copies to Manny, Dr. Sam and Trang Nguyen," Darius said. "Send me a copy too. I'll add it to my collection."

Darius didn't have a collection of reports filed against him; it was just the most smartass thing he could think to say without running the risk of really getting into trouble. Maslon's pathetic attempts to get him thrown out of Second Chance had been tiresome from the beginning. After a year, it had become a game that Darius still hated playing.

Halfway between the entrance and the nearest elevator an alarm sounded signaling a Red Alert. Less than a second later, Darius's Personal Communication Unit went off. He heard a commotion behind him at the entrance that let him know the guards had also been signaled.

"Darius, where are you?" asked a voice coming from his PCU. Darius immediately recognized the voice of Oegheneo-chuko, his Fast Response Unit partner.

"I'm at the rear employee entrance, AA6828," said Darius.

"We've been dispatched to Detention, double time."

"Copy that. I'll meet you there in three minutes."

As much as he hated running, Darius had no choice. The complicated elevator system at HQ made getting from one place to another fairly easy as long as speed wasn't required. The Red Alert made time crucial. He could get to where he needed to be faster by running.

Darius had taken the time to familiarize himself with every part of Super Justice Force Headquarters—every corridor, hallway and stairwell. He knew what doors led to where, which shortcuts to use when time was of the essence. He had Manny to thank for that.

"Always know where you are, and always know three ways to get to where you need to be—the easiest, the safest and the fastest," Manny had told him.

Darius took the fastest route possible to Detention. Walking would take five minutes. Running less than that. He didn't know what triggered the Red Alert, and it didn't matter. Whatever the emergency, it would be dealt with.

Darius ran as fast as he could down the service corridor that led to Detention. There were only two ways into Detention, either by way of the elevator, or by way of the service corridor. Up ahead, Darius could see a team of security guards gathered at the end of the long passageway where a door opened directly into Detention.

This can't be good, he thought. The guards were armed. Most security guards at HQ didn't carry weapons.

Two of the guards aimed their guns at Darius as he approached. Darius screeched to a halt, gasping to catch his breath, holding out his identification badge for the guards to see.

"He's good to go," said one of the guards, motioning Darius past.

Darius pushed his way past the guards gathered in the corridor outside Detention. They talked amongst themselves, while a second chorus of voices came from PCUs—an overwhelming noise of status reports, security checks and confused voices all wanting to know what the hell was going on. One voice drowned out the rest of the noise. Darius heard Manny barking orders from inside Detention before he could see him.

"Divert everyone from MAS and team them up with SAO. Tell CAD to scramble all SAO employees immediately—I want everyone here in under an hour. I want teams of five conducting full manual sweeps of every inch of every building in this facility. High-security areas get top priority," said Manny. "Someone get Chuck Maslon on the line. We need him here right now."

Darius squeezed passed the cluster of security guards. He couldn't believe his eyes. Someone or something had trashed detention. Medics from MTSU were working on one of the guards. A white sheet, slowly soaking up blood, covered another guard.

What happened here?

Manny caught sight of Darius standing in the doorway, but he didn't miss a beat. "Each team will be led by someone from the Fast Response Unit," said Manny. He pointed directly at Darius. "I want one FRU leading the search, and reporting back directly to their partner. Understand me—nothing goes through CAD. Everything goes through FRU. I don't care who you are, if you ain't a L4 Supervisor or Fast Response Unit, you ain't callin' the shots."

Darius looked around Detention. He still had no idea what happened or what was going on. He saw Oegheneo-chuko on the other side of the room talking to Amina, the other Operations Crew supervisor. Both Oeghe and Amina were talking into their PCUs while carrying on a conversation with each other.

"Does anyone have any questions?" Manny asked.

Darius knew better than to ask what was going on. He'd get caught up to speed soon enough.

"Search team assignments will be coming through to your PCUs any second now," Manny said. "As far as I'm concerned, this search started five minutes ago, which means I want these murdering pendejos caught four minutes ago."

38

The five buildings that made the World Headquarters of the Super Justice Force made it the largest manmade structure in the world. A complex system of corridors, hallways, tunnels and elevators that moved up, down, sideways and diagonally connected all five buildings in a way that made the entire New York City subway system look simple. Between the offices and the apartments, the museum and storage closets, the Kurtzberg Center for Metahuman Training and Research and all the other aspects of SJF that could be found in HQ, there were literally millions of places to hide.

Looking for a bio-morph only made things more complicated. A bio-morph could be anywhere, assuming the appearance of anyone or anything. And somewhere inside HQ there were two bio-morphs hiding.

Darius had never seen a bio-morph before—at least not that he was aware of. Part of him had trouble believing they even existed. Bio-morphs were the only extraterrestrials banned from the planet Earth, and not because they were practically impossible to keep track of. They were loyal to the Ad-Ahlen Empire. Bio-morphs were, in fact, genetically engineered Ad-Ahlen that carried out counter intelligence and suicide missions during the War of Tessaria, and had played a part in the Battle of Enceladus. Darius read all about both.

He didn't feel comfortable hunting for a pair of bio-morphs hiding somewhere in HQ. Darius felt even more uncomfortable leading the search team. Manny said all the search teams would be led by someone from the Fast Response Unit, which left Darius in charge of a team that included his FRU partner Oeghe handling all communications, Rodney Thaxton and Omar Manigo, two crew guys from MAS, and Coleman, Maslon's Long Arm crony from security.

Darius knew Thaxton and Manigo in passing. Rodney Thaxton was a Chancer, Omar Manigo wasn't, but he was EZ Manigo's cousin. Both worked on the Service side of MAS. Thaxton worked mostly as a Scrubber. Manigo spent most of his time working in Facility Services doing laundry. Both of them were out of their element looking for a bio-morph. And neither gave Darius a sense of security. Still, he preferred their company to that of Coleman.

Coleman wasn't happy with Darius leading the team. Darius didn't even have clearance to carry a weapon. Neither did Coleman, for that matter, even though he'd been given an UltraStun 500, which gave him the sense of being better suited to lead the search party.

Darius and his crew searched a large storage room in the corridor leading from Vehicle Maintenance Bay 1. Thaxton and Manigo carried a portable scanning unit that could, in theory, identify a bio-morph. The fact that no one on his team really knew how to use the unit did little for Darius's confidence.

Thaxton and Manigo fumbled with the security scanner, trying to get a reading on a bucket and mop. A shape-shifting bio-morph hiding in a storage closet disguised as a mop and bucket seemed ridiculous to Darius. But that didn't mean it wasn't possible. A bio-morph could take on the shape of anything that appeared to take up approximately the same mass of space as a human being—at least that was the theory. No one knew for sure. For all anyone knew, a bio-morph could shift into a mouse, although it would be a mouse with the molecular density of a man, making it the heaviest mouse on the planet. And even that was uncertain.

The fact remained that no one knew enough about bio-morphs to assume anything one way or the other. There weren't supposed to be bio-morphs on Earth, and there certainly weren't supposed to be any running loose in HQ.

"You guys sure you know how that thing works?" Darius asked.

"Not really," said Thaxton.

"Not really? Then what good are you?" asked Coleman.

"You wanna work it?" Darius asked.

Coleman glared at Darius without saying a word. The security guard didn't know how to work the scanner either. He didn't even have a high enough clearance to carry a gun. The only thing he had going for him was his unspoken allegiance to Maslon and the UltraStun 500 he clutched like a child holding on to its favorite toy.

"I want everything in this room scanned and cleared in less than ten minutes, including the cases of toilet paper," said Darius.

"Anything out of the ordinary?" asked Oegheneo-chuko over the PCU.

"Nothing. Did you run a cross check on what was stored in this room?" Darius asked.

"Everything you reported is supposed to be there. How many cases of toilet paper did you say there were?"

Darius looked around the storage room and counted the cases of toilet paper.

"Five."

"Then it is not pretending to be a case of toilet paper," said Oeghe. "Keep a sharp eye. All the surveillance monitors went offline in that sector, which means there is as good a chance as any that they are hiding near your location."

Darius stepped out of the cramped storage room and into the long corridor. He looked around, wondering if any of the other teams were having any luck. He stared at a door on the other side of the corridor, less than ten feet from the storage room.

Something's not right, he thought.

He walked down the corridor and stood in front of the other door.

"We'll be done here in a few minutes," said Darius. "We just need to scan a few more things. Where do you want us to go from here?"

"There are two teams searching the Maintenance Bay. Join up with them once you're done," said Oeghe.

"What's the point? There's nothing to find there. My guys don't even know how to work the scanning unit," said Darius. "These things could be anywhere—right in front of me even—and we wouldn't know it. You know what I mean?"

Oegheneo-chuko did not respond for a moment. Darius hoped his message had been clear enough.

"Yes, I know that they could be anywhere," Oeghe said. "They could be in the Vehicle Maintenance Bay, take your team there next."

"Great."

Darius walked back to the storage room. Thaxton and Manigo continued scanning everything in the room. They struggled with the portable unit while Coleman watched in amusement. Darius didn't have a problem with Thaxton or Manigo—they seemed nice enough. He hoped he could count on them if anything dangerous happened.

Thaxton will go down swinging in a fight. He's a Chancer. No matter what, he'll back me up, Darius thought. *Not so sure about Manigo.*

Darius's biggest concern wasn't how Thaxton or Manigo would handle themselves in a bad situation. He'd already started hatching a plan to keep them as safe as possible. It was Coleman who worried Darius. He didn't know if Coleman could keep his cool, and with an UltraStun 500, a bad situation could become worse.

"You guys done here?" Darius asked. "Let's move on."

Thaxton and Manigo looked up from the security scanner that wasn't working properly. They were confused. "We're still…"

Darius held his finger up to his lips, signaling Manigo to be quiet. "We need to move on—meet up with the other teams in VMB1."

"Okay," said Thaxton, still looking confused.

"You guys get down to VMB1," said Darius. "I'll secure this place."

Thaxton and Manigo gathered up the portable security scanner and headed out of the storage room. Coleman followed behind them, but Darius grabbed him by the shoulder before he could get out of the room.

"Walk out of here and go towards the Maintenance Bay," whispered Darius. "Wait sixty seconds after you leave this room, radio in that we found one of the bio-morphs, and then make sure you cover my ass."

"What? What are you talking about" asked Coleman.

"Just do what I say," Darius said, shoving Coleman out the door.

Darius began a mental countdown. He had sixty seconds to act. He grabbed the mop in the bucket and snapped off the head, his anger rising. Forty-five seconds. The mop handle with the head broken off looked like a spear. It was the only weapon he could think of. Thirty seconds. *The bio-morphs killed Len Vittmier,* he thought. *Someone has to tell his kids that their dad is dead.*

Darius walked out into the corridor, holding the broken mop handle close to his side. Twenty seconds. The others were much farther down the corridor, well past the other door. He couldn't see what Coleman was doing. *Is he on his PCU? Please let him be doing what I told him to do.*

Darius stopped in front of the other door down the corridor from the storage room. Ten seconds. He thought for a moment about Len Vittmier. Len had been a Chancer. Darius only knew him passing, but Len had stopped by his birthday party.

Len was a Chancer. A Chancer with kids. The bio-morphs killed a Chancer with kids. Chancers look out for each other.

"I didn't know Len Vittmier that well," Darius said to no one in particular, his rage reaching a critical mass. "But I know he had kids. And now his kids don't have a father."

Coleman turned around. He couldn't figure out who Darius was talking to. "What did you just say?" he asked.

"This is for Len Vittmier and his kids," said Darius.

Darius jammed the broken end of the mop handle into the door.

The door screamed in pain, and in the blink of an eye it wasn't a door anymore. It became a man—or at least it looked like a man—with a broken off mop handle stuck in its shoulder. And it was pissed off.

39

Even before coming to work for Super Justice Force, Darius saw some incredible things. Living side by side with unregistered metahumans in the abandoned subway system introduced him to some of the stranger things in life. A kid with giant wings growing out his back, an old woman who could control light and a guy with four arms were among the more "normal" things he had seen. But nothing Darius saw before or after coming to Super Justice Force HQ compared to an enraged bio-morph with a broken mop handle jammed into its shoulder.

The bio-morph pulled the broken handle from its shoulder, roaring in fury and pain as a thick gray substance sprayed from the wound. The alien swung the mop handle wildly at Darius.

Darius ducked a blow that would have caved in his skull had it connected. His pumping adrenaline kept his fear in check. He tackled the bio-morph, and together they fell to the floor. Darius tried to hold on to the creature, but it kept changing shapes, making it impossible. He tried to punch it in the face, only to pull back as the head morphed into that of an alligator and snapped at him. Darius managed to get the alligator mouth in an arm lock, pounding it in the head with his free fist.

Rodney Thaxton joined the fight first. The bio-morph transformed one of its arms into a huge snake and wrapped it around Darius's neck. Thaxton struggled to break the snake's hold on Darius.

Coleman watched in terror unable to move. Omar Manigo rushed past him, grabbed up the broken mop handle and speared the bio-morph with it.

The shape-shifting alien let out another roar of rage and pain. It threw Darius and Thaxton to the side, slamming them against the wall of the corridor. It grabbed the mop handle and used it against Manigo.

Omar Manigo let out a gasp as the mop handle jammed into his stomach and came out his back. The bio-morph lifted Manigo off the floor like he was a toy, flinging him down the corridor.

Darius knew fighting the bio-morph was a losing proposition. It was too strong and too unpredictable.

"Coleman! Use the stun gun!" Darius shouted.

Coleman pointed the UltraStun 500. His hands shook violently as he aimed the weapon at the bio-morph.

Darius could swear he heard the alien laugh.

"Kill you all," growled the bio-morph. It loomed in the corridor, taking the shape of some extraterrestrial beast that looked like a cross between a grizzly bear and a tarantula.

"I don't think so, puta," said Manny, grabbing the creature's head from behind.

Manny seemed to appear out of nowhere, moving faster than Darius could have ever imagined. Manny slammed the creature's head into the wall with so much force it sounded like a cannon ball slamming into concrete.

The bio-morph's lifeless body slumped to the floor as is shifted back to its original form. It looked like a human, only with less developed features and with an entire side of its head caved in. Manny stood over the bio-morph. Gray liquid oozed out of the smashed head of the alien.

"That's one down," said Manny. "Let's hope we catch the next one alive. We got some questions that need answerin.'"

40

Chuck Maslon yelled at Darius, which was nothing new. He always yelled, or threatened, or sneered with contempt. This time he screamed something about Darius "not following proper protocols" and "endangering the lives of his team."

Darius did his best to ignore Maslon. His head pounded, and the last thing Darius needed to hear was a list of everything he'd done wrong, prattled off by someone who hated him.

Maslon showed up at HQ less than an hour after the Red Alert had been signaled. Still dressed in his pajamas, while wearing his shoulder holster, he looked like a bad joke. And to hear Maslon, everything done since the Red Alert started had been done wrong.

Maslon took out his anger, first on Darius, and then on Manny, whom he held responsible for the "ineptly handled breach of security."

"You're not the head of security, I am," barked Maslon. "You had no right to do what you did."

"Manny is a ranking supervisor on duty, he did everything the way it should have been done," said Captain Freedom.

"We've got one security guard critically injured, a dead bio-morph and another on the loose somewhere," said Maslon.

"Then what're we doin' wastin' time here?" asked Manny.

Darius looked around the Medical Trauma and Surgery Unit. He'd only seen it this busy when Kid Spectacular had been brought in. Now the doctors hurried as they tried to save Omar Manigo's life.

Manny, Thaxton and Darius had carried the badly injured Manigo to MTSU, leaving Coleman behind to watch over the body of the dead bio-morph. Manigo remained conscious the whole time, saying over and over again that he didn't want to die.

"You ain't gonna die, amigo," Manny assured Omar.

Darius didn't have the same level of confidence as Manny. Omar looked terrible, a broken mop handle skewered through his body, blood pouring out of his mouth, snot coming out of his nose. And who knew what sort of nastiness was in the bio-morph's blood, which had been all over the mop handle that went through Manigo's body? Darius thought they should wait for a medical team from MTSU to come get Manigo, but Manny said otherwise. "It'll take too long," he said.

Captain Freedom met Darius, Manny and Thaxton at MTSU as the team of doctors whisked Omar Manigo off to surgery. Maslon stormed in a few moments later, exploding into a rage the moment he spotted Darius.

He's more pissed that I'm here than he is about the bio-morphs, Omar being hurt, or Len getting killed, Darius thought.

"Chuck, I need you to calm down. Manny did the right thing," said Captain Freedom. "You need to concentrate on making sure these search efforts are being properly coordinated."

"It's going to take days to search this entire facility," said Maslon.

"We don't have days," said Manny.

"Tell me something I don't know," Maslon said. "We don't have a choice. We don't have the manpower. Hell, searching the Tower alone will take forever."

"We don't need to search the Tower, or the Mansion for that matter," said Manny. "The bio-morph ain't there."

"And you know this how?" asked Maslon.

The tone is Maslon's voice made Darius want to puke. The throbbing pain in his head didn't help the situation. He needed to sit down, just for a moment. Darius wandered over to a wheelchair a few feet away and sat.

"Because we're under attack. Two bio-morphs went out of their way to get into HQ, and they did it for a reason," Manny said. "What're they gonna do, steal stuff from the gift shop or ransack the corporate offices? They came here for a specific reason. We figure that out, and we've got a good chance of catching the other one."

"How do we figure out why they broke in here?" asked Captain Freedom.

"Just before our friends escaped Detention, surveillance monitors all over HQ started goin' offline," said Manny. "Something like that ain't unheard of—three years ago we had a massive system failure and we went blind on over half the monitors. The reason I dispatched so many teams to VMB1 was because we'd gone blind in all the units that track the area, and that can't be random."

"You played a hunch and you got lucky," said Maslon.

Manny started to respond, but Captain Freedom stopped him. Manny and Maslon could argue for hours, every second of which would be a pointless waste of time. Too much time had already been wasted. Each minute the remaining bio-morph roamed free meant another minute it came closer to achieving its goal.

In all the years Captain Freedom had led Super Justice Force, Headquarters had never been compromised like this. There would have to be a full investigation as to how it happened and what went wrong. But for the moment, finding the bio-morph was all that mattered.

Darius could see Captain Freedom weighing his options, trying to come up with a plan of action. Captain Freedom's eyes looked tired. He seemed different—uncertain of himself. Darius wondered if the Captain had just woken up, had not been sleeping, or if he had been drinking. It bothered him to think of his childhood hero as a drunk. But ever since that night in his apartment, when Darius thought he smelled booze on Captain Freedom, the possibility that Jake Kirby Jr. was an alcoholic plagued him. And then there were the rumors—bits of gossip Darius tried to ignore.

Being a superhero can't be easy, Darius thought. *Maybe he needs to take the edge off every now and then.*

Captain Freedom looked over at Darius, who sat in the wheelchair fighting the intense pain in his head. "What do you think?" asked Captain Freedom.

"Why are you asking him?" demanded Maslon.

"Because he's right here," Captain Freedom said. "And because he was the one who found the other bio-morph."

"He got lucky, just like his friend here," said Maslon, pointing at Manny.

"It wasn't luck," Darius said. His voice came out like a low growl. He didn't mean for it to sound that way, but the pain was killing him.

"I found the bio-morph because I was looking for something that didn't belong. I've been down that corridor hundreds of times—maybe thousands. I know it like the back of my hand. When I saw that door, I knew it didn't belong."

"You expect me to believe that you knew a bio-morph could turn into a door? I didn't know that, and I've seen bio-morphs," Maslon said. "You've never even seen one!"

"Chuck, we don't have time for this," said Captain Freedom. The confident tone returned to his voice. He sounded like a superhero—like the leader of Super Justice Force. It gave Darius his own sense of confidence, although it did nothing to ease the pain in his head.

"Here's what we are going to do," said Captain Freedom. "We will continue to search HQ, but I want a full analysis of all blind spots caused by the surveillance monitors going down. Run cross references to find out what areas with Level 3 security ratings and higher were affected. That includes everything leading to and from L3 areas. We'll concentrate efforts in those spots. Have CAD get someone from the Galaxus Alliance Corps on the line—someone who's dealt with bio-morphs. I want them here as soon as possible, which means right now."

Captain Freedom laid out the rest of the action plan, which included Manny and Darius rejoining the search efforts, and Maslon working out of O3C, where everything was being coordinated. Captain Freedom's plans didn't sit well with

Maslon. Darius could tell this much because reading Maslon was easy. He cursed the head of security under his breath as Maslon followed Captain Freedom out of MTSU, complaining all the way.

"You okay, amigo?" Manny asked.

Manny stared down at Darius, still sitting in the wheelchair. The lines around Manny's eyes looked more pronounced. He looked as if he had aged ten years in the last few hours.

Darius nodded. "My head is killing me."

"You want to stay behind?"

"No," said Darius, getting up from the wheelchair. "I'm feeling better already."

Darius and Manny left the Medical Trauma and Surgery Unit. They both checked in on their PCUs, Darius with Oeghe, and Manny with Amina. Oeghe told Darius that they had been ordered to work with the teams searching the Tower.

There won't be any action in the Tower, Darius thought. *I bet that order came from Maslon.*

Both Darius and Manny moved slowly through the corridor leading from MTSU into the other parts of Headquarters. They looked like battle-weary soldiers returning to war.

"You know you screwed up, right?" Manny asked.

"I know. I should've radioed in the moment I suspected it was one of the bio-morphs," said Darius. "I'm sorry."

"I'm not. They killed Len Vittmier. Len was good people."

"We could've captured it. Found out what it was doing here."

"They killed Len Vittmier."

"If we capture the other one, we can question it," said Darius.

"That's one option," said Manny.

They walked in silence for a few moments, each lost in their own thoughts. Manny didn't seem to be bothered by the fact that he had killed the bio-morph. There would be some sort of investigation, of that Darius had no doubts.

"I tried to kill it. You know that, right? When I jammed it with the broken mop handle, I wasn't trying to stop it or capture it. I wanted the damn thing dead," Darius said.

Manny said nothing, just nodded his head.

"I've been in a lot of fights before," said Darius. "But I never wanted to kill someone. And it was a someone, wasn't it?"

"Yeah, it was a someone, amigo. And it killed Len Vittmier," said Manny.

"Did you want to kill it?" asked Darius.

Manny stopped in his tracks. He looked at Darius, a grim hardness etched in his face. Darius often wondered what Manny had been like back in his El Toro Loco days. Darius imagined a younger Manny, tough as hell, with a cold stare and not a care for anything in the world. And as hard and as tough as El Toro Loco looked in the imagination of Darius Logan, it didn't even come close to how Manny Ortiz looked in that moment.

"No, amigo, I didn't want to kill it. Not really," said Manny.

"Then why did you?"

"It was gonna kill all of you, amigo. It's gonna be bad enough tellin' Len Vittmier's family that he's dead. Only thing I could think about was explaining to Elladia how I let her boyfriend get killed. That wasn't a conversation I was willing to have."

41

Darius slept for two restless hours and was awake for twenty minutes when the alarm on his PCU signaled he had a message. He didn't have to look to know it had something to do with the events that took place hours earlier. A video message from Manny simply said, "Emergency meeting today in the Situation Room. Noon. Be there."

It had taken three more hours to find the other bio-morph, and neither Darius nor Manny was there to see it happen. Details were sketchy at best and only two things were certain. First, Nightwatcher and Lady Themis captured the other bio-morph. Second, the bio-morph apparently had been caught exactly where Manny said it would be, at one of the blind spots caused by the surveillance monitors going offline.

Darius crawled out of bed, took a shower and got dressed. He went to MTSU to check on Omar Manigo's status, but opted out of visiting him—the memory of Kid Spectacular was still too fresh. After MTSU, Darius went to get something to eat before heading to the Situation Room, passing the security teams actively patrolling every corridor of Headquarters.

The Situation Room looked like a smaller version of Operations Crew Command Central—a leaner, meaner version of O3C. Designed for the most essential operations during emergencies, the Situation Room could comfortably seat up to three hundred people. Darius looked for an empty seat, but couldn't find one.

Standing near the back of the Situation Room, Darius looked around at the most remarkable gathering of individuals he'd ever seen. By his count, every member of Super Justice Force was present, including auxiliary and reserve members, and Teen Justice Force. He counted six members of the Galaxus Alliance Corps, including Z-Boe, who wasn't due back on Earth for another two weeks. He saw members of the European Alliance, the leader of Israel's Children of Abraham, and Steel Monkey from China's People's Guardians. And then there were the others—two dozen or so costumed heroes from all over the world that he didn't recognize.

The brightly colored costumes of superheroes and crime fighters from six continents were not the only uniforms in the room. On the opposite side of the crowded room, a small group of military officers stood talking to Otto. Darius couldn't hear the conversation from that distance, but he could tell they were talking about Otto's bionic arm. Otto had designed the arm himself—he was considered one the world's leading biomechatronic engineers—and Darius knew that he'd been offered jobs by the military and private technology firms.

A conference table had been set up in front of the wall of video monitors that lined one side of the Situation Room. Captain Freedom sat at the table, along with Chuck Maslon, Manny, a member of the Galaxus Alliance Corps that Darius didn't know, and four others—three men and a woman. Darius didn't recognize the men, but he could tell they were high-ranking military. The woman needed no introduction—Elizabeth Banks, President of the United States.

The dull roar of dozens of conversations filled the room. Darius lingered in the back, listening to everything being said, and hearing nothing. He picked up bits and pieces of the conversations closest to him, but nothing complete. Just fragments of ideas, parts of questions, moments of declaration, moving from one person to the next, sweeping through the room like weather systems from all over the globe.

It should have been the most exciting time in Darius's life, standing in a room with the most powerful beings on the planet. But he couldn't help but feel he didn't belong. He had no power, be it the enhanced ability that came from being born with Kurtzberg-24 Syndrome, the mutated effects of being metahuman, the artificial enhancements of taking Adrenaccelerate, or that of an elected official. Darius commanded no armies, and had no bionic body parts. In a room with this much power, Darius Logan knew that no one was weaker than him.

Captain Freedom stood up from the table to address the room. It took a moment for the dull roar to fade to a faint whisper and then to the silence of undivided attention. "I want to thank you all for making it here on such short notice," he said. "This meeting, of course, is above top secret. Everything said in this room is not to be repeated. We've managed to keep this out of the media, and a leak would all but ensure a global panic."

Darius felt a nervous energy that quickly spread through the room.

"Approximately fourteen hours ago, two individuals were apprehended by Super Justice Force member Slambang and brought here to Headquarters. They were placed in the holding facility we call Detention, until such time that the police could take custody of them," said Captain Freedom. "This is a common practice at SJF, and there was no reason to suspect that these individuals were anything other than the muggers they initially appeared to be. These individuals were, however, not what they appeared to be. They were, in fact, bio-morphs."

The entire room exploded in words. Thousands of words, maybe millions, strung together and flowing like tidal waves forming the panicked thoughts of everyone in the room. And the strings of words, each one ending with either a question mark or an exclamation point, were hurled to the front of the room.

It took more than a full minute for Captain Freedom to calm the crowd. He assured everyone that there would be time for questions. Darius doubted it. *There might be time for questions, but there's no answers,* he thought.

"The bio-morphs were being held in Detention, which they managed to escape from, killing a member of the SJF security crew," said Captain Freedom. "We still don't know for sure how they escaped. One of the bio-morphs was killed in a confrontation with one of our Operations Crew supervisors and another employee."

Several heads turned to Darius. A few nodded at him, acknowledging that he had played a pivotal role in taking down one of the aliens.

"A short time later, the other bio-morph was captured. It is being interrogated, as we speak, by members of the Galaxus Alliance Corps," Captain Freedom said. "The second bio-morph was apprehended near a high security area known as the Cage."

Darius felt like someone punched him in the stomach. A feeling he seldom felt gripped every fiber of his being. He'd known the other bio-morph had been captured, but he didn't know where. The fact that it had been caught near the Cage could only mean that it was trying to get to the ACU-64 Killbots. And that scared the hell out of him.

"The Cage is a state-of-the-art containment facility located five stories underground. We employ a Class One containment field designed by Tess-Tech, which as many of you know is based upon Tessarian technology. I'm sure most of you have seen their ads—'With Tess-Tech, nothing goes in and nothing comes out, unless you want it to.' In fact, most of you are probably using Tess-Tech containment fields at your various bases of operation," said Captain Freedom.

"In addition to the standard containment barriers using a Tessarian configuration, we use a cold fusion techno-plasm-infused reinforcement layer, which provides an extra level of security. As most of you know, cold fusion techno-plasm reinforcement is also used at all Galaxus Alliance Corps operations facilities and the Enceladus Colony. Literally, there is no place on the planet Earth more secure than the Cage."

Captain Freedom paused for a moment. Darius picked up on the hesitation. He knew what was next. He knew that the next words out of Captain Freedom's mouth could change the course of human history.

"Although the interrogation of the bio-morph is on-going, we must assume that the mission was to gain access to what is being held in the Cage," said Captain Freedom. "This means that for reasons we don't yet know, the bio-morph was trying to gain access to the decommissioned Automatic Combat Units, Model 64, that are currently contained in the Cage."

A murmur of whispers passed through the room. Darius felt the knot in his stomach grow.

Then the Situation Room exploded with the sound of voices, all talking at the same time, shouting accusations, asking questions, and expressing fears.

Darius stood quietly processing everything as the chaos raged around him. Many of the same questions being shouted out also ran through his brain. Was this the work of the Ad-Ahlen? Did Earth need to be preparing for a war no one thought they could win? How were two bio-morphs able to get loose in HQ in the first place?

Darius couldn't answer the first two questions. The third question, however, had an answer. He knew it did. He just had to figure it out.

Reviewing the facts, Darius tried to figure out what had happened. Slambang apprehended two muggers. Rather than waiting for the police to come pick them up, Slambang had been instructed to bring the muggers back to HQ, where they would be held in detention. Shortly after the muggers were dropped off, surveillance monitors throughout HQ went offline. During this time, the muggers escaped from Detention, killing a guard.

None of this makes sense, Darius thought. *There's no way two muggers who just happen to be bio-morphs get caught by Slambang and are brought to Detention. There's no way they manage to escape from Detention just as surveillance monitors all over HQ decide to take a dump and go blind. There's just no way any of this can happen.*

And in that moment, Darius realized that none of it had *just* happened. None of it had been a coincidence. It had all been planned. Somehow the muggers had been a plant—they were meant to be caught by Slambang and brought to detention.

It all made sense. Getting into HQ without going through security was impossible. And even if you got in, without the proper security clearance, there were only a handful of places you could go. You would be locked outside of the most secure areas within HQ. But Detention was located inside one of the most secure areas. You wouldn't even need the proper security clearance to get into that part of Headquarters, as long you had been picked up for mugging and brought to Detention to wait for the cops to take you away.

Darius scanned the Situation Room, looking for someone, though he wasn't sure who. There were no real discussions taking place. No civil discourse or even polite conversations. Instead there were arguments, accusations, and unwavering demands. The people gathered in the Situation Room at Super Justice Force HQ represented some of the most powerful people on the planet, both physically and politically—a global force to be reckoned with. Yet they were screaming at each other, arguing like children, and refusing to communicate in a manner befitting adults. *And at least one of them helped planned everything that happened.*

In order for the two bio-morphs to get brought back to HQ and held in Detention, someone had to make the call—someone in CAD, Darius thought. *And someone had to make sure that the monitors went offline—someone in SAO.*

Darius needed to tell someone about his theory. It needed to be someone he trusted. Someone who would take him seriously and not think he was being paranoid.

Manny was locked in a heated argument with Chuck Maslon.

Don't even want to get within spitting distance of Maslon.

On the opposite end of the Situation Room, Darius could see Z-Boe and the rest of the Galaxus Alliance Corps. They were talking to several of the military men.

Darius didn't think twice about interrupting the conversation, pushing his way through the crowd. He had to get to Zander, pull him off to the side, and explain everything to him.

Z-Boe will listen. He won't think I'm being paranoid.

Darius came up from behind Zander, placing a hand on his shoulder. He had almost gotten used to the odd surge of energy that pulsed through his body. The first one or two times it had surprised him, but Darius had gotten to the point where it was expected. He just assumed it was always like that, some sort of side effect of being exposed to the cosmic power bands that endowed all the Galaxus with their special abilities.

"I need to talk to you," Darius said.

Z-Boe turned around to face Darius. "What's up, dude?" Zander asked.

The words didn't sound right to Darius. They came out of Zander's mouth like he was talking in slow motion with the volume turned all the way down.

Darius felt weird. He felt dizzy, his heart pounding, his brain feeling like it was shutting down. He couldn't concentrate on anything, as if his mind had lost the ability to focus. He wanted to say something, to tell Zander that he suddenly felt ill, but he no longer knew how to form words. One of the other Galaxus placed his hand on Darius's shoulder, but Darius wasn't sure if it was really his shoulder or not. He felt a surge of energy pulse through his body, but it was not the same as the times with Z-Boe. But who was Z-Boe? Who was Darius?

"Aaaaaaarrrrrreeeeeeeyyyyyyoooouuuuooookkkaaaaayyyyyyyy?" asked the other Galaxus.

Somewhere, in the back of Darius's mind, he had a distant memory of being surrounded at a playground by a group of bullies. They had formed a circle around him, taunting him, pushing him around, grabbing at him. The same thing was happening to him now, only it wasn't happening to his body, it was happening to his mind. No, not his mind, Darius realized, it was happening to his very being. Whatever made Darius who he was—his soul, his spirit, his essence—was being pushed around. Bullied. Something was shoving him out of his own body.

"Wwwwwhhaaaaatttsssswwwrrrrroooonnnggggg?" asked Zander.

Darius couldn't understand what the words meant. They were sounds that somehow he sensed were addressed to him, but at that moment he wasn't quite sure of who he was.

Darius screamed. At least he thought he screamed. But even that wasn't clear, because he had lost the ability to understand everything. And then, everything went black.

42

When Darius Logan woke up, he had no clue where he was. He did, however, know who he was, and that was an improvement. His last memory, if it could be called that, had been a sense of complete loss. He had lost everything, the ability to process all conscious thought, including his own identity. And he remembered every moment of it, as if it were a bad dream. But somehow he knew it hadn't been a dream.

He looked around, realizing he lay in some sort of room.

A hospital room? MTSU?

Darius tried to move, and felt the sharp pain of an IV needle stuck in his arm.

How long have I been out?

"Oh god, you're awake."

He knew the voice. Elladia sat in the corner of the room, curled up in a chair, a blanket wrapped around her. She moved from her position, rushing to Darius's side. She stared down at him, reaching out to gently stroke his face—checking to make sure it was all real. "Thank you for coming back," she said.

Before Darius could utter a sound, Elladia rushed to the door and opened it. "He's awake!" she called out into the hall before rushing back to his side.

Darius's mouth felt dry—his throat parched. "What happened?" he asked, his voice raspy and cracked.

Elladia shushed him, "Don't try to talk."

A doctor and a nurse came into the room. Darius recognized the nurse. She'd been there when he had undergone all of his physicals and medical tests over a year ago. He didn't recognize the doctor, who politely pushed past Elladia, and flashed a light in Darius's eyes.

"How do you feel?" asked the doctor.

"Thirsty," said Darius.

"We'll get you something to drink in just a moment. Do you know where you are?"

"MTSU," Darius said, even though he wasn't sure.

"Do you know *who* you are?"

What kind of stupid question is that? Darius thought. *Of course I know who I am.*

"Darius Raymond Logan," he said. "I just turned eighteen. I'm L2, assigned to the SAO service team."

Darius looked over at Elladia, and weakly raised his hand to point at her. "And that's Elladia Ortiz," he said. He wanted to add, "She's my girlfriend," but he didn't.

He wasn't sure why wanted to say it, it just felt right. Something had happened to him. Something bad. And when Darius had woken up, Elladia was there. The way he figured, that made Elladia his girlfriend.

Within moments, Manny and Zander were in the room.

"How you doin', bro?" asked Zander.

"Gracias a Dios que están vivos," said Manny.

"We can't have this many people in the room," said the doctor, and then he sent the nurse out to get Darius some water.

Manny and Z-Boe simply ignored the doctor. They were in the room. They weren't leaving. Elladia hung out in the corner, trying to keep from being noticed. She wasn't going to leave either.

Darius still felt groggy and a bit disoriented. Part of him felt like he'd just woken from a bad dream. At the same time, he felt so exhausted it was almost as if he hadn't slept in days.

"What happened?" Darius asked.

"You blacked out, only not really," said Z-Boe.

"When you were brought in here, you were in a highly agitated stated, completely incoherent," said the doctor. "Do you remember anything?"

"We were in the Situation Room, and I had a strange feeling, at least I think I had a strange feeling. I'm not sure," said Darius.

"Can you describe the feeling?" asked the doctor.

"It was like—I don't know. Like I had forgotten how to be me. It felt like I was losing myself. I know it sounds crazy."

The nurse returned to the room with some water. Darius took a small sip, enough to get rid of the dry wasteland that his mouth had turned into. He took a second sip to irrigate his throat.

"How long have I been out?" Darius asked.

"Technically, you never were out," said the doctor. "Your heart rate, respiration and brain wave patterns, none of them were consistent with someone who is either asleep or unconscious. I've never really seen anything quite like it—and I've seen a lot. You've been in a state that can only be defined as conscious for nearly thirty-six hours…"

"But you weren't here with us," finished Elladia. She had moved next to the bed, gently taking Darius's hand in hers.

"We're just glad you're back," said Manny.

It took some doing, but the doctor managed to push the visitors out of the room. They all promised to be back soon, as the doctor wanted to hold Darius for observation.

"I'm feeling pretty good," Darius told the doctor after the room had cleared. Honestly, he felt bad. He just didn't want to stay in the hospital bed.

There wasn't much discussion about the matter. The doctor wanted to keep Darius for another twenty-four hours and run some more tests. In his professional career, he had seen everything from radiation poisoning to alien parasites to possession by demons of the dark dimension. He once had to perform emergency surgery on Nightwatcher, when Microbe Jones had flown up his nose and got stuck in his sinus cavity. But he'd never seen anything like what had happened to Darius.

Over the next few hours, the doctor ran a series of tests. First, he wanted to make sure Darius hadn't been exposed to some alien virus during the confrontation with the bio-morph. When the tests showed no signs of alien virus or infection, they thought of more tests to run, asked more questions, and continued to poke and prod.

During this time, Darius received a small army of visitors. Dr. Sam looked less like an old drill sergeant, and more like a concerned old man. He didn't say much, but Darius got the sense that Dr. Sam was extremely worried about him. Maybe he felt somehow responsible for having recruiting Darius into Second Chance, or maybe he knew something Darius didn't know. Whatever it was, Darius sensed that something had changed with Dr. Sam.

He regrets bringing me into Second Chance, Darius thought.

The conversation consisted of nothing more than idle chitchat, which struck Darius as odd, especially considering the meeting in the Situation Room that had just taken place. Darius didn't know how to broach the subject, so he steered clear. But that didn't change the fact that Dr. Sam seemed distant.

"I'm really feeling better, Doc," Darius said. "I just want to get out of here and get back to work."

"Maybe this was all a mistake, Darius," said Dr. Sam. "This life, the things you see and the things you're exposed to, maybe it's no place for a young man. Maybe I did you more harm than good by bringing you here."

"If you hadn't brought me here, I'd just now be starting the second year of a fifteen-year bid," said Darius. "You saved my life."

Dr. Sam nodded his head, but it seemed like he was convincing himself more than agreeing with Darius.

After Dr. Sam left, Otto Rekker came by. He brought two hand-drawn "get well" cards from the twins, and a batch of homemade cookies from Anna.

"How you feeling, Big D?" Otto asked. "Anna and the kids, they're worried sick about you."

"I'm good. I just want to get out of here," Darius said. He'd said the same thing to every visitor who came by.

Elladia returned a little after five. She could only stay for few minutes. A few minutes were better than no minutes.

She hovered over his bed, looking down on him with a concerned look that reminded him of the way his mother looked at him when he felt sick. It was a look that as a child brought Darius comfort when he didn't feel well. As a young man, and coming from Elladia, it brought a different feeling.

For too long, Darius had stared at Elladia from a distance, afraid to say anything to her. And even when she finally came close enough to hear him, and he could say something—anything—he still said almost nothing.

The problem wasn't that Darius didn't have anything to say. He had plenty to say. He just didn't know how to say it. He was eighteen, and had never had a girlfriend before. Never been on a date before. He had no sense of romance or relationships, other than the distant memories of how his parents treated each other. Sure, he had desires, but those desires—like nearly everything else—had taken a backseat to survival.

Maybe I should've taken the time to read some romance comics, Darius thought, Elladia standing over him. *If I had only picked up a few issues of "Burning Love", or "Lost in Love," or "Tales of True Love," then maybe I'd know what to say.*

Elladia told him about her day, as she did whenever they spent time together. She always did most of the talking, and never demanded he say anything in return. Darius realized, as he lay in the hospital bed, that whatever he had with Elladia was because she had made all the first moves. Suddenly, he felt very selfish for doing little to let her know how much he cared. And not knowing what to say or how to say it was no longer an excuse.

"Will you be my girlfriend?" Darius blurted out.

Elladia had been mid-sentence, talking about how one of her co-workers had dropped a case of Black Fist and White Dynamo salt and pepper shakers, breaking all of them. "What?" she asked, stunned and confused.

Try as he might, Darius could not think of anything romantic or poetic. "Will you be my girlfriend?"

Darius had no possible way of knowing what Elladia thought at that moment. He had seen her happy—or at least pretending to be happy—and he had seen her sad, but he had never seen this look before. He worried that maybe he'd made a mistake. And then Elladia began to smile, and though Darius had seen her smile a million times, both when he was spying on her from the safety of the library and then when they began spending time together, he had never seen her smile like this.

"Of course," Elladia said.

She could have said more, but she didn't need to.

43

Elladia left Darius alone in his room at MTSU. She kissed him on the forehead before she left, promising to be back tomorrow. She hadn't been gone long, when Darius fell asleep. The nightmare started soon after.

The nightmare had been with him since his parents had been killed, and as he dreamed it countless times before, Darius saw everything as if he were watching a movie. An army of ACU-64s always chased after him while the world around crumbled and burst into flames. In the nightmare, Darius was always nine—the age he was at the time of The Attack. But as this nightmare played out like so many others, something new happened. The child that had been Darius Logan ran into a man who was much older. He looked a bit like Dwayne Logan, Darius's father. Only it wasn't Darius's father.

The man blocked young Darius's path of escape from the ACU-64 Killbots, the deadly automatons closing in fast. The machines left in their wake a path of destruction the likes of which young Darius had never seen.

"Please, I need to get past, or the robots will get me," said the young boy.

"These things can't hurt you," said the man. Something seemed oddly familiar about him.

"You don't understand," said young Darius. He glanced back over his shoulder at the ACU-64s closing in. "Those robots are going to kill me."

"I do understand," said the man. "But what you need to understand is that you are already dead. And you have been for a long time. It's time to stop running."

"Please! I need to get away," begged young Darius.

"I wish I could have come sooner, and brought you the peace you deserved," said the man. "I'm sorry it took me so long to get here."

Young Darius felt confused. The sounds of destruction from the ACU-64s were overwhelming. He could hear the screams of dying people. He could feel the heat from the flames devouring the world. He sensed that his death was imminent.

"Who are you?" asked young Darius.

The man reached down and placed his hand inside young Darius's chest. Surprisingly, it didn't hurt. The man began to pull something out of young Darius, a shimmering mass that glowed a million colors, and the boy realized that his very life was being pulled from him. He felt terrified even though it didn't hurt. And then the man said something that brought an odd sense of comfort to young Darius, as the last bit of his life was pulled from his body.

"I'm you, and I've come to bring you peace," said the man.

Darius woke with a start. He'd been having the same nightmare for close to a decade. Impossible to ignore, it took little effort to figure out where it came from and what it meant. To that end, Darius gave little thought to his nightmare, except for the moments before he went to sleep, when he dreaded visiting the dark fears of his subconscious, and the moment he woke up, glad to be done with it. This nightmare, however, was different, which meant that it couldn't be ignored the same way he had learned to ignore the others.

A knock on the door of his room thankfully pulled Darius away from the thoughts of the moment.

"Come in," said Darius.

Manny entered the room, dressed in his work uniform. He pulled up a chair and sat beside Darius.

"How you feelin'?" asked Manny.

"I just wanna get out of here. Get back to work."

"That might take a while. Chuck Maslon wants an investigation. He thinks you might be on drugs."

"You're kidding me."

"I wish I was kiddin' you," said Manny.

"What about my drug tests? I've been pissing into a cup every week for over a year."

"I know. Believe me, I know. We'll get you through this."

"I'm not on drugs," said Darius. "I don't know what's happened to me. All I know is that I want to get back to work."

"Let's just make sure you're fine," said Manny.

"I'm not the one to be worried about. I'm not the threat."

"What's that mean?" asked Manny.

"Back in the Situation Room, before this happened—whatever this is—I had an idea," said Darius. "I needed to tell someone I could trust. You were with Maslon, so I tried to tell Zander."

"Maslon ain't here now," said Manny.

"There's no way bio-morphs could just get into Detention. There aren't even supposed to be bio-morphs on Earth," said Darius.

"I know. We're still investigatin' what happened."

"It was an inside job," said Darius. "Think about it. Slambang catches two muggers, who happen to be bio-morphs, and CAD tells him to bring them back here. Whoever issued that order from CAD is in on it. And I hate to say it, but Slambang might even be in on it. And whoever disabled the surveillance monitors—someone in SAO—they were in on it too. The way I see it, there are at least two people working in Operations Crew that had to be working with the bio-morphs. Maybe even more."

Manny nodded his head, letting everything Darius said sink in.

"You been talkin' to Nightwatcher, amigo?" asked Manny.

"No. Why?"

"He says pretty much the same thing."

"And?"

"And this is some scary cagada, esai," said Manny. "Someone hacked into the main computer and deleted key files. We don't know who in CAD made the call to have those bio-morphs brought to Detention. There's no record of who in SAO took the surveillance monitors offline."

"So, it could be anyone," said Darius. "We could have an army of bio-morphs running around HQ, and not even know it."

"Like I said—this is some scary cagada."

Darius thought about the situation for a moment. If more bio-morphs were in hiding, it would be impossible to know whom to trust.

"Is this it?" asked Darius. "Are we at war with the Ad-Ahlen?"

Ever since he was a kid, Darius had heard about the Ad-Ahlen Empire. They had waged war with every known species in the universe—conquered many, destroyed some, and terrorized all. The closest the Ad-Ahlen ever came to attacking Earth had been the Battle of Enceladus on the moon of Saturn twenty years earlier. But the threat remained a constant, thanks to politicians and military leaders who used the specter of an Ad-Ahlen invasion as a means to garner votes and get more money for weapons.

"I don't know if we're at war," said Manny. "But we've got people around here acting like we are. Things are going to get ugly."

"How ugly?"

"Maslon is usin' what happened as an excuse to take full control of security. He says security is compromised with two teams."

Security responsibilities at HQ were divided amongst two specific teams. Maslon oversaw Security One, the primary unit of security forces that answered directly to him. But a secondary security unit, Security Two, operated within the larger body of Operations Crew. Maslon's Security One forces were the armed police of HQ, while Security Two was like the unarmed rent-a-cops at the mall. Security One guarded the Cage. Security Two helped lost children in the SJF Museum find their parents.

Among the many things Maslon had problems with at HQ, Security Two was at the top of the list. Maslon handpicked all the Security One forces, most were ex-cops, all were Long Arms. The Security Two unit consisted of a mix of SJF employees, including more Chancers than Maslon could ever feel comfortable with.

"They'll never let him take over all of security," said Darius.

"I ain't so sure about that," said Manny. "Two bio-morphs got into HQ undetected, escaped from Detention and killed someone. Things like that don't happen without mierda golpea el ventilador. But honestly, amigo, it ain't Maslon we need to be worrying about."

Darius already knew where Manny was taking the conversation. Lying in the hospital bed, he'd had plenty of time to think about it—the reason the bio-morphs had broken into HQ.

"The bio-morphs were after the ACU-64s," said Darius.

"That's what it looks like," said Manny. "Can't quite figure out why. They've got everyone questioning that shape-shifting puta, and it ain't said a thing."

"Let me ask a question or two. I'll get it to talk," said Darius.

"No doubt," said Manny. "And you know I got your back."

"Okay, the freaky monster won't talk. All we need to do is figure out what it wanted based on its actions."

"Soundin' more and more like Nightwatcher," said Manny.

"Look, you were the one that figured out where they were headed," said Darius. "That thing wanted to get to the ACU-64s why?"

"Ain't but a few possibilities."

"The Ad-Ahlen want to know how they work, to come up with a way to stop them," said Darius. "Or maybe just destroy them completely."

Darius stopped talking for a moment, trying to gather his thoughts. Thinking about the Ad-Ahlen made him feel sick. Thinking about the ACU-64 Killbots made him feel sicker. But something made him even sicker still—an idea that had only just started to form in his brain.

"They want to reactivate the ACU-64s," said Darius. "That's what you meant a few minutes ago when you said Maslon wasn't what we should be worrying about."

"The meetings have already started," Manny said.

"They won't work."

"I know."

"They need to be destroyed."

"I agree."

"Who doesn't agree?" asked Darius.

"The usual suspects," said Manny. "The president ain't weighed in on it yet, but her advisors want to begin lookin' for a way to make the damn things work properly."

The sick feeling in the pit of Darius's stomach grew. The ACU-64 Killbots simply could not work properly. Unless the wholesale slaughter of innocent human lives could be considered "working properly."

The ACU-64s were a variation of the ACU-52, an automated combat unit that had been deployed by the United States government successfully in several military campaigns. The 52s were sent in on missions deemed too dangerous for humans, and could be programmed to incapacitate or kill enemy hostiles. They had been deployed during the Battle of Enceladus, and effectively used in the fight against the Ad-Ahlen. With the continued threat from the Ad-Ahlen, the government sought to improve the ACU-52.

Twelve models later, the ACU-64 was unveiled. Designed as a weapon to protect the human race, the ACU-64 Killbots became mankind's biggest threat when Doc Kaos, the armor-clad dictator from a parallel universe, gained control of the deadly machines, using them as weapons in what people came to know as The Attack.

The ACU-64s featured a central processing computer that had been created with a dynamic modulating self-programming feature. This meant that the Killbots had been designed to program themselves as needed in combat situations. These sophisticated machines could, in theory, act and react in a way that closely resembled "thinking."

As if a "thinking" machine loaded down with an arsenal that included techno-plasm blasters weren't bad enough, the ACU-64 Killbots had been designed with a secondary power drive that could run on bio-organic fuel. This new feature meant that if an ACU-64 ran low on its primary fuel source, it could consume and process bio-organic material, turning it into fuel. Unfortunately, the ACU-64s did not differentiate one bio-organic fuel source from another, meaning an ACU-64 Killbot looking to refuel would consume and process a dumpster full of garbage, sorting out all the organic matter, the same way it would consume and process the corpse of a human being.

During The Attack, as the battle waged on and the fuel reserves of the ACU-64s began to run low, the machines began to consume and process any and all bio-organic fuel sources. The sight of a Killbot tearing off an arm or leg of dead person and shoving it into its fuel-processing receptacle only served to make a nightmarish situation even more gruesome.

Under the control of Doc Kaos, the deadly machines killed thousands of people, including the father, mother and newborn baby brother of Darius Logan. His life had been destroyed in every way imaginable by the monstrous creations. And no matter what the potential threat from the Ad-Ahlen may have been—or anyone else for that matter—using ACU-64 Killbots was not a good idea.

"Reactivating those things will be a mistake. It'll be the death of us all," said Darius.

"Let's hope you're wrong about that," Manny said. "Chuck Maslon has agreed to open up the Cage and let the military see what they can do to fix our friends down there."

44

Things could be worse, Darius told himself, trying to remain optimistic. He had been placed on "forced medical leave," pending a full investigation as to why he had lost consciousness—or whatever it was that happened to him. He couldn't work for thirty days, and the security limitations on his movement outside of Headquarters made him a prisoner. Within twenty-four hours, the walls began to close in, followed by a bad case of cabin fever. *Things could be worse,* he told himself over and over again.

With nowhere to go, nothing to do, and angrier than usual, Darius started spending more time in the Fight Rooms in the training facility at Super Justice Force HQ. As part of his regular routine at HQ, Darius had started going to the training facility, located in the Tower. Complete with weights, cardio machines and heavy bags, the high-tech gym also had five Combat Simulation Training Rooms—Fight Rooms— that were used by Super Justice Force members to hone their fighting skills. After the incident with Francis "the Safecracker" Feeney, Butchie suggested that Darius check out a Fight Room and maybe blow off some steam.

With padded walls, floors and ceilings, each Fight Room used automated combat simulation robots that everyone called "Bruisers." The Bruisers looked like something out of a low-budget science fiction movie—the bizarre creations of a mad scientist with limited imagination. Standing on four legs, with two articulated arms that extended from its torso, and a head that looked like a large cooking pot with electronic eyes looking in multiple directions, they were powered by a computer using random sequencers in a combat mode scenario.

It took three trips to the Fight Room, with the training control modes set to the lowest level, before Darius could stay on his feet for more than fifteen seconds. He became increasingly frustrated. *This should be easy,* he said to himself. *These are just machines. How hard can it be to fight a machine, especially one set to the lowest skill level?*

He had returned to the Fight Room for a fourth time, only to be knocked down again and again. The Bruiser knocked him to the padded floor one more time, and

Darius lay there. He swore under his breath, mad that a machine had gotten the better of him, trying to figure out what he had done wrong.

His father had trained Darius how to fight—how to defend himself against the bullies at school. *But what would he say about defending myself against these stupid machines?*

He'd say that these stupid machines are smart enough to knock me on my ass. So maybe I'm the stupid one.

Darius got back up on his feet, ready to call it quits, frustrated that he couldn't figure out how to keep from getting knocked down. In the back of his mind he could hear the voice of his father. "Some fights you can't walk away from."

As much as he wanted to quit, he simply couldn't do it. Dwayne Logan had trained his son too well. Darius had managed to stay alive for years thanks to the training of his father, and he knew that somewhere along the line he had been taught what he needed to know in order to fight the Bruisers.

Okay, what's the first rule in a fight? Darius asked himself. He thought of the many lessons his father had given him. Darius could practically hear Dwayne Logan saying, "Never underestimate your opponent."

"But how do you underestimate your opponent when it is just a machine?" Darius asked out loud.

And in that moment, he knew the answer. It almost felt like his father was there, pointing out the obvious. All along Darius had been thinking of the Bruisers as machines like any other. But the fight-training robots were far more than toasters on legs or clothes driers that could punch him in the stomach. He had been underestimating his opponent.

The Bruisers were an early generation of the ACU-64—the ACU-12—which made beating the crap out of them especially satisfying to Darius. After months of training, he had improved considerably as a fighter, and instead of getting knocked down in a matter of seconds with the training level at its lowest setting, Darius was working out at the maximum skill level possible for a non-powered human.

Four days into his medical leave, Darius arrived at the Fight Rooms only to find Kaebel Kaine training. Things had not gone well since Nightwatcher's bad eye had been replaced with a high-tech bionic one. An infection had slowed his healing process considerably, followed by a lengthy rehabilitation. "It's like learning to see for the first time," said Nightwatcher.

Darius watched Kaebel Kaine going through his workout. Training at level eight, which was meant for low-level superpowers, Nightwatcher was more than impressive. From his own standpoint, Kaine considered himself slow and sluggish—a result of getting used to his new eye—but to Darius, he was a marvel to behold.

Darius had never seen anyone fight quite like Nightwatcher. He moved like a wild animal and a graceful dancer, often at the same time. Criminals lived in fear of running into him on the streets, and Darius could see why—even in sweatpants and a t-shirt he was a monster.

I can't imagine what he looks like in action, decked out in his full outfit, Darius thought.

Nightwatcher wore black body armor, allowing him to blend into the shadows of the night. If light hit the sculpted armor in just the right way, it looked like a skeleton. His helmet looked like a jet-black skull carved out of onyx with reflective red eyes. The eyes made it possible for criminals to see their own reflection as Nightwatcher beat them senseless.

Nightwatcher trained with two Bruisers at the same time. One Bruiser grabbed him from behind in the robotic equivalent to a bear hug, while the other attacked from the front. Kaine kicked out his legs, and caught the second Bruiser in a scissor lock around what would have been its neck. He then managed to pry apart the arms of the Bruiser that held him, slipping out of its grip while maintaining his scissor lock on the other. He twisted his body in such a way that he dragged the Bruiser with him down to the padded floor. Nightwatcher smashed the downed Bruiser with the heel of his foot, and then did a backspin that seamlessly transitioned into a leg sweep of the other Bruiser that only seconds before had been crushing him from behind. The second Bruiser lost its balance, and came crashing down on Kaebel Kaine before he could move out of the way.

"End program!" shouted Kaine. He struggled to get out from underneath the robot.

Darius came into the Fight Room to help Nightwatcher get free of the inactive Bruiser resting on his left arm and leg. He lifted the monstrous machine enough for the crime fighter to slide out from underneath it.

"The new eye," said Nightwatcher. "Doesn't work the same as a real one."

"Looks like you handled yourself pretty well to me," said Darius.

"Saw that thing falling on me, but the damn eye took too long to measure distance and speed. Misjudged how far I needed to move to get out of the way."

Kaebel Kaine picked himself up off the floor. He didn't thank Darius for helping him lift the Bruiser off of him, but he offered a barely noticeable nod, which Darius recognized as the closest thing to courtesy Nightwatcher ever offered anyone. Kaine had notoriously bad social skills, and he seldom talked to anyone. Perhaps that's what Darius liked most about him—Nightwatcher didn't go out of his way to be liked.

"You've been training," said Nightwatcher.

"Some," Darius said.

"Can you handle yourself?"

"I know a thing or two."

"Show me," said Nightwatcher.

Darius set the program controls for level six. He tried on several occasions to move up to Level Seven, but at that level the Bruisers were too much to handle.

You either needed to have low-level powers, or you had to be a supreme badass who could take getting hit with the force level equal to getting kicked by a mule.

One of the things Darius's father taught him about fighting was to do only what needed to be done, and nothing more. "Some guys are all about showing off their skills," said Dwayne Logan. "But a display of technique doesn't amount to much in a fight for your life." Darius remembered that every time he fought. *Looking good is no substitute for being effective.*

Nightwatcher watched Darius fight for a solid six minutes. That in and of itself was impressive. Professional boxers only fought in three-minute rounds, and even the most physically fit had trouble going more than a minute or two when something attacked hard enough to knock them out. But the thing Nightwatcher found especially impressive about Darius was his ability to avoid being hit, and turning his opponent's attacks into his offensive strikes. True fighting required a simultaneous blend of defensive and offensive skills to a point where the two were one and the same. Some people were good at blocking a hit, while others were good at hitting. Darius had both skills in equal measure, and there was something vaguely familiar about his fighting style.

Nightwatcher knew Darius had developed some of his skills in the Fight Room, but there was more to it than that. To fight like this, you had to have been trained, and you had to have traded blows for real. Training in the Fight Room had sharpened Darius's skills, but Kaine could see that Darius had progressed far beyond the limits of the program. Sure, Darius pushed himself, working up a sweat and breathing hard, but from what Kaine saw, Darius's true capabilities as a fighter had yet to be tested. The problem was that the pre-programmed training modules were not designed to work for someone like Darius. Nightwatcher had the same problem, forcing him to custom-design his own programs.

The fight program ended when the Bruiser delivered a one-two combination that Darius ducked. Darius caught the Bruiser in its midsection with an uppercut, causing it to double over—the robots were programmed to react as if they felt pain. Darius then grabbed the Bruiser by the back of its head, and drove his knee into what would have been the machine's face. It collapsed to the floor in a computerized equivalent to being knocked out.

"Not bad," said Nightwatcher.

"Thanks," Darius said.

"Who trained you?"

"My dad."

"Who was your dad?"

"Dwayne Logan—just a guy who knew how to fight."

Kaine nodded his head ever so slightly. His icy stare made Darius uncomfortable. Of all the members of Super Justice Force, Nightwatcher was the one who intimidated Darius the most, which seemed ridiculous, considering Kaebel Kaine had no super powers.

"Let me show you something," said Kaine.

In watching Darius fight the Bruiser, Nightwatcher spotted a critical tactical error. Despite handling himself exceptionally well, Darius repeatedly left himself open to a powerful blow that could be delivered to his left kidney.

"It's a dirty fight technique. These things aren't programmed to fight dirty. Some guy in an alley, he'll pop you in the kidney. You'll think you're dying," said Nightwatcher.

Darius and Kaine went over more fight techniques. They met up the next day, Nightwatcher showing Darius more moves. This went on for three weeks, and in between combat training Nightwatcher would talk to Darius. At first, the conversations with Darius were little more than lessons quoted from Sun Tzu's "Art of War," which Darius had practically memorized already. Eventually, the conversations became more personal.

"Who do you trust?" asked Nightwatcher.

"What?"

"You've made friends since you've come here," said Nightwatcher. "But who do you trust?"

Darius shrugged. "I don't know. Z-Boe for sure. Manny. He saved my life from that bio-morph. Maybe Dr. Sam. Why?"

"These last few weeks, people haven't known who to trust. The bio-morphs didn't get in here on their own," said Nightwatcher.

"That's what I said to Manny."

"I know. He told me," said Nightwatcher. "Why do you think they broke in?"

"I'm not really sure. I think they wanted to get to the ACU-64s. Maybe find out how they work."

"What would be the point of that?"

"Killbots are the most powerful weapon on the planet. If the Ad-Ahlen knew how they worked, maybe they could build something stronger," said Darius.

"The Ad-Ahlen already have something far more powerful than an army of ACU-64s, and they've already used it on us," said Nightwatcher.

"What's more powerful than a Killbot?"

"Fear. They've made us afraid. And fear is the most powerful weapon of all," said Nightwatcher.

45

Despite the fact he'd been given a laptop computer on his birthday—a Super Justice Force Signature Series Intellipad—Darius continued to go to the library. Having been placed on medical leave, he had even more time on his hands. When he wasn't working out his hostilities in the Fight Rooms with Nightwatcher, he developed his mind in the library.

Darius blazed through his online courses, and it eventually dawned on him that he was a college student. He had simply thought of himself as someone taking a few random courses, but somewhere along the way he'd become an undergrad.

After the encounter with the bio-morphs, Darius became increasingly interested in the Ad-Ahlen. He read every comic book he could find that featured tales of the alien race, including "Adventures of the Galaxus Alliance Corps" and a Captain Freedom graphic novel. And while the comics were entertaining, he found that none of the stories went very far in explaining the complexities of human and extraterrestrial relations. Knowing the difference between real life and how comic books portrayed real life, Darius knew he needed to look elsewhere for information.

He started with "A Complete Moron's Guide to Extraterrestrials" and followed it up with "An Earthman's Understanding of Aliens and Outer Space." Neither book was nearly as exciting or entertaining as the massive twelve-issue maxi series "Super Justice Force: Space Battle," which chronicled the conflict between SJF and the Ad-Ahlen Empire during the Battle of Enceladus. At the same time, the comic books Darius had read seemed to gloss over some rather significant historical and scientific facts.

For one thing, Zander Boeman and his family didn't appear in "Super Justice Force: Space Battle." Darius knew for a fact that Z-Boe had been one of the colonists to survive the Enceladus conflict. Chuck Maslon had been there as well, although Darius didn't care that he wasn't in the comic.

Darius had come to grips that the real life in comic books didn't always look like real life. The biggest difference he could see had to be space travel. In comic books and movies like "Star Trek" and "Star Wars," adventurers zipped through the universe in ships faster than the speed of light. There were no problems with the lack of gravity in space, and unless the plot called for it, fuel never posed a problem. Real life was nothing like that.

Human beings without powers, and even some with powers, simply could not travel for prolonged periods of time at speeds approaching that of light. The strain on the body was too great, and the longest trip anyone could survive without relying on cryostasis was Saturn's moon Enceladus. Reality transformed the glamour of space travel into a time-consuming, cost-prohibitive endeavor that posed countless dangers. And it was no different for those that had traveled to Earth from other solar systems.

Only the Galaxus Alliance Corps moved through space by a different set of rules. Through technology created by the Mhadra Turas, the elite guardians of the galaxy possessed the power to manipulate the fabric of space itself, creating Quantus Portals that made it possible to move from galaxy to galaxy as if moving from one room to another.

By comparison, it had taken refugees from Tessaria—the nearest civilized planet to Earth—two full generations to make it to Earth, traveling in ships moving close to the speed of light. By the time their ships arrived, so much time had passed that there wasn't a single being that had started the journey left alive. In fact, over half of the Tessarians who originally arrived at Earth were born on the ship.

Earth played second home to five of the seven known alien races—the Tessarian, the Sesstarian, the Zzngth, the Elbanev and the Quoor. Some considered the Mhadra Turas to be a sixth alien race, but it was more complicated, given they were a symbiotic life form living through a parent host. Only Tessarians and Sesstarians, from twin planets in the same system, lived on Earth in any significant numbers. Each race had come to Earth for the same reason, they were fleeing the Ad-Ahlen, bringing with them technology and science that had since been incorporated into human life.

During the month of his medical leave, Darius learned more about the aliens living on Earth than he had ever known. He studied the Tanhauser Peace Accord, the shaky treaty that most believed to be the one thing keeping the Ad-Ahlen Empire from declaring war on Earth. There were, however, other factors, not the least of which being the Galaxus Alliance Corps and a small army of super-powered humans ready to slug it out until the bitter end.

For millennia, the Ad-Ahlen had waged war with other planets, enslaved other races, and terrorized multiple galaxies. They dominated weaker planets, ruling several systems through their colonies. The long history of their atrocities had been recorded thousands and thousands of years before the human race ever made contact with any extraterrestrials.

The first human contact with the Ad-Ahlen came during the final days of the Tessarian War, just before the fall of Tessaria. Human members of the Galaxus Alliance Corps fought alongside other races before falling victims to a stunning defeat.

Ten years later, the Ad-Ahlen attacked the Earth colony on Enceladus—a research facility and military outpost that was home to several thousand humans and an equal number of extraterrestrials. A fleet of a dozen warships entered the galaxy, threatening a massive invasion of Earth, only to be dealt a devastating blow by a computer glitch. A system failure on seven of the ships killed more than half of the invading force while still in cryostasis. The remaining five Ad-Ahlen ships engaged in what became known as the Battle of Enceladus.

Captain Freedom led a team of Earth's most powerful heroes during the Battle of Enceladus, fighting alongside the Galaxus Alliance Corps and the colonists. The battle raged on for weeks, with both sides taking heavy casualties. If not for Zzngth forces that joined the fray, the Ad-Ahlen would have destroyed the Enceladus Colony, moving on to Earth.

For twenty years the inhabitants of Earth lived in fear of another Ad-Ahlen attack. The United States government built the ACU-64s as a means of defending the planet from the threat of an invasion that never came. Instead, the human race had a new monster to fear—the ACU-64 Killbots—which was more real and deadly than the Ad-Ahlen.

Darius remembered what Nightwatcher had told him about fear being the greatest weapon of all. The Ad-Ahlen had never set foot on Earth, but they created a fear that resulted in unthinkable devastation. And now, with the attack on HQ by bio-morphs, fear once again led the way.

46

Despite the best efforts—or at least the greatest desires—of Chuck Maslon, Darius Logan returned to work after a thirty-day medical leave. Thirty drug screenings over the course of thirty days failed to back up Maslon's assertion of Darius's drug abuse. Maslon's unwavering dislike for Darius and his efforts to get the young man sent off to prison, however, did succeed in further alienating the head of security from a staff that already didn't like him.

Darius felt good about being back at work. As much as he enjoyed working out and studying, his days had been a bit too long without his job to keep him occupied. Of course, Elladia took up his time as well, but she had her life to live, and the time they spent together was always limited one way or another.

While he was away on forced medical leave, much had changed around HQ. Increased security protocols meant more bio-scan screenings, random checks and a greater sense of impending doom. Maslon managed to successfully wrangle complete control of both security teams. He increased the Security One team, expanding the number of Long Arms working for him, and implemented a new policy regarding firearms for guards with L3 ratings and higher. Maslon had a bunch of ex-cops walking around HQ fully armed, all under the pretense of "increased security." The Chancers working security weren't allowed to be armed, and were all transferred to nonessential areas. Long-term employees like Butchie suddenly found themselves issuing citations in the parking lot, inspecting mail, and holding the doors open for tourists.

Maslon's new policies upset Manny, who felt that if security threats did exist, all guards needed to receive the same training and carry weapons. Maslon couldn't have disagreed more, and the argument between him and Manny quickly became one of modern legend at Super Justice Force HQ.

"The last thing we need is a bunch of trigger-happy ex-cons running around armed, posing even more of a threat," said Maslon. At least that's what he was rumored to have said.

Manny supposedly responded by calling Maslon a particularly unpleasant twelve-letter word.

Darius chose to believe the stories about the argument between Maslon and Manny, even though he had no proof, and Manny wouldn't confirm.

The one thing Darius did know to be true was that tension ran high at HQ, compounded by the government sending in a team of "pencil-neck geeks" to work on the ACU-64s. They had been charged with determining if the killing machines could be made to "work properly." The assumption, of course, being that "work properly" meant the ACU-64s could only be controlled by the "good guys," as opposed to someone like Doc Kaos.

The pencil-neck geeks spent long hours down in the Cage, working in a makeshift lab—locked inside with a team of armed security guards handpicked by Maslon. Even though the guards were loyal to Maslon, Darius felt sorry for them as they worked on a rotating schedule so that everyone had a fair turn at dying should the Killbots become active.

Maslon had fought hard to have the ACU-64s taken to another facility, where they could be worked on properly without placing undue burden on his security forces. He felt the machines should be repaired as best as possible, to be effectively used as weapons of mass destruction—he just didn't want to be bothered guarding them. Fortunately, Captain Freedom shot down Maslon's rallying to have the ACU-64 Killbots transferred someplace else. No one really wanted the things at HQ, but no one would let them be removed either.

Darius had been back on the job for a week when Manny called him into the supervisor's office.

"I got good news and bad news and then some more good news for you," said Manny.

"Good news, bad news and more good news?"

"Yeah. The first bit of good news is I'm promoting you to Level 3."

Darius was stunned. It took most employees at least two years to get to Level 3—sometimes three years. He had been promoted to L3 in just over a year, which was cool, and a real honor, but he wasn't sure he was ready for the responsibility.

"Manny, I'm not ready to go to Level 3. There are guys here three years and more who aren't L3s."

"Darius, listen to me. This increased security has got us stretched thin in SAO. Maslon pulled a dozen people out to put them on his new goon squad. I'm pulling bodies from CAD, but it still ain't enough to fill in all the gaps. I need L3s that I can trust, and whether you think you're ready or not, I need you."

"Maslon won't like it," said Darius.

"Who cares what Maslon likes? That stupid pendejo is the reason SAO is at the breaking point."

"What's the bad news?" asked Darius.

"Well, there's two bits of bad news, amigo" said Manny. "First, you're going to be training new crewmembers. We've got seven new people starting next week, and I'm giving you two of them."

"Man, I don't know the first thing about training anyone," said Darius.

"You know the job better than you think," Manny said. "The second bit of bad news is that I need to transfer you to day shift."

Manny may as well have punched Darius in the face. This was more than bad news. This was terrible news. Darius liked the night shift—he belonged there.

"Manny, you can't take me off night shift," Darius said. He prepared to prattle of a list of reasons why he couldn't work the day shift, but Manny held up a hand and gestured for Darius to be quiet.

"You think I wanna transfer you?" asked Manny. "Believe it or not, vato, I actually like you. You work hard, you don't talk that much and you laugh at my corny jokes. But the reality is that over half of day shift has been assigned to that special security detail, and that's where our butts are really exposed."

Darius thought of a million reasons why he didn't want to go to day shift. None of them mattered though. Manny had made up his mind. And though Darius wasn't too happy with the decision being made, he couldn't deny the significance of it all. Moving up a level in security status meant a pay raise. Being trusted to train new employees and moved to day shift meant being groomed for an assistant supervisor position somewhere down the road.

Darius wasn't sure if he wanted to be an assistant supervisor or not. He'd only recently started thinking about maybe being a lawyer or a teacher. He couldn't do either of those while being an Operations Crew assistant supervisor.

Still, the thought of being an assistant supervisor held a certain appeal. At his current pace he could have the position by the time he was twenty-one. That would make him the youngest person to ever hold the position at Super Justice Force. It would also prove that Dr. Sam and Captain Freedom were right to let him in the program. And it would really upset Chuck Maslon.

"When do I start?" Darius asked.

"Monday."

"That doesn't give me any time to prepare."

"You're forgetting to ask me what the other piece of good news is," said Manny.

"I'm afraid to," Darius said.

"You can leave HQ any time you want, and go anywhere you want. The two-block limit is lifted," said Manny.

"Don't even joke around that way. I'm supposed to wear this STATU for another two years. There's no way Maslon is letting it come off."

"You're right, there ain't no way Maslon is gonna let it come off, and it ain't comin' off," said Manny. "But you've earned a bit more freedom than you've been given. The STATU stays on, but it's more of a formality."

"In case I try to escape?" asked Darius.

"Something like that."

"In a million years, Maslon won't approve this."

"I went over his head and he didn't have much of a choice," said Manny. "It helps that the big guys like you, amigo.

"The big guys?"

"The supes. Captain Freedom. Nightwatcher. Lady Themis. Black Fist. Smoking Ace. Rocky. Marvelous Man. White Dynamo. Stixx and Stone. All of 'em. They all signed off on givin' you some freedom," said Manny. "With that kind of support, ain't a thing Maslon can say."

Darius was at a loss for words. He couldn't believe he finally could move around like a free man.

"What did you tell them?" asked Darius.

"I told 'em the truth," said Manny. "I told 'em that Elladia's boyfriend needed to take her out in style."

47

At eighteen years old, Darius Logan had faced more hard times than most people three times his age—orphaned at age nine, bounced around from one abusive environment to another, and more than his share of fights, he had the scars to prove it. In addition to the abuse and the physical confrontations, there was other trauma. The memory of the first time he had to dig through the trash to keep from starving stuck in his mind like it had just happened the day before.

Darius thought of all these things and more—the moments when he questioned whether he would live to see another day—and somehow all of it seemed to pale in comparison to his first real date with Elladia.

They stood outside a movie theater, trying to decide what to see. Over a dozen movies were showing, and Darius had no clue what to watch. He didn't know anything about the big stars in Hollywood or what was popular. There were three different sequels playing to movies Darius had never even heard of, and as he and Elladia discussed what to watch, he felt hopelessly out of touch with everything.

Things were much easier when all Darius did was stare longingly at Elladia. And things had been relatively easy when their relationship—if you could call it that—had been restricted to the confines of HQ. Darius didn't have to think about where to take Elladia for dinner, or what movie they should go see, because he couldn't take her to the movies or out to eat. Their relationship was largely defined by the restrictions of the world he live in. But with those restrictions gone, he had no excuses. Or at least the old excuses weren't going to work anymore.

They decided to watch one of the silly romantic comedies playing at the multiplex. Not because Darius wanted to see it, but because it was easier to say yes.

"Know how to pick your battles," his father used to say.

The movie wasn't nearly as bad as Darius had feared it would be. For one thing, it was fun just to be in a theater. For another thing, Elladia holding his hand and resting her head on his shoulder was just about the greatest feeling in the world. Darius thought about the time he fought with the giant rat over the hamburger he'd picked out of the garbage, and how he would do it again if it meant being with Elladia. Then he laughed at the whole ridiculous idea, and Elladia thought he was laughing at the movie.

After the movie they went to eat at a pizza parlor. It had been many, many years since he ate pizza at a place like this one, which reminded him of a place his father would take him. They would go to this one comic book store, followed by a slice of pizza, and then return home to a mother who pretended to be jealous that they were having fun without her.

Working at Super Justice Force had given Darius a new life, complete with friends and family—things he had given up on having. Slowly but surely he grew into his new life, though it hadn't always been easy. Then again, life seldom was easy. But as comfortable as he had become in this new reality of his, it wasn't complete. And sitting across from Elladia, as great as it was, served as a reminder that Darius still struggled to fit in with the rest of the world.

Elladia sensed something was wrong with Darius. His moods generally ranged between "tense and brooding" and "more tense and brooding." Sometimes he would lighten up, which was his "happily tense and brooding" mood—the most fun time to be around him. And though he seemed to be happily tense and brooding, Elladia sensed something more.

"Are you okay?" Elladia asked.

Darius had two choices. He could do what he normally did, saying practically nothing and pretending nothing was wrong. Or, he could be honest and say what was on his mind. Elladia did, after all, ask. Clearly she sensed something.

"I don't know how to do this," said Darius. "And I don't want to blow it."

"What are you talking about?"

"I haven't been to see a movie in a theater in ten years. It's been almost that long since I sat in a place like this and ate a slice of pizza," said Darius. "I've never been on a date before. I've never been a boyfriend before."

"I've never been a girlfriend before. And you know Uncle Manny—I've never been on a real date before," said Elladia. "As for seeing a movie in the theater, you haven't missed much the last ten years. Those new 'Spider-Man' movies were pretty bad. But I did like the originals."

"Spider-Man is so fake," said Darius. "There's no way you can get powers from being bitten by a spider."

"I know it's all silly, especially compared to real life, but the original movies were awesome—especially 'Spider-Man 2.' I have it on my computer, and I always cry at the end," Elladia confessed. "You really should see it."

"Okay, maybe we can watch it together some day," Darius said.

Elladia reached across the table and grabbed Darius's hand. "See, you've already got the good boyfriend thing down," she said.

Their first real date came to an end, and Darius and Elladia stood outside the home she shared with her Uncle Manny. Manny was at work, which meant Darius had no reason to be nervous about prying eyes. Of course, Manny's best friend and co-worker Otto Rekker lived just across the street, and Darius wasn't so sure Otto wasn't doing reconnaissance.

"This was the best date of my life," said Elladia.

"I thought you said you'd never been on a real date before," Darius said.

"Why did you have to ruin the moment?"

"Sorry."

"This is where I say, 'This was the best date of my life,' and then you say, 'This was the best date of my life.' Okay?"

"Okay."

"This was the best date of my life," said Elladia.

"This was the best date of my life," Darius said.

"Now, this is when you kiss me."

Darius pulled Elladia close, and though it wasn't the first time they had kissed, it may as well have been. It was not a peck on the lips, but rather a deep, soulful kiss that lay to rest any doubts and fears either of them had about the other. It was a long kiss, full of passion that sought to bring to an end years of loneliness felt by both Darius and Elladia, in which both of them wondered if they could ever feel whole again. It was an end and a beginning that signaled the rest of their lives had just started.

48

If Darius Logan could have only seen himself, he wouldn't have recognized the goofy teenager he had become in the minutes and hours following his date with Elladia. His head swimming in a silly ocean of hopeless romanticism, he took a bus to the subway, riding aimlessly until the rattling car of the train started to feel like a prison. Sitting still, on a downtown-bound train, just made the world seem small. And at the moment, he needed the world to be big—big enough to handle the energy inside of him threatening to explode.

The train crossed the river back into the city, and Darius decided to get off and travel the rest of the way on foot. The walk back to Super Justice Force HQ would be long, but he had freedom to enjoy.

Darius stepped on to the platform of the subway station and a rush of memories came flooding in. He hated subway stations—the smells and dirt and the crushing feeling of being underneath a city. It all reminded him of the world he had come from. He stood on the platform, deserted except for the homeless man asleep on a bench, and made sure that he saw enough and smelled enough and remembered enough of his life from before that he would never forget how far he'd come.

Outside the subway station Darius found himself in a grim neighborhood that looked too much like No Man's Land. This neighborhood had not been decimated by The Attack, which wiped out entire parts of the city in the blink of an eye. Instead, it had been crippled by the diseases of poverty and crime, left to slowly wither and die along with the people who called places like this home. Crime ran rampant in these neighborhoods. The laws of the urban jungle were in full effect, survival of the fittest on every block and in every decaying building with rusty pipes and crumbling stairways. It was no place for a love-struck kid fresh from playing kissy-face with his girlfriend.

There are worse stops I could have gotten off at, Darius told himself. *But not much worse.*

Darius started his long walk back to HQ. The energy he felt from his date with

Elladia still had him charged up, just as the dying neighborhood he walked through had his senses on high alert. Darius felt great. He felt alive and invincible and ready for anything that came his way. And then he heard the scream.

For a moment, Darius thought his imagination was working overtime. It wasn't his imagination. A woman screamed for help. Darius never stopped to think about how much he hated running as he ran toward the sounds of the screams.

This is not good, Darius thought.

Halfway down the block and across the street, an older woman struggled in a late-night game of tug-of-war with some punk over her purse. A few feet away, a man lay in a pool of blood. And watching all of this were three other punks who seemed endlessly amused by their companion wrestling with an old woman for her purse.

Four against one aren't the best odds, Darius thought. He looked for some sort of weapon as he quickly moved toward the gang. The only thing he saw was an old trash can. Darius grabbed the metal lid.

Darius quietly snuck up behind the punk closest to him, bringing down the trash-can lid on the punk's head with such force that it sent him to the ground, out for the count.

Odds just dropped three to one, and the fight hasn't even started.

The remaining punks turned to see what had happened. Darius stood over their fallen friend, holding a garbage-can lid like it was some sort of shield.

The punk wrestling with the woman for her purse loosened his grip. The old woman ran to the side of the motionless man. Darius couldn't tell if the man was dead, which only made him angrier.

In comic books and movies, right before a fight breaks out, someone usually said something cool. Darius couldn't think of anything cool to say. He was too busy sizing up his three opponents. They had been surprised by Darius's attack on their companion, but with a little luck he might still have some surprises left.

The punks thought their numbers gave them an advantage. They weren't expecting Darius to do much of anything other than get his ass handed to him when they jumped him. And that was where Darius still had the element of surprise—he hadn't stopped by to get his ass handed to him.

In one fluid motion, Darius moved toward the punk closest to him, while flinging the garbage-can lid at the punk second closest—this would buy time before the third, who was the farthest away, could get into the mix.

The garbage-can lid hit the second punk in the face, just as Darius leapt into the air and came down on the other punk with a Muay Thai elbow strike to the nose. The punk screamed in agony, his nose broken. The pain and the blood would slow him down, and Darius could finish him off later if need be.

The third punk rushed to the side of his friend, who had gone down the moment the lid hit him. Darius hadn't counted on that happening, but it helped, making his job easier.

Darius rushed the third punk, who managed to get himself into a defensive pose, pulling a switchblade from his back pocket.

Darius stopped short. He noticed the knife, but was careful not to look at it. The knife posed no threat. It was the guy holding the knife that represented the danger. Darius stared the punk in the eye. If he was older than Darius, it wasn't by much.

The punk with the knife rushed Darius, who side-stepped the attack, tripping his opponent at the same time. The punk dropped the knife when he hit the sidewalk, but managed to get back on his feet more quickly than Darius expected.

Darius and the punk circled each other, like two hungry animals getting ready to fight for a scrap of food. Darius couldn't tell if the punk was a good fighter, or if he had just been lucky so far. He was, after all, the last of four still on his feet, but that didn't necessarily have anything to do with skill. It may have just been the luck of the draw.

The punk moved toward Darius, swinging his arm wildly, and Darius knew for sure that he faced a bad fighter whose luck had run out. Darius waited until the last possible second before he bobbed out of the way of a sad-looking punch—the goal to make his opponent think he stood a chance. The punk's arm whooshed over Darius, and then Darius came back up and delivered a right uppercut to the punk's stomach.

The punk gasped for air, stumbled back a few steps, and never really knew that the fight had ended. That realization didn't register with him until Darius's foot connected with the side of his head, turning the lights out.

Darius looked around to see if any of the rest of the gang had some fight left in them. The punk he'd taken out with the garbage-can lid was still down for the count. *That's one.*

The punk whose nose he'd broken cowered, crying like a baby. *That's two.*

Where's three?

Darius's head exploded in pain.

The third punk—the one who went down when the trash-can lid him in the face—didn't stay down for long. He brought the lid down on Darius's head a second time.

Darius lost all sense of balance, dropping to the cold sidewalk. Stunned and confused, he rolled over on to his back, vaguely aware that he needed to focus his attention. He saw the bottom of a shoe rushing toward his face, and thought enough to move out of the way.

Darius grabbed the punk's leg and held on tight, trying to clear his head enough to regain his focus. The punk kicked Darius with his free leg, but lacked the leverage to do any damage. The punk struggled to free his leg, bent down, and smashed his fist into Darius's face.

Darius loosened his grip on the punk's leg. The punk went to hit Darius again, but Darius caught the blow, and dragged the punk to the ground.

His head throbbed, his face hurt, but Darius had his focus back. He got back up his to feet, backing away from the punk he'd just brought to the ground. Darius needed distance, a moment to fully collect himself.

The punk picked himself up off the ground—ready for more.

Well, at least I know which one can fight, Darius thought. *If I'm not careful, this guy is gonna kick my ass.*

The thought of getting his ass kicked—maybe even getting killed—on the same night of his date with Elladia amused Darius. He started laughing.

"What's so damn funny?" growled the punk.

Now would really be the time to say something badass.

Darius didn't say a word. He had to end the fight, check on the old couple, and get going before the cops showed up. If the cops showed up.

Darius moved toward the punk, pulling back his right arm to throw a punch. He moved in, started to throw the punch—slower than he normally would have—and waited for the punk to block the punch. The punk moved to protect his head from Darius's punch, but it was too late. Darius shifted his stance, whipping his body around with a full-force roundhouse kick.

Darius's foot smashed into the punk's ribs. Darius snapped his leg back, pivoted on his other foot, delivering a side-kick to the punk's face, dropping him to the ground.

His adrenaline raced, his face and head throbbed, and Darius felt great. He turned to check on the old couple.

A black skeleton stood over the old woman. The old man still lay motionless, but his head had been bandaged.

Darius walked over to Nightwatcher and the older couple. "How's he doing?" asked Darius.

"Hurt, but alive. Ambulance is on the way. So are the police," said Nightwatcher. He pointed to the Nightmobile. "Wait in the car. Don't touch anything."

Darius sat in the Nightmobile—which had more legroom than he imagined—and watched as the ambulance arrived, taking the old couple away. Nightwatcher talked to the police who arrived on the scene, and then disappeared from view. A moment later he appeared, got in the car, started the engine and drove off.

"How much of that did you see?" Darius asked.

"Enough," said Nightwatcher.

"So your eye is all healed up?"

"Mostly."

"Good. That's great," said Darius.

"You had a date with Elladia," said Nightwatcher.

"Yeah. It went great. Thanks for asking."

"I didn't ask."

"No. No, you didn't," said Darius.

"I took credit for what happened back there. I'm licensed. You're not. It's easier that way," said Nightwatcher.

"That sounds reasonable."

"Don't make a habit of this."

"I won't. This just sort of... happened," said Darius.

"Be careful. Playing hero can get addictive," said Nightwatcher.

Nightwatcher and Darius drove in silence the rest of the way back to HQ. Nightwatcher pulled the car to a stop on the far side of the park in front of Headquarters. "Get out here," said Nightwatcher. "I still have work to do."

Darius got out of the car. "Thanks," he said.

Nightwatcher drove off without saying a word.

Darius went to his apartment, cleaned up, and tried to get some sleep.

49

No matter how hard he tried, Darius could not think of an odder couple than Monica Firor and Doug Baum, the two new employees he had been assigned to train.

Before she came to work for Super Justice Force, Monica had been a cop. Shot in the line of duty, damage to her spinal cord left her a paraplegic. There were plenty of injuries that could be repaired with various types of biomechatronics and bionics, but a spinal injury was one of the few exceptions. She could have stayed on the force doing modified duty, but there were too many memories attached to the job, and she needed to start a new life.

Doug was a car thief who started his life of crime at the age of twelve. A career criminal who never worked an honest day in his life, he had operated one of the biggest chop shops in the tri-state area. The cops had spent close to a decade trying to bust up his operation, but it took an angry ex-wife to bring down his empire. While in prison, Doug realized he needed something to do when he got out, leading him to Second Chance.

Darius worked directly with Monica and Doug three days a week, and the other two days they spent "floating" in other sections. He made sure that they took their meal breaks together and sat together while they ate. He wasn't sure why he did this, other than the fact that Manny trained him that way, and Darius wanted to be like Manny.

They didn't socialize much during their meal breaks, because that wasn't Darius's style. If Monica and Doug wanted to talk about their private lives, Darius wasn't about to stop them—he just wasn't going to talk about himself. Instead, he tried to keep most of the conversations centered on aspects of the job.

Darius had little doubt that Monica could do well at SJF. Despite the fact she was no longer a cop, she still had the cop mind-set—a deep-rooted commitment to the law that made her a Long Arm through and through. If anything threatened to hold her back at SJF, it was her prejudice toward guys like Doug. Not that Darius could blame her—it was, after all, some criminal who had shot her and left her paralyzed.

But the fact remained that Monica had to get used to working alongside ex-cons. For all anyone knew, the day might come where she would be working with whoever shot her.

Doug's success at SJF was more questionable than Monica's. Darius wondered if the former car thief would amount to anything more than a Scrubber. Doug knew a lot about cars, but he would have to make L2 before he could actually do any mechanical work in the Vehicle Maintenance Bays, and Darius wasn't sure if that would ever happen. Doug's problem, and it was part of what rubbed Monica the wrong way, was that he didn't take anything seriously. Everything was a joke to him, and he had an annoying habit of finishing other people's sentences with "that's what she said."

Monica and Doug were nearing the end of their four-week training time with Darius. Monica still couldn't hide her disdain for Doug, and Doug could not stop cracking silly and inappropriate jokes. Darius knew the chances of them ever working together after training were slim to none. He planned on recommending Monica for a position in SAO, while Doug would be recommended for a low-level position in MAS. But at the same time, both of them were going to have to work with others, and Darius felt responsible for preparing them for more than just the routine aspects of working for Super Justice Force.

Darius decided to start with Doug, because Doug seemed easier to deal with. One day after their shift was over, Darius asked Doug if he had time for a brief conversation. The two men sat down in the employee cafeteria, while Darius figured out what to say. Doug was at least fifteen years older than Darius, which made any conversation about maturity and ambition at the work place a little awkward.

"Doug, you're nearing the end of your training, and I'm recommending you for placement in MAS," said Darius.

"Really? Wow. That's great," said Doug.

"You'll make L1 after training, no problem. But honestly, I think you're gonna have trouble moving up to L2," said Darius.

"Yeah, so?" Doug said.

"I don't know what your plans are for the future, but you don't want to spend years working here as a L1."

It felt weird for Darius to be giving anyone advice about their life of career.

"I got an ex-wife and two kids, and I need to make sure I meet my financial obligations," said Doug.

"I get it," Darius said. "But do you want to do that by mopping floors and washing dishes? Second Chance isn't just called Second Chance because it sounds good. It's called that because it gives guys like you and me a Second Chance."

Darius couldn't believe the words coming out of his mouth. Not only did he think he sounded like some sort of guidance counselor, he actually believed what he told Doug. Second Chance was just that, a second chance.

"What do I need to do?" Doug asked.

"Learn how everything works around here. Show that you actually know it. And be a little more serious," said Darius. "Otto is always looking for guys who know what they're doing, but he doesn't have time for jokers. He's die-hard Second Chance. If he doesn't think you take the program seriously, he won't let you put air in the tire of a company car or wash a windshield."

Darius had no idea if his little talk with Doug did any good. Doug thanked him, which was all Darius could really hope for.

Dealing with Doug was easy compared to Monica. Darius had no clue how to handle her. She wasn't as bad as Chuck Maslon when it came to her visible disdain for the criminal types like Darius—in fact she didn't even know Darius was in Second Chance—but she did wear her prejudices on her sleeve.

Darius knew it would take something more drastic than a conversation to reach Monica. She carried around a lot of hostility—justifiable though it may have been—and if she faced potential undoing at SJF, it was from the same thing that had threatened to destroy Darius: emotional baggage.

He had to check with some others to make sure it was cool to do, and when he got the approval, Darius took Monica to a group counseling session for Chancers. Personally, he hated the sessions—it wasn't all that long ago that he punched out Francis "Safecracker" Feeney at one such meeting—but as time wore on, Darius understood their importance. Even though he didn't participate much in the dialogs that went on, there were occasions that he got something useful out of the conversations.

It had been quite some time since Darius had been to a group session. His required attendance had long since passed, and he chose to stop going. He got more out of working out in the Fight Rooms and his one-on-one sessions with Dr. Sam.

Darius had Monica meet him at the group counseling session. Butchie led the group, and Darius recognized some of the faces, while some were new to him, including the Shake and Bake Sisters, who had been a notorious supercriminal team.

The session started out like most, and quickly turned into the thing Darius hated most—a group of ex-cons whining about this, that and the other. He hated the lack of emotional honesty in the meetings. He was guilty of it as much as the others, but at least he said almost nothing, as opposed to complaining about his nagging wife or the difficulty of going legit.

Darius invited Monica to the meeting because he wanted her to see that Chancers were more than ex-cons. Unfortunately, the session didn't prove her wrong. No one had anything of merit to say, which would leave Monica justified in her mistrust and disdain, and Darius wasn't cool with that.

Without realizing he was doing it, Darius raised his hand to say something. He had gone out of his way to say as little as possible during the countless group sessions he'd endured. He never felt the need to explain himself to anyone, or to be understood by anyone. And even in that moment, he wasn't looking for acceptance or understanding from anyone in the room. He was who he was. The things that happened to him in the past, as well as the things he had done, were all part of Darius Logan, and had helped to shape him, but that wasn't who he was. Darius couldn't be defined merely by his past, and he was not about to be judged for it either.

The rest of the group sat silently as Darius opened up for the first time. Many of them had been in meetings with him, had heard his occasional comments, and some remembered the incident with Safecracker. But with the exception of Butchie, none of the people in the room knew much about Darius other than the rumors that had circulated HQ.

Darius told the group about his family, and how they were killed in The Attack. He told them about Uncle Kenny, and the foster homes and juvenile detention. He told them about the fights and living in the abandoned subway stations with the junkies and the unregistered metahumans. And then he told them about Karlito and the Adrenaccelerate, and assaulting the police officer, and about how Captain Freedom had saved him from a certain death, and in doing so had given him a second chance.

None of it was easy for Darius to talk about, but with each word he spoke, with each new detail he shared, a tremendous weight lifted off him. *Is this how the group sessions are supposed to be, and if so, why haven't I done this sooner?*

Everyone in the room stared at Darius—even Monica—hanging on his every word. It was like they were all seeing him for the first time. Darius looked over at Butchie, suspecting that under that giant walrus mustache was a smile. Butchie gave Darius thumbs up.

"The thing about this program is that it wasn't the first choice for any of us," said Darius. "Every choice we made before coming here—good or bad—led us to this. Those choices didn't work out. And so here we all are. Where we go from here, what we do from here, it's all open to possibility."

50

It only took one trip for Darius to move all of his belongings out of his apartment. When he'd moved in to apartment 11-J in the Tower at Super Justice Force, all of his worldly belongings fit in an old pillowcase. He didn't have much more in the way of possessions—some more clothes, an impressive collection of books, a laptop computer, and a singing fish that didn't sing—but owning things had little appeal for Darius. Maybe it was because he had grown used to living with so little for so long that he'd become comfortable living that way.

Darius wasn't moving very far, just down the hall, straight up, and down another hall to the apartment of Zander "Z-Boe" Boeman, member of the Galaxus Alliance Corps.

It all happened quickly. Darius had been living in his studio apartment at Super Justice Force HQ, an apartment normally used for Transitional Employee Housing. And if things had gone as planned, with Darius serving three to five years under "house arrest" at SJF, he wouldn't have moved out of his apartment fifteen months after moving in. But things seldom worked out as planned—as Darius discovered on a regular basis. When TEH faced a shortage of apartments for Chancers, Zander Boeman suggested that Darius move in with him.

As it was, Darius spent a fair amount of time in Z-Boe's apartment watering plants and feeding the Vissoam aqua-singers—he had even placed his own aqua-sing, which he named Randy, in the tank with the others. And the extra bedroom got no use other than as a storage room for surfboards that collected dust and cases of trade paperback collections of "Adventures of the Galaxus Alliance Corps" that didn't even feature Zander.

Darius and Elladia had discussed the issue of privacy. If he moved in with Zander, how much privacy would they have? It was common knowledge that the two were a couple, despite the fact neither of them made a big deal out it. Still, people saw them together, and it was only a matter of time before someone figured it out, and then word began to spread throughout Super Justice Force.

Manny had already talked to the two of them separately, and had given the young couple his blessings. He made it very clear, telling them both that he didn't want to know what they did, as long as they were "careful." It had been an awkward conversation for Darius, and he couldn't imagine how Elladia felt.

After Manny had his talk with Darius, a line began to form of others with warnings of their own. Elladia was beloved at SJF, with no shortage of people willing to hurt Darius if he broke her heart.

"Treat her right, 'cause if you don't, I'll rip your arms off and beat you to death 'em," said Otto Rekker.

Lady Themis, who had confided in Elladia her dating problems for years, had her own warning for Darius: "For every tear you make her shed, I'll see to it you lose a thousand times that amount in blood."

And then there was Kaebel Kaine, a man of even fewer words than Darius. "Hurt her, and I'll kill you," was all Nightwatcher had to say.

Darius loaded all of his stuff—mostly books—into three boxes, borrowed a hand truck from MAS, and moved all of his stuff in about ten minutes. Elladia helped him, not that he needed any help, and unpacking his stuff at the new apartment took about as long as packing, which wasn't very long at all. By the time they were done, the aqua-singer Darius had named Randy and placed in the tank with the others, was singing along with the other five.

A few days after he moved in, Anna Rekker insisted on there being a housewarming at the new apartment. Although he had grown in many ways, Darius still wasn't the most social person on the planet. He would have rather spent the evening alone with Elladia than with a dozen people—even if the dozen people were his friends.

The Rekkers—Otto, Anna and the kids—came by with enough food to feed an army, and a present for "Uncle Big D." Reinier and Aziza had made a scrapbook full of pictures for Darius. They knew that Darius had no family of his own, and the nine-year-old twins felt it very important that Darius know he was a member of the Rekker family.

The party had been a pleasant enough gathering, but Darius felt ready for people to leave. The last guests to leave were Manny and Elladia, and though he wished he'd had more time alone with his girlfriend, he really needed some time to himself. Elladia understood this about Darius—that at times he just needed to be alone—and she respected that. The thing Darius had yet to understand was that Elladia didn't take it personally—she loved him in spite of his brooding and his occasional need for solitude. To not accept that would have meant not accepting him.

Darius sat alone in the apartment for a long time. He had spent many hours here in the past as a guest, but now it was his home. The Vissoam aqua-singers, which tended to be shy around large crowds, had started to sing. Although Darius loved the fact they sang Jackson Five songs, he had started playing other things for them, in the hope that they might expand their repertoire. As the aqua-singers began to sing the opening notes from Marvin Gaye's 'What's Goin' On,' he felt a lulling calm overtake him.

Hours later, Darius woke up to the sound of the front door opening. Confused at first, uncertain of where he was, or if he was in danger, he leapt to his feet ready for action.

Z-Boe stood in the dark living room. The stars that glowed throughout the fabric of his costume cast an odd light in the room. It was like having the night sky standing a few feet away.

"Always ready for a fight," said Zander.

"Sorry. You woke me," Darius said.

"No need to apologize. The day may come when always being ready for a fight will come in handy."

Zander went into the kitchen and prepared himself a plate of leftovers. He came back into the living room and sat on the couch across from Darius. Before he started eating, Z-Boe pulled off his boots and let out and audible sigh. "Sorry I missed the housewarming, bro," Zander said.

"No worries," said Darius.

Darius watched his superhero roommate as he ate. Z-Boe looked exhausted. Darius couldn't recall any other time that he'd seen his friend looking so tired.

Darius wanted to ask Zander why he didn't just take a break. Why not take a vacation and get some rest and relaxation? But Darius knew that if you're a member of an intergalactic police force protecting multiple galaxies and an alternate dimension as well, there isn't always time to take a break.

Still, Darius felt bad for Z-Boe. He wasn't sure what motivated guys like Black Fist and Captain Freedom—and even Nightwatcher, who didn't have real powers—but Darius knew it was something he lacked. If Darius had a choice, even if he had the powers, he wasn't one to play the hero role. Z-Boe, on the other hand, didn't have much of a choice. At least he felt pretty sure Zander didn't have a choice.

The glowing bands around each of Zander's wrists were a constant reminder of his lack of choice. Being banded with the Mhadra Turas was no small deal—it was a lifetime commitment to fight for justice. There were times, when Darius wondered if Zander regretted being in the Galaxus Alliance Corps, dealing with the pain of all the sacrifices he'd been forced to make because the Mhadra Turas had chosen him.

I think I would rather die than give my life up that way, Darius thought.

After Zander finished eating, he and Darius talked into the night. Z-Boe asked about how things were going with Elladia, and Darius thought he heard a hint of sadness in his friend's voice. Perhaps Zander thought about his own failed relationships. Darius had only witnessed the end of Z-Boe's last romance, but he knew there had been others that had fallen apart.

"It's not easy, doing this thing that I do, and trying to have a normal life," Zander once told Darius. "I wish I knew how guys like Captain Freedom do it—staying in a solid relationship for years. He's kind of the exception, even though the drinking keeps him from qualifying as being well adjusted. Lady T can't make it work with anyone. Nightwatcher doesn't even try."

Darius had seen and heard enough at Super Justice Force to know the magic of superhero life balanced out with sad realities. He often thought of the scene in "Wizard of Oz," when Dorothy pulled back the curtain and saw that the wizard was just some old man flipping switches. Working at SJF pulled the curtain back on the world of superheroics. In comic books, the heroes always had girlfriends or boyfriends. Sometimes the villain would kidnap the loved ones of heroes, but they were always rescued in the end. And the endings were always happy. At least in the comic books. Darius didn't know about real life. There certainly hadn't been a happy ending for Kid Spectacular and his wife.

"You know what the worst part is?" Zander had asked once before. "The worst part is that you have to learn to push them out of your mind. You can't think about the woman you love when you're in a fight for your life. It becomes a distraction, which is a weakness. So instead, you've got to push them out. But once you do that, you can't really let them back in all the way. At least that's how it is for me."

Darius thought back to that conversation with Zander as the two of them sat in the apartment they now shared, listening to their Vissoam aqua-singers. It struck Darius as sad when the creatures began singing "Who's Loving You."

Zander fell asleep on the couch, still dressed in his Galaxus uniform, the stars of some galaxy twinkling. Darius got a blanket and covered his friend. As he headed to his new bedroom, he thought he heard Z-Boe thank him. But Zander was asleep, and Darius figured he must have imagined it.

PART III: BLACK THANKSGIVING

51

Summer turned into autumn, the days grew shorter, and nearly all of the leaves had turned yellow and brown and red and fallen from the trees. It was November, and production had begun on a movie based on the life of Kid Spectacular. Black Fist and White Dynamo ended their crime-fighting partnership over "creative differences," though they remained co-stars on a hit reality show. Manny had been secretly dating someone for months, but no one knew who she was. And Darius Logan felt like life was just a little too good to be true.

For a second year, he spent Thanksgiving with the Rekker family. Anna was pregnant with their third child, and she and Otto asked Darius to be godfather.

Who would've thought any of this would be my life?

Manny and Otto watched football in the living room. Anna and Elladia prepared the meal in the kitchen. Darius, Aziza and Reinier played with action figures—pretending the villains were really the good guys. Between the lot of them, there were incredible stories to be told, and they were not, by any stretch of the imagination, the typical American family, extended or otherwise. But they were family none-the-less.

Anna called Darius into the kitchen to help. Elladia peeled potatoes and Anna chopped vegetables for the salad. "Can you cut the potatoes?" asked Anna. "The turkey will be done soon, and we need to get going on the mashed potatoes."

Darius started cutting the potatoes up into small pieces—they cooked faster that way, according to Anna. He stood next to Elladia. She leaned her body next to his, and for a few moments they stood there, supporting each other.

"Guess what," said Elladia.

"What?" asked Darius.

She leaned in even closer and whispered in his ear. "I love you."

It was the first time either of them had ever said it. Darius thought about saying it many times over the past few months, keeping it to himself out of fear. Few things scared him, because few things were all that important to him. His love for Elladia, being the most important thing in his life, terrified Darius in ways he never imagined.

But hearing Elladia say that she loved him brought a sense of ease to Darius. Knowing that she loved him made him no longer worried about telling her the same.

"It's funny you should say that," said Darius.

"Why is that?" asked Elladia, smiling.

Darius loved her smile.

"Because I have something I want to tell you."

"And what would that be?" Elladia asked.

Before Darius could respond, the alarm sounded on his Personal Communication Unit. "Hold on a second," he said.

Darius pulled his PCU from his pocket, aware of the sound of two more units going off at the same time. Both Manny and Otto's PCUs were ringing. *Something must be wrong*, he thought. His heart sank when he saw the Code Red alert.

From the living room Otto bellowed for everyone. "Get in here now!"

Anna and Elladia rushed into the living room, followed by Darius, trying to access security feeds on his PCU to find out what was going on.

Anna Rekker screamed in terror.

Darius looked up to see what was wrong. The football game had been interrupted for a breaking news story. A thick black cloud of smoke billowed up from Super Justice Force Headquarters. At least one part of the facility was engulfed in flames. And though there was no way it could be real, ACU-64s moved around outside the buildings.

"What's going on?" Elladia asked. She sounded like a frightened child.

The news reporter on the scene said something about an attack on SJF Headquarters. That had to be a mistake.

Elladia started crying. Darius took her in his arms.

Anna hurried the kids out of the room so they couldn't see the television.

Manny tried to reach someone, anyone, from HQ on his PCU.

It was like something out of a nightmare—a nightmare they all shared—and none of them could deny what the television showed them. The ACU-64 Killbots were on the attack.

Without a word, Otto bolted out of the room. He ran through the kitchen, and down into the basement. It seemed like he was gone for hours, or at least long enough for the others to see the first defensive line of Super Justice Force engage the Killbots.

The television news camera shook, making it difficult to fully make out everything happening. White Dynamo went down—that was definite. The fact that his head had separated from his body meant he would not be getting back up.

Otto came back into the living room carrying a massive metal trunk with his bionic arm. He dropped the trunk to the floor, and the whole house shook. It must have weighed a ton.

"What've you got?" Otto asked, opening the trunk.

Inside the trunk were three of the biggest guns Darius had ever seen and what looked like part of a bionic arm. He had never seen portable techno-plasm cannons like those in Otto's trunk before. *Otto must've built them himself.*

"It's bad," said Manny. "Half the security feeds are offline. I can't raise CAD."

"Anna, you and the kids get in here now!" yelled Otto, pulling the bionic arm from the trunk.

Anna came back in the room, the kids looked scared, but they had stopped crying.

Otto worked to remove his bionic arm, detaching it just below the mechanical elbow joint. "You two want to help daddy?" he asked Reinier and Aziza.

The Rekker twins went to their father, helping him attach the bionic arm that had been in the trunk. "I need the both of you to be brave," said Otto. "Can you do that for me?"

Aziza and Reinier Rekker nodded.

Otto locked the new bionic forearm into place, punched in a series of numbers on the keypad located on the wrist, and it hummed to life. He flexed the wrist and moved the fingers, making sure everything worked. Confident his new arm was operational, Otto grabbed Anna firmly by the shoulders, taking care not to squeeze too hard with his bionic hand. "I don't know what's going on," he said. "But we need to get to HQ. You remember how to use one of those things?" Otto motioned to the guns.

Anna nodded her head.

"There's no danger here. Yet. But you take one of these things, and you protect our babies. Understand?"

Otto handed one of the plasma cannons to his wife and kissed her on the forehead. He then reached out and took Elladia by the shoulder and turned her around to face him. Otto reached inside the trunk and pulled out a second cannon. "Anna is going to show you how to use this," said Otto handing her the giant gun. "Please, help protect my family."

Elladia nodded, even though she wasn't really sure of what was going on.

Everything happened so fast, Darius didn't know what to think. He didn't want to leave Elladia, but there was trouble at HQ, and he was needed.

Otto handed Anna his PCU, giving her and Elladia more instructions on what to do. "You're not in immediate danger," he said. "Don't panic. Load the car with food and clothes in case you need to make a run for it. Under no circumstances do you hide in the basement. You won't be able to get out of there if you need to."

Despite the tears, Anna and Elladia put on their most courageous faces. Manny said goodbye to his niece, while Otto kissed his family and told them to be brave.

Darius didn't know what to say. Literally minutes earlier he had been cutting potatoes, Elladia telling him that she loved him. Now, the nightmare he'd been having for over ten years was coming true.

Manny and Otto rushed out of the house and into the garage. Manny carried the third plasma cannon. Darius followed, but not before he told Elladia, Anna and the kids that everything would be fine.

Somehow, he felt like he was lying.

52

The Rekkers' garage had been built for three cars, but only one car was parked inside. Otto keyed in a sequence of numbers on the touchpad near the door leading into the house. The floor of the garage opened, a hydraulic lift rose from below ground, carrying something amazing.

The sleekly designed machine looked like a cross between a minivan and a fighter plane. The vehicle had sliding doors on either side that opened horizontally, with half the door retracting into the roof, and the other into the lower part of the body.

Otto jumped into the driver's seat, Manny into the front passenger seat. Darius piled into the backseat, as Otto and Manny strapped themselves in.

Otto started up the machine, which barely made a sound. He pulled out of the garage, peeling out as he took to the streets.

"This thing street legal?" asked Manny.

"Don't ask, don't tell," said Otto.

"It's going to take forever to get there," Darius said. The Rekkers' suburban house was near an hour from HQ.

"Not quite," said Otto. He flipped a switch on the dashboard, and pressed a series of buttons.

The g-forces pushed Darius back into his seat, as the car shot into the air.

"What is this thing?" asked Darius.

"Weekend project," said Otto. "Hold on."

The car swerved hard to the left as Otto worked to avoid overhead power lines. He missed the lines, but did some damage to a tree. They weren't more than sixty feet off the ground, going well over one hundred miles per hour. Darius was convinced they would die long before they got to HQ.

"Either of you guys got anything for me?" Otto asked.

Manny checked his PCU to see if he could catch some sort of information. Darius also checked his PCU. What both of them saw was not pretty.

"Go faster," Manny said.

Darius used his PCU to tap into the main communication grid at CAD. He was sure that a call for help had already been placed, but he sent out a Code Red distress signal to all members of SJF, the European Alliance, and the Galaxus Alliance Corps. He didn't know if any of it would make a difference.

Within a few minutes they could see the clouds of black smoke coming from SJF Headquarters. Darius fought back the fear that clawed at his soul. He could feel the stone in his stomach getting bigger. He just wanted to have Thanksgiving dinner with his girlfriend, not rush off into the face of death.

"Do we have some sort of plan?" Darius asked. It seemed like as good a time as any to ask.

"Stop the Killbots and look for survivors," said Manny.

"And how are we going to do that?" asked Darius.

"By stopping the Killbots and looking for survivors," said Otto.

It wasn't much of a plan, but it made sense.

The closer they got to HQ, the more of the full nightmare they could see. The Bunker was engulfed in flames, as were some of the lower floors of the Dome. People were evacuating from whatever exits they could find. Someone, probably Nightwatcher, used the SJF Hovercraft to get people off the roof of the Tower.

Captain Freedom slugged it out with three Killbots, while Lady Themis, Blue Shield, Smoking Aces and Black Fist each seemed to have their hands full with one. Stixx and Stone tried to help people through the smoke.

Armed security forces were engaging the ACU-64s, but their weapons were having little effect. A lone Killbot fired a blast at a group of guards, exploding them into a million pieces.

"How many of these things are we up against?" asked Otto.

"Good question," said Manny. "There were twenty-six intact models in the cage, and fourteen disassembled."

Darius scanned the area trying to get a count of how many of the killing machines were in action. "I count fifteen in action—make that seventeen. And at least three down for the count," said Darius.

"Okay, I'm bringing this thing in fast and hard, so hold on to your panties, ladies," Otto said.

They passed over the park across from the main entrance to HQ. Otto maneuvered the flying car toward the main entrance of the Bunker. It looked like this was where the ACU-64s had breached the building.

Before Otto could bring the vehicle down for a landing, a massive explosion rocked the Bunker, shooting something out that flew toward the car.

It moved so fast Darius couldn't make out what it was, but it looked an awful lot like Rocky Feldman, speeding toward them like a missile. Whatever or whoever it was slammed into the flying car with so much force that the car slammed into the ground, but not in one piece. The front part of the vehicle tore away from the rear section, and it lay upside down, burning in flames.

Otto was thrown clear of the driver's seat. He was a bloody mess, unconscious, but alive.

Still strapped into the backseat—the only intact part of the car's rear half—Darius regained consciousness. He felt woozy, and at first could only hear a terrible ringing in his ears.

He managed to get free and surveyed the damage around him. They had crashed in the park, less than 500 yards from the main entrance. Darius was right. It had been Rocky Feldman hurtling toward them. The remains of his body splattered amid the wreckage of the car. He looked like a broken sculpture oozing some sort of red mush.

Seeing what was left of Rocky reminded Darius that he was alive, with work that still needed to be done. *Mourn later*, he told himself, the ringing in his ears finally dying down enough to hear the screams.

Darius turned to the direction of the screaming, coming from what was left of the car.

Manny was trapped inside the burning wreckage, surrounded by a raging inferno, his crushed legs pinned underneath the twisted metallic remains of an ACU-64. The car had crashed into the Killbot, and now it had Manny trapped.

Darius tried to pull Manny from under the wreckage, but it was no use. Manny screamed in agony while blood poured from his mouth. Darius didn't have long to get Manny out of the car before the flames completely engulfed him.

He rushed over to Otto, who struggled to get back to his feet. Blood poured from the gash in his head, blinding him. Darius guided him over to the wreckage.

"I can't see!" shouted Otto.

"It doesn't matter!" Darius shouted back. He guided Otto's bionic hand to the twisted metal that pinned Manny in the burning car. "When I tell you to, lift," Darius said.

Darius raced around to Manny. He reached in and undid the seatbelt. The heat burned Darius's hands. "Okay, now!" Darius shouted.

With his powerful bionic hand, Otto lifted the destroyed ACU-64. Manny screamed in pain. Darius grabbed Manny under his arms, and pulled him from the wreckage. Manny screamed even louder. His legs were bent, twisted and burned to the point they no longer looked like they belonged on a human.

Otto tried to wipe the blood from his eyes and stop the flow of crimson that poured from his head. Darius tore off his own shirt, and wrapped it around Otto's head. "Come on, we have to get Manny out of here," said Darius.

As he guided Otto over to Manny, Darius caught sight of the techno-plasm cannon. He grabbed it, but had no idea what to do with it. Otto could barely see. Manny couldn't walk and needed immediate care if he was going to survive. All around Darius could hear the sounds of battle.

Darius looked around for some sort of cover. Less than twenty yards away there was a tree—not much, but it would have to do. Otto picked Manny up, and Manny screamed again in agony. Darius led Otto to the tree.

This is where we'll make a stand, Darius thought. *Not that it'll be much of a stand.*

He looked back over toward the burning headquarters of Super Justice Force. Darius knew he wouldn't be much help hiding with his back against a tree. He had to do something. There was the gun. The portable techno-plasm cannon—or whatever it was.

"How do you use this thing?" Darius asked.

"Flip the safety switch, wait for it to charge, aim and fire," said Otto. "It will take a few seconds to recharge after you fire."

"You mind if I take this, or do you want it?" Darius asked.

Otto held up his bionic arm. "I've got a techno-plasm blaster built in to this thing."

Darius pulled back the safety switch, and the gun began to vibrate in his hands. He quickly scanned the front lines of the battle, and spotted Captain Freedom doing his best to fight three Killbots. Darius aimed his weapon, and fired.

The techno-plasm charge caught one of the ACU-64s in the arm and tore it right off. Unfortunately, it didn't stop the machine, which turned to see where the shot had been fired. It zeroed in on Darius, and in one giant leap covered the almost five hundred yards that separated them.

Darius waited for the cannon to recharge, but it took too long. The ACU-64 loomed over him, ready to deliver a deathblow with its remaining arm. Before it could strike, Otto Rekker tackled the killing machine, and both fell to the ground.

Otto wrestled with the ACU-64. The Killbot reached for Otto's throat, which it could have crushed with ease, if Darius hadn't managed to destroy its other arm with a blast from the cannon. Otto fired a blast from his bionic hand, pulverizing the Killbot's head and shutting it down once and for all.

Before Otto could pick himself up off the ground, another ACU-64 leapt through the air, landing near him and Darius. For whatever reason, the ACU-64 ignored Otto and moved for Darius. Otto scurried to get between Darius and the machine. And then another ACU-64 landed from the sky, followed by another and another. Otto stood between Darius and four ACU-64 Killbots.

There was no knowing why, but Otto knew, just as Darius did, that the Killbots were after Darius. "Run!" shouted Otto as he dove at the ACU-64s, his bionic arm letting lose a blast of techno-plasm.

Darius stayed still long enough to fire a charge at one of the Killbots. He didn't stand around to see what sort of damage he had caused. He heard another scream. This time it sounded like Otto. Darius couldn't look back. He couldn't bear to see if Otto was dead, torn apart by Killbots.

The main entrance to HQ lay straight ahead—with only a small war between Darius and the entrance. Backup had started to arrive, for all the good the city's

S.W.A.T. teams would be able to do. The high-caliber weapons used by the cops were having no effect at all. It was like throwing grains of sand at charging rhinos. An energy blast from a single ACU-64 took out three cops at once. A moment later the same Killbot brought down a police helicopter.

Darius stopped in his tracks as the flaming helicopter fell from the sky. It barely missed the statue of the original Super Justice Force that stood in front of HQ. The flaming mass of wreckage did, however, slam into the front entrance. Darius couldn't hear any screams coming from inside the inferno. He prayed his own death would be as quick and painless as he hoped the helicopter crew's had been.

Insanity surrounded Darius. He felt like he stood in the eye of a hurricane. He tried to survey his surroundings. Maybe he could inflict a little more damage on some ACU-64s before he went down. But first, he had to have a better sense of the situation.

How many ACU-64s did Manny say there were? Twenty-six intact. Fourteen disassembled. How many are active? How many have been taken down? Darius knew of at least five that had been destroyed. But that meant there could be twenty-one more to deal with—maybe more if the other fourteen had been reassembled. *What the hell did those pencil-neck geeks do down there in the Cage?*

His quick assessment of the surrounding area revealed what he knew before the car crashed into the park—things were not good. Darius saw Captain Freedom take two energy blasts from a pair of Killbots. The blasts threw his limp body back so far that it slammed into a building on the other side of the park. Darius thought of Rocky. *What kind of energy blast did it take to turn him into the missile that took down Otto's flying car?*

Darius leveled his techno-plasm cannon at one of the two machines that had blasted Captain Freedom. *This is for Rocky and White Dynamo*, he said to himself. *And Captain Freedom and Manny and Otto.*

Darius fired his cannon at one of the ACU-64s. He must have hit it near its fuel source, because it exploded, knocking its companion to the ground. Darius took aim at the second Killbot, but it was back on its feet before the techno-plasm cannon could recharge. It locked its targeting sensors onto the cannon and fired.

The energy blast hit the cannon, exploding it into a million pieces. The force of the explosion threw Darius at least twenty yards. His body slammed into the statue of the original Super Justice Force.

Darius lay at the base of the statue, gasping for breath. He was on fire. Or at least it felt like he was on fire. His brain registered a pain the likes of which he had never felt before. He looked down at his hands. They were burned beyond recognition. He could see bone.

A fire burned in Darius's torso. He saw that his undershirt was soaked in blood. A piece of shrapnel from the destroyed cannon had managed to tear through his abdomen. If he had anything that resembled hands, maybe he could apply direct pressure to the wound. Not that it would do any good. He could slow the bleeding from his guts, but all that would do was prolong his life by maybe ten or fifteen minutes. Darius knew he didn't have long to live.

He had thought about this moment so many times, wondering how and when it would happen. His nightmares had been filled with moments just like this one. But he never thought it would really end like this—killed by the same machines that killed his family.

For years he had wished he died with his family. That was before he became a Chancer. Before he met Zander and Manny and Otto. Before he met Elladia.

Elladia. She told Darius that she loved him. It was one of the last things she had said to him—no more than an hour ago. A lifetime ago. He had run out of the house with Otto and Manny, and not taken the time to tell Elladia that he loved her. And now he was going to die.

How will she know?

Darius looked around. Was there anyone near him he could tell? He just needed someone to tell Elladia that he loved her too. That he was sorry he didn't talk more. He needed to tell someone, so she could know that as he lay dying, the only thing that mattered to Darius Logan was his love for Elladia Ortiz.

The only sign of life in Darius's view came from the ACU-64 that had blasted the cannon in his hands. It moved toward him with what could only be described as a limp. A limping robot. Darius found it amusing. He must have damaged it when he blasted its companion.

The ACU-64 Killbot loomed over Darius. It locked its sensors on him, but it did not fire.

What're you waiting for, you mechanical piece of shit?

Darius faded fast. Sounds became distant and muffled. His vision blurred, but he could still see the murdering machine that stood in front of him. Darius coughed up some blood as he found the strength to curse the ACU-64, calling it the worst twelve-letter word he knew.

As if it understood what he said, the ACU-64 responded. "Darius Logan. Target acquired."

53

Darius Logan moved closer toward death. He lay at the base of a statue that represented the good of humanity. A machine that represented the bad of humanity loomed over him.

The Automated Combat Unit, Model 64, the most expensive weapon ever designed by any world government—and the most deadly—had never worked properly. Hijacked by the nefarious Doc Kaos, a small army of ACU-64s carried out the most brutal attack on American soil in recorded history. Among the victims were Dwayne and Janae Logan, and their newborn son. Now, nearly ten years later, the ACU-64 Killbots were about to finish what they'd started—killing off the Logan family.

Three more of the automated killing machines joined the one that stood over Darius. Each one of the machines scanned him, but none attacked. Instead, each said the same thing: "Darius Logan. Target acquired."

"Life signs at thirty-five percent," said the mechanical voice of one of the Killbots. "Probability of death, one hundred percent."

In turn, each of the ACU-64s repeated the same thing. Not that Darius needed some damn machines to tell him what he already knew. He could feel himself fading. He felt like his guts were on fire, but the rest of him was freezing.

Still, he had some fight left in him. Darius eyed the four Killbots in front of him as best he could given his blurred vision. He tried to do the math in his head—tried to remember how many of these things there were, how many he had personally taken down. More important, he tried to figure out how to take down the four that stood in front of him.

The ACU-64s formed a perfect line in front of Darius, scanning his steadily dwindling life signs.

Let's just get this over with, Darius thought. With no strength left to fight, Darius spit at the deadly machines. "Kiss my skinny black ass," he said.

Suddenly, as if obeying an unheard command, the ACU-64s moved. Two stepped to the right and two stepped to the left, clearing a path for someone or something to move in between the two pairs.

Darius's vision blurred badly—the air thick with smoke made it even more difficult to see. And yet something seemed familiar about the man who stood between the four Killbots. Darius couldn't be sure, but he felt certain he knew the man.

Or was he just hallucinating? Was the pain so intense that his mind was creating an image appropriate to this moment? Maybe that was it. Moments like these needed a villain to come along and explain everything to the fallen hero. Then the villain would triumphantly exclaim, "All my life I have awaited this moment of glory!"

But all Chuck Maslon did was look down at Darius and say, "Yeah, that's him."

Maslon, or the hallucination of Maslon, walked away, leaving Darius to die, blood steadily leaking from the massive gash in his abdomen, his head resting against a placard that read, "Justice for all."

Darius saw a bright light, and thought that it must have been the bright light people claimed to see at the moment of their death. Loved ones were supposed to be waiting at the end of the light, waiting to greet you as you crossed over to the other side. A smile crept to his face at the thought of seeing his family.

But the light disappeared as quickly as it had appeared, and Darius didn't see his family. Instead, he saw something better. It wasn't a light beckoning him to the afterlife that Darius had seen. The light in the sky was a Quantus Portal, an opening in the fabric of space signaling that the Galaxus Alliance Corps had arrived.

Zander raced down toward Darius, like some sort of rocket fired from a massive launcher. He slammed into the four ACU-64 Killbots, as the night sky began to light up as if there were a massive electric storm. Only it wasn't lightning, it was Quantus Portals opening all throughout the sky above Super Justice Force HQ. And through each gate came a Galaxus ready for action.

The battle must have been great—like something out of the best comic book. Unfortunately, Darius couldn't see much of it. In fact, part of him wasn't even sure if it was real. It could all be part of the pain, part of some deathbed hallucination. He couldn't be sure the Galaxus Alliance was any more real than Maslon had been.

Everything started to fade to black. His time had come. Death was at hand. In the distance he heard a voice. "Darius, I need you to hold on," said the voice.

Darius felt a sudden, yet faint surge of energy. He opened his eyes. His vision cleared, though the excruciating pain remained. Darius could see Zander standing over him, reaching down and touching his shoulder. "Hold on, Darius," Z-Boe said.

Something strange was happening to Darius. Mind-ripping pain tore at him, but he could feel strength, as if some energy surged through his body, giving him enough strength to fight off the death that moments before had been a given.

An energy blast of some sort knocked Zander off his feet. Darius struggled to turn and see the source of the blast. It was not an ACU-64. It was something else. Something bigger.

The Cage had been filled with ACU-64s, both intact and disassembled. The thing that blasted Z-Boe looked liked it had been built out of two or three Killbots. It was a giant, standing close to twelve feet tall. Where there should have been two arms with energy blasters, there were four. And the energy blasters looked to have been modified. The massive machine locked its sensors on Zander, aimed its four arms, and fired four energy blasts that converged into a single bolt of destruction that slammed into Z-Boe.

Amazingly, Z-Boe stood his ground. He even fired back his own energy blast, which managed to disable one of the four arms. Unfortunately, the other three arms fired another blast that knocked Zander flat on his back.

The giant super Killbot lumbered toward Zander, no doubt going in for the kill. Three Galaxus slamming into it at the same time knocked it off balance.

If it all were a comic book with "to be concluded next issue" on the last page, Darius would have wanted to know what happened next. But there was no next issue—only an immediate need to survive, to stay alive, to help his friends. Darius needed to get to Zander, who lay motionless only a few yards away. Darius needed to help Z-Boe.

All the strength Darius had inside was being used to stay alive. His hands were burnt, mangled and useless, his body torn open and leaking blood. None of that mattered, though. One of his best friends needed him. He had already failed Manny and Otto, who were most certainly dead. He would not fail Zander as well.

His mind exploded in searing pain as he picked himself up off the ground. Darius stumbled over to Z-Boe, oblivious to the battle raging around him, and collapsed. Darius lay on the ground next to Zander Boeman. He looked over at the fallen hero.

Zander was stunned and in bad shape. The combined energy blasts that hit him must have been incredibly strong to inflict this much injury. Still, Z-Boe wasn't nearly as bad off as Darius.

At least he's going to survive this night, Darius thought.

Darius could feel himself growing weaker. Whatever strength he had found, wherever it had come from, it left him. He faded fast.

Zander stirred, his head clearing from the impact of the blast he had taken. He saw Darius on the ground next to him, the life quickly draining away.

"Darius!" screamed Z-Boe.

Darius didn't know what to say. Should he ask Zander to tell Elladia he loved her? Or was it better to go as he had lived much of his life, in silence?

Zander moved so that he could cradle Darius in his arms. Darius was too weak to cry out in pain. The physical contact with Galaxus brought with it a surge of energy, just like it always did. Darius wondered what caused the odd feeling. He wanted to ask, but it was too late, he was already dead.

54

Darius Logan breathed his last breath, and the world around him went black. Death embraced him like an old friend.

A moment later, an explosive force jolted Darius, as if waking from a deep sleep. Only he had been dead. He knew this. Darius *knew* that he'd stopped living, even though he now found himself alive.

Darius opened his eyes, uncertain of what he would see. He half expected to see his parents and baby brother. Instead, Darius saw Zander kneeling at his side, holding his hands—only there were no hands. Darius's hands were no longer there, nor were Zander's hands. Instead, a glowing mass of power, burning brighter than the sun but without blinding, bonded them together, making them one.

A power like he never felt before surged through Darius, impossible to describe, completely foreign, while at the same time completely familiar—like life itself. He could feel the wounds that had killed him healing. He could feel the blood that had drained out of his body being replaced with something else—something that he could not fully comprehend.

"What's happening to me?" Darius gasped.

"I hoped it wouldn't be like this. I'm sorry," said Zander.

Darius didn't understand what Z-Boe had said.

What doesn't he want to be like this? What's he sorry about?

And then Darius saw it in Zander's face, and he knew. He didn't know how he knew, but he knew—like the way his lungs knew how to breathe and his heart knew how to pump. Thoughts and the ideas appeared in his mind as if they had always been there, only forgotten like a box full of old letters hidden in the bottom of a closet. Darius looked into the face of Zander Boeman, and he could see the life draining from his friend. Z-Boe had sacrificed his life so that Darius could live.

Darius struggled to break free of Zander's grip, but that was not what held him. The Mhadra Turas gripped Darius, and as the massive ball of energy that had merged his hands to Z-Boe's hands began to fade, the truth was revealed.

The Mhadra Turas, the symbiotic life forms that appeared as bands around the wrists of Zander, were now around Darius's wrists. The mix of technology and organic life that gave every member of the Galaxus Alliance Corps their powers had become part of Darius. Darius became part of it. They were now one and the same. And Zander, instead of Darius, lay on the ground lifeless.

From deep within the core of Darius's being a rage began to grow. It was a rage that started on the playground where he had been bullied. It grew when his family had been killed, growing even more as he lived a life of hopelessness and fear. Looking down at the body of a man who had sacrificed himself for Darius, and then looking around and seeing the death and destruction destroying the new life he had created for himself, the rage exploded.

Darius could not deny the rage. He could not force it back down inside where for years it had eaten at him like a hungry animal trying to gnaw its way free. In that moment, the rage defined Darius—it informed his every thought—but unlike so many other times when it reared up and threatened to make him lash out, this time Darius knew what to do with his anger. He had to make the nightmare stop. And though he could not explain or understand it, he knew he had the power to do what needed to be done.

Darius leapt into the heat of the battle. His mind and body were one. Action and reaction were the same. There was no offensive or defensive action, just rage providing the fuel to carry Darius to the only thing that had to be done—the complete and total destruction of the ACU-64 Killbots.

The first Killbot fell with ease. Darius simply punched through the nearly indestructible metal casing of the head and ripped out the central processing unit, grinding it to dust with his bare fist. The second and third ACU-64s were brought down with energy blasts that Darius shot from his hands with such force that the Killbots were vaporized. The powerful force of destruction came with ease—a natural instinct—serving as an introduction to Darius of what he'd become.

The other heroes that fought the ACU-64s inflicted damage on the deadly machines, but it could not compare to the destruction rained down by Darius. He transformed into a blur of pure fury unleashed. He had become the living embodiment of revenge. Revenge for his family. Revenge for Zander and Otto and Manny. Darius was a weapon of retribution—payback for every human being who had suffered because of the machines that had chased him in his dreams for a decade.

The remaining ACU-64s, locked in combat with Super Justice Force and Galaxus Alliance Corps and an army of cops, all paused for a moment, their mechanized sensors all locking on to the same thing at once. The machines spoke in a single voice. "Darius Logan. Target acquired. Terminate. Terminate. Terminate…"

Over and over again, in an endless chorus, the ACU-64 Killbots repeated one word—terminate—breaking away to engage Darius. It made no sense. Everyone stopped and watched, confused by the sudden tactic change of the machines, unsure of what had happened. Captain Freedom and Lady Themis, the cosmic-powered Galaxus Alliance Corps and the heavily armed S.W.A.T. officers, everyone who could still see watched the battle in amazement—Darius Raymond Logan versus mechanized death. And none of them had ever seen anything quite like Darius in action.

The last of the ACU-64s crossed the battlefield outside Super Justice Force Headquarters, converging on a solitary target. A target that moved faster than any Galaxus had ever moved. A target that hit harder than any Galaxus had ever hit. A target that fought with a deadly combination of cosmic powers and animalistic rage.

Darius produced an energy stream from his hands that he wielded like a massive sword, using it to chop one of the Killbots in half, while simultaneously dodging techno-plasm blasts from two other machines. A moment later, Darius transformed the sword into a pair of whips, one in each hand. One whip lashed out, wrapping around a Killbot that Darius slammed into the ground. The other whip caught a Killbot around its neck, a sharp snap decapitating it.

And so it went, until the battle between supermen and supermachines came to an end. None of the ACU-64s remained intact. Darius stood on ground littered with the parts of nearly two dozen machines, and the lifeless remains of even more human beings. It was a terrible sight, and not even the victory seemed worth the cost. And then the ground shook, and Darius knew that the war had not yet ended.

Every head turned toward the sound of the mechanical rumble, Darius included. They all looked at what had once been the Bunker of Super Justice Force Headquarters—a smoldering heap collapsing in on itself. The escape route of the ACU-64s had taken the machines up from the fifth sub-basement, and straight through the Bunker. At one point the machines had poured out from the ground like giant bugs. Now, only one emerged from deep beneath the surface.

The modified ACU-64 that had attacked Zander Boeman had stood twelve feet high, and looked like it had been put together using the parts from two or three different machines. Its twin emerged from the fire and moved toward Darius.

Someone built this thing, Darius thought. *On purpose.*

The Super Killbot looked its sensors on Darius. "Darius Logan. Target acquired. Terminate."

Four robotic arms locked in unison, firing four energy beams that converged into a massive bolt of deadly force aimed directly at Darius. If the blast had hit him, even with his newly gained powers, it would have killed him. Somehow he instinctively knew this, just as he instinctively leapt into the air, flying directly at the Super Killbot as the energy blast hit the spot where he'd been standing.

Darius slammed into the gigantic robot with enough force to topple a building. The Super Killbot struggled to stay upright on its massive metallic legs. It furiously swung its mechanical arms at Darius like swatting at a bug. Darius swerved to avoid being hit, caught one of the robotic arms, tearing it off. The shower of sparks was almost as good as blood for Darius. He took the arm and used it like a giant bat, swinging it at one of the legs.

The robot's arm tore through its leg. The giant machine toppled to the ground, its second leg snapping in two as it fell. It struggled to set itself back up, but with both legs broken in two, it couldn't stand. Instead, it found a compromise in a seated position, its bottom two arms serving as supports holding it upright.

Darius took off into the air, flying a hundred yards above the ground. He turned to face the Super Killbot, holding the severed arm like giant lance. The machine locked its sensors on Darius and fired an energy blast from one of its remaining arms. Darius swerved, dodging the blast as he flew at top speed toward the Super Killbot. He drove the metallic arm into the chest of the killing machine with such force the two bottom arms snapped and it fell backwards. Another shower of sparks brought a twisted smile to Darius's face.

The Super Killbot struggled to move, looking like an animal that had been hit by a car. It was a twisted mess of damaged circuitry and malfunctioning sensors, but it was still functioning—still alive. And it needed to be put out of its misery.

Darius stood over the fallen machine, staring at what would be considered its face. The mechanical eyes locked on Darius and the sensors kicked in. "Darius Logan. Target acquired," it said.

The remaining mechanical arm moved and pointed at Darius. He grabbed it by the wrist, and without flinching, tore the entire arm off.

The Super Killbot tried to bring one of its other arms around to bear on Darius, but the arm had been snapped in half, a mangled stump of damaged circuitry. The machine continued to scan Darius, unable to do anything else.

Up until this moment, no one had ever seen a machine like the modified ACU-64. That was because it didn't exist. Someone had put it together from disassembled parts stored in the fifth sub-basement at SJF headquarters—one of the most heavily secured places on the planet. And whoever had managed to put this thing together—right under the nose of Super Justice Force—also activated it, along with all the others. This was no accident. They knew what the deadly machines were capable of. And they specifically targeted Darius for termination.

Darius wondered if whoever reactivated the Killbots was watching him through a video feed built into the eyes of the last ACU-64.

"I don't know if you can see me or hear me," said Darius. "But if you can, know this: I will find you. I will kill you."

And with that Darius let loose an energy blast from his hands that turned the head of the Super Killbot to dust.

55

The media started calling it "Black Thanksgiving" before the day ended. Mere hours had passed, the rescue operation well under way, and the world, having watched much of the horror unfold while it happened, reeled in a state of shock and mourning.

The list of casualties boggled the mind. Zander Boeman, member of the elite Galaxus Alliance Corps. Rocky Feldman, beloved hero and international spokesman for metahuman rights. White Dynamo, television star and former partner of Black Fist. All of them were dead. Also dead were Speed Skater, Limelight and the Jackhammer, three trainees of the Teen Justice Force, and four other unlicensed superpowers no one ever heard of. The media focused on the fallen heroes, their names coming up over and over again in the worldwide conversations about Black Thanksgiving.

Twenty-five of the city's finest police officers and twelve emergency rescue workers had been killed in the battle. Their names were hardly mentioned, and instead of individuals, they seemed destined to be remembered by history as the "Black Thanksgiving Thirty-seven." Although their names would not be known, they would be honored in some parade, or some police memorial, and the mayor would make a speech.

The biggest losses of life, however, were not among heroes of Super Justice Force, the twenty-five cops, or the twelve emergency rescue workers. The hardest hit by Black Thanksgiving was the Operations Crew of Super Justice Force. Their death toll hit eighty-two, and that did not include family members attending the annual Thanksgiving dinner for employees who had to work. All told, there were one hundred and seven deaths that the media all but ignored.

Darius knew most of the casualties from Operations Crew. He had worked with many of them, passed them in the halls; he even trained one of them.

Doug Baum was working in the kitchen on Thanksgiving, helping prepare the meal for employees and their families. His own family was there—his ex-wife, with whom he was reconciling, and their two kids. After Doug helped his family and those in the employee cafeteria escape, he went back to help evacuate the other buildings. Monica Firor, the other employee Darius had trained, was among those helped by Doug. She had been knocked from her wheelchair during a blast, and lay unconscious on the floor when Doug found her and carried her to safety. Monica was still unconscious when Doug went back to help others. A few minutes later, a wall collapsed on him, and he died instantly.

The media, and by default much of the world, dwelled less on the dead than on one person in particular. People became obsessed with the mysterious figure spotted battling the ACU-64s. Footage of what looked like a black kid in a bloody t-shirt, single-handedly taking on the deadly Killbots and laying waste to the machines, captured the imagination of the world. He was, by all accounts, the hero of the hour. Unfortunately, no one knew his identity.

That kid, who became the instant subject of message boards, chat rooms and news broadcasts, had assisted with the rescue operation immediately following the battle. Side by side with those he knew and didn't know, Darius sifted through the rubble, looking for survivors. He lost count of the hours and the dead bodies he found, each one a reminder of the similar tragedy that robbed him of his own family. Finally, when Darius lifted the collapse wall, and saw the lifeless body of Doug Baum, he'd had enough. He quietly slipped away, and left to be with the people who needed him most.

Amidst all the tragedy was bits and pieces of good news, or perhaps it was slightly less tragic news. Otto Rekker had survived the battle. The last time Darius saw him, Otto was slugging it out with four ACU-64s. The machines had done their worst damage to Otto, but miraculously, he had lived. He lost his human arm in the fight, which he'd regularly referred to as his "good arm."

Manny survived as well, but Darius didn't know if it was a good thing or not. Manny sustained severe burns on over seventy-five percent of his body. His legs and spine were crushed. The legs could be replaced with new bionic ones, but science and modern medicine still had no biomechatronic repairs for a spinal injury, which meant Manny still wouldn't be able to walk. And that was if he lived. Uncertain of Manny's chances, the doctors had him in a medical-induced coma.

Elladia sat at her uncle's bedside, praying for him, though she doubted it would do any good. She had spent years praying for her parents, and they were still dead.

Lady Themis sat next to Elladia, the two women holding hands. Neither had slept in almost twenty-four hours. Both were ravaged by fear and sadness, exhausted from no sleep, too much crying and the mental anguish of preparing for the worst.

Manny had been secretly dating someone for months, but no one knew who. Everyone wondered who she was, what she did for living, and how she and Manny met. Seeing Lady T sitting at Manny's bedside, crying like she'd lost her lover, Darius knew all those answers. For the briefest of moments Darius overflowed with happiness. And then reality set in. Manny might not live.

Darius stood behind Elladia and Lady Themis, looking down on Manny. Before coming to the hospital—MTSU had been destroyed—Darius had pulled more dead bodies from the rubble of HQ than any eighteen-year-old should ever have to. None of the broken and battered dead bodies looked as bad as Manny.

Elladia sensed Darius's presence in the room, but Lady T was lost, nearly catatonic. Darius had seen her on the battlefield in front of Super Justice Force HQ. She'd fought hard and strong. She survived when others had not. Now she looked weak and defeated.

"The doctors say he can't feel anything," Darius said. He couldn't think of anything else emotionally comforting to say.

Elladia got up from her seat and guided Darius to the entrance of the hospital room. There was no need for Lady Themis to hear the conversation—if she could hear through her dazed emotional state.

"If he lives, he won't ever walk again," Elladia whispered.

"He'll live, and we'll deal with it."

Darius cautiously put his hands on Elladia's shoulders. Would she feel the same energy surge he felt whenever he had physical contact with Zander?

If Elladia felt anything, she didn't let it show. "Have you seen Anna and the kids?" she asked.

"Not yet," said Darius.

Elladia's eyes were weak and bloodshot from hours of crying.

"I don't know what to do," said Elladia.

"First, you need to be strong for Manny. You are the most important thing in the world to him. Be strong for him, so he can concentrate on healing," Darius said.

"I don't know if I can do it," said Elladia.

Darius took Elladia by the hand. "You're strong. That's one of the reasons I love you so much."

"You love me?"

"I love you."

Darius had never said it before. He'd meant to say it barely twenty-fours ago, before the world was torn apart. Given a second chance, he had to make sure she knew how he felt.

Darius leaned forward and gently kissed Elladia, and she knew that every choice she had made about Darius had been the right one. She lifted one of his hands to her lips and kissed it. That's when she saw his wrist.

The Mhadra Turas glowed bright, and Elladia stared in disbelief. She looked at his other wrist, equally stunned, as if the two were more of a shock than the one.

Darius could see Elladia trying to process everything. Her boyfriend—the man she loved—had Mhadra Turas fused to his wrists. You only became joined with Mhadra Turas when it separated from the host— someone in the Galaxus Alliance Corps. It meant a Galaxus had died.

"Who?" asked Elladia.

"Zander."

Elladia looked like she wanted to cry, but there were no more tears left. She knew how much Zander meant to Darius. And she knew that Darius's life had changed forever. Suddenly, she felt small and insignificant. Darius had become part of the most elite group in the universe.

"Why are you here?" Elladia asked.

"Because you need me."

"Don't you have somewhere to be?"

"Not as long as you need me."

"I will always need you," said Elladia. "But right now, others need you more. Go. I give you permission. I'll be strong."

Elladia kissed Darius goodbye. "I'll be fine," she said.

Darius left Elladia and Lady Themis in the hospital room to worry about Manny.

Before he could leave the hospital, Darius had to see Otto. He quietly entered the room. Anna Rekker sat curled up in a chair. The twins, Reinier and Aziza were nowhere to be seen.

Anna stirred, looking around the room for a moment, disoriented and uncertain where she was. She saw Otto in the bed next to her, then turned and saw Darius. She smiled a tired smile, but behind the exhaustion, Darius saw a strength that he envied.

"Where are the twins?" Darius whispered.

"I took them to my mother before I came here. They don't need to see their father like this," said Anna.

"How is he?" Darius asked.

"He's doped up pretty good," Anna said.

"I cannnnn hhhearrrr youuuuu," said Otto. "Issssh that Biiiiig D?"

"It's me."

"C'mere sssho I can sssheee yyyyooou," Otto said.

Otto didn't look as bad as Manny, but only because he was conscious, which made him look like the walking dead. His face, a mass of pummeled flesh, had been stitched back together, and both of his arms—organic and bionic—were missing. An IV tube steadily dripped painkillers and antibiotics into his leg.

Darius moved closer. Otto being alive was a miracle—even if he wasn't in one piece.

"Yyyooou ssssshaved Maaaaannyyyyy," said Otto. Tears flowed from his eyes. "Yyyooouuu shhhaaaaaved my besssssht frieeeeend."

"We saved him. Together. You and me."

"Yyyyou sssshaaaaved my besssssht frieeeend. Yoooooou sssssshaved usssssh aaaaall."

Otto drifted off into a drug-induced sleep brought about by a morphine drip.

Anna joined Darius at Otto's side. She looked down at her husband and did not see the broken wreck of a man that lay in the bed. She saw the father of her children—alive. Nothing else mattered.

"The doctors say he'll be fine," said Anna. "It will just take time."

"How are Aziza and Reinier?" Darius asked.

"They're Rekkers. They'll get through this. How is Elladia?"

"Not good," said Darius. "I just left, but I need to be with her."

"Then why aren't you?"

Darius held his hands up in front of his face so Anna could see what encircled his wrists. Her eyes grew wide, and though he wasn't sure, Darius thought he saw a hint of sadness.

"There's all this stuff in my brain, and I don't know what most of it is. I know things that I don't understand, and understand things I don't know," said Darius. He looked at the Mhadra Turas around his wrists, more uncertain than any other time in his life. Everything had changed. "I have to leave Earth. I don't how I know this, but I do."

Anna pulled Darius close, holding him tight like a mother holds her frightened child. It had been years since anyone held him that way—not since his mother had died. Anna whispered soothingly, "It'll be alright. We love you. You've got our love to keep you strong. Don't ever forget that."

Anna released Darius, kissing him on the cheek.

"Promise one thing," Darius said. "Promise that if anything happens to me—today or ten years from now—make sure you tell Elladia that I love her. Tell her every day."

Anna wanted to tell Darius that nothing would happen to him—that everything would be fine. But the events of the last twenty-four hours would only make her a liar. And the Mhadra Turas that had become part of Darius served as an even greater reminder of the uncertainty ahead. Anna had been with Otto too long, had heard too many stories about the lives of the people he worked with, and so she knew that anything that made Darius like the others—the ones who saved the day so that people like her and her kids could be safe—might not always be a good thing.

Anna looked at Darius and saw little more than a child, a young man not even nineteen years old. Her children called him Uncle Big D, and loved him like family. He was family—the godfather to her and Otto's unborn baby. And now Darius had become Mhadra Turas—part of the Galaxus Alliance Corps. Anna Rekker worried that he would not live to see the birth of his own godchild. The least she could do, in the very likely event something happened to Darius, was remind Elladia that he loved her.

"I'll tell her every day," said Anna.

"And tell Aziza and Reinier that I love them, too," said Darius. "I really do."

"And they love you," said Anna. "They love their Uncle Big D more than you'll ever know."

Darius fought back tears as he thought about the Rekker twins. He didn't want to be robbed of watching them grow up. His heart ached, and even the cosmic power that he now possessed could not stop the pain. Darius wanted to stay with them—with all of them. They were all his family—Elladia and Manny, the Rekker family—and they were all hurt and scared, uncertain of the hours and days and weeks to come.

Darius wanted to stay and protect all of them. He had the strength to protect them. But he had other things to do.

He left Anna Rekker alone in the hospital room, as Otto woke from his sleep, mumbling to himself, "He sssshaved usssh all."

56

Captain Freedom waited for Darius in the hallway outside of Otto Rekker's hospital room, sitting on a plastic chair that strained under his mass of muscle. He looked battered and exhausted, like a war-weary soldier fresh from the front lines. His rugged face—streaked with dirt and soot and dried blood—belonged to a man who had seen too much, done too much, and wanted nothing more than a chance to rest. Captain Freedom stared deep into his cup of coffee, as if the steaming dark liquid held the answers to all the questions of life.

An Asian woman, dressed in the uniform of the Galaxus Alliance Corps, sat next to Captain Freedom. By comparison, her diminutive size almost made her look like a child. But the blood and dirt that streaked her face identified her as a veteran of the same war as Captain Freedom.

Captain Freedom blew on his coffee to cool it down, not that it could have burned him. He took a sip, and closed his eyes. "How long have you known?" he asked.

"Not long," said the woman. "Zander told me over the summer."

"You're telling me that he knew, and he didn't tell anyone?"

"It's complicated."

Captain Freedom took another sip of coffee. He had more to say—more he wanted to know. Exhaustion kept him silent.

The door to Otto Rekker's room opened, and Darius stepped out into the hallway, showing no surprise at finding Captain Freedom waiting.

"I was wondering when someone would come looking for me," said Darius.

"We knew where to find you. And we knew you had things to attend to," said Captain Freedom. He didn't bother to get up from the chair. "How is Manny?"

"Not good," said Darius.

"And Elladia?"

"Pretty bad. I should be with her now."

"There's always going to be times when we have to leave behind the ones we love, in order to do what needs be done," said Captain Freedom.

"Yeah, Zander told me something like that once," Darius said. "It was almost like he was trying to prepare me for…this."

Darius held up his hands and stared at the bands around his wrists. He looked at the Asian woman standing next to Captain Freedom. "You're here for me," Darius said.

"Darius, this is Mee Vang Pao," said Captain Freedom.

"I know," Darius said. He had never met Mee Pao—never even heard of her—but still he knew her. A steady stream of thoughts flowed through Darius's mind, informing him of things he otherwise did not know. "You were Zander's unit leader."

Mee Pao stood up and moved in close, reaching out her hands. Instinctively, Darius did the same, joining Mee Pao in an ancient greeting. His right palm touched her right palm, his left palm touched the right side of her head, and her left palm touched the right side of his head. He had never seen it done before, but somehow he knew what to do.

"One as Wholeness," said Mee Pao.

"Wholeness as One," said Darius. Like the touching of the palms and the head, he had never heard the saying, and yet he knew it.

Mee Pao stepped back. Despite her small stature, she radiated the great strength of a leader and a fighter. Her face, too serious to be beautiful, nonetheless had an exquisite quality. Mee Pao looked like beauty sculpted from the hardest stone.

"You have a lot of questions, I'm sure," said Mee Pao.

"A few," said Darius. "But first I have things that I need to take care of."

As odd as it seemed, Darius thought of the aqua-singers back at the apartment. He could do nothing for Manny or Otto that the doctors weren't already doing. And even though he wanted to be there for Elladia, she could take care of herself. But Michael, Jackie, Marlon, Tito, Jermaine and Randy were alone—if they were alive—with no one to take care of them.

Darius turned and headed for the nearest exit. He needed to know that something he cared about was safe and unhurt, even if that something was a tank full of alien creatures that sang Jackson Five songs.

Mee Pao followed two steps behind Darius. Captain Freedom rose from his chair, following three steps behind her.

"I'll need to go with you—for training," said Darius. He kept walking, not bothering to look back to see if Mee Pao and Captain Freedom were behind him.

"Yes. You'll have time to get your things in order, and then we'll be leaving," said Mee Pao.

"I understand. I don't know how, but I do," said Darius. "But first, you'll want to talk about what happened."

"We're still picking up the pieces and sorting through everything," said Captain Freedom. "Right now we have more questions than answers."

All three passed through the main lobby of the hospital, walking out into the cold air. People outside were bundled up against a bitter cold that Darius didn't feel. While others shivered, their teeth chattering, the cold had no effect on Darius, even though his only protection was a torn t-shirt, caked in dry blood.

"I'll go wherever I need to go. I'll talk about whatever needs to be talked about," said Darius. "But first I need to get myself cleaned up and take care of something."

"We'll go back to HQ. The area has been secured," said Captain Freedom. "I'm joining the president for a press conference in an hour. After that, I'd like to talk to you."

"Fine," said Darius.

"Do you need a ride back to Headquarters?" asked Captain Freedom.

"Why would I need a ride?" Darius asked, taking off in the air in a single bound.

Captain Freedom and Mee Vang Pao of the Galaxus Alliance Corps took off after Darius, flying beside him, one on his right, the other on his left. People on the street below looked up and pointed.

Darius didn't know how he could fly, just that he could. It was really that simple—no different than walking. From the moment the Mhadra Turas fused with Darius, bringing him back from the dead, it had changed him.

He couldn't explain it, because he didn't understand it. His thoughts and feelings and memories were still his, but more informed Darius than the sum total of experiences and knowledge that made him the person he had been. The person he had been died at the base of a statue. The person that came back to life was something more.

Deep inside the core of his being, Darius could feel the collected knowledge of hundreds, maybe thousands of lives that had bonded with the Mhadra Turas. It felt like Darius had opened a cabinet full of files in his mind, suddenly discovering things that he already knew, but simply didn't know he knew. It was almost overwhelming—this seemingly endless flow of information—and he worried about getting lost within everything inside of him.

Darius, Captain Freedom and Mee Pao flew in a tight formation toward Super Justice Force Headquarters. It had still been dark when Darius left the rescue operation and went to the hospital. In the cold gray daylight of November, he saw what remained of HQ for the first time. The fires had been put out, but a thin layer of smoke still filled the air. Much of the great architectural achievement of HQ had been transformed to a smoldering mass of rubble. The Bunker and the Dome, the two main strongholds of daily operations at SJF, were destroyed.

"It looks worse than I thought," Darius said. He had to almost shout to be heard over the rush of air.

"It's not pretty," said Captain Freedom. "Thank God it's not worse."

On the ground below, the National Guard patrolled a secured perimeter surrounding Headquarters. Armed soldiers stood beside barricades that blocked all entry points to Super Justice Force HQ.

Hundreds of people gathered outside the barricades. Some were mourners, come to pay their respects to the dead. They carried handmade signs that read, "R.I.P. Rocky," "We Will Never Forget, "I ♥ Super Justice Force." A smaller group of protestors carried signs reading "No More Lies" and "Unmask the Truth."

Television news crews surrounded the area like vultures feeding off the death and destruction. Looking for more ways to tell the only story that would be told for days to come, the reporters went into a frenzy when they saw Captain Freedom, Mee Pao and Darius flying overhead.

A sea of people—mourners, protestors and reporters—erupted into a dull roar of hundreds of voices shouting at the figures who flew past. When they realized that the mysterious black teenager was part of the flying trio, the shouts became louder. No one knew who Darius was, but they all loved him. Even the protestors forget that they were protesting, calling out to the kid who stopped the mechanical monsters.

"Wave to your fans," said Captain Freedom.

Having spent much of his life being ignored or abused, avoiding others as much as possible, Darius didn't know what to make of the people cheering for him. They didn't even know his name, but still they cheered him on.

Darius waved, and the crowd cheered louder.

The trio flew past the crowd outside the barricade, past the soldiers standing guard, landing on the scorched ground inside the secured perimeter.

Two-dozen soldiers and six Galaxus stood guard over a massive scrap heap of ACU-64s, while a team of National Guardsmen scoured the area with metal detectors. A truck with a full-size techno-plasm cannon mounted in the back sat a few yards away from the remains of the Killbots.

Darius stared at the motionless pile of metal and circuitry—the destroyed remains of the nightmares that haunted him over half his life. *Twice you've destroyed my life*, Darius thought.

Captain Freedom placed his hand on Darius's shoulder. "Come on," said Captain Freedom. "Get yourself cleaned up. Maybe get some rest. We'll move on from there."

Captain Freedom, Darius and Mee Pao walked together toward the devastated ruins of HQ, passing the statue of the original Super Justice Force. The fact that it still stood, despite the death and destruction that had gone on all around it, struck Darius as bittersweet at best. And despite all that had happened, Darius felt like he had returned home.

57

The damage to Super Justice Force Headquarters had been extreme, but not complete. Of the five buildings that made up the facility, only two were complete losses. The total destruction of the Bunker and near total destruction of the Dome would leave SJF crippled for a long time. Located in the Bunker, O3C had been completely wiped out. Likewise, everything in the Vehicle Maintenance Bays housed in the Dome was gone. The estimated loss of equipment from the two buildings would be well into the billions of dollars.

The Tower, which housed MTSU, Personnel, corporate offices, living quarters and more, took considerable damage, but it wasn't a total loss. The Mansion sustained the least damage of all the buildings in the main complex. On the other side of the park, the Kurtzberg Center for Metahuman Research and Training remained relatively untouched.

The official story in the news was that Super Justice Force had been attacked by ACU-64 Killbots. The part of the story that had been glossed over was the fact that the killing machines had been stored in a secret warehouse called the Cage, located beneath SJF Headquarters. As far as the general public knew, all the ACU-64s had been destroyed ten years earlier. It wouldn't do for people to know what really happened, so it was covered up.

The one thing that remained unclear for the public was where the ACU-64 Killbots had come from. News reporters quoted unnamed sources that speculated terrorists had somehow gotten their hands on the original designs and built the robots, while other sources claimed the attack was the work of Doc Kaos, bringing a small army of killer machines with him from a parallel universe. Both stories sounded good, so some news outlets ran with the terrorist angle, while others went with Doc Kaos. And the public, with two villains to choose from, was thoroughly captivated by the entire spectacle.

The President of the United States delivered a moving speech, and vowed that "our fallen heroes will not be forgotten." President Banks stood, stoic and resolute,

Captain Freedom by her side, and she eased the shattered nerves of a terrified public. "The vile cowards who committed this act of terror will be made to pay dearly for their actions. We will not bullied, made to live in fear and cower in the shadows like scared children. We will fight back, and we will prevail."

It all sounds great, Darius thought, *except for one thing. Terrorists didn't build the Killbots. And Doc Kaos didn't bring them from a parallel universe. Those damn things were here the entire time.*

Darius returned to the apartment he shared with Zander. Had shared with Zander. He wasn't sharing it anymore.

All of the apartments in HQ were to be cleared out until a damage assessment could be conducted. Darius wasn't even supposed to be in the apartment, but no one bothered to stop him.

The Vissoam aqua-singers were fine, seemingly unaware of the devastating battle that had recently transpired outside the confines of their tank. Cleaned up and wearing fresh clothes not caked in his own blood, Darius watched the aqua-singers while they hummed an unfamiliar tune. Something sounded different about the creatures, and Darius realized that he understood the sounds they were making. Before, he had only heard their melodic humming, but now he understood their language. And in their song Darius heard them mourning the death of Zander. Somehow they knew. All six of the aqua-singers lined up, side by side, their wings and tails moving in perfect unison, and they sang.

Darius pressed his hand gently against the glass tank. "Who's gonna take care of you when I leave?" he asked.

In the background, the president continued her speech on the television. "Now, more than ever, we must stand firm in our fight for freedom," she said.

Darius listened to some more of the president's speech, but he had to stop. He needed the truth, not feel-good catch phrases or lies in response to more lies. He turned off the television and left the apartment.

Darius passed other SJF employees as they roamed the halls, solemn faced and diligently trying to pick up the broken pieces of Super Justice Force. Some nodded as they passed, others kept to themselves. Everyone looked tired, yet determined. Life had to go on, work still needed to be done, despite the tragedy.

The main foyer of HQ had been converted to a staging area, first for the rescue operation, then for the salvage operation. Normally hustling and bustling with tourists and visitors, the foyer had been transformed into mission control for employees from every department and service team, guarded by heavily armed soldiers.

Darius stared out the front entrance doors. A crew worked to clear away the charred remains of the helicopter that had literally crashed on the front steps of Super Justice Force Headquarters.

For so long, Darius had been alone. All of that changed when he came to Super Justice Force. He'd made a life for himself, with friends and family. And in one instant it all crashed down around him like the helicopter that fell from the sky.

He stood silently, piecing together the events of the last twenty-four hours. Part of him wanted to believe the story being peddled by the media. Terrorists would be a pleasant treat compared to the truth. So would Doc Kaos. At least if it had been Doc Kaos or terrorists, no one would be looking for answers within the crumbling walls of HQ. But the truth—as difficult to accept as it may have been—was that the Automated Combat Units that attacked Super Justice Force came from the fifth sub-basement.

58

With the Bunker destroyed, Operations Crew Command Central had been relocated to the Situation Room. A small army of security guards—armed with a variety of weapons ranging from machine guns to portable techno-plasm cannons to UltraStun 500s—stood outside the entrance to the Situation Room. Darius recognized the guards, they were all Chancers. None of them had the authorization to carry weapons, not even Butchie. But just like the glowing bands around Darius's wrists, the armed Chancers were a sign of the drastic changes that had taken place.

Butchie grabbed Darius, hugging him strong and tight. "Glad you're alive, kid," said Butchie.

"Me too," said Darius.

The other Chancers all shook Darius's hand, or patted him on the back, thanking him for all he'd done.

Even though the Situation Room had not been damaged in the battle, it still looked like a disaster area. Far from being a cramped space, the room overflowed with equipment and people who'd hastily picked a spot and gone to work. On a busy day, O3C looked like controlled chaos. By comparison, the Situation Room looked like chaos without the control.

Darius stood in the corner of the room, watching the frenzied activity that swept through the space like a force of nature. Both SAO and CAD teams were crammed together off to one side of the room. One section of the space had been set up with large maps, photographs and diagrams taped to the wall. The center of the room had a large conference table, cluttered with papers, photos and computers. There was even a portion of the room where two or three people lay on the floor sleeping.

Everyone in the room focused on the task at hand, none of them noticing Darius. As near as he could tell, there were close to one hundred people in the Situation Room—an eclectic mix of people that included heroes in costumes and SJF employees seemingly out of place. Miss Evelyn, the librarian, sat at the conference table in the middle of the room, explaining something to a dozen members of Super Justice Force, three members of the Galaxus Alliance Corps including Mee Vang Pao, and another ten or fifteen superheroes and crime fighters from all over the world.

The first person to notice Darius enter the room was Oegheneo-chuko, his Fast Response Unit partner. Oeghe looked up from a surveillance monitor, caught sight of Darius, stood up and started clapping. It took a few seconds for the people working near Oeghe to realize what was going on. As soon as they realized, they joined in the standing ovation. Before long, every man, woman and non-gender-specific entity in the room stood and applauded Darius, the room echoing with the thunder of clapping hands and loud cheers.

The attention overwhelmed Darius. He could feel his face flush, his heart fill with pride. The screaming crowd outside Headquarters had been one thing—and that thing was pretty much just weird. But to have his co-workers treat him this way meant something else altogether.

"Alright, that's enough! We all have work to do," said Nightwatcher.

The room quickly quieted down, and everyone returned to work. Some people waved at Darius, others gave him the thumbs up as he walked by, making his way to the large conference table in the center of the room.

Kaebel Kaine still wore part of his costume, covered in dirt and dry blood, but he had removed his mask. Even after more than a year, Darius still had trouble recognizing Nightwatcher without his mask.

A cluttered mess of books, papers and photos covered the table in the middle of the room. Darius stepped to the table without saying word, not wanting to interrupt the librarian, who had something important to share with the costumed heroes who surrounded her.

"I've spent the last three hours combing through every source I can find, but there are only a handful of references to the Khadku Turas, and those only make reference to them as legends," said Miss Evelyn. "Honestly, there's not enough information to support the theory."

"The stuff of legend Khadku Turas are not. Real are the Khadku Turas," said one of the Galaxus Alliance Corps. He was the biggest Zzngth Darius had ever seen, standing well over six feet tall. One of his four arms was missing just below the second elbow joint.

"That may be the case, but I can't find any verified proof, or an explanation of what they are," said Miss Evelyn.

"Khadku Turas are 'the Broken Ones.' They aren't like us," said Mee Vang Pao. "They're not balanced."

"But are they real?" asked Nightwatcher.

"Real are the Khadku Turas," repeated the Zzngth.

"I've never met one—at least not that I was aware of," said Mee Pao. "They are supposed to be rare."

"But they are real," said Darius.

All eyes turned toward him. Once again, Darius was the center of attention. He didn't like how it felt.

"How do you know?" asked Nightwatcher.

"I just do. I don't know how," Darius said. "Someone long before me fought them. And I know this. I feel this."

It didn't make sense to Darius any more than it made sense to anyone else gathered around the conference table. The only ones who seemed to understand Darius were the other members of the Galaxus Alliance Corps. They all nodded their heads. Except for Mee Vang Pao, Darius didn't know the others, yet somehow he recognized them.

"Together we were," said the giant Zzngth, pointing toward Darius. "Khadku Turas we defeated at the Swamp of Suffering."

Darius looked at the Zzngth unsure of anything the insect-like creature had just said. Darius knew nothing about the Khadku Turas, and he had never been to a place called the Swamp of Suffering, and yet he had vague notions of both, and that he had been part of something significant. "I've never been to the Swamp of Suffering," said Darius. "I don't even know where it is."

"Many Ones ago this was. Saved my One you did," said the Zzngth.

"Look, I hate to break up whatever this is that you two are having, but we all have jobs to do," said Nightwatcher. "Miss Evelyn, please keep looking for anything that might be useful."

"I'll do my best," said Miss Evelyn. She smiled at Darius. "Thank you, Mr. Logan. Oh, what I wouldn't have done to be in your shoes, for just one minute. The things I would have done to those monsters."

The group gathered around the table split up, going their separate ways. Nightwatcher came around to the other side of the table. "Good work," he said, extending his hand to Darius. "Dr. Sam needs to talk to you. I'll have someone track him down. In the meantime, come with me."

Darius followed Nightwatcher to a corner of the Situation Room that had been turned into a tactical command post. A map of Headquarters had been taped to the wall, covered with handwritten notes. Along with the map were pictures—frame grabs from surveillance feeds, photos of two-dozen SJF employees. Darius recognized most of the people in the photos.

"There were twenty-six intact ACU-64s locked in the Cage, and another fourteen disassembled," said Nightwatcher. "So far we've found parts from twenty-four units. That's including those big bastards that had been pieced together from multiple units. We've only salvaged parts from four down in what's left of the Cage."

"That leaves two possible intact units, and the parts to piece together another six," said Darius.

"Or something bigger and nastier than what we tangled with last night," said Nightwatcher.

"There's no way anything could have slipped past us."

"Look at this," said Nightwatcher. He led Darius to the map of HQ hanging on the wall. Immediately to the right were pictures of what remained of the Cage. "The 64s punched through the Cage here, using this as their escape route."

Nightwatcher used his finger to trace a path from the fifth sub-basement, up through the Bunker, and out into the courtyard.

"What's that there?" asked Darius, pointing to a second hole in the Cage.

"That's the second escape route. It leads under the Dome, and out to the river," said Nightwatcher. The attack last night wasn't just designed to do as much damage as possible, it was meant to create a diversion."

Darius studied the pictures of the Cage. The containment facility and the force fields surrounding it were supposed to be the strongest on the planet. Nothing could break into the Cage, but apparently something could break out.

"We've got people checking all satellite imagery from the time frame we're looking at," said Nightwatcher. "But nothing has turned up so far. I think they have some sort of device that deflects imaging."

"You mean something that makes it invisible?"

"We can't rule anything out at this point. They went to a lot of trouble to get access to the 64s. Spent a lot of time and energy into getting them up and running, modifying them. Someone goes to all that trouble, you can believe they've got a good escape plan."

On either side of the map of HQ hung dozens of pictures—images grabbed from surveillance footage, photos from the aftermath of the battle, and even shots of SJF employees. The photos from the aftermath of the battle were difficult to look at, as many showed people who had been killed. O3C was littered with bodies. It looked like over half the crew on duty died in the blasts that tore up from the sub-basement.

Darius thought of everyone who died, and his anger began to build. They deserved better than that. Even the Long Arms who had harassed him deserved better than being blown up while guarding the Cage. And that's when Darius noticed something odd about the photos from the cage—something very different than the photos of O3C.

"Where are the bodies?" Darius asked. "What happened to the bodies of the guards at the Cage?"

"We can't find them," said Nightwatcher. "They've disappeared."

That didn't seem possible to Darius. There should have been twelve guards posted at the Cage—that was the new standard protocol. And twelve bodies didn't just vanish without a trace. There should have been a random ear stuck to the ceiling, or some guts splattered on the wall.

Bit by bit, Darius began to put together a picture in his mind. "The guards were in on it," said Darius.

"That's what it looks like," said Nightwatcher.

"And the research team. They were in on it too."

It seemed almost impossible to believe, yet no other scenario made sense. The guards and the research team were the only ones with the sort of access to the Cage that would allow for such a complex plan to work. The only thing that remained unclear was how and why.

Darius studied a series of images lifted from a surveillance feed. Each of the images looked exactly the same, but all had different time stamps. All the images showed one of the research team in the far background of the frame, spilling coffee on himself. One of the printed images appeared to have been taken from a surveillance feed recorded at eleven in the morning on July 30, while another seemed to have come from August 18 at three in the afternoon. Four more images—all exactly the same—each with a different day and time stamp.

"This is the same thing, repeated over and over again," said Darius.

"As near as we can tell, the first month the research team spent in the Cage was recorded—much of what they did was staged for the cameras," said Nightwatcher. "After that first month, someone hacked into the system, and uploaded the recorded footage, placing new time stamps on everything. They even edited footage together, so that it never looked completely the same. Even if you were paying attention, you might never notice."

"You mean to say that for four months SAO monitored activity in the cage that wasn't live?" Darius asked.

"Not just in the Cage, but outside as well. Surveillance feeds showing the guards, it's the same thing—old footage, spliced together, and uploaded with new time stamps," Nightwatcher said. "That's how those damn machines got up and running, right under our noses."

It would have been funny to Darius, if it weren't so tragic. Someone had conspired to bring two bio-morphs into HQ, setting off a panic. Everyone assumed the bio-morphs had been trying to gain access to the ACU-64s, when in reality it had all been part of a much larger plan.

"They used fear against us," said Darius, recalling something Nightwatcher had told him. "They made us think the bio-morphs wanted to do something with the Killbots, which is stupid. Even if they got in the Cage, how could two bio-morphs get those machines up and running? But we were so scared, that we gave them the keys to the Cage."

As the words came out of Darius's mouth, a memory came flooding back, filling in another piece of the puzzle. So much had happened so fast over the last day—much of it a blur—that Darius had trouble recalling everything. One memory in particular was especially vague, something easily dismissed as a deathbed hallucination. Darius recalled being badly injured. His hands melted down to the bone, his guts spilling out on to the ground. He could feel himself dying. And in his hazy memory, he remembered looking up and seeing someone standing over him.

"Chuck Maslon is behind it all," said Darius.

"I'm afraid you're right," said Dr. Sam.

Darius turned to see Dr. Sam, looking as tired and worn out as everyone else.

Dr. Sam walked over to Darius and placed his hand on the young man's shoulder, shaking his head with a sad resolve. He recalled meeting Darius for the first time, thinking of the possibilities of taking Second Chance in a new direction. He had put so much great importance on Darius's success, and now Dr. Sam Omatete couldn't help but think the young man might have been better off in prison.

"I've known Chuck for many, many years. He was a difficult man to get along with," said Dr. Sam. "But never in a million years would I think him capable of this."

"Maslon was always an asshole," said Nightwatcher. "I don't put anything beyond an asshole."

"That doesn't explain why he had it out for me," said Darius. "Why he did all of this..."

Darius pointed to the photos of the devastation wrought by the ACU-64 Killbots. He thought of Manny and Otto, hurt and crippled for life. He thought of Zander, dead. And himself, forever bound to a symbiotic life form. *Is Maslon really the one responsible for all of this?*

"It also doesn't explain why all the machines specifically targeted you," said Nightwatcher.

The memory of Maslon, surrounded by ACU-64s chanting "terminate," became clearer in Darius's mind.

"Maslon hated me from the beginning," said Darius. "I never knew why."

"Khadku Turas is he."

They all turned to see the giant Zzngth. Darius had never seen the odd looking bug-like being until only a few minutes earlier—he didn't even know his name—but something felt familiar to him.

"You can't be sure of that," said Dr. Sam. "You can't be sure of any of them."

The Zzngth didn't bother responding. Instead, he walked over to Darius, who reached out and greeted the towering insectoid the same way he greeted Mee Vang Pao. They separated and the Zzngth stared at Darius with his large, unblinking black eyes. "Magic Bronson I am," said the Zzngth introducing himself. "Many Ones we go back."

Darius nodded his head, sensing a bond with Magic Bronson that went back decades, maybe even centuries. "I know."

"Dhaisam are you," said Magic.

"What exactly is going on here?" asked Nightwatcher.

"Dhaisam is this One," said Magic, pointing to Darius. "This, Khadku Turas could know."

"I have no idea what you're saying," said Nightwatcher, his patience wearing thin.

"He's saying there's something special about me," said Darius. "And somehow Maslon knew."

"Khadku Turas is he," repeated Magic Bronson. "Broken Ones are all. Killed many Mhadra Turas were on Enceladus. Some Ones are not dead. Some Ones are Mhadra no more. Khadku some Ones become."

Darius struggled to understand Magic. His mind filled with ideas and information that was not his, and he fought to keep track of the things he knew, versus the things the Mhadra Turas knew. Darius was certain he had never been to Enceladus, and yet he had distinct memories to the contrary.

"All the Mhadra Turas on Enceladus died except me. I know, I was there," said Darius, even though he knew he had never been there.

"Memories of your One, not of you," said Magic.

"Is this about something that happened on Enceladus?" Nightwatcher asked. Kaebel Kaine studied the photos of the death and devastation that had befallen Headquarters. "Are you saying that what happened here today has to do with something that happened twenty years ago on another planet?"

"I was on Enceladus. So many people died, I can't bear to think about it," said Dr. Sam. "We lost most of the First Earth Infantry—Chuck Maslon was one of the few survivors. The Galaxus Alliance Corps lost twenty, maybe thirty of their own. The only Mhadra Turas to survive bonded with Zander Boeman."

Darius knew the story of what happened on Enceladus all too well. He had read about it at length, and even talked about it with Z-Boe. And now that he was bonded with the same symbiotic life form that had once been attached to Zander, Darius had an even greater understanding of the Battle of Enceladus—part of him had lived through it, almost died in it, and been reborn during it.

He looked around the makeshift command post that had been set up in the Situation Room, and Darius saw people diligently and desperately looking for answers. He heard the sounds of voices buzzing all around him, trying to make sense of everything that had happened. Everyone wanted to know the reasons for all the death and destruction that had crashed down on their lives.

Darius didn't care what the reasons were. Reasons would not change anything. Reasons would not bring back the dead. Darius had enough reasons to know that he would hunt down Chuck Maslon. And despite the flood of ideas and information that seemed to be drowning out who Darius was, he had never been more positive of anything in his life than he was about killing Chuck Maslon.

59

Darius Logan sat alone in his apartment, struggling to hold on to himself. His entire world had changed in the short span of a day. The world itself had changed. And he had changed too.

Before he left the Situation Room, Dr. Sam handed Darius a data storage vid-disc. "Watch this right away—it's very important," Dr. Sam said.

Dr. Sam looked Darius in the eye. He could see no trace of the boy he had met a lifetime ago. Try as he might, he could not hide the regret that ate at his soul. He had tried to save Darius's life, to give him a sense of purpose in place of hopelessness. He had helped to build Darius up, only to have him knocked back down again.

"It's okay," said Darius.

"If I knew then what I know now…" Dr. Sam's voice trailed off.

"I don't blame you. None of this is your fault, Dr. Sam," said Darius. "This just is… how it is."

Darius held the vid-disc in his hand as he walked back to his apartment. He wasn't sure he wanted to know what was on it. He smiled as he remembered something his mother used to say, "A little bit of knowing is better that a lot of not knowing."

He booted up his Super Justice Force Signature Series Intellipad computer—the one Captain Freedom and the others gave him for his birthday. Darius inserted the vid-disc into the drive. His heart pounded when Zander appeared on the screen of the computer.

"Hey, Darius, it's me, bro" said the recorded image of Zander. "I'm afraid I have some bad news. I'm dead. That's why you're watching this video. Hopefully, my death won't come for quite some time, but just in case, I need to explain some things to you—especially these."

Z-Boe held his hands up in front of the camera to show off the glowing bands around his wrists. "You're wearing these now. One is knowledge, the other is strength—though I can't remember which is which. These are what give me my power. Now that I'm dead, they are what give you your power. They're part of you now, for the rest of your life. You're Mhadra Turas—the Balanced Ones. I hope you'll think of 'em as a gift and not a curse—although at times it'll be difficult.

"The Mhadra Turas pick their hosts. No one knows how or why they pick who they do. To this day, I don't know why my Mhadra Turas picked me, and I don't know why it picked you. But I knew from the moment we met, and shook hands, that you were to be my replacement. I'm sure you felt it too."

Darius thought of the surge of power he felt every time he and Zander had physical contact. He thought it was normal—that everyone who touched a Galaxus felt the same power. Now that he was one with the Mhadra Turas, Darius realized how ridiculous that sounded.

"Normally, it don't happen like this. Normally the Mhadra Turas makes its choice closer to the death of its current host. I can't tell you how freaked out I was when we first met. But here we are, a year later, and I'm still alive and kicking," said Zander. "It's been weird getting to know you this last year, knowing you've been chosen to replace me after my death, bro. I don't think of my death often, and I hope that when I died, it was doing something good for someone else. My only real fear is that when I kick the bucket it won't have any real meaning. But the thing is, I don't want you to mourn me. What you need to understand is that I'm now part of you. You know the things I know, just as I know the things the host before me knew and on and on down the line for thousands of years. That's part of how the Mhadra Turas works. Knowledge becomes part of the whole and is passed on, always to be part of the whole. One as Wholeness. Wholeness as One.

"There are so many things I want to tell you, bro. But I don't know when you're watching this. It could be a week from right now, or it could be ten years from now—there's no way of knowing. Maybe we've already discussed the Mhadra Turas, and maybe I've told you that you've been chosen to replace me. But I doubt it. Dude, this isn't the sort of thing you can really tell someone, and just expect life to go on as usual. Not that your life is going to go on as usual. But right now, as I sit here recording this message, it seems best that you don't know. That you live your life as much as you can before…well…before everything changes. And if I'm wrong for not telling you while I'm alive, then I'm sorry, bro.

"Up until two days ago, I hadn't told anyone you were chosen. But then you collapsed at that meeting the other day. Well, not really the other day, but the day after your birthday, how ever long ago that was. Dude, I keep forgetting you might not be watching this for a long time. Hopefully a very long time.

"Anyway, I don't know exactly what happened to you that day you collapsed, but I have a theory. The Mhadra Turas are very selective about who they choose. When I was chosen, there were twenty Mhadra Turas all in need of a new host surrounding me. But only one chose me. That's how it works—one symbiot chooses one host.

But there are a few—the Dhaisam. I've never met one, and I don't really know how to describe it, bro. The Dhaisam are like the holy chosen Ones—they'll be chosen by every Mhadra Turas they come in contact with. I'm worried that might be what happened to you, bro. You got too close to a posse of Galaxus, and every symbiot in the room tried to reach out and choose you. That might also explain why my Mhadra Turas chose you, even though I wasn't near death.

"If that's what happened—if you really are Dhaisam—it means you've got some serious mojo, and you need to be extra careful. If half a dozen symbiots can sense you, and all of 'em want to dance with you at the prom, then there are other things that can probably sense you, too.

"I've only told two people about our connection—Dr. Sam and my unit commander, Mee Vang Pao—and those are the only two people I'll tell. You know Dr. Sam, and Mee is good people, so you can trust them.

"Two more things I want to tell you. First, no matter what is happening right now, you need to go through training. I don't care if you feel you need to avenge my death, or you're married and are about to have your first kid—in which case congratulations. But no matter what the circumstances; you have to leave Earth and go through Galaxus training. I know you can feel the power running through you, I know you can sense all this knowledge and information. But if you don't learn how to control it, all of it will consume you, and everything that makes you who you are, it'll be lost, bro. Even as you listen to this recording, it's happening. You'll be able to deal with it for a while, but without training, you'll be lost to the Ones—the others that came before you. I've seen it happen. There are guys in the Galaxus Alliance Corps who don't really know who they are.

"Finally, I want to tell you that you should never doubt yourself. You're Chosen for a reason. The Mhadra Turas saw in you something incredible. Trust in that."

The recording stopped. Darius played it three more times. There was so much to think about. There was so much more he needed to know. He looked down at the glowing bands around his wrists. One gave him knowledge. The other gave him strength. Together they made Darius Logan one of the most powerful beings in the galaxy, but if he wasn't careful, he could be lost within himself.

Darius began to understand the magnitude of himself, of what he had become and what he was becoming. He understood that he was part of life, and that all things that lived were connected to an intricate mosaic of existence. But more important, he saw life itself.

For years he only thought of life as something cruel, that had to be endured as it heaped misery upon him and him alone. Now he understood it to be something more complex, while at the same time simple.

Life simply was what it was. It was the culmination of all the things that happened to all the creatures that had ever lived or would live in the future—all of it connected.

It was impossible for anyone to conceive of the totality of the connection of life, and most people never reached a point of awareness that they could even comprehend the connection. This lack of understanding made people act selfishly. It fueled hatred and mistrust, making people think that they were alone, when all around them there was life, and they were part of it.

How could I not have seen it before? But he also knew it was because he had not been ready to see it. And as Mhadra Turas, as one of the Galaxus Alliance Corps, Darius was beginning to understand his role in protecting life.

His mind, which had been cluttered with so much information that wasn't his, became clear as he pushed aside all thoughts but the most important to him personally. He thought about all he had to do. All of his things needed to be packed up. A home had to be found for his aqua-singers. Aziza and Reinier Rekker needed to be reminded to do their homework, and to be strong and brave while their daddy healed. Elladia Ortiz needed to be held one more time, and told how much she was loved. And then Darius Logan had an appointment with the stars.

Acknowledgements

There are way too many people to thank, but I need to name a select few. My mom, Bonnie Walker, who bought me my first comic book and has never stopped believing in me. Geoff Kleinman and Mike Russell who let me bounce ideas off of them. Becky Ohlsen and Margaret Seiler for helping out in their precious free time. Robert Love for providing a cover when no one else would (and Diego Simone for coloring it). Jim Hill for designing everything and being a good friend. Reggie Hudlin for believing in this thing from the very beginning. Cort Webber and Bobby Roberts for not telling me to shut up. Brian Bendis for yelling at me to write a book, even though I don't think this is what he had in mind. Chelsea Cain for yelling at me to let her read this book before it was done, and then yelling at me to finish it. My friends and family who have stood by me all these years (you all know who you are).

And finally I want to thank you, the person reading this book.

About the author

D.F. Walker is an award-winning journalist, filmmaker and comic book writer (although technically he has never won an award for writing comic books). He was born in Hartford, CT, the insurance capital of America. Walker grew up reading comic books, watching too much television, and performing poorly in school. Most of his  teachers told him he would never amount to anything. He decided to prove them wrong. Walker currently lives in Portland, OR, where he divides his time working as a freelance writer and begging strangers for spare change. When he is not doing either of those, he is hard at work on the further adventures of Darius Logan.

Justice For All

Made in the USA
Charleston, SC
08 July 2011